BAHAMAS SURPRISE

BY

National Award Winning Author

WILLIAM VALENTINE

WILLIAM VALENTINE

Published by Shutterplank Publishing LLC
6800 Gulfport Boulevard, Suite 107
South Pasadena, Florida 33707

Cover Design by David Tarlepon

Cover photos: Front-Shutterstock License
              Rear-Alamy License

Printed in the United States

ISBN-978-0-9894754-6-4 (Print)
ISBN-978-0-9894754-9-5 (E-Book)

Author's Note :
You might consider tracking the plot with
Google Earth to enhance your reading experience.

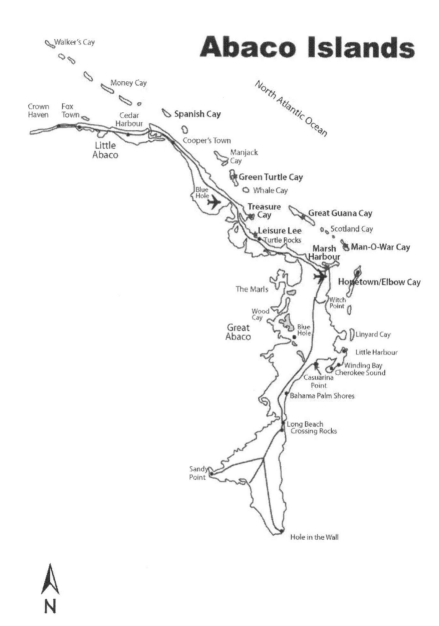

1 Fathom = 6 feet

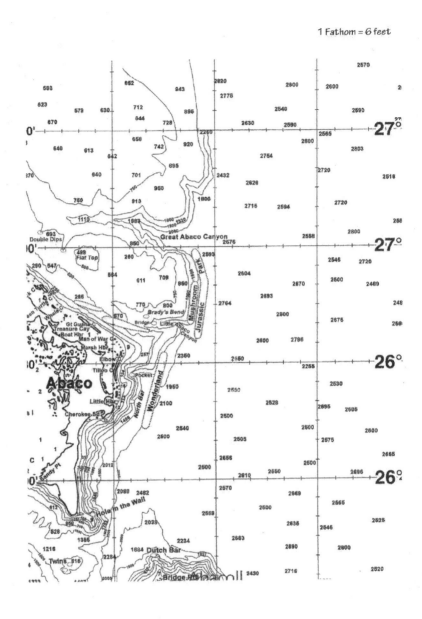

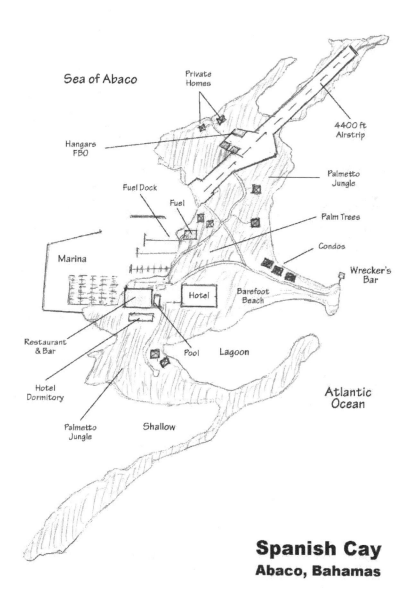

Sea of Abaco

Private Homes

4400 ft Airstrip

Hangars FBO

Palmetto Jungle

Fuel Dock

Fuel

Palm Trees

Condos

Marina

Wrecker's Bar

Hotel

Barefoot Beach

Restaurant & Bar

Pool

Lagoon

Hotel Dormitory

Atlantic Ocean

Palmetto Jungle

Shallow

Spanish Cay
Abaco, Bahamas

WILLIAM VALENTINE

OTHER NOVELS – by *WILLIAM VALENTINE*

SALT CREEK JUSTICE ......

Winner 2014 -Next Generation Indie Book Awards -1st place- Regional Fiction
Winner 2014-National Indie Excellence Book Awards-1st place-Crime Fiction
Indie Book of the day March 13th- 2014

COSTA RICAN REPRISE ......

Finalist- 2016-Next Generation Indie Book Awards-Action/Adventure
Finalist- 2016-National Indie Excellence Book Awards- Crime Fiction

CAICOS CONSPIRACY ......

Winner-2017- Beverly Hills Book Awards-1st place-Action/Adventure
Winner-2017- National Indie Excellence Book Awards-1st place-Crime Fiction

CUBAN CHARADE ......

Finalist-2018-National Indie Excellence Book Awards-Crime Fiction
Finalist-2018-National Indie Excellence Book Awards-Action/Adventure

WILLIAM VALENTINE

THANK YOU ...

To my crack crew of eagle-eyed editors who keep me on track: Andy Arnold, Bob Astley, James Byrne, Debbie Hayden, Dean Karikas, G. Louise, Lee and Page Obenshain, Norm Ogan, and Johnna Roberts.

Also, to all my fishing and hunting buddies who have traveled with me in small planes and boats halfway around the world ...and to all my readers and reviewers.

WILLIAM VALENTINE

DEDICATION

First and foremost, this novel is dedicated to my two good friends Dr. Harvey and Pat Partridge. I flew on countless hunting and fishing adventures with Harvey in his Piper Lance or Malibu, and many times our wives accompanied us as they shared our adventurous spirit. From the Out Islands of the Bahamas to the jungles of Panama we pursued big fish and sampled different cultures. Harvey and Pat "crossed the bar" last fall while flying out on another adventure. They will both … always be alive in my mind.

And … I am certain they also would join me in dedicating **Bahamas Surprise** to the courageous and hospitable people of the Abacos, who are battling back from the severe destruction that was wreaked upon them by Hurricane Dorian in September of 2019. Throughout history, the Bahamians' strength, character, and resiliency to overcome obstacles has always served their diverse society well. I'm confident that all of America joins with me in knowing that the Abacos will soon be restored and once again be a beautiful and orderly place in paradise.

WILLIAM VALENTINE

CHAPTER ONE

Late Spring – 2015 – Spanish Cay, the Abacos, Bahamas

Gene Johnson turned off *TAR BABY'S* shower, quickly dried himself, then slipped into a clean pair of tan Tunaskin shorts and a black Columbia PFG long sleeve T-shirt. Only his hands, face and lower legs were tanned as the sun was not his friend. It had been a great day of fishing on Seth Stone's 46-foot Hatteras, 12 nautical miles straight out to the *Double Dips,* two V-shaped pockets at the tail end of *Great Abaco Canyon*. The 5,000-foot bottom rises up there as a sheer wall to 4,000-feet, and the up-welling of confluent currents off those sheer walls holds bait in the two pockets. Gene's was the larger of the two blue marlin they caught that day and was estimated at 550 pounds. Both were tagged and released. John Harvey's was half the size of Gene's at 275 pounds.

Scotty caught a 150-pound yellowfin tuna to start the day. Freddy and John both caught large dorados, and Scotty finished the day when he missed a third blue marlin bite with a pitch bait chance behind the left bridge teaser. Local Captain Justin, an old friend of Seth's, was along to shorten their learning curve in this new area north of Abaco. *TAR BABY* looked good at Spanish Cay Marina's dock flying two blue marlin release flags and one yellowfin tuna catch flag from her starboard outrigger halyard. Rookies who flew their dorado or wahoo flags are told that in the Bahamas it would be more appropriate to fly their underwear.

Gene brushed his hair back and looked in the mirror … *Maybe I'm ten pounds overweight, and my full head of curly hair is turning a little greyer … But I'm feeling pretty fit for an old, retired police detective who lived on coffee and donuts for 40 years.* Before leaving, he plugged his cellphone into one of Seth's chargers … Freddy Buckley had videoed his entire marlin fight with Gene's iPhone. It was the biggest marlin Gene had ever caught, and Freddy got it all. Between videoing and then watching it all the way in, the battery was spent. When they returned from Wrecker's Bar, they would grill today's tuna for dinner. Gene planned on watching his whole video, from the hookup through tagging and release, over and over on the boat's new 42" LED TV.

Gene hurried off *TAR BABY* and jumped into the six-seat golf cart the boys had left him. He drew the last shower and Seth and the rest of the crew had already left to walk the half mile to Wrecker's, which was on the Atlantic Ocean side of Spanish Cay. The marina was full, in anticipation of the upcoming Bertram-Hatteras Shootout tournament, and the small hotel restaurant and its TIKI BAR was packed with marina and hotel guests. There was still a line waiting for showers at the marina restrooms. Darkness fell as he started down the sandy path to Wrecker's. The path navigated east through a patch of jungle that opened up onto Barefoot Beach, then meandered across a grassy knoll past three two-story condos that were close to the path. Two hundred yards beyond was picturesque Wrecker's Bar, that was built out over the Atlantic Ocean on pilings at the end of a rock jetty.

As he approached the second condo, the front door burst open amidst some shouting … Gene slowed the cart, turned his head, and noticed several men kneeling on the living room floor … with their foreheads on the floor. The two men closest to the door were bickering loudly and pushing each other. When they noticed Gene slowing down and looking at them, they turned each other loose, jumped off the porch and ran out after him. Both of them were waving short machete-like knives at him. He stomped the pedal down and headed for Wrecker's, but the two men steadily gained on him. Just as they reached for the cart, Gene took a sharp right turn and headed across the grassy knoll. He glanced in his rear-view mirror … he'd gained a bit and steered back towards another path that lead northwest to Spanish Cay's airstrip. Three private residences, with some empty wooded lots in between, whizzed by on the Atlantic Ocean side. A stretch of palmetto scrub jungle still fully covered the land on the Sea of Abaco side. Gene finally reached the paved airstrip and turned north, but even in the increasing darkness he could see the men were still hard on his tail, even though he'd gained quite some distance. Both men had close-cropped black hair, wore khaki shorts and white T-shirts, which made them easy to see. He noticed that the blades of the knives they were brandishing had more of a curved shape. The main hangar and plane parking area went by next. Gene soon ran out of paved runway which left a few hundred feet of mowed clearing that ran to the water, with scrub palmetto jungle on both sides. There was no moon, but he knew the island ended at the ocean a few hundred feet ahead. The little stretch of island ahead was only twice the width of the runway.

Gene abandoned the golf cart, which was beginning to run low on charge, and ran into the palmetto scrub on the east side of the mowed area. He turned and saw his pursuers white T-shirts running towards him about 100 yards behind on the runway. Whoever they were, both men were in superb physical condition. His black shirt would help conceal him, but his only chance to escape was to double back on his assailants and work his way down the 4,400-foot runway while concealing himself in the scrub jungle. He slipped into the palmetto scrub and started running. A narrow trail provided direction, but Gene was being scratched and pricked by the palmettos and underbrush with each step. He slowed down and picked his way towards the end of the island. Gene thought about making it back to *TAR BABY* where Seth had a weapons cache. Policemen were not accustomed to being chased. His many years of police training were based on pursuit. As he worked his way down the trail, he wondered why he was being chased. All he had seen was a group of men appearing to be exercising ... or maybe praying? What the fuck had he stumbled upon ... and why did they want to kill him over what he saw?

In spite of that, it wouldn't matter unless he could outsmart his two pursuers. They would probably figure he would head back down the wider western edge of three-mile long Spanish Cay. The widest part of the island was only a half mile wide where the marina, hotel, the beginning of the airstrip and the condos were located. If he could cross them up, maybe they would divide and comb both sides of the runway. Gene moved east in the darkness. Soon after, he could hear the waves lapping on the narrow beach. Four steps later he tripped over some brush and fell to the ground. He stayed still and listened for any sound. Gene didn't hear any out of place sounds, so he got up and picked out a stout branch from the pile of brush. He continued south at a slower pace, picking his way down the jungle shoreline in the pitch dark.

Finally, the heavy foliage and beach petered out on both sides of the runway just a few hundred feet above the main hangar's location. Only two mercury vapor lights lit that entire area. Gene stayed still for 10 minutes and heard nothing but insects buzzing and music wafting from the marina's dockside bar. The sky was clear and filled with stars. The dark of the moon and strong tides were another reason the marlin bite had been so voracious that day. Gene didn't want to chance walking up on the runway with no cover. He knew at his age he could not outrun them, so he slipped silently into the water and slowly breast-stroked across the 200-foot stretch, carrying his club in his right hand. Gene rightly hated to swim at night, fearing the nocturnal feeding sharks in these waters, but it was a percentage decision. He crawled out of the water and headed for the first clump of the palmetto jungle at the edge of the beach. He worked slowly towards the airplane parking area, across the runway from the main hangar, stopping to listen for any sound every couple of minutes. Gene felt that attempting a crossing over the 70-foot wide airstrip would be suicidal. He continued thru the palmettos to the end of the runway and stayed still for another ten minutes. Suddenly, he heard a twig break near him and one of his pursuers popped out right in front of him moving east. The man did not see Gene and he continued past him. Gene rose up and hit the man across the back of his kidneys with his stout branch. He swung it like a batter swinging for a home run. The blow knocked his assailant down and left him gasping for air. Before he could recover, Gene hit him in the back of his head with the club and drove his face into the ground. The man made no sound and lay motionless. Gene waited a few moments, then reached down and felt for a pulse in the man's neck. No pulse.

Gene broke out of the jungle on to the narrow beach and started running south. As he reached the hard sand near the water, a shape hurtled out of the dark jungle and tackled him. The force rolled both of them into the water. Gene lost his branch and he fought for the upper position as they went under the water. He maneuvered his pursuer into a headlock and held him underwater. The man struggled mightily but could not pull loose. Gene kept his own head above water and applied maximum pressure. When he saw the bubbles stop, he shifted his weight and twisted his attacker's head sharply to snap his neck. He heard the *snap* and started to relax. All at once, something grabbed the hair on the top of his head and pulled him straight up. He felt a searing pressure, then intense pain, across his throat and neck. A strange floating sensation came over him. Gene looked down and watched his dead assailant, still in the headlock, slip beneath the dark water … along with his own headless body. Gene tried to turn his head and eyes towards whoever was gripping his hair, but his world suddenly turned to black ……

FIVE MONTHS EARLIER

HAKIM AL-RASHID stood on the airport's tarmac runway and watched a full moon rise over the rugged Uzbekistan mountains. His borrowed Gulfstream G-500 jet was being refueled at the Tashkent International Airport FBO for the destination flight back to Africa. Hakim paced nervously back and forth as he checked his watch anticipating the arrival of the commander of the Uzbekistan military. Weeks of careful planning, fundraising and negotiation with General Victor Cheryazova were only mere minutes from fruition. A few seconds later, he saw the headlights of three black Chevrolet Suburbans and a Mercedes Sprint heading towards him on the access road leading to the remote FBO. The gate was opened, and Hakim strode toward the motorcade approaching the Gulfstream jet. Armed paramilitary troops spilled out of the SUVs, securing the area. The rear door of the middle Suburban was opened and out stepped General Cheryazova in full uniform.

Hakim's men, outfitted in flowing robes and head scarfs, did not openly display their weapons and spaced themselves along the Gulfstream. He walked up to the General, bowed respectfully, and said, "I am Hakim Al-Rashid, your excellency."

The General said, as they shook hands, "We finally meet … I trust you brought the gold."

"And I trust you have brought the Soviet RA-230S suitcase nukes in working order."

"Even better than that my new friend … they all have a battery backup monitor that sends a text message if the batteries get low. I have included new batteries and spares on all five of them."

"Thank you, General, the five million U.S. dollars in gold bars is ready for you to assay and weigh."

"Inspect the suitcase nukes first," said the General, with a wave of his hand, as he ordered his men to open the Sprint.

Hakim walked to the Sprint and produced a Flir R440 handheld radiation isotope scanner, the same scanner used by port authority and customs personnel around the world. The scanner buzzed and beeped and pegged its scale, validating his purchase. He signaled to his men to bring the 400 Troy ounce *Good Delivery* gold bars from the airplane. Each gold bar weighed 25 pounds and was worth $480,000. The General's personnel fluoroscoped the gold in the Sprint with a portable x-ray machine and weighed each bar. The exchange was made; 262.5 pounds of gold bullion (10.5 bars) for 600 pounds of nuclear explosives contained in Louis Vuitton Stratos 80 retro suitcases.

Hakim's men struggled to load the 125-pound suitcases in the Gulfstream's cargo bay as two of the General's men stacked the gold bars in an empty wooden mortar shell box in the Sprint. The General made a phone call to clear the runway and within minutes the Gulfstream rolled down the tarmac as General Cheryazova's motorcade disappeared through the FBO gate and into the night.

"Shall I run the tail numbers on the Gulfstream?" asked the General's attaché.

"It would be a waste of time, Serge. It will be leased to a myriad of untraceable shell corporations. But my guess is it belongs to somebody with Middle East oil money."

***

As the Gulfstream lifted off the runway and left the Tashkent airport and Uzbekistan behind, Hakim breathed easier and relaxed in his seat. Stage-one of his plan was complete. Now he had the means in his hands to move on to stage-two. He thought back to the events that had brought him this far. ... Hakim was just a teenage boy in Afghanistan when 9/11 went down. He was already training with the Osama Bin Laden led Al-Qaeda in the rugged Afghan mountains. Having outlasted the Russian occupation of Afghanistan, Al-Qaeda turned to governing Hakim's country after the Russians had been driven out. Bin Laden and his co-conspirator, Egyptian eye surgeon Dr. Ayman al-Zawahiri, expanded their terrorist activities outside Afghanistan to promote radical Islam worldwide. They cooperated with the Taliban, Iran, and other splinter terrorist groups in Africa and other parts of the world, forming a shadow cult of Islam. Hakim spent years fighting against the American coalition troops in his own country and hiding out in the border tribal regions of Pakistan, where Al-Qaeda got a free pass from the Pakistanis. Finally, American intelligence found Osama Bin Laden hiding in plain sight and killed him in 2011 in Abbottabad, Pakistan.

Hakim left Afghanistan, where the Taliban and Al-Qaeda had been tamped down and joined up with ISIS leader, Abu Al-Baghdadi in Syria, as one of his top lieutenants. After some initial success creating a large caliphate in the Iraq and Syria oil fields, the European, Western, and Kurdish military coalitions decimated and defeated ISIS and sent them scurrying back into their remote desert hideouts. Hakim contacted Al-Zawahiri with a proposal: *Let's go back to Al-Qaeda's roots.*

He met with Al-Zawahiri in Pakistan's Karachi city, the fourth most populous city in the world, and pitched his proposal. Hakim still remembered their meeting word for word: "Al-Qaeda has not had a major terrorist event in the United States or anywhere else since 911. We still have our organization in place, less concentrated, but now spread all over the world. When we come out of the shadows with any force, we are no match for the free world's military forces. Why not let me deal a major blow to the infidels. I envision something even greater and a thousand times more destructive than 9/11, to the United States of America. It will jumpstart a whole new Al-Qaeda era," said Hakim.

"What do you have in mind?" asked Al-Zawahiri.

"My plan centers on planting five Russian suitcase bombs on America's eastern seaboard. They will all be set off at the same exact time. The cities I want to hit are Washington D.C., Charleston, Jacksonville, Miami and Tampa."

As Al-Zawahiri listened to his detailed plan, Hakim saw his eyes light up for a moment. Then he said, "We have tried unsuccessfully several times to ship those type of bombs into the U.S. on container ships. The world's shipping companies, ports of entry and customs inspection agencies have hardened themselves with radiation detection devices both large and small. I'm afraid that they've gotten ahead of us on that score," said Al-Zawahiri.

"I have a way figured to get the suitcase nukes close to our chosen targets. We will use private charter yachts."

"Tell me more, Hakim," said Al-Zawahiri.

"First let me tell you I have located three caches of Russian suitcase nukes. Over a 100 were left outside of Russia when the Soviet Union disbanded in 1991. Countries like Armenia, the Ukraine, Kazakhstan, Uzbekistan, and Moldova took back their independence and militaries. They all kept the weapons that had been deployed by the Soviet Union. The best deal for quality and price that I've found is 10 RA-230S's in Uzbekistan. They are controlled by the head of its military and are for sale at one million dollars each."

"The suitcase nukes that Osama and I procured and lost years ago were from Belarus," said Al-Zawahiri.

"We will need a base of operations in the Bahamas Islands, some of which are less than 100 miles from Miami. There are many islands in the Abacos chain that have sufficient infrastructure, dockage and airstrips. We will also need a temporary remote island base somewhere in the Caribbean to train our charter crews away from prying eyes. Explaining what we're doing there for three or four months of yacht handling and hospitality training is not an option."

"I probably can set that up for us in Venezuela," said Al-Zawahiri. "I understand Washington, Charleston, Jacksonville, and Miami, but why Tampa?"

"Central Command at MacDill."

"Of course. What about your charter captains?"

"I plan to use native Bahamian internationally licensed captains, and English-speaking Al-Qaeda operatives from England and Cameroon for crew. No passport or communication problems there. All the charters will embark and disembark from Nassau."

"Why don't you train your own captains, so you can totally control them? I have an Egyptian operative who is a master captain with an unlimited tonnage license. He can teach your inner circle and educate them to get certified," counseled Al-Zawahiri.

"That will take some time?"

"It can be done on the internet in less than a month while you train your recruits. All they need is a what they call an offshore 'six-pack' certification."

"I agree, that will tighten our security."

"How will you hide the nukes?"

"Inside a fiberglass, lead-lined, 12-man life raft cannister on each yacht's foredeck."

"May Allah be with you my son, that's brilliant! How much financing will you need for the yachts and expenses?"

"Fifteen million dollars, which includes the suitcase nukes, and also gratis use of a couple of long-distance jet aircraft."

"We should be able to round up a few of our more radical Saudi princes for the financing and all of them have the latest jet aircraft that take them to their blond girlfriends in Europe and the West. They're in need of some religious recompence"

"I want to set up a legitimate British corporation with credentials, a bank account, and a couple of yacht brokers on our board who will supply the boats and also add credibility. We'll pick an upstanding Muslim English citizen who will be willing to disappear back into the Middle East after this event is all over. I will act as General Manager. We'll call the charter company, *Britannia Yacht Cruises Ltd*, London/Nassau."

"It sounds inviting."

"We'll create a website and brochure featuring our fleet of five, fifty-two-foot catamaran motor yachts and offer multiple Bahamas and U.S. locations for two-week luxury coastal cruises. Once we advertise in the boating and cruising magazines, we should attract mostly wealthy British and some American couples."

"How many guests will you accommodate."

"Three couples in equal cabins, or six friends or family, and a crew of two … plus the captain's cabin. There is a separate crew cabin."

"What kind of itineraries will you offer?" asked Al-Zawahiri.

"'Nassau to Key West to Naples to Sarasota to Tampa to Captiva to Miami and back to Nassau, on the west coast of Florida … On the east coast, Nassau to Palm Beach to Jacksonville to Charleston to Savannah to St. Augustine to Miami to Key West and back to Nassau. We will also offer a three-week cruise in the summer months only from Nassau to Palm Beach to Jacksonville to Charleston to Washington D.C., and back to Savannah, then Miami to Nassau. That's when we'll detonate."

"Who builds the yachts you plan on using?" asked Al-Zawahiri.

"Robertson and Caine power catamarans. They're 52 feet long, have a 25-foot beam, and are 20 feet 5 inches high. They have economical twin Yanmar 350 horsepower diesel engines and can cruise at 32 kilometers per hour (20 mph)."

"Will we buy them new?"

"No, these power cats are already in charter at eight or ten locations around the world. Several come on the market every year after being replaced by new owners within those charter companies. Our brokers will find them, and we will refit them as needed in 4-6 weeks under our brokers paid supervision. Used, they run $700,000 to $800,000, and we'll have close to $1,000,000 in each one after the refit."

"So, what do we get for each $2,000,000 bang?" asked Al-Zawahiri, smiling.

"The Russians rate the RS230 at 2 Kilotons, which translates to a 1-mile diameter of severe damage, a 2-mile radius of moderate damage and a 4-mile radius of light damage. Depending on the wind, 3-6 miles from ground zero could be radioactively uninhabitable for three years or more. In a city like Washington D.C., the blast and radiation could kill upwards of 80,000 people or more."

"How far is the capitol from the marina you plan on using?"

"Less than a mile."

"Will you and our people perish in this holocaust?"

"Only if necessary, great leader. I plan to detonate the bombs with a cell phone trigger. We can pick up our crews in a matter of a few hours with two jets at the closest FBOs and fly them back to our African headquarters in Cameroon. Remember, there is no customs check to fly anybody out of the United States. The charter guests will remain with the yachts. Our talent pool is spread thin enough as it is."

"What about communication?"

"Once we start this mission there should be no communication between us or any other Al-Qaeda operatives. The loaned aircraft will be made to look like charter company business. Our communications are what have exposed us in the past. I will take an ad in the Sunday New York Times to signal you: *Camel Hair sport coat 50 long $500, 941-555-1212.* The holocaust will take place sometime in the following 14 days. Weather at sea or mechanical breakdowns could alter our plans by a few days. But once we have the boats in the chosen cities at the right time … it will happen. The nukes will always be ready and aboard the yachts."

"You bring joy to my heart, Hakim. I have an old man's desperate final wish for one last big attack against America, before folding my eyes … you have my blessing and Allah's."

***

Hakim's thoughts turned to the six men he had aboard the G-500. His assistant, Marwan had been with him since the Bin Laden training camp days. Marwan, Shareef, Jabbar and Naser were from Afghanistan, Aksleel and Abdul were Iraqis he picked up from ISIS. All but Marwan would remain with him in this new endeavor. Marwan would command the African network of Al-Qaeda operatives left behind in Cameroon. Al-Zawahiri was sending a former Suez Canal pilot turned Al-Qaeda operative from Egypt to train Hakim's inner circle captains and teach all of them maintenance skills in case they were needed in any situation. The cooks and stewards would be selected from England's fast-growing Al-Qaeda ranks. In addition to refining their hospitality and fine cuisine talents, they would be taught basic seamanship and deckhand skills.

By this time, the men were hungry, and Marwan was pouring a little olive oil into a hot skillet before heating up some refrigerated falafel and braised lamb shanks in the aircraft's galley. After eating and kneeling for early prayers in the aisle, Hakim's crew slept in their seats. He was too wired to sleep and took a *Google Earth* tour of Spanish Cay on his laptop. The island looked ideal, much better than closed-down Walker's Cay that he'd checked out on Google during the trip in, although it was 50 miles further from Palm Beach. The marina would be busy with transients, but there were only seven isolated residences on the island, and the new hotel, pool and restaurant were built on the south side of the marina. The three, four unit, condos were remotely located east of the runway and marina in an area devoid of any foliage. They would need golf carts for transportation on the three-mile-long island that was about a half-mile at its widest point (158 acres total). Hakim scribbled a note to himself; they would also need access to a forklift to handle the lead-lined life raft canisters.

Hakim leaned back in his plush leather seat and tried to relax. The plane was headed west at 500 miles an hour for N'djamena International Airport, in Chad, 3,826 miles away. Al-Qaeda's African headquarters is in the mountains above the city of Koussei, Cameroon, directly across the Logone river from N'djamena. The river forms a natural boundary between the two countries and cities. That gave him about six hours to catch up on his sleep. Hakim had not slept in two days.

He sat back and tried relaxing to no avail. Finally, Hakim Googled and started reading a brief history of Spanish Cay that he pulled up on his laptop. It had been a deserted island in the Bahamas, bought in 1952 by millionaire Texas oilman Clint Murchison. Murchison built a fisherman's paradise there, complete with a large house, boat docks, a caretaker's cottage, and a runway long enough to land large airplanes full of friends, politicians, and business clients. By the 1960's, he owned the Dallas Cowboys football team and had hired the famous and controversial sportfishing Captain Ray Stancil and his top mate Billy Caldwell out of Gulfport, Florida. Long standing IGFA records started to fall. Clint had three boats docked at Spanish Cay in those days, foremost a 40 ft Andy Mortensen twin engine sportfish named *CENTEX* with a tower that was designed to troll for marlin and chase down giant blue-fin tuna. Later in the 60's, new owners constructed a small marina and hotel .... at that point Hakim dozed off as the Gulfstream continued to fly towards the west and his destiny at 500 miles per hour.

CHAPTER TWO

SETH STONE checked his scuba tank's pressure gauge. He swam over to Dino Vino, tapped him on the shoulder, then kicked hard and headed up to the surface of the Blue Hole 100 feet above. After decompressing on his ascent, he swam to the small sandy clearing on the south side of the Blue Hole where John Harvey helped him shrug out of his tank and buoyancy compensator vest (BC).

"I was wondering if you were going to stay down there until you ran out of air," called out John, as Dino's head bobbed above the surface in the middle of the Blue Hole. He swam over to the sandy spot from the middle of the150-foot diameter Blue Hole, owned by their favorite bonefish guides wife's Uncle Jake, and joined his mates. Except for the narrow path coming in from the old logging road and the small sandy clearing, the rest of the Blue Hole was ringed by mature pine trees and palmetto scrub as far as the eye could see in any direction. Albury A. Albury Jr., (known as JR) was rated as the top bonefish guide in the Abacos. John and Seth had been fishing with him for over 20 years. JR's wife's mother was Jake Snood's sister. Jake had inherited the largest pine tree logging operation in the Abacos. The Snood's, originally from New York City, were given land grants from England's King George III dating back to 1783, when the British loyalists were forced to leave the fledgling United States.

"Lots of bones in the caverns below," said Dino.

"Could be old Arawak Indian bones," said John. "Or the pirate's bones who lugged the treasure that's supposedly hidden down there. They had to carry it in from the Atlantic side, it would be too shallow to bring through *The Marls* even in a longboat. They say the Captain always buried the diggers with the treasure."

"Might be a few locals down there too," said Seth.

"If there is treasure down there, it's got to be fairly close to the surface … I mean the pirates had to free dive," said John.

"Let's figure it this way," said Seth. "I'm not an alarmist, but the ocean mean high tide has been increasing. Might be climate change or global warming, but my marks on the seawall at the boatyard and the data at the

NOAA tide station in Bayboro Harbor show a 10-inch rise in sea level in the last 100 years. The pirates Charles Vane, Calico Jack Rackham and Wyannie Malone were active in the Abacos around the start of 17th century. That means the water is about 3 feet deeper than it was then."

"So, we might have been diving right past the treasure," said Dino.

"I think John's right. Let's check the limestone walls down about 8-12 feet all around the perimeter of this Blue Hole on our next dive. But starting tomorrow, the moon is right for some marlin fishing off the lighthouse in Hope Town."

"Well, I'm glad we're keeping our priorities straight," said John, laughing. "Gold just translates to money, but each hooked-up marlin is a unique and priceless thing!"

The three divers carried their gear out to JR's black pickup truck and headed out the old logging road on *The Marls* side of Abaco Highway. Seth drove through the dense pine forest and stopped to unlock the metal bull gate at the highway. He turned north towards Marsh Harbour and headed for the Cherokee Sound settlement.

"Remember to drive on the left side, Seth, we're in the Bahamas," said John, smiling. "There's nothing like a roundabout to ruin your day!"

"Let's stop at Pete's Pub for a cold one, Seth," said Dino. 'I'm powerful thirsty."

"Not a bad idea, JR won't be back from bone fishing with Gene Johnson for at least another hour," said Seth, turning down the road to Little Harbour. "We can't get the Hatteras out of the anchorage between Casuarina Point and Cherokee Settlement until the morning high-tide."

The boys got settled under the shade of Pete's thatched roof and started on their ice-cold Kaliks.

"I guess we'll fish from Winding Bay all the way north to the lighthouse," said John.

"Then we'll go in through Tilloo Cut and put *TAR BABY* in her slip at Sea Spray," said Seth.

"When will we dive the Blue Hole again, Seth?" asked Dino.

"Depends on the weather and the marlin, the fishing has started out slow. I mean, one missed marlin bite and a few small dorados for three full days fishing is slow for the Bahamas. But we'll be back here diving for sure next weekend when your girlfriend, Zoey, and Billy and Kitty Chandler fly in from Florida. The Bahamas Billfish Tournament is fishing out of Boat Harbour Marina next weekend. There'll be 60 boats fishing the *Bridge* and the *Pocket* out front of Elbow Key. It'll be a zoo."

Pete Johnson, the pub's affable, 40-something owner delivered another round of cold ones to the table and said, "Saw you come in with JR's black truck, John, been bone fishing?"

"Naw, just exploring the Blue Hole on his uncle's pine forest land."

"Yeah, I noticed the dive tanks in the back of the truck. You guys must be special, the only divers Jake Snood let in there were from National Geographic Magazine. Be careful, that cave diving 'might could' kill you."

"Pete, do you remember Seth Stone? He's fishing his Hatteras, *TAR BABY*, up at Sea Spray for the next few weeks."

"Yeah, I remember you and your boat. Haven't seen you for a while," said Pete while shaking Seth's hand.

"Got too busy with family issues, but I'm back now … I missed these islands and the marlin."

"And Pete, this is Dino, he has a dive business in Key Largo. He wanted to dive the caves in the Blue Hole," said John.

Pete smiled and said, "Maybe old Snood is smarter than I thought, I always thought he could make some serious tourist money off his Blue Hole. Well, nice to see you guys and stop in whenever you get down this way."

Seth and the boys finished their beers and returned JR's pickup to his house in Cherokee. Gene and JR were sitting in the shade on his porch with JR's wife, Winona.

"How was the bone fishing, boys?" asked John.

"Saw a hundred," said Gene, "Caught 15, eight of them on flies."

"How was the dive?" asked JR.

"No luck today, but we covered a lot of territory in the caves. I think we need a better metal detector. I've got one coming over with Billy Chandler this week. We'll be back on Friday and will need your truck for three days."

John said to JR, "We stopped for a beer down at the pub and Pete *kind of* questioned us about diving the Blue Hole. I guess some people must have an interest in us. We said we were just diving the caves for fun."

"Everybody on this island thinks that pirate treasure is fair game. But if the treasure is found on Uncle Jake's land it's his," said JR shaking his head.

They motored Seth's inflatable dinghy back out to *TAR BABY,* and Seth fired up the Onan generator, to power up the A/C, refrigeration, lights and water heater. John hit the shower first and Dino said, "How are things at the boatyard, Seth?"

"I'm lucky to have a son like Jeb. He's doing a great job running it, so I don't go in much anymore … my girlfriend, Lori, and I have been traveling to Italy, Australia and Spain. But I missed the fishing, my boat, and the Caribbean. I'm glad John put this fishing and diving combo together for us.

I have quite a few of our 'Geezers' crowd coming over to fish while I'm at Sea Spray Marina. How about your dive business?"

"It's doing well, and Zoey and I are getting married soon. I have learned a lot about Marine Biology from her and she's become a great business partner. She loves living in Key Largo. We still see your buddy Jock, in the Turks and Caicos twice a year, when we run dive trips there using his dive boats. I'm glad to get the chance to dive this Blue Hole down here and fish with you again. Now that Zoey and I have experienced employees, we can get away to hang with the 'Geezers'."

"Invite me to the wedding, Dino, and just remember the Tampa Mafia and the Dominican gangsters ... you saved my life a couple of times with your karate and combat skills, so you're responsible for me. Here comes John, you get the shower next."

"The shower felt great, Seth, and it's good to be back on *TAR BABY*", said John, while cracking open another cold Kalik.

"What do you think motivated old Jake Snood into wanting us to search for pirate's gold in his Blue Hole?" asked Gene Johnson.

"Well, he's paying for Winona and JR's son, Walt Whitman Albury, and two of Jake's other sister's children's college tuition and expenses at Florida State University. His father left all that land to Jake with some stipulations. With all three of them in school at once it's probably an astronomical number. The profits he makes from harvesting the timber isn't getting it done. JR said, 'I told him I knew some guys with a good cover who were good **and** lucky enough to maybe find the treasure'."

"That would be us. Especially the lucky part!" smiled Gene, as he headed for the shower.

"More probably because I said we would take only 35% off the top if we found it, plus expenses ... and if we came up empty, we'd get zero," said John.

"We'll have fun either way, and it ain't like we need the money," said Seth smiling. "Speaking of money, how is your new partner doing at your dermatology practice?"

"He's working hard and paying the bank off for the loan to buy the practice. I still own the building, so he pays me rent, and I see patients two days a week and do Mohs surgery on Thursdays. He pays me by the hour, so I can take off when I want."

"You and I have always had the best deal," said Seth. "I have the boat and you have the airplane."

Seth finally took a shower, grilled some hamburgers, and the foursome watched the Rays beat San Diego on *TAR BABY'S* new KVH satellite TV.

BAHAMAS SURPRISE

***

The next morning Seth waited to pull the anchors until 10:00 a.m., when the tide was high enough. The sun had risen enough in the east to help him read the water. The narrow and rocky channel out of shallow Cherokee Sound demanded full concentration. John and Dino pulled both anchors that had been deployed Bahamian-style to hold the boat in the same spot regardless of the tide phase. Seth idled south following the narrow dark blue ribbon of the channel that led out to Winding Bay and the Atlantic Ocean. The channel edges were light blue and beyond that dark brown melded into yellow and stark white. Seth turned east as he passed tiny Duck Key and stayed at idle speed until he reached the ink blue deep water.

"Put four ballyhoo out under Islander lures, on the outriggers, John," shouted Seth from the flybridge as Gene let down the riggers. "Then put the bridge teasers in and get a pitch bait ready."

There were some birds working in front of the cliffs just before Winding Bay and Seth headed *TAR BABY* straight for them. Ten minutes later Dino was reeling in a 40-lb. dorado that ate the left short rigger Islander blue & white. John gaffed the big bull and slid him in the fish box before he could cause any havoc in the cockpit.

"Now that we've caught dinner, I'll troll out and work the 3,500-foot drop-off … all the way up to the *Pocket*. Put the marlin spread out boys."

The conditions were ideal for marlin, a light chop in 8 knots of wind from the northeast. The inky blue water color was magnificent. Seth set his new Raymarine auto pilot to an automatic zig-zag pattern and concentrated on adjusting the lures, so they smoked and popped. The long riggers ran Moldcraft wide range seniors with #11 hooks, and the short riggers sported 8-inch Pakula Prowlers with #9 hooks. The lures had extended skirts and hooks at maximum length, *ala* famous marlin guru Captain Skip Smith. *Seth had fished with Skip in Quepos, Costa Rica the year before on a two-day, three-night Seamount/FAD trip with Bobby Thompson, Toby Warner and Billy Chandler. The "Geezers" released 23 marlin out of 28 hook-ups in two unbelievable days of fishing, 100-miles offshore. Most of the marlin were hooked on pitch baits. Seth had learned a lot from Skip over the years.* TAR BABY'S left bridge teaser was a pink surface squid chain, and the right was a mirrored bowling pin with a Melton Cherry Jet trailing. The rods and reels were identical Tiagra 50- wides on 7-foot Crowder bent butt rods with a tip roller and one stripper, with eyelets in-between. Seth used Captain Harry's orange fluorescent 400 lb. wind-on Dacron/mono leaders. The pitch bait was a nose-hooked horse ballyhoo with a #8 forged circle hook.

After two hours of trolling they were approaching the middle of the *Pocket* off Tilloo Cut. Suddenly, Seth saw a dark shape come up behind the right long rigger. It quickly disappeared but resurfaced behind the right short rigger.

"Right short!" yelled Seth. "Small marlin, maybe a white ... get the pitch bait John."

John grabbed the pitch bait rod and stood at the transom. Dino moved behind the right short rod holder in the fighting chair rocket launcher. The marlin trailed the Pakula for a moment and then swam across the boat's wake and tried to eat the squid chain. Seth reeled in his over-head teaser reel pulling the squid chain up and away, while John free spooled the pitch bait right in front of the lit-up white marlin. The hungry white ate the ballyhoo, then turned and swam slowly away. John pointed the rod at the marlin and free spooled the reel for 4 seconds. Then, he slowly pushed the reel's lever up to strike and let the fish hook itself. When the line came tight, the white jumped, twisted, and put on quite an acrobatic show. But the circle hook held fast in the corner of his mouth as he sped away from the boat. Dino and Gene cleared the rods and Seth started to back down on the white as the reel's drag took its toll. Soon, Dino had the leader in his gloved hands and the white made a few more jumps to try and escape. Finally, Dino held him by his bill, as Gene de-hooked the game little marlin, before releasing him back into the Atlantic.

"Nice white, John. Good hook-up. and good release, guys. I'd guess him about 60 lbs."

"It was fun watching the bite, and he was quite an acrobat," said Dino.

"Well, we got the marlin skunk off us quick this trip," smiled Seth.

They fished the *Pocket* for two more hours and caught a small wahoo before calling it a day. Seth wanted to get in before the dockmaster closed the fuel dock and headed home. They ran in at Tilloo Cut and up past palm tree laden Tahiti Beach and made the turn for Sea Spray at the Abaco Inn Channel at White Sound. Sea Spray Marina had changed and improved since Seth and his late wife, Lisa, made their last trip to Sea Spray almost 15 years ago. Shortly after returning to Saint Petersburg that July, she unexpectantly died from an undiagnosed heart condition, catching everyone by surprise. She was full of life, a great fisherman, and Seth would never get over her. But in time, he found a steady girlfriend, Lori Gudentite, with whom he could share some of his life with. Although they were compatible, each had their own grandchildren and neither saw a reason to marry again.

The new owners added more docks at Sea Spray, and the restaurant, Tiki-Bar, rest rooms, pool and grounds had been improved. The new dockmaster was pleasant, as all dockmasters are, and the former dockmaster, Juvenal Menard, now owned a small restaurant and bar catering to the fishing clientele on Elbow Cay. The surroundings had many bittersweet memories for Seth, and he had avoided coming back for many years. But now that he was here, he felt Lisa's presence and her approval. His reunion with Juvenal Menard, a seven-foot tall, 350-pound man of Haitian descent was emotional, as they had become friends over those early years. But soon they were bantering as if Seth had been back every year.

Seth fueled *TAR BABY* and piloted her back into her slip. The boys scrubbed the decks with salt water and soap, then hosed her off with 40 cents per gallon fresh water.

"We can rinse the boat with 20 gallons at those prices," laughed Gene.

"If we had these meters in Florida and charged half that price, we wouldn't have a water shortage in Florida," said John.

"We're already maxed out on water in Florida. Look for this in the near future," said Seth. "With millions of people flocking to Florida for our low taxes and good weather, we'll be using reverse osmosis and paying these same high prices for water soon."

"Looks like another slow fishing day here," said Seth. "I only saw two blue marlin flags flying, and no white marlin flags flying except ours."

"I hope the moon phase will turn them on this week," said Dino.

"That's not many marlin for a 50-boat marina … at least half these boats fish every day."

"Let's clean the fish we brought in and hit the Tiki-Bar for a cold one. Then we'll take the fish up to Juvenal's and have him cook it for dinner," said Seth.

John busied himself at the fish cleaning table across from the docks, with the large dorado, and the little wahoo. After parrying away the inevitable "Ziploc" fisherman (cruisers who didn't fish but would unabashedly ask for a fish filet and produce a Ziploc® bag from their back pocket), he joined Dino, Gene and Seth at the bar.

The Tiki-Bar was busy, and the main topic of conversation was the slow fishing.

"See you guys released a white marlin today, congratulations," shouted a sun-tanned, wizened old salt from across the bar.

"Thanks, did you fish today?" asked Seth.

"No, we're waiting until it picks up on the new moon. We've been burning a lot of diesel for nothing."

"What boats are flying the two blue marlin release flags?"

"Captain Jack Bixby on *HAD 'EM*, his owner's in from Charleston, and Jim Crofwell from Stuart on *STINGER*."

"Both are good fisherman."

"Are you going out tomorrow?"

"We'll probably go out deeper, might try *Jurassic Park*."

The boys threw back their cold ones and headed for Juvenal's in their rental golf cart.

Juvenal had one of his picnic tables filled with fisherman and Seth could smell burgers on the gas-fired grill. It was Jim Crofwell, his mate Kevin, and the rest his crew.

"Nice to see you Seth," said Jim getting up to shake hands. "Saw you come in flying the white marlin flag."

"Congrats on your blue marlin ... any size?"

"No, he was a rat, but it's been slow and my crew's going back to Stuart in a couple of days ... so it's better than being skunked. You and I have some catching up to do. What's it been, close to 15 years since you've been back here?"

"Yeah, not since Lisa's been gone. I want to thank you for coming to St. Pete for her funeral."

"Well, we all had a lot fun here back in the day ... when I was dating the Sheriff of Okeechobee."

"Yeah, Marla ... she was a piece of work! I always wondered if she let you handcuff her. Do you still see her?"

"Never indicted, never convicted," laughed Jim. "I understand that you've been fishing down island since Lisa passed away."

"That's right, too many good memories here. But I'm glad I came back."

"Is this crew the "Geezers" I've been hearing stories about?"

"Yes, we've all been to Key West, the lower Bahamas, the Turks and Caicos, and Cuba. Unfortunately, we've crossed paths with some of the local underworld and shady politicians there, but we've been lucky enough to dodge any bullets."

"How did you get the name?" asked Jim.

"We were fishing a July marlin tournament in Providenciales, a few years before our trouble there, and we were the only visiting boat that wasn't staffed with professional captains and mates. Most of those 55 to 70-foot sportfish boats were on their way to the "Boy Scout" Marlin Tournament in Tortola, BVI, in August. Their owners and anglers would fly in to fish on the weekends. Well, we caught and released five marlin the first day and added four more over the next two days. The average age of our amateur crew was 62 years old, and our boat was Toby Warner's 25 year old Hatteras 52. The night of the awards banquet, the top three crews were called on stage. When we were presented with the first place trophies and check, one of the second place mates turned to his captain and said loudly, "**The fucking Geezers got us!**"

"That's a great story," said Jim, laughing.

"Yeah, there's eight or ten more Geezers back in Florida … we're kind of interchangeable."

The crews were introduced all around, and the irrepressible Kevin, wearing one of his colorful Dr. Seuss fuzzy top-hats, helped Juvenal provide each crewman with the drink of their choice. Then Juvenal took the fresh fish into the kitchen. His bar/restaurant had a six-seat bar built under a side porch, out of the weather. In the sandy side yard stood three picnic tables that were shaded by mature breadfruit and palm trees. Juvenal stretched a couple of retired sailboat sails above the tables tied to the taller palm trees. Underneath the sails, he ran strings of lights festooned over the tables. From his vantage point, up on the hill overlooking White Sound, he'd circled six Adirondack chairs around a log burning firepit built from limestone bricks. It was a pleasant place to spend some time. Dinner was brought out for both crews and their appetites for good food and conversation ensued. Juvenal baked the dorado slathered in island spices and mayonnaise, then dredged it in panko. He served it with fresh steamed broccoli and a baked potato with sour cream. It was superb.

Juvenal said, "Dorado always tastes best on the day it's caught, so I'll grill the rest and have lots of dorado salad for tomorrow, gentlemen."

After a couple more cold ones around the fire pit, the crews called it a night anticipating an early departure from the dock the next morning.

***

Dawn broke to a beautiful morning in Abaco. The marina teemed with early activity as a majority of the boats made ready to leave the dock for a day of marlin fishing. *TAR BABY* was one of the first to leave, coasting by the busy fuel dock where three boats waited to be fueled. Seth idled out of White Sound with the sun at his back and throttled up to 22 knots planing south towards Tahiti Beach and Tilloo Cut. The crystal-clear water mirrored the pastel blue and pink shades radiating from the rising sun. Seth's first look at the Atlantic revealed calm water in Tilloo Cut and an ebbing tide. He took the Hatteras through the shallow cut on a plane and headed for the bottom of the *Pocket* and its 6,000-foot drop-off, less than two miles away. Soon, the tide would turn and start to push the ever-present bait schools against the drop-off. The plan for this morning was to troll the *Pocket's* northeast rim and follow the 3,000-foot ledge north to Hope Town Lighthouse. Closer to the lighthouse, Seth had some wreck numbers in 1,250 feet that had consistently produced marlin on the high tide.

Seth slowed the *TAR BABY* to 7 knots and Gene let the outriggers down. Dino and John set out four 50-wide equipped rods, using the outrigger clips. In the meantime, Gene climbed down from the flybridge to bait and ready the pitch rod and put in the bridge teasers. Flocks of birds were working closer to shore in 700 feet of water.

John pointed them out to Seth saying, "Probably those football sized yellowfin tuna that are always there."

"If things are slow today, we'll troll in there later."

Seth zig-zagged to the east along the edge of the *Pocket* and noticed another early-bird sportfish backing down hard and belching black diesel smoke a mile further out to the east near the 12,000-foot drop off entering *Wonderland.*

"Looks like somebody's hooked up out in *Wonderland.* Can you see the smoke?"

"Yeah, maybe they're biting today?"

Seth turned the boat to the north and bucked the incoming tide as the tide changed. At that moment, a large dark shape came up behind the long-left rigger and pounced on the pink and white Moldcraft wide range. The clicker on the reel started to scream and Dino eased into the fighting chair and set the rod in the chair gimbal as Gene helped him clip the Tiagra reel to the bucket harness straps. As Seth slowed the Hatteras to idle, the marlin broke water several times and grey-hounded towards the horizon.

"She's a big one, Dino, let her run while we clear the rods, and then we'll go after her with the boat."

Seth wound up the two bridge teasers, while John and Gene brought in the other lures and cleared the rods.

"Starting into the spider-wire backing, Seth," squeaked Dino as the big blue jumped 250 yards off the transom.

"I'm going to turn the boat now, Dino. Let the drag off a little for the line catenary and get ready to reel."

Seth turned the boat gradually to port until the bow pointed at the fish, then he increased his speed to 10 knots. Dino reeled hard while layering the line back on the spool equally with the side of his thumb. Within a few minutes the tiring marlin was 150 feet from the boat.

"I'm going to try and get her to swim up sea, Dino. Put some pressure on her through my turn, then we'll backdown on her," called Seth from the bridge. He turned the Hatteras 180 degrees to starboard and the marlin began to rise, ripping the catenaried line out of the water. When the marlin came tight, she rose up from the depths and jumped 100 feet off the stern. Seth backed-down hard on her, knowing that the 500-pound fish was easier to catch on the surface than pulling her up from below. Seawater splashed high off the transom and flooded the cockpit. Dino was a big man, six feet tall and 235 pounds of muscle. His dark hair glistened, and his shirt and shorts dripped with sweat as the big marlin tested him. Dino finally broke her will and reeled her to the boat. John put on his leather gloves and waited for the orange dayglo wind-on 400 lb. leader to appear, while Gene kept the fighting chair turned towards the marlin's frantic jumps.

"Double-line," yelled John as the Bimini twist cleared the rod tip. Then John had the mono leader in his hand. Seth slowed, and shifted into forward as John controlled the tired marlin through a couple more jumps. Then he led her up the starboard side of the cockpit, finally grabbing her bill. Gene retrieved the lure and dehooked the fish cleanly. Seth continued to idle forward moving water through the tired fish's gills and Dino struggled out of the chair for a closer look. Gene tagged her and took a picture of the lit-up marlin with Dino's iPhone as John released her. The big marlin swam slowly away then disappeared with a flick of her gigantic tail. The crew erupted in a flurry of high-fives and loud hoots.

"I got some nice pictures of the jumps, Dino, and a video of John wiring her," said Gene as he handed Dino back his iPhone.

"Great job with the boat, Seth. If you hadn't chased down all that line and forced the fish up sea … we could still be trying to pull her up from the depths," said John.

"Yeah, I knew she'd be tired after that long initial run against the drag, no sense in letting her recover. Now let's put the spread back out and we'll work our way up to the Hope Town Lighthouse."

The rest of the day produced two more marlin bites, but neither fish was caught. The left rigger pink and white was hit again, but after a short fight the hook pulled out with Gene in the chair. Later, a white marlin appeared behind the squid teaser and John could only manage a *sanschoho* (only the ballyhoo's head was left on the bare hook) after his masterful hookup the day before. *That's why they call it fishing and not catching,* thought Seth.

On the way into Sea Spray, Seth idled around Tahiti Beach and thought about the promise he had made to his son Jeb. He promised he would no longer get involved in righting wrongs that law enforcement, mercenary forces and courts of law should handle and would spend his retirement fishing, diving, hunting and traveling. Seth had to admit he and his Geezer buddies had been involved in some serious life-threatening situations with the Florida drug dealers, Tampa Mafia, Dominican Gangsters and the Cuban Government. So here he was, on a trip that wasn't even his idea ... fishing, diving and traveling in one of his favorite places in the world. What was the worst that could happen ... maybe engine trouble or somebody getting poked in the eye by a marlin ?

CHAPTER THREE

THE GENTLE BUMP of the Gulfstream's tires on N'djamena International's runway woke Hakim from his deep sleep. His body instinctively braced as the plane's brakes were applied and the jet engines reversed their thrust. The pilot taxied quickly toward the FBO where several vehicles and a full squad of armed Al-Qaeda militia awaited their arrival. Chad customs ignored Al-Qaeda and Boko Haram activities in the northern mountain areas, as did Cameroon, which shared a common border. Chad is a former French colony and is Muslim in the north and Christian in the south. Cameroon is of similar religious persuasion but is a combination of a former British colony in the south and a former French colony in the north. The governments change frequently, due to open warfare between the English and French speaking factions, but the religious, language, and tribal influences are maintained, which makes the situation all the more complicated. Hakim realized that Africa's and the Middle East's present political and ethnic tensions were a direct result of colonialism after World Wars I and II. The Europeans divided up both territories between England, France and the rest of Europe based on their natural resources, rather than their tribal and religious boundaries. Those decisions became a recipe for disaster, fomenting the present unsolvable discord in both regions.

The trucks and vans were loaded, and they quickly left N'djamena (500,000 population), for smaller Koussei (90,000 population), Cameroon, directly across the Logone River. The Al-Qaeda convoy crossed over the bridge and was let through the Cameroon checkpoint with impunity.

Al-Zawahiri had established the Al-Qaeda headquarters stronghold 10 miles outside Koussei, in the mountains above the city, with the knowledge that this area was the center of the Muslim stronghold in Africa. The ancient Baggara tribe cut through all strata of the state and local governments in both of the countries. Hakim was appointed its commander when he returned from Syria.

Soon, they were ascending a single mountain road that passed through guarded switchbacks and led to an elaborate system of ancient catacombs. The compound had tunneled escape routes and was undetectable from the sky. The trucks and equipment were parked and stored inside the mountain.

As they stopped at the main entrance, scores of operatives greeted the convoy cheering and firing their AK-47s in the air.

"Marwan, stow these 'suitcases' deep in the mountain behind locked and guarded doors … then arrange a quiet celebration after sunset prayers and the evening meal," said Hakim. "Tomorrow, I will start preparing for my trip to London to recruit crew for *Britannia* and the move to our Venezuelan training camp."

"I wish I was going with you, my leader."

"You are needed here in Africa while I am away. There are many factions that need our help to continue the *Jihad* on this continent."

"I understand, my leader," said Marwan as he organized a work crew to move the nukes into the bowels of the mountain.

The mountain complex had served the Baggara tribe for centuries as a hideout, fortress and relief from the oppressive heat in the Sudan summer. The temperatures during April through June exceeded 100° Fahrenheit daily. Hakim and his men used the catacombs as an indoor running track, a rifle range, obstacle course, lodgings, garages, storage, kitchens, dining rooms, prayer rooms, dungeons and a command center throughout the long hot and short rainy seasons. Natural springs provided water and the farms in the valley below supplied foodstuffs. An alternate international airport was an hour and fifteen minutes to the south of Koussei in Salak, Cameroon.

***

Early the next morning Hakim went right to work. Since securing Al-Zawahiri's financial support and now obtaining the suitcase nukes, he forged ahead. Hakim was optimistic about the possible success of his planned mission. He also felt confident after seeing the doctor's new hideout in the rugged outskirts of populous Karachi City that an American extraction, missile attack or assassination attempt would not be probable in that location. Moving his three wives, seven children and an entourage of assistants from the remote tribal section of Pakistan had been a smart move.

The necessary funding had been put in place quickly and was funneled through London. *Britannia Yacht Cruises Ltd.* was formed in Nassau by Abdul Qshear, a respected London barrister, and an account was opened in the Royal Bank of Canada, Nassau, Bahamas branch and in Miami, Florida. Al-Zawahiri contacted Hugo Chavez, Venezuela's President, and arranged for the use of a deserted military base on Orchila Island, 100 miles from Caracas in the Caribbean. The island was off-limits, had a working freshwater cistern system, diesel powered electric, a full-time caretaking crew and a beach house belonging to Hugo Chavez. Hakim would have the run of the military base and airstrip, free diesel and jet fuel and the use of the supply docks for up to 12 months.

Hakim fired up his laptop and started outlining and emailing as Harry Muneer, General Manager, of *Britannia*. He emailed the two yacht brokers he'd installed on *Britannia's* board of directors, Robert "Honest Bob" Willingham in Nassau, Bahamas, and Phillip Oliver Holz, in Southampton, England. He asked for a list of possible purchases from their for-sale market research, including the price, age, location and refit estimate on each available RC-52 power cat. Hakim instructed Robert and Phillip to collaborate, as their commissions on the purchases would be split fifty-fifty.

Next, he called by sat phone to the real estate agent he'd selected based in Hope Town, in the Bahamian Abacos, to find boat dockage, shore and office accommodations and access to a paved airstrip.

Christian Thomason answered, "Hello, Mr. Muneer, I think I've found what you are looking for with our first choice. I did check out the abandoned Walker's Cay property, but the hotel is in serious disrepair from the last two hurricanes and the marina docks, as I mentioned previously, are condemned. Robert Abplanalp's heirs will restore the hotel and rebuild the loading dock only if you sign a five-year guaranteed lease. I checked out the airstrip and it is only 2500 feet long, and that won't handle your aircraft. But we're in luck at Spanish Cay. They have finished rebuilding their boutique hotel after an off-season fire last summer. The new construction has freed up three remote quad-plex condos which formally housed their hotel staff. Their new employee quarters have been built behind the hotel on the south end of the island. The 4,400-foot airstrip is on the north end of the island."

"Are there any storage buildings near the airstrip?" asked Hakim.

"Yes, there are two small plane hangars available."

"What about slips for the Power Cats?" asked Hakim.

"None are wide enough, but there is a 200-foot beam-to dock next to the fuel dock that can be leased. Both sides are usable. The rest of the 80-slip marina is transient in nature."

"What about provisioning?"

"Marsh Harbour is close, where three other yacht charter outfits are located. The downtown has two supermarkets, three liquor stores, and is 45 minutes by motor launch."

"Work up some mix and match lease costs … say on a three-year lease basis plus a three-year renewal. If I like the terms, I'll fly in for a look."

"Thank-you, Mr. Muneer, I'll start putting it together in an email tomorrow."

At that moment, an email came in from "Honest Bob" and Phillip Oliver Holz:

"We have located five RC-52s. Two in the Exumas, two in the BVI, and one in Grenada. We can have the BVI and Exuma yachts delivered to boat yards that can handle their 25-foot beam in San Juan, Fajardo, or Ponce in Puerto Rico. The Grenada yacht can be refitted in Trinidad and be used for training near there. Your refit dollar will go further in those yards. We'll make offers (subject to survey) directed by your wishes, and order repair and refit surveys on each vessel you approve. After reviewing each buyer's survey, we will recommend a negotiated offer and repair and refit time frame for your perusal."

The mundane facets of Hakim's plan were starting to come together. Not fast enough for an Islamic soldier who was used to chaotic war zones and non-stop action. But Hakim knew it would take patience to make his plan work. His mission's success hinged on planning, precise schedules and the appearance of *Britannia's* operation looking wholly legitimate.

He would not permit his operatives to show any outward signs of religion during this operation. Public prayer would be prohibited. Dress codes and haircuts would be strictly western style to arouse no suspicion. All written and verbal crew communication would be in English. They all would have British passports and speak English. Facial hair would be prohibited. Suddenly, for a fleeting moment, the enormity of the possible death toll he would be responsible for in America flashed across his mind. Over 400,000 people could perish. That many Americans died in World War II. **Only** three thousand died in 9/11. He shook the thought off quickly, buoyed by his radical Quran schooling in Afghanistan. The mullahs had brainwashed him from grade-school age. The Quran exhorted Muslims to kill infidel non-believers who would not convert to Islam. There is no other God but Allah, and Hakim could not wait for the day of the Holocaust when the Mahdi would descend from heaven, bringing Jesus Christ with him. Jesus would then renounce Christianity and embrace Islam thus converting the millions of earthly Christians to Islam. This had all been prophesized by Muhammad. The radical mullahs had done their job … and Hakim was not aware that he had become a religious sociopath.

After prayers and a mid-day lunch Hakim got back on his sat phone. He called London to arrange a meeting with Al-Qaeda's Great Britain coordinator, Fareed Dawoud.

"Fareed, I have personnel needs inside an upcoming project for 15 to 20 young operatives who speak British accent English and have hospitality backgrounds. Cruise ship experience would be most excellent. Six need sous chef experience; the rest can be waiters, stewards, bartenders, or doormen.

They have to be fit, and we will train them to be soldiers of Allah. But of number one importance- none of them can suffer from mal-de-mer."

"Does this *jihad* business include Jamaal Sayed, the Egyptian Captain who Al-Zawahiri sent to London?"

"Yes, but I would prefer to discuss the rest of the details when I get there. They'll need passports and clean police records. Jamaal will return to Africa with me."

"This shouldn't be too difficult to assemble considering we have 3,000,000 Muslims living in Great Britain, and almost 1,000,000 live in London. In fact, the whole of Europe has become a haven for Muslim refugees. Many are in step with our Islam thinking and would jump at the chance to aid our cause."

"Good. What airport should I use to fly in a private jet?"

"Avoid Heathrow-LHR ... use London City Airport-LCY, it's international, and has a small jet FBO. It is also close to Newham where I live, where you can stay at the same safe house with Jamaal ."

"I'll call or email you in three days with our ETA, after we're on our way. These Saudi princes have every luxury imaginable on their aircraft, KVH tracking Sat phones, Satellite TV and Wi-Fi. I'll be travelling as Harry Muneer and will be clean shaven and dressed in western business attire. Please outfit Jamaal similarly and arrange for him to have a westernized name on a British passport. Something easy to pronounce along with a first name of James. That first name makes an easy comeback if he forgets and says Jamaal. Additionally, I need five other British passports for my African operatives who will join me on this mission. I'll have their clean-cut photos with me when I arrive."

"Consider it done, Hakim. We have a talented forger on our London staff."

Hakim went to the mountain's commissary and asked the barber to shave off his beard and cut his thick black hair in a western style. He took along a GQ magazine he'd found in his seat pocket on the G-500 to help his barber.

When he was clean shaven and coiffed the barber gave him a mirror and said, "You look like a young Omar Sharif."

With his chiseled features, compact build and smoldering eyes, Hakim could easily pass for Omar.

***

Hakim sat glued to his passenger seat window as the Gulfstream-500 flew low over London on a windy grey morning. The number of houses and the population density staggered his sensibilities. The plane landed without incident at London City Airport and taxied to the FBO. Fareed met him and they were red carpeted through the airport's small customs facility. Jamaal waited outside in Fareed's Range Rover with Fareed's driver.

"Pleasant trip, I hope?" asked Fareed, who was tall and thin, and in his early fifties.

"Not a bad hop from Africa, but it is chilly here compared with Cameroon."

"We may get a little sunshine this afternoon if we're lucky. Have you ever been to London, Hakim?"

"No, this is a first for me," said Hakim, as he got in back behind the driver.

Fareed said to Hakim, "This is Jamaal, who's been expecting you."

Hakim shook hands in the back seat with the burly Jamaal as Fareed slid in up front.

"Well, why don't we do some sightseeing on the way to the safe house."

"Sounds good to me," said Hakim.

"I very much look forward to working with you, Hakim. Al-Zawahiri has briefed me on some parts of your project," said Jamaal. "I am glad to be part of it, praise Allah."

"We can't share any of that information, Jamaal, even with Fareed. Although he will get a clue or two during my visit, it is safer for all of us if he doesn't know."

"We all understand that," interjected Fareed. "Let's head west and see some of London," said Fareed, turning to his driver. "Jamaal has been sequestered at a safe house and hasn't seen much of London himself." They made their way out of the airport and away from the Royal Thames Dock and headed west on Newham Way.

Fareed pointed out the Tower of London as they crossed the Thames River on the Tower Bridge. Next was the London Bridge, which was closed to traffic because it had been the recent sight of a successful *Jihad* massacre that killed eight tourists and injured 48 others.

"This is where three of our operatives drove a rented van through a peak busy period and ran over scores of tourists. When they crashed, they jumped out and stabbed several others until the security guards shot them dead."

"Praise Allah, those three martyrs are now in heaven with 52 virgins for comfort," said Hakim, smiling.

"Notice all the concrete bolsters they've installed to prevent cars or trucks from jumping the curbs now," said Fareed. "In a year or so, when the authorities cut back on the troops they've deployed throughout this area, we'll launch more armed death squads here, and simultaneously at Buckingham Palace's changing of the guard."

"Mohammed taught us that time is on our side," smiled Hakim, as he noticed William Shakespeare's Globe Theatre to his right.

Soon they crossed back over the Thames passing the Houses of Parliament and Big Ben, then Westminster Abbey and Westminster Cathedral. The Range Rover turned north and motored alongside Hyde Park, then through the great Marble Arch, where they turned east on Oxford Street and headed for Muslim dominated Newham.

"The architecture is interesting, and impressive, and someday it will belong to Islam. As you know, Islam is much different than being just Muslim. True Islam allows no other gods on this earth, no other god but Allah. But we give all non-believers a choice, they either embrace Islam and the true Quran ... or they die."

Jamaal, who had been silent until now said, "What the western world democracies don't understand is, *Islam does not melt in their pot.*"

"Right-on, Jamaal ... or should we use your passport name, James Raskin?" said Fareed.

"At least Raskin means respectful in Arabic," laughed Jamaal. "But we must get accustomed to using our westernized names in public."

"I followed Hakim's instructions. If someone slips, the first sound is similar and can be easily corrected. Jamaal-James ... it could be a nickname. Actually, it is easier here in England, where many of our operatives have already westernized their first name to help them gain employment. Every name I use for your forged passports is a brother who was killed in the Isis wars. No one traveled directly to Syria, they all went through Egypt, Qatar, Lebanon and Bahrain, so they could return to Great Britain unimpeded."

"That makes sense," said Hakim. "Look at the problems the young Muslim women, who traveled to Syria to marry and support our warriors, are having getting back into their native countries. Especially those who have dead husbands and new babies."

"Live and learn for the next go-around," said Fareed.

The two-story safe house was on a quiet street in the predominately Muslim suburb of London. The first five blocks past the Village of Newham welcome sign were typically English. The houses, built close to the road, were neat, clean and freshly painted. The small front yards were well-kept with small manicured lawns, rose bushes and flowers. Each home had a picket fence around the yard and all the sidewalks appeared to be broom clean. Turning east towards the safe house, the neighborhood architecture remained the same, but the houses were in different stages of disrepair.

Pickets were missing in many of the fences. Roses, flowers and grass had given way to weeds and browning bushes.

"Is this the poor side of town?" asked Hakim.

"Not really," answered Fareed. "It's a cultural anomaly actually. Muslims are more interested in the walled and solid fenced interiors of their property, than in the outer appearances."

The safe house was unassuming and had a walled backyard with an alley behind it. The backyard had a brick patio and two large shade trees and was well-kempt. The rooms were spartan and all their meals were delivered. A Muslim woman did the cleaning and changed the beds.

"I will pick you and Jamaal up at dawn tomorrow and we will interview candidates between the five prayer sessions at the Masjid-e-Ilyas Mosque, just a few blocks away. I have 36 men set up for your first round of interviews. The candidates comings and goings will not be noticed there. They were picked as finalists after being interviewed, first by me, and then by the famous British/Mediterranean chef Abdulla Razaaq from Chennai Dosa in Stratford. All the finalists were taken out on the North Sea yesterday on Abdulla's 110-foot Horizon yacht, in four to six-foot seas. Fifty candidates were quickly reduced to 36."

"Jamaal and I will revert to desert robes and headscarves for the Mosque. Jamaal will do most of the actual interviewing. We will work on the questions and protocol tonight," said Hakim. "Thank you for all you've done so far, Fareed."

After an eastern dinner taxied in from Kebabish and evening prayers in the safe house living room, Jamaal and Hakim set up their interview protocol and turned in. The next morning Fareed took them to De Café, on Barking Road, for an early Halal breakfast, then delivered them to the mosque in their flowing robes and head-scarves. The mullah personally set them up in a private office, and Fareed stayed to greet and organize the finalists. They started interviewing and asked questions beginning with: *Would you be a martyr for Islam? Do you have a problem espousing western ideals to make infidels trust you? Will you shave your beard and cut your hair in the name of Allah? Are you comfortable at sea? Do you have mechanical aptitude? Will you train physically and militarily for service to Islam? Will you kill infidels in the name of Allah?*

After a full day they selected 16 ... 6 sous chefs and 10 waiters/stewards. Adding these 16 to Hakim's quintet of battle-hardened operatives in Africa would more than fill out his crew. He was taking more operatives than needed to allow for sickness, injury, or attrition. His plans included having Jamaal train five captains from his inner circle, five chefs, and ten stewards/deckhands. Jamaal will train Jabbar, Naser, Aksleel, Shareef and

Abdul, plus a few of the other recruits who showed aptitude, to captain and navigate the charter yachts. In addition, they all will be trained as maintenance and equipment troubleshooting engineers. The chefs and stewards will be cross trained as deckhands. Everyone will be trained as bartenders. The new operatives will start arriving in Cameroon in a week, first passing through Qatar, Bahrain or Lebanon. Their physical training will begin upon their arrival.

After returning to the safe house, Hakim and Jamaal changed into western clothes and sat down for a dinner from Chennai Dosa."

"The day went better than I could have hoped for," said Hakim.

"We have some first-rate recruits to work with," agreed Jamaal.

"Abdulla's food is excellent. Fareed told me that he will be sending one of his sous chefs and a mixologist to Orchila Island to teach our chef recruits and stewards. Most of his employees are radicalized and are used as operatives when needed."

"I look forward to more of this food in Venezuela, Hakim."

"Abdullah has invited us for a late afternoon cruise on the Thames and a private dinner on his yacht tomorrow. Our Gulfstream is not coming back until the day after tomorrow. He says we deserve some 'special' R&R for working so efficiently today. Fareed will also be joining us."

"It sounds like a nice day to me and I would like to meet Abdullah. He seems to thrive in the western world."

"Fareed says he has not forgotten his roots," said Jamaal.

"Let me ask you a question, Jamaal. How is it that you were able to stay in Egypt after 9/11, when Al-Zawahiri was sentenced to death there in abstention."

"I was never connected to him by anybody. The Doctor was careful in that respect. He wanted me inside for a plan to blow up a portion of the Suez Canal."

"I see. Being a pilot, you were his inside man."

"That's right—He wanted me to blow up a military munitions ship I was piloting in a lock and disable one the world's busiest shipping routes. The only problem ... I would also be a martyr."

"Like our airplane pilots in 9/11."

"Right ... I would have done it for Islam, but I like your reasoning better."

"We **are** creating a brainpower shortage by killing our smartest operatives. By the way, where did you acquire your excellent command of the English language?"

"Two years at the United States Merchant Marine Academy at Kings Point, New York, through a foreign exchange program back in the 1980's with the Egyptian Naval Academy in Abu Qir. The Americans are generous to a fault with their educational opportunities."

"Yes, they might be their own worst enemies. I mean, the 9/11 hijackers, Mohamed Atta, Khalid al-Mihdhar, Hani Hanjour and others learned to fly in Arizona, California and South Florida."

"You're correct. Where did you learn your English?"

"Running errands for Bagram Airforce Base personnel, in Kabul, when I was in grammar and high school."

"I know I will be teaching seamanship, among other things, on a remote island 100 miles off Venezuela, but I'm curious to know what our overall plan is Hakim?"

"I will reveal it in pieces, as you need to know, but there should be no martyrs. The day after tomorrow we leave for our headquarters in Africa."

"I understand, Hakim. I will follow you into this battle and you can count on me. But I wonder what Abdullah meant by *special* R&R?"

"I wondered the same thing, Jamaal. We are in the western world, and I won't ask Fareed. I guess we'll just have to be surprised."

CHAPTER FOUR

Billy Chandler sat on the edge of Jake Snood's Blue Hole, assembling the $1800, state-of-the-art Fisher CZ-21 underwater metal detector. He brought it with him on his flight from Fort Lauderdale the day before. Depending on its performance the older Fisher, $650, 1280X, might be relegated to finding dimes and quarters on the beach. Fisher claimed the newer model could read through limestone and mineralized rock. Billy's wife, Kitty, and Dino's girlfriend, Zoey Fugazi, flew over to Marsh Harbour on the same Silver Air flight with Billy. After a welcome dinner last night at the Abaco Inn with Seth, Gene, Dino and John ... the whole crew bunked on *TAR BABY* at Sea Spray Marina.

They left Sea Spray, for the Cherokee Sound anchorage, just after first light that morning. After a bumpy ride down the coast, they anchored and immediately went ashore and took JR's loaner truck to the Blue Hole. Gene and JR headed for *The Marls* for a day of bone fishing.

"Seth, this metal detector caused quite a stir in customs yesterday," said Billy. "Everything that lands on or sails to these islands goes through customs' scrutiny."

"What did they ask you?" said Seth.

"What did I pay for it, and where was I going to use it. They brought out another agent to look at it, even though I had the sales receipt, and he went and looked up the retail price on the internet."

"How did you answer the question?"

"I told them I was going to scour their beaches for pirate's doubloons. They suggested I contact their Department of the Interior in Nassau to get a treasure permit. They made me leave a $200 deposit, refundable when I leave the island."

"I guess they want to make sure you don't sell it," laughed John.

"Precisely," said Billy. "I explained I bought it for you, Seth, and they said the receipt was transferable. They copied the serial number on the receipt."

"No problem. I'll just add $200 to the sales receipt. But now they know we're looking for treasure. I didn't declare the old Fisher detector when I checked in at Spanish Cay. The agent there didn't search the boat … just asked about guns."

"What did you tell him," smiled Billy.

"I declared one and showed him a 9mm Glock and three clips locked in the ship's safe. Let's not talk about it anymore."

Everyone laughed and made the *zip your lip* sign.

"I think there is an unhealthy curiosity on this island about us diving Jake's Blue Hole," said Seth.

"I agree," said Dino. "I thought it was weird the way Pete acted the other day at his pub, when we told him we were diving the Blue Hole for fun."

"Maybe I ought to ask Jake to put a guard down there?" said John.

"That would make what we are doing too obvious," said Seth. "Let's not get paranoid and jump to conclusions. Look … Blue Holes are plentiful in the Bahamas. There are five or six on Great Abaco alone, one at Treasure Cay, the Bight of Old Robinson, Hole in the Wall and a few more on private land like this one."

"The whole Bahamas chain is limestone … look at the Thunderball Grotto on Staniel Key in the Exumas and Dean's Blue Hole, the world's second deepest Blue Hole, on Long Island at 665 feet," added Dino

"Right. John and I, along with some of the Geezers, dove there on our way to the Ragged Islands and Cuba a couple of years ago. It was spectacular," said Seth. "Let's get to what we want to accomplish in the next five days while we have Billy, Kitty, Dino and Zoey here. We have our best group of divers now, so we want to dive three of those days and fish the other two. We'll dive today, Saturday, fish Sunday, dive Monday, fish Tuesday and dive Wednesday. Then we'll run back to Marsh Harbour Thursday morning so you can catch your flight home that afternoon. We'll hang out at Boat Harbour and pick up Scotty and Freddy who are flying in later that afternoon. Any questions so far?" asked Seth.

"Can we make it out and back during the day from fishing? I know the channel in Cherokee Sound is shallow." asked Billy.

"During this full moon tide, we can make it two hours either side of high tide."

Dino stated, "We could use another truck to bring us and our equipment out to the Blue Hole from JR's house. His truck alone is too small. I'm not complaining, just asking."

"I'll see what I can do about that … so, I hope the accommodations are OK with everybody on the Hatteras. Both couples have their own cabins,

Gene is bunking with me, and John prefers to sleep on the pull-out couch in the salon. At dinner time space is kind of tight, but the cockpit or flybridge should handle the overflow. If you think it's too tight, JR and Winona have offered a couple of spare bedrooms in their house."

There were no takers and the meeting progressed.

"We are going to dive in the deep caves first, using the new metal detector, to make sure we haven't missed something in our preliminary dives last week. Basically, we're starting over. The cave floors are 100 feet deep and we have four caves and their connecting passageways to scan. The dive teams will be Dino and Zoey, Billy and Kitty, and John and me. We will have two rounds of diving today; each dive team's bottom time will be 30 minutes. You will be relieved at that time by the next team. Each team will take a dive safety line with them, tied to this metal piton I hammered in up here in the limestone last week. When your time is up, wind up your dive line on the way out. Turn the metal detector off when it's not scanning to conserve the battery. We can't charge it out here. Any questions?"

Billy raised his hand and asked, "Is Dino going to mix the nitrox so we can stay down longer?"

"Yes, but not so you can stay longer. We'll use the nitrox as a safety factor. Dino, please elaborate."

"I've mixed EAN32 nitrox/oxygen in each tank; it will give you 10 to 15 minutes longer at 100 feet. You can dive down right to 100 feet, but when you come up use regular decompression protocol ... stop at 50 feet for 3 minutes, then 1 minute at 10-foot intervals up to the surface, just to be safe."

"Thanks Dino," said Seth. "A couple more rules. One-hour surface interval time between dives and use your buoyancy compensator to suspend yourself above the cave floor so we minimize the silt for visibility. Let's get started ... our professionals will go first. Then Billy and Kitty and finally John and me. Zoey brought a box of slates and pencils. Sketch what you've scanned in each cave. Number the cave and hammer in a piton on the wall where you started and finished. Show your last slate to the new crew as you leave. John has a large composite sketch... hold it up, John ... that he will modify as we go."

Dino and Zoey adjusted their equipment, set their dive computers, and turned their battery powered headlights on. Dino picked up the new metal detector and tested it on the metal piton. Zoey tied a pink fluorescent roll of cord to the piton and they swam to the middle of the Blue Hole. After giving their companions watching from the sandy patch an OK sign, they dove, and power kicked down for Cave #1. Billy and Kitty set their dive watches for 30 minutes.

John unfolded his tall lanky frame as he stood up. He was slim for an old guy and some said he looked a lot like John Wayne with his brown hair and easy smile. He just fit in the pilot's seat in his Piper Saratoga, which was parked at the Marsh Harbour FBO. He'd flown in a couple days after Gene Johnson and Seth made the trip from St. Petersburg to Sea Spray on Elbow Cay in *TAR BABY*. He and Seth walked out the narrow path to the truck to bring in a couple more tanks and their BC's. Gene didn't dive and was bone-fishing today out in *The Marls* with JR Albury.

When they returned Kitty said, "Seth, you're walking better than you have in the 30-some years I've known you."

"Medical miracles, Kitty. They gave me a new knee a couple years ago and a new hip last year. It straightened me up and my back has quit hurting me. All that pounding I took playing football at St. Pete High and the University of Virginia in the 70's had taken its toll. Even though I've kept my weight at 180 pounds and have shrunk an inch or two from 6 feet, I was starting to have trouble getting around. Those operations made me feel 20 years younger."

"Tell me the truth, Seth, do you dye that beautiful head of blonde hair?"

"No, but I'm thinking about mixing in a little gray around the temples, because so many people ask me that question," said Seth with a smile. "Old Robert E, my daddy, left me good genes. He had a full head of hair when he passed in his late 80's and was still down at the boatyard working three days a week. I think the common denominator of all the Geezers is something that Clint Eastwood just said lately, 'Get up early and go do something every day, and **don't let the old man in!**'. We Geezers would rather die doing what we love or believe in, than sitting in an assisted living or a nursing home … you never know when your number's up for a heart attack or worse."

"Get ready to go, Kitty and Billy, we're coming up on 20 minutes," cautioned John.

Billy tied a fluorescent green cord to the piton and Kitty got her slates and pencils. They set their dive computers and positioned themselves in the center of the Blue Hole. Seven minutes later they were on their way to Cave #1 following the pink safety dive line. Once they kicked to the bottom, Billy led Kitty along the pink dive line while she spooled out their green tracer. Their head lamps cast eerie shadows off the main grotto and lit the stalactites and stalagmites around the edges. Five or six Blue Angelfish swam by. They both inflated their BC's to stay off the bottom and Billy followed the pink line through a tight tunnel into Cave #1. Dino gave him a thumbs up and handed him the metal detector. He motioned to a narrow chasm in the back wall that led to a chamber about the size of a walk-in closet. Zoey showed Kitty the slate it was identified on with the written notation, NO GO.

Dino hammered a piton into the wall at their stopping point, and they left winding up their safety line as they went. Billy started sweeping the craggy walls of the cave with the metal detector and Kitty kept a record on her slates. The water was getting a bit silty from the change out, but the visibility was still good. Dino and Zoey stopped at 50 feet and waited 3 minutes. They continued with their decompression protocol and finally broke the surface 5 minutes later.

"How did it go?" asked Seth as Dino waded ashore.

"We covered the passageway in and then almost half the cave. There is a small anteroom about a quarter way across the back wall, accessible only through a tight chasm type opening. Zoey couldn't get through it, even with her tank off. The room was full of Parrotfish and Red Coney."

"Maybe Kitty can squeeze through, she's a little smaller than Zoey. I don't remember seeing that the first time we dove Cave #1," said John.

"We hadn't started adjusting our BC's the first time we dove, and there was a lot of silt and the visibility was pretty bad," interjected Seth.

"Let's start to put our tanks and equipment on," said John.

Dino shrugged out of his tanks and turned to help Zoey. Suddenly he dropped her tank and yelled in surprise, **"What the hell is that ??"** looking up behind Seth and John and pointing.

Everyone swung around and looked, but nothing was there.

"What did you see, Dino?" questioned John.

"It looked like a small white four-engine drone … like the kids play with. But it took off fast when I looked up."

"Maybe it was a little white heron flying by?" said Seth.

"No, it was plain as day against the dark green background of pines," said Dino. "Maybe somebody is watching us, and we should ask Jake for a guard?"

"I don't know?" said John. "The only road back here has a locked bull gate across it. We might be overreacting."

"There are no fences. Anybody can slither in here through the pine forest or even run a drone from across the main highway," said Dino.

"Well, for now let's just stay alert, and tell Billy and Kitty when they come up," said Seth. "Let's get ready to dive John."

John and Seth kicked down the Blue Hole at the appointed time following the fluorescent green dive line. John continued to spool out their

Day-Glo orange safety cord as they progressed through the passageway to Cave #2. Billy and Kitty had just started scanning the east wall. They made the exchange, and Seth started scanning after adjusting his BC to handle the metal detector. They alternated every seven minutes and covered half the cave before their time was up. Seth hammered in a piton and tied their orange line to it. They both followed the dive line out of the cave, dodging a few scattered stalactites, and swam up to 50 feet to start decompression. The rest of the crew sat waiting in the sandy spot as they swam, then waded ashore. John turned the metal detector off and laid it on a dry beach towel.

"Guess what?" said Billy. "Dino wasn't seeing things. We all saw the drone fly over about 10 minutes ago."

"Yeah," seconded Zoey. "It paused for a moment then shot over the trees towards the highway."

"Then it looks like someone is keeping tabs on us," said Seth. "Maybe Gene and JR can take a day off from bone fishing while we're diving and slip around this forest and its surroundings and figure out who's so interested … meantime, we're half-finished scanning Cave#2. Let's do another round of dives. Dino and Zoey, you can go down in about 20 minutes. When we finish this round, we'll update the cave sketches from the slates and call it a day."

Zoey followed the Day-Glo orange cord down to Cave#2, with Dino right on her tail handling the metal detector. This is how their romance had started a few years ago in the Turks and Caicos. Zoey was one of Jock Baffert's dive masters and Dino went diving on Providenciales' spectacular reefs after the Geezers rescued Jock's wife, Kat, from the Dominican criminal element in Provo. Dino was smitten by what he saw above and below the water. Zoey was a five-foot three-inch voluptuous ball of energy. She was a marine biologist by training and a natural under water. When that adventure was over Dino lured Zoey back to Key Largo to be his partner in his dive business and his life.

Kitty and Billy made a flawless change out with Dino and Zoey into Cave #2 and finished it 30 minutes later.

John and Seth covered two-thirds of Cave #3 and left a piton in the west wall of the stalactite filled cave. They exited the Blue Hole with the metal detector and their fluorescent green dive line.

While Dino and Billy made a number of trips back and forth to the truck with the spent air tanks and gear, John, Seth, Kitty and Zoey worked on updating the cave sketches, from their slates.

"Now tune me in on the little anteroom in Cave #1 that Zoey couldn't fit in," asked John.

"No way with her tank on, and I don't think she could squeeze in with it off either."

"Any chance Kitty could get in there with her tank off? She's smaller than Zoey," said Seth.

"I think she might," said Billy. "We'd need an auxiliary tank with 20 feet of hose with its own regulator and second-stage."

"I'm game to try," said Kitty.

"Let's wait until we cover all the caves. We still may find the treasure in #3 or #4. No sense taking a risk for nothing," said Seth.

Everybody agreed and headed for the truck. John drove, Zoey rode shotgun, and Kitty sat in between. Seth, Billy and Dino rode in the pickup's bed surrounded by tanks and the other dive equipment.

"We need to ask JR for a second truck," reiterated Dino, as the truck pulled out.

"No argument from us!" chorused Seth and Billy as several tanks toppled over on them as they bumped up the rutted dirt road towards the locked gate.

Seth shouted through the open back window, "Dinner on the boat tonight, and a crack of dawn start for marlin fishing."

***

At first light, John Harvey and Gene made ready on the bow of *TAR BABY* to retrieve the two anchors that were set out the previous day "Bahamian Mooring" style. Because of the strong tides ebbing and flowing across the shallow banks of the Bahamas every six hours, a special technique is required. A lone anchor will be rotated 180 degrees on the bottom at each tide change and the anchor will subsequently break loose and drag. In any anchorage a boat could end up on the beach, nearby reefs, or worse. The double anchors have to be deployed, one into the prevailing tide, then the second 180 degrees from it, with the same anchor line scope from each one. Some adjustment might be needed if the wind is brisk, but generally the tide prevails. This maneuver entails precise boat handling from the helmsman, and timely anchor rode slacking and retightening by the crew. When done correctly, the slack anchor should be visible straight down under the vessel's stern in the gin-clear Bahamian water. Gene pulled the slack anchor's rode in and weighed the anchor. Seth then slowly motored up to the tight anchor as John gathered in that rode and secured the anchor in the pulpit. When the second anchor was secure, Seth idled into the narrow channel leading out of Cherokee Sound. The Cherokee anchorage was small and shallow by any standards, being 175 feet in diameter and five feet deep at low tide.

The sun was rising in the east as Seth turned the Hatteras towards it at Duck Key. He idled down the channel carefully as the sun helped mark the darker shades of blue. The wind was calm and when Seth reached the deep water of Winding Bay, he turned north towards some birds that were working a school of bait. Gene let the outriggers down and Seth called for skirted ballyhoo on the short riggers and small blue and white Pakulas on the long riggers.

"Let's catch some wahoo or dorados for dinner tonight," said Seth from above. "We'll head out to *North Bar* and *Wonderland* after we put something to eat in the fish box."

They trolled up-sea along the edge of the jumping bait and wheeling birds. The sheer cliffs of Winding Bay were a cacophony of pastel pink and blue reflections, a spectacular sight in the early morning light. Seth neared the big rock breakers off Little Harbour and turned back south and crossed through the bait school. On his third zigzag both of the long riggers went off.

"Fish on!" yelled Seth as he pulled the throttles back to idle. "Give these dorados to Zoey and Kitty."

Kitty took the left rigger and Zoey took the right. Both reels screamed as the boys fitted fighting belts on each girl. After a few minutes both fish settled down and started their tug of war.

From his vantage point on the bridge, Seth shouted, "Kitty has the cow and Zoey has the big bull. Zoey, keep your line tight and reel when you can. If he takes line don't reel against him, but when he stops ... reel."

Seth shifted the boat into neutral, then reverse and started to head for the cow ... they'd catch her first ... the boys all yelled to Kitty, "Reel, reel, reel!"

Kitty worked hard and soon the 35-pound cow was right off the transom. The lit-up dorado jumped a couple of times. Seth kept backing and John put his gloved hand on the leader. After two more jumps he led her up the starboard cockpit gunnel and Dino made a nice headshot with the gaff. John opened the fish box, as Dino lifted her over the gunnel and slid the cow smoothly into the box. John slammed the lid. No time for celebration, just some "Good Job-Kitty's", as Seth switched his attention to the bull.

"Zoey, I can see from here you don't have much line left on your reel. I'm going to spin the boat and run towards the fish and get almost all your line back ... are you ready to reel?" asked Seth.

She nodded *yes* and Seth spun the boat towards the fish. Dino moved next to Zoey to coach her, as Seth started after the big bull at 6 knots. Zoey was a strong girl and started to reel fast. She kept up the pace and Seth pushed the throttles up to 8 knots which didn't faze her. Five minutes later she had the bull right off the transom. Tired and perspiring, Zoey climbed into the fighting chair and put the rod butt in the gimbal. The bull finally saw the boat and managed a few half-hearted jumps, but the drag and Zoey's persistence had worn him out. Dino put on his gloves, grabbed the leader and led the big dorado up the port side gunnel. John was ready with the gaff and buried it in his head. Billy opened the fish box in anticipation, as John lifted the 50 lb. bull over the gunnel and started him toward the fish box. Suddenly, the big bull flipped himself off the gaff and rebounded off the transom gunnel. Billy jumped up on the flybridge ladder as the dorado flew by. John retreated into the port cockpit corner with the gaff and Zoey ducked and cowered in the fighting chair. Dino was trapped in the starboard cockpit corner. The huge bull made a series of twisting jumps, caromed off the fighting chair, and headed for John. He took a batter's stance and tried to hit the dorado with a home-run swing but missed. The big bull went airborne again as Dino vacated his corner and rushed to protect Zoey. The big bull and Dino met tail to crotch halfway to the fighting chair. Dino went down like he was shot with a Colt .45. He clasped both hands between his legs and let out a blood curdling scream as he landed on the deck in the fetal position with his face turning red and then purple. Dino's hands stayed clasped over his throbbing *cojones*. Billy rushed in with a wet towel and threw it over the dorado's head and eyes, which had a calming effect. John retrieved the pre-made dolphin calmer (a 4-foot length of 400 lb. mono leader with an adjustable loop in one end and a large hook on the other) from the tackle station and looped one end over the fish's tail and pulled it tight. While Billy held the wet towel over the fish's eyes, John slipped the #9 hook, at the other end of the leader, in the corner of the dorado's mouth. This bent the fish's body in a crescent shape. Billy pulled the towel off the fish's head and the big 50-pound bull could no longer move. John slid the dorado into the waiting fish box and Billy shut the hatch. For a moment nobody knew whether to laugh or cry. Gene helped Dino off the cockpit deck and put him in the fighting chair as Zoey hastily exited. It was an awkward moment … Zoey couldn't very well hold Dino's *cojones*, so she soaked a towel in the cooler and applied it to his forehead. He started to come around and said in a high-pitched falsetto, "It ain't easy having fun!"

That broke the ice, and the whole crew cracked up laughing. The girls were congratulated for catching two dorados of a lifetime, Dino limped into the salon to lie down for a while, and the rest of the crew laughed and rehashed the highlights of the ballet in the cockpit.

Seth had the crew put the "Big Boy" spread out and turned *TAR BABY* east to head for the *North Bar*. He was counting on the full moon, heavy tides and perfect weather to give him a marlin bite. The long riggers pulled the senior Moldcraft lures, pink and white to look like large squid. The short riggers had large Pakula lures, with blue and white skirts that resembled a skipjack or mackerel. Both dredges were smaller skipjack clones, and the bridge teasers sported a squid chain left and a hookless Black Bart green and yellow marlin candy lure right. The transom teaser today was three mirrored bowling pins that flashed, danced, and generally made a ruckus in the whitewater. Billy brought along his Braid big game fighting belt and harness in hope of fighting a big marlin standing up. Seth would love to see him try it. Billy was average height and on the lean side. But he worked out daily in a gym in Boca Grande where he and Kitty lived. Billy also practiced in the Gulf of Mexico reeling up 300-plus pound Jewfish off wrecks in 35-feet of water. He'd caught a couple of yellowfin tuna over 300 hundred pounds in Costa Rica, and countless 200 to 300-pound marlin, stand-up, with light tackle. Seth hoped he could hook him up with a big one on this trip.

As *TAR BABY* worked east at 7 knots the water depth went from 85-feet to 3,600 feet in three nautical miles. The drop off was 8,700 feet at 9 miles out entering the *North Bar* area, and 12,000 feet crossing into *Wonderland*. The water color was a stunning deep indigo blue and the water temperature between the two had *Wonderland* at -1.5 degrees. Seth settled on this temperature break after three hours of fruitless trolling and followed the break both north and south. Right before lunch, John and Billy picked up two sailfish on the Pakulas while fishing the break. But no marlin showed up. Seth hoped there would be an afternoon bite and by 2:30 p.m. he had the Hatteras back in the area where they caught the sailfish earlier.

The crew was nodding off in the cockpit from their lunch of pulled pork and black beans. Seth sent Gene down to cut up a cold watermelon he'd put in the fish box after they ran the Eskimo crushed ice machine to cover-up the dorados. Gene rinsed it, cut it up, and passed it out to everyone in the cockpit and flybridge. Fifteen minutes later a blue marlin came up behind the Black Bart green and yellow teaser.

"Billy, pitch a mackerel to the right teaser ... nice blue marlin!" yelled Seth.

Billy grabbed the pitch rod out of the rocket launcher and pitched the carefully rigged bait back toward the right teaser and held the spool still with his thumb. Seth reeled the hookless lure up about 3 feet. The marlin lit up and tried to swat the lure with his bill.

"I'm pulling it out of there, Billy. Drop your bait all the way back to him," said Seth, as he wound the teaser up and out of the water quickly. Billy stopped the bait right in front of the lit-up fish. The marlin pecked at the bait a couple of times then slashed it with his bill and went under. Billy held his rod high over his head which made the bait skip, making it easier for the fish to see. Through a ten count, the marlin did not reappear. Seth turned the boat in an easy circle, trying to reconnect with the marlin, but to no avail. Billy reeled the untouched bait in, and Seth resumed zigzagging.

"Tough one, Billy. That fish just couldn't find that bait. Maybe his eyesight was bad? Bad luck ... but we'll get another chance," said Seth.

TAR BABY trolled in and did not raise another billfish. The crew reeled in the lines and pulled up the outriggers when they could see the cliffs at Winding Bay. Seth hoped for some luck on two fronts: diving tomorrow and raising another big marlin the next day.

CHAPTER FIVE

ABDULLAH'S 110-foot Horizon Yacht was a stunning sight floating in its slip in the shadow of the twin Tower Bridge at St. Katherines Docks Marina. The Dickens Inn cast its actual shadow on *HAZA EATHIR'S (Pure Luck)* transom. The Tower of London was a block away, and the marina's basin was ringed with quaint shops, outdoor cafes and marine service businesses. His uniformed staff welcomed Fareed, Jamaal and Hakim as they filed up the yacht's gangplank, after the 15-minute drive in from Newham. Abdullah rose and greeted his guests as they were shown to the yacht's fantail.

"Gentlemen, find yourself a comfortable seat, Ali will take your drink order as *HAZA EATHIR* casts off. We are at the mercy of the high tides this far up the Thames and we can only lock in and out of our basin two hours on either side of the high tide. It will take about 20 minutes to lock through, then we'll head down the Thames towards the North Sea."

"How far is that?" asked Hakim.

"Forty miles to Southend-on-Sea. We'll sail half of that to East Tilbury and turn back around," said Abdullah. "The boat will average 8 knots."

Abdullah had adopted western dress and was clean shaven. His thick black hair was moussed and combed straight-back, and his sidewalls were stylishly shaved. He wore pegged linen trousers on his slim frame and an untucked white silk designer shirt with black Gucci driver's loafers. His choice of a watch was a Brietling Navitimer 41.

The yacht entered the lock with a smaller 55-foot Sunseeker as the lock closed slowly behind them. The riverside lock slowly opened, and the water level began to match the rising river. While they waited for the lock to fully open, and the Sunseeker to exit, Hakim asked, "How did you get started in the restaurant business, Abdullah?"

"My family came here from Iraq, where we were persecuted Shiites. My family started a small Mediterranean restaurant across from Wembley Stadium. It was small but the sidewalks were wide, and we had more seating outside than inside. As I got older, in my teens, I did most of the cooking. I started to experiment with western spices and created a following for westernized Halah food. Although my family didn't drink alcohol, I talked my father into getting a license to serve English beer. We became a soccer fan's favorite pub. I took over the restaurant in my early 20's and opened a second restaurant at Emirates Stadium, then a third at London Stadium. I kept my same formula going forward and now have 12 locations at London soccer stadiums, all staffed and managed by Shiite refugees. I have franchised 21 locations throughout Great Britain, and some were even purchased by native Englishmen. And of course, I have my two upscale Chennai Dosa restaurants here in London."

"Why did you name your yacht, *HAZA EATHIR?*" asked Jamaal.

"Why, it was *pure luck* that we opened that little restaurant across the street from Wembley Stadium," said Abdullah laughing.

They all laughed as the yacht cleared the lock and started down the river passing the Isle of Dogs and Canary Wharf. They spied the famous old three-masted warship the *CUTTY SARK,* moored alongside the Old Royal Navy College. Soon they were abreast of the Royal Docks and the London City Airport where one of the Gulfstreams would be picking up Hakim and Jamaal tomorrow. From that point the landscape became industrial, then more rural, as the Thames wound towards the North Sea. East Tilbury, where they turned around, was actually pastoral. The time passed quickly, and two hours had gone by. The Thames had seen hundreds of years of history at this one-time center of civilization, and it still had the feeling of greatness. Darkness fell as they started back. The four men gathered in the ornate main salon for drinks before dinner.

"I don't usually drink alcohol unless I'm with infidel guests. And when I do … I prefer French wine. I practice different forms of *taqiyya* (a Muslim's denial of religious beliefs in the face of persecution) to further my relationships with the infidels. When we are in the majority in this world, I will strictly adhere to the Quran. But until that day we must move forward using whatever means possible. Forgive me for 'preaching to the choir' as the Christians are fond of saying," said Abdullah as he supervised his steward who was opening two bottles of 20-year-old Baron Rothschild Bordeaux.

"I hope you will all join me in toasting the Prophet Mohammed."

Abdullah tasted the offering and proclaimed its excellence. His three guests all took a glass and all four toasted in unison, "To Mohammed."

"This is very special," said Hakim, proposing another toast. "We must all work together to make Allah the only god in the universe."

They toasted, then sat for a sumptuous dinner.

As the dinner neared its end, Fareed said to everyone at the table, "We have made great progress in the past 10 to 15 years in Great Britain and the rest of Europe. Our people have taken advantage of the middle eastern wars and flooded these countries with our brothers. According to Mohammed's original 632 A.D. plan, we Muslims will be the majority in Great Britain, Germany and France by 2050. The other countries won't be far behind. We may only see it from paradise, but the world will belong to Islam in the near future."

"In honor of our meeting here today, I have a special surprise, also sanctioned by the Quran," said Abdullah. "Notice that Khaldoon, my steward, has a camel skin bag in his hand. Inside are four smooth stones. Each one has a number etched on it – **1, 2, 3**, or **4**. This yacht has four guest cabins. Waiting in each cabin is a gift for each of you. We have an hour and a half until we dock. Choose a stone and go to that cabin. The cabins are through this forward door. Hakim chooses first, then Jamaal, then Fareed. We will meet on the fantail when the yacht is docked."

Hakim put his hand in the bag held before him. He felt each stone, then pulled out the smallest one. Room #4. He didn't look left or right, and only concentrated on the exit door. Khaldoon opened the door which led into a passageway. Hakim took a deep breath and passed by room #1, then #2 on the left, then #3 on the right. He turned and faced room #4 ... he felt a little light-headed from the two glasses of wine, but he steadied himself and opened the door. He went in and closed the door behind him. He looked at the empty king-size bed and moved towards the head door. Before he could get there, the head door opened and out stepped a young, beautiful, blonde, white woman wearing a sheer black negligee and high heel shoes.

"Oh, aren't you a handsome one. I'm here to do whatever you want me to do ... my name is Holly," she said while smiling.

Hakim was not surprised; he had suspected something along these lines. He was a student of the Quran and knew the rules. Basically, with an infidel woman there weren't any rules; they just couldn't be your friend. You were required to rape and humiliate them. If he were married, which he was not, the Quran granted him four wives and an hour a day with a prostitute, and/or unlimited sex with any number of slaves. A second look at Holly convinced him that he might as well categorize her as unlimited. It had been a long time since he'd been with a woman, and he'd never been with a milk-white, blonde-haired girl before. This was Saudi Prince territory. Hakim's sex life had consisted, up to now, of raping Iraqi, Syrian, and Kurdish women that had been captured during the Isis battles. He had consorted with concubines in Afghanistan and Pakistan. But nothing close to this level. Hakim could see Holly's rosebud pink nipples through the sheer fabric of her negligee. He felt his member swelling. Holly dropped her negligee with a slight movement of her hand to her shoulder. She stood before Hakim in all her dazzling whiteness. Holly looked almost ethereal to Hakim as he ran his eyes back and forth from her cherry lips to her perky breasts and her perfectly shaved camel-toe. *Allah must have meant this to be a preview of what awaits me in paradise,* thought Hakim.

Holly sensed his nervousness and started unbuttoning his shirt with one hand, while zipping down his fly with her other. As Holly dropped to her knees, *Jihad* was put on hold for an hour and a half.

The four *Jihadists* met on the Horizon 110's fantail beneath the venerable porches of the Dicken's Inn. The host was thanked for his hospitality and help with the vetting and testing of the candidates. They looked like four friends or business associates out for a relaxing evening cruise. No mention was made, nor any discussion ever took place, of the host's special gift. Not now, or anytime later. The participants left and shortly after the yacht owner's chauffeured car picked him up. Late that night four shapely figures disguised as the "help" were escorted to an unmarked white van by Khaldoon and were spirited away to an unknown location.

***

"I had no idea that Cameroon and Chad would have mountains like this," said Jamaal as the armed van navigated the guarded switchbacks leading up to Al-Qaeda's mountain headquarters.

"Wait until you see the ancient catacombs —— this is truly a mountain fortress," said Hakim. Two more armed vans and a machine gun equipped pickup truck completed their convoy from the N'djamena Airport.

"Do you always travel with this much firepower?" asked Jamaal.

"Loyalty is a fragile commodity in this part of the world; your ally yesterday may be your enemy today."

The convoy reached the encampment and quickly disappeared into the catacombs. Hakim introduced Jamaal to Marwan as they stepped from the van, "Marwan meet Jamaal, the canal pilot that Al-Zawahiri sent to work with us." Marwan extended his equally large right hand and Jamaal shook it.

"Good trip, my leader?" asked Marwan as he leaned down and kissed Hakim on both cheeks.

"The trip was productive; 16 operatives will be arriving here over the next two weeks. You will need to set up temporary quarters for them. I plan to move the whole operation to Venezuela in about four to six weeks."

"I'll set them up in the north cavern area next to the soccer field."

"I want them to have physical training twice a day, indoor shooting instruction, obstacle course experience, laps on the indoor track and hand to hand combat training while they're here."

"I'll see to it, Hakim."

"I need to work in my office for the rest of today arranging my next trip. Jamaal and I will be leaving to check out the Bahamas and Venezuela in a couple of days. Please get him settled and give him a tour of the entire compound. Include the secret exits and hidey-holes … and arm him."

"Follow me, Captain. There's a room close to my quarters where you can stow your gear," said Marwan. They turned and walked away down the tunneled corridor and Jamaal fell in step as he pulled his small roll-around suitcase behind him.

Hakim went to his office, turned on his computer and checked his *Britannia* email. Phillip Oliver Holz had forwarded the Grenada-based RC-52 yacht refit estimate of $215,000 U.S. along with the owner's asking price of $750,000 as is. Phillip recommended offering $695,000 and settling at no more than $710,000. Hakim okayed the strategy, as his goal was to keep each refitted yacht's cost under $1,000,000. He emailed his instructions to Phillip in South Hampton. Phillip closed the Grenada deal and arranged for immediate delivery to Peake Yacht Services in Trinidad. "Honest Bob" Willingham had negotiated a similar deal with the British Virgin Islands representing broker on the two RC-52s located in Tortola. Hakim gave him a go/no price and "Honest Bob" negotiated the sale. Those two vessels were delivered to Puerto del Rey Marine in Fajardo, Puerto Rico for their refits. The yachts were booked to be finished in six weeks with a bonus payment for each day earlier and a penalty for each day later. "Honest Bob" and Phillip were still waiting for a buyer's survey on the two RC-52s located in the Exumas.

The next email was from Christian Thomason's Hope Town Realty. Christian attached a PDF Excel spread sheet with three-year lease options, including renewals, covering several rental scenarios. Hakim circled the options he wanted and emailed it back to Christian authorizing him to sign an option with a non-refundable $2,500 deposit which would be used towards the first month's rent when the long-term lease was signed. The deal was contingent on Harry Muneer's personal inspection of the property later that week. When Christian confirmed the deal, Hakim would authorize a $2,500 e-deposit from *Britannia's* bank in Nassau.

Next, Hakim emailed the Venezuelan Defense Minister for flight protocol and permission to land on Orchila Island later that week in a Gulfstream 500. With that accomplished, he turned his efforts to logistics planning. All foodstuffs will be supplied from Caracas and La Guairá using the Venezuelan Navy supply boat that ran twice a week to service the Island's maintenance crew. One of his chefs will make that trip weekly. Western clothing and aboard-ship uniforms will be purchased in Caracas by Jamaal. Five Winslow 12-man offshore life rafts in fiberglass cannisters and stainless-steel deck brackets, along with 5 soft pack valises, will be ordered from Safety-One Supply in Tampa, Florida. A G-500 will pick up the Winslow order in Tampa and deliver it to the charter base. Once in Hakim's hands, the new life rafts will be transferred to the soft pack valises and stored in the Captain's quarters. The existing life raft and brackets will be discarded, and the new Winslow cannisters will be installed in their place, after first being insulated inside with .032 inch thick lead sheets. The Soviet RA-230S suitcase nuclear bombs will be removed from the Louis Vuitton Stratos suitcases and placed in the lead-lined cannisters. One 'Winslow' will be installed on the foredeck of each charter vessel. The total weight of each 'life raft assembly' will be 365 pounds (35 lb. cannister, 80 lb. RA-230s, and 250 lbs. of lead). They will be moved by forklift or crane, as necessary. All armaments, including pistols, automatic rifles, grenade launchers, surface to air missiles and ammunition will be smuggled in by airplane. Each charter yacht will have a secret weapons locker installed under the Captain's berth.

Hakim broke for prayers and walked briskly towards the amplified call to prayers that echoed through the mountain's catacombs. He arrived at the large cavern that served as the mountain fortress's prayer Mosque. After prayers Marwan and Jamaal joined him in his quarters for supper.

"So, what do you think of our mountain home here in Africa, Jamaal?"

"It's amazing, Marwan found me a room near the soccer field. After I stowed my gear, I joined a pick-up game for an hour or so. Good exercise and fun. When the call to prayers started on the loud speakers the game broke up, but each man had a task. Two groups wheeled the goals into the tunnels and another group pulled the boundary tapes and brought them in. In ten minutes, the soccer field disappeared."

"As I said earlier, we make this fortress hard to find from the air."

"The size of the catacombs on different levels and the number of connecting tunnels is overwhelming. The Mosque, the indoor running trail, the obstacle course and the rifle range were totally unexpected."

"You haven't seen it all yet, Jamaal," said Marwan.

"The electric golf carts are a nice convenience."

"Yes, they charge off the generators that run at night to power the lights and refrigeration. We also have solar panels on the south side of the mountain for emergencies, but they are covered by camouflage netting until we need them," said Marwan.

"We black out all the entrances with tarps after sunset," added Hakim. "Also, we have forklifts, bulldozers and other heavy construction diesel equipment to shape the mountain to our needs."

After supper Hakim went back to work. He had a new email from Christian informing him that any day was a good day to land on Spanish Key's airstrip to tour the small island. Hakim immediately sent deposit instructions to his bank in Nassau. There was also an answer from Antonio Mendoza. He was given a phone number at Generalissimo Francisco de Miranda Airforce Base in La Carlota, just outside Caracas, with instructions to call at least an hour before entering or leaving Venezuela's airspace. Hakim had also been granted impunity at the Orchila Airbase, where the tower was not manned. His planes could come and go at will as long as they notified the tower at Miranda by phone. Jet fuel would be gratis on Orchila. The Defense Minister also reiterated their use of the twice-a-week supply boat. If any problems were encountered on Orchila, Hakim was instructed to call Antonio Mendoza directly. Hakim wondered how much Al-Zawahiri had told Hugo Chavez.

CHAPTER SIX

ZOEY broke the surface of the water first with Dino right behind her. They swam quickly to the sandy patch.

"We are into Cave #4," said Zoey to John, as she wound up the rest of her pink safety line. "We didn't get a beep from the metal detector except for a couple of the old pitons down there among all those stalactites. It's funny how each of these caverns is different."

"Yeah, Cave #4 is just full of boulders," said Seth.

"Has our new guard seen anything up here today?" asked Dino while he shed his gear.

"Yes," said Seth. "The drone flew over twice so far today. The guard's name is Rex Malone and he's out searching for the pilot right now."

"On the highway?"

"No, the drone came from *The Marls* side and went back out the same way. The guard figured they came around by boat. He drove down that way."

"I hope Rex finds whoever it is. He certainly looked armed and dangerous with that hog rifle and shot gun when he exited his truck," said John.

"I thought his rottweiler was impressive. He reminded me of my Spider, who guarded the boatyard for years. This one's name is Mozart."

"Yeah. Spider was a nasty one, " agreed John.

"Rex said he'd use the shotgun to knock the drone down, I guess the hog rifle is for the pilot."

"He said he'd just shoot holes in his boat and sink it. JR said he was Jake's best man."

"We better get ready to dive," said John.

"You're right," said Seth looking at his watch. "We're getting this finished a little faster than I thought we would."

"I wish we'd find the treasure, that would slow us down," said John.

Halfway through the second round of dives, Rex and Mozart trudged up the path onto the sandy spot.

"No luck, gents. He must have doubled the drone back to make it look like he was in *The Marls*. Mozart and I will head out to the highway in my truck."

As he left, he took the shotgun off his shoulder and slung the hog rifle up there. He put his Benelli 12 gauge semi-automatic in the crook of his right arm, then started down the trail to the logging road where his truck was parked.

"With this northeast sea breeze blowing in here this afternoon, Mozart should smell him if he's hiding near the highway," said Seth.

Seth, John and the others heard the shots about an hour later, when the diving crew was updating the large map of the Blue Hole caves and tunnels.

"Dino and Billy, take Snood's truck, that JR gave us this morning, and run up to the highway and see if Rex needs any help. There's a 9 mm Glock and two ammo clips in the glove compartment."

Fifteen minutes later both trucks pulled up out on the logging road and Mozart, Rex, Billy and Dino all filed up the path to the Blue Hole. Rex carried what was left of the white drone.

"Nice shot, Rex," said John.

"Where did you shoot it?" asked Seth.

"Right at the bull gate, we didn't find nothin' up on the road. But when we was comin' back, and I was dialing in the combo to the gate, I looked up, and there it was. It hightailed across the highway, but I swung my shotgun up quick and nailed it."

"We ran back and forth on the highway for a couple of miles and found a spot back off the east side behind some bushes where a car or truck might have been. The grass was tamped down by tires, and a few Marlboro filter cigarette butts were scattered around," said Dino.

"What's the drone's brand name?"

"Potensic D-85," said Billy, turning it over. "I've seen these at the fishing tournaments. They have about a mile range."

"We've got the perfect guy to watch the highway next time we dive. We'll put Gene out there in the second truck. He's probably getting bone fished out about now anyhow. You know what I always say!" said Seth.

"Yeah, Fucking-A," said Dino laughing.

"That's it for today, guys. Let's pack it up and head for the Hatteras. The day after tomorrow we have a few tunnels that lead to nowhere to check, and the Blue Hole's main grotto wall - and we're done. Everyone keep your fingers crossed that we find something."

"Don't forget that difficult spot in Cave # 1, Seth," said John.

"Right, we'll let Kitty give it a try. But, tomorrow's a marlin day."

***

Seth was ready to leave but the second anchor's flukes would not pull out of the bottom. Whenever he anchored in the Keys or the Bahamas, Seth always dove on his anchors to make sure they were securely in the bottom. Because of the limestone, instead of having a mud or sand bottom, there was just marl. Marl is finely ground limestone and clay that does not stick together. It acts more like a fine gravel. An anchor will hold in marl until about 12 knots of breeze pipes up, and then the anchor drags. Seth, or one of the crew, would dive on the anchors and move the 6 to 8-inch deep marl from around each anchor by hand, looking for a crevice or small hole in the limestone. Once one was found, they'd shove one or both flukes of the Danforth anchor into the crevice. While they were busy doing that, they always had supervision. In every anchorage there always seemed to be a territorial, 5-foot long, toothy barracuda watching from 10 or 15 feet away. John took the early morning swim and 10 minutes later Seth idled *TAR BABY* out of the narrow, shallow Cherokee anchorage.

The east wind was a little brisker than two days before, and Seth ran 20 knots out to the *North Bar*'s 12,000-foot depth, about 13 miles offshore. Once there, he slowed to 7 knots and Gene put down the outriggers. The crew quickly put out the dredges, teasers and lures. Seth started zigzagging northeast towards *Wonderland* and a small canyon three miles away. The water color was deep azure blue. Soon, Seth spotted four frigate birds soaring high above the water about a mile away. This was a long way offshore for a frigate as they could not land on the water and could only swoop down and pick up scraps floating on the surface. Normally they followed large pelagic fish like tuna, dorado and billfish closer to shore, depending on their keen eyesight for a meal. When Seth got closer to the frigates, he saw five sperm whales alternately blowing, then slipping back under the water and showing their gigantic tails as they descended below. Seth estimated there were at least 10 to 12 whales in that pod. The long riggers had on the senior Moldcraft pink and white wide ranges that simulated the squid he guessed the whales were feeding on. Seth knew these 90,000 lb. whales ate about 2,000 pounds of squid a day. It took a lot of squid to keep these huge whales interested. The two large dorados they caught two days ago had squid in their stomachs when they were cleaned. Seth felt he was in the right place, and he steered right under the circling frigates. He turned down sea as he approached the pod of whales and that's when the big blue marlin showed herself.

The long right rigger had slowed the most during the wide turn, first dropping down and slowing, then rising and speeding up as the boat straightened up. Mama marlin came in like a freight train and literally pounced on the pink Moldcraft, which acted like it was trying to escape her.

"Big marlin — right rigger," yelled Seth as the 50-wide Tiagra's clicker screamed and the rod bent almost in-half in the rocket launcher behind the fighting chair.

"Let Billy have it on stand-up," yelled Seth.

Billy let the big fish run and shrugged into his Braid shoulder harness and drop-down power play belt. He knew too many big fish had been lost by snatching the rod out of the rod holder prematurely. Seth's reel drags were set just below 8 pounds. Billy took a deep breath and lifted the rod out of the rod holder and transferred the butt smoothly into the fighting belt's gimbal. He slowly bent his knees until he was almost in a sitting position, distributing the fleeing fish's speed and power across his entire body. He kept the clicker on so Seth could hear when the fish's initial run was over. The crew had almost finished clearing the other rods, teasers and dredges when the marlin broke water and greyhounded from right to left across the horizon. She slowed down and took two surprisingly acrobatic jumps for a fish this size. The crew, male and female, whooped and hollered with each jump.

"How big do you think she is, Seth?" asked Gene, leaning in next to Seth's ear.

"Around 600 pounds … **Easy**," said Seth, as he knocked the throttles down to idle and shifted the port engine into neutral.

Billy switched off the clicker and rotated the reel his way for the first time. He reeled the fish tight and the big girl started to take more line immediately. They played a little tug of war back and forth and then she jumped a couple of times and took off again.

"Billy," shouted Seth. "When she stops this time, I'm going to spin out and run her down. I don't want her to sound in 12,000 feet of water or we'll lose her for sure. Are you into the braided backing yet?"

"Yes, half-way."

Billy soon fought her to a stalemate, and Seth motored into an 180° starboard turn and pointed the bow right at the big marlin. Billy reeled like he was possessed, as Seth throttled *TAR BABY* up to 9 knots. Within 8 minutes he had most of the line back and the dangerous catenary loop was out of the line.

"When I turn the boat back around, reel her up tight, and move to a corner. I'm going to try and get her to swim up sea. Let John put your knee pads on so you can brace your legs against the inside of the transom."

Billy waved ... he'd been here before.

The big girl surged 60-feet behind the boat, and jumped a couple of times, but she didn't gain on Billy. He slid across the transom to the starboard corner, as the fish started to go down.

"Push your drag up to 10-pounds. I'm going to turn down sea and turn her around," yelled Seth.

He turned the boat on its axis and powered past the fish below. Seth pulled the throttles back to idle and the big fish was now swimming up sea away from the boat. She would tire more quickly now. Billy put short jabs to her and kept her head turned as he gained some line. Finally, the taut line started to slowly rise up and she broke water behind the boat with a series of small jumps. As soon as she jumped Seth started backing on her.

"Keep the pressure on Billy, we're going to try for a quick release on this fish, we don't want to wear her out and kill her ... Get your gloves, John."

Billy reeled and slowly moved back from the transom It took three or four *almosts* to get the 400-pound wind-on leader close enough for John to grab it. Then he lost it twice before he took control.

"It's a catch!" yelled Seth. "Gene, go down and get the tag stick and try to get a tag in her. Take some more pictures girls — before we release her. WHAT A FISH!"

John held the big mama at the transom and Dino slid the Moldcraft lure up the mono leader. Billy kept a short leash on the fish in case she surged, as Gene put a tag in her shoulder. John held her next to the boat by her bill as Seth sped up a little to push some water through the tired fish's gills, while Zoey and Kitty snapped scores of pictures. Kitty had taken pictures of some of the closer jumps and Seth hoped there were some good ones.

Finally, John reached down with his pliers and snipped the leader just above the # 11 hook that was embedded in the corner of her mouth. The hook would rust away in a matter of days. She turned on her side and looked at the crew assembled on the port side with her huge eye, then dropped back behind the boat. Seth shifted into neutral and watched her slowly swim away. She looked all right and would continue to breed and live to fight another day.

The whole crew was patting Billy on the back and giving Seth the thumbs-up sign as they started to put the spread back out. Billy took off his harness gear and climbed to the flybridge to shake Seth's hand.

"Good work, Cappy," said Billy smiling. "How big did you make her?"

"I would say close to 600 pounds, Billy. She was quite a fish to catch on 50 lb. test ... standing up. But I knew you could do it."

"I was thanking God the whole time that you know how to run a boat with a big fish on like that. Thanks."

Seth called down to the crew, "Good job everyone. What we all just witnessed is why we travel to these locations. None of this would be possible without the teamwork that takes place on this boat. You should all be proud of yourselves. Now, we're going to troll northwest in towards the Pelican Cays, then back to Winding Bay and Cherokee Sound. I hope we pick up another billfish, and later this afternoon some dorado and wahoo for dinner tonight. Remember, tomorrow is probably our last diving day at Snood's Blue Hole, unless we find the treasure."

***

Gene Johnson dropped Kitty and Billy off at the Blue Hole with their diving equipment and six extra dive tanks. He drove Jake Snood's work truck back up the Great Abaco Highway past the Leonard M. Thompson Airport to Marsh Harbour. Gene stopped and filled the truck with gas at the Rubis Gas Station, owned by JR's cousin Percy Futch. He didn't pass but a few trucks and cars, even in downtown Marsh Harbour, if you could call it a downtown. To coordinate information, JR set Gene, Rex and Seth up with three of Winona's official Bahamas Constabulary snap phones. Gene and Seth were surprised to learn that Winona was the Constable for the Cherokee and the Casuarina settlements. Her superiors were located in Nassau. Gene felt like he was back in the saddle. He checked the two supermarkets and two small neighborhood convenience stores and all of them sold Marlboro cigarettes. Winona informed him it would take a whole day to run a license plate if the drone's transportation was a truck or car. Undaunted, Gene drove back towards the logging road and set up about a mile and a half north towards Marsh Harbour at the turn off for Winding Bay. From there to the logging road the highway was as straight as a poker. Gene parked facing south across from the turn, then checked in with Seth at the Blue Hole, and with Rex, who was stationed today at the end of the logging road at *The Marls,* on a three-way call. Jake supplied Rex with a bonefish skiff in case he needed to give pursuit.

"Nothing to report here," said Seth. "John and I are about to dive. We should have this Blue Hole exploration completed in the next three hours."

"Rex here ... Mozart and me don't see nothin' yet. Not one boat back here — which don't surprise me. Standin' by."

"Gene here ... standing by at the Winding Bay turnoff."

Seth and John dove down and relieved Billy and Kitty, who were working their way up the north and east walls of the main Blue Hole grotto. Seth and John covered the east and south walls up to twenty feet from the surface.

"Pretty disappointing," said Seth as they all helped fill in their master chart of the hole, while waiting out the required surface interval for their second round of dives.

"Well, you said it might come down to the last twenty feet." said Dino, looking at his dive watch. "Let's find that treasure."

Each team took their turn and worked the more powerful metal detector back and forth over the rocky surface, but to no avail.
Seth turned the metal detector off and handed it up to Dino.

"Well, I don't know what to say." said Seth dejectedly.

"Don't say anything Seth, until we check out the crevice in Cave #1," said Billy

"Yeah, Seth. Stranger things have happened," said Dino.

"OK, set up 25 feet of air hose with a mouthpiece and regulator, and we'll give it a go. Are you ready Kitty?"

"As ready as I'll ever be. I want Dino and Zoey to dive with us."

Dino went out to the truck, put the hose assembly together and was back in ten minutes. The four of them synchronized their watches and dove down to 100 feet. They all adjusted their BC's to keep their fins off the cavern's silty floor. As Zoey played out the fluorescent green safety line, Dino carried the hose assembly, a spare weight belt, spare BC and the air tank. Billy turned on and carried the metal detector. Kitty conserved her energy. Once they entered the cavern their head mounted dive lights quickly found the crevice. Zoey tied off the dive line, then helped Kitty shed her tank. Dino turned the valve on the small auxiliary air tank and handed the mouthpiece to Kitty. She changed out her mouthpiece and headed for the crevice. Her slender body almost fit through, but her weight belt kept her out. Kitty stepped back and dropped her weight belt without looking back to see Dino making the *NO* sign. She stepped through the crevice into the small cave and immediately floated to the ceiling losing her mouthpiece. She looked down with terror in her eyes. Dino kept his cool and pointed at her, then grabbed the spare BC and inflated it with his mouth. He pulled in her air hose and mouthpiece and quickly tied it to the BC with one of its straps. He floated the air hose back up to her and she put it back in her mouth. Kitty coughed and sputtered but started breathing again. Dino grabbed the auxiliary air hose near the tank and started to pull the hose through the crevice slowly. Kitty held on and Dino pulled her within reach. Billy pulled her through the opening and put her discarded weight belt back on. She was breathing but was visibly in distress as she probably had ingested some water into her lungs. Dino signaled to go up, *NOW!* They stopped at 50 feet for 3 minutes and worked up in 10-foot intervals probably quicker than they should have ... but what's right in a crisis?

Zoey broke the surface first, carrying Kitty's dive tank. She yelled, "**Help**! Kitty's in trouble."

Billy came up next, holding Kitty and the auxiliary tank. Seth and John dove in and helped pull her up onto the sandy patch. Dino came out last with the new metal detector and threw it back into the underbrush in his haste to get to Kitty.

"Stand back and give her some room," exclaimed Dino.

Kitty had passed out and looked unresponsive.

John took over, saying, "Billy, run out to JR's black truck and get my black doctor's bag from under the front seat."

Billy was back in a flash with the bag and John started listening to her lungs and heart with his stethoscope.

"Her heart sounds OK, but she definitely has fluid in her lungs. Stretch her out so I can clear her lungs."

John turned Kitty's head to the side and checked her breathing passages.

"They look clear and she is breathing ... but very shallow," said John.

Billy said, "I was a lifeguard all through high school and college, let me give her CPR."

Billy blew five breaths in Kitty's mouth, followed by pressing with his hands clasped together on her chest and she immediately coughed up quite a bit of water and regained consciousness. She coughed some more and sat up. Everybody clapped their hands and patted Billy and John on the back.

Seth's phone rang and he fumbled for it in his duffel. "Seth and Rex; a pickup truck came out of the Winding Bay turnoff and dropped a man off about a hundred yards from the logging road," said Gene. "He's carrying a duffel, medium build, Caucasian, short black beard, tan ball cap, tan fishing shirt and blue jeans. Rex, drive your truck up to the highway; I'm going to follow the truck."

"Gene, we have an emergency here, and I don't know how serious it is yet," said Seth. "Kitty almost drowned. John's checking her out right now."

"If you need me there call me. This driver can't go far since we're on an island. Rex can handle the drone if that's what's in the passenger's duffel. I want to tail his chauffeur. Keep me posted on Kitty. What's that beeping noise I hear in the background. It sounds like an alarm," said Gene.

Seth hadn't noticed it in all the excitement, but he heard it now. A noise was coming from the bushes on the west side of the sandy patch. Seth walked into the underbrush and found the discarded metal detector, beeping and blinking, and pegging its treas-o-meter. Seth picked it up and it continued to beep in a six-foot square. '*Well ain't that some shit!*' thought Seth, '*that wily pirate knew everyone would concentrate on the Blue Hole but not on the limestone rock around it … and it would be easy to find the treasure at a later date if you knew exactly where it was. We've all been turning the metal detector off as we left the water to conserve the battery*'. Seth turned the detector off and set it back on the sandy patch.

"How do you feel Kitty? You gave us quite a scare," said John.

"Not so good, Dr. John. My joints all hurt, I have a splitting headache, and my fingers and feet are tingling. I feel like there's a rash or something all over my chest."

"Billy, do you think the decompression cycle was compromised?"

"It could have been. But no one else is ill. We were more interested in getting her up here and making sure she could breathe."

"I think it would be smart to fly her to Miami Mercy Hospital and get a Neurologist to look at her, but we have to do it quick. If she is suffering from the bends, it's nothing to fool with. They have a decompression chamber there."

"She dropped her weight belt and lost her air hose inside the crevice. Kitty almost drowned … but Dino floated her air hose back up to her and we were able to pull her out. I think the trauma brought this on … she was stressed to the max," said Zoey.

"Well, that could have done it. Sometimes just repetitive diving can get you bent, even when the decompression protocol is followed to the letter. Every dive you make increases your odds of getting the bends," said John.

"Isn't there a decompression unit in Nassau?" asked Billy.

"Yes, but they won't take your medical insurance, and it's the same distance as flying to Miami."

"Can you fly her there, John?"

"No, a bends victim shouldn't fly higher than 500-feet. High altitudes will just exacerbate her symptoms and it could be fatal. I'll call a helicopter from South Florida Helicopter Charters right now. I can write her flight and decompression prescriptions."

Billy filled Seth in about Kitty's condition, as he walked back from loading some gear into the pickup.

"They're going to have to fly Kitty in a helicopter sent from Miami ASAP. John just ordered a helicopter for her; It should be at the Marsh Harbour Airport in two hours. John suspects she has the bends," said Billy.

"There's that fucking drone again!" yelled Dino as he was loading tanks into JR's truck.

As fast as it flew over it was gone, and ten seconds later two shotgun reports were heard out to the east.

Seth grabbed the Constable phone and called Gene and Rex, "Gene get back here. The drone just flew over here again. I need you to take Billy and Kitty to the airport; Kitty likely has the bends."

"Hey Rex, did you shoot?"

"Yes, I did, Mr. Seth. Drone #2 just bit the dust."

"Rex, Gene here — that drone pilot is in the brush on the other side of the road, not too far from you. Let Mozart loose over there and see if y'all can run him down."

"Roger that, Mr. Gene."

"Seth, the truck that dropped off the drone pilot, drove into the private high dollar section of Winding Bay. I've got the address and the truck's license plate. I'm on my way back for Kitty and Billy now. We should have time to get their gear off the TAR BABY. How did the treasure hunt go today?"

"I'll tell you when we get a minute alone."

Seth walked over to Billy and Kitty and said, "Kitty ... I want you to know how much I appreciate your courage. And Billy, it's been fun fishing with my old pal. What a fish! And thanks for bringing over the new Fisher metal detector."

"Well, we didn't find anything. But, thanks for your hospitality, and that big marlin," said Billy.

"This treasure hunt is not over, you know. I have a feeling that it's just starting ... and everybody that's participated is going to share equally. Get your girl well, so you can come back with us soon."

"We'll be back, Seth," said Kitty.

"I'm going to miss those grilled dorado dinners," said Billy, with a smile.

Gene pulled in at the Blue Hole with Snood's truck.

"Hey Billy and Kitty, come on over and get in the truck," said Gene. "First, I'll take you down to JR's so Billy can gather your stuff off of *TAR BABY*. Then I'll drive you to the FBO at the airport to catch the helicopter."

"Do we really have time to go to the Hatteras?" said Billy as he and Kitty approached Snood's pick up.

"Get in, the helicopter isn't due to arrive for two hours, and they're not going to leave without you. No problem."

As Gene pulled out, Zoey, Dino and John said their goodbyes to Billy and Kitty ... Rex pulled in with Mozart sitting in the front seat of his pickup truck.

"Any luck?" yelled Gene through the passenger window.

"Nah, he gave Mozart and me the slip back in the brush. He must have high-tailed it when I got the first shot off. But I got what's left of Drone #2 back in the truck's bed."

"Did you hit it with your first shot?"

"Both shots."

"How'd you get so good with that shotgun?" asked Gene.

"Shootin' doves on Andros."

***

Later that night Seth was having a nightcap up in the flybridge with Gene and John. Dino and Zoey were packed for their flight home and asleep in their cabin. It was a calm night, and the water looked like glass. A few lights still twinkled in Cherokee Settlement and over on Casuarina Point. Earlier, Winona had phoned in Gene's information on the Winding Bay address and the white pickup truck's license number to Nassau Police Headquarters. Billy called from Miami and reported that Kitty was in the chamber at Miami Mercy for her first decompression session. He thought they'd be there at least a week.

Tomorrow morning, they would drop off Zoey and Dino at Boat Harbour Marina, in Marsh Harbour, where they would take a cab to the airport. Later that afternoon, Scotty Remington and Freddy Buckley were scheduled to fly in and meet them at the Boat Harbour Marina pool bar. They would all ride the four miles back to Sea Spray and fish the following day.

Seth took a sip of the Turley Cedarman 2008 Zinfandel he'd uncorked for the three of them and savored it for a few seconds before saying, "Gene and John, I think we found the treasure today."

What... w-w-where?" stammered Gene, setting down his wine glass.

John laughed nervously and asked. "What kind of treasure, Seth — like *treasure* our friends?"

"Well that too, of course. But when Dino came out of the Blue Hole behind Billy and Zoey while we were all dragging Kitty up onto the sandy patch … he cast the metal detector aside and rushed to help us get her onto dry ground. Because of Dino's adrenalin, the metal detector ended up way back in the bushes. After a few minutes, when all the commotion was finally calming down a little, I heard a beeping sound back there in the underbrush. Actually, you tipped me off on the phone, Gene. I followed that sound. It was the metal detector beeping. Dino had not turned it off before he tossed it. I picked it up and the meter was pegged, and the red light was flashing. I moved it around that area and found about a six-foot square where the detector stayed activated — outside of that, no beeping. I turned it off and put it back into JR's truck."

"I get it," said John. "Each time we came out of the water we turned the metal detector off to preserve the battery. Actually … you asked us to do that."

"Right … Except, I'm not sure what's down there. It could be an anchor or a cannon. But … I do think it's too much of a coincidence. I think, in the Pirate Captain's mind, the Blue Hole was a diversion."

"So, what do we do now, start digging?" asked John.

"We need to keep to our schedule; fish and dive every other day like we have been. I would string up a camouflage net over the suspected area and carefully excavate by hand until we know what's down there. It has to be fairly close to the surface — I mean there's only 12 to 18 inches of soil in that pine forest, then it's all limestone. We'll dive a little just to satisfy the next drone fly-over … we can get Rex and more guards to watch it 24/7 when we know what's buried there."

"Winona should get the information on the owner of the Winding Bay house tomorrow, along with whoever owns the pickup truck," said Gene. "It will be nice to start finding out who's been watching us and why."

"There's a lot to find out. We'll brief Scotty and Freddy when we get over to Sea Spray, tomorrow," said Seth, before finishing off the last of his Turley wine and heading below.

CHAPTER SEVEN

MARWAN followed Hakim and Jamaal off the Gulfstream jet and walked across the barren runway to the main hangar that also served as the terminal. He quickly sized up his surroundings — the Bahamian air was almost as hot and humid as the weather they'd left behind in Cameroon. There was, however, a nice sea breeze blowing in off the Atlantic Ocean that made it more bearable. A tall, blond, good-looking gentleman was shaking hands with Hakim and then Jamaal. "James" was introduced as *Britannia's* yachting operations manager. He heard himself being introduced to Christian Thomason as Harry Muneer's personal secretary, Marvin. He shook hands with Mr. Thomason and continued to size up Spanish Cay. The runway was devoid of any foliage at this central location but had scrub jungle along both sides of it otherwise. Except for a couple of small prop planes that were tied down, there was no aviation traffic and only one airport employee was chocking the Gulfstream's wheels. He saw no security system cameras outside the main hangar and offices.

Marwan was clean shaven and had a close-cropped western haircut. The barber in their mountain fortress was getting good at giving western haircuts. His five counterparts had already been shorn. Each day more of the new British recruits filtered in and the first thing they did was visit the barber. Marwan wore a blue Brooks Brothers button down oxford shirt, with tan slacks, a Brighton belt and a pair of Clark's cordovan driver loafers with no socks. His Maui Jim aviator sunglasses topped off his portrayal of the casual understated elegance that *Britannia* wished to convey. His appearance was a far cry from the flowing robes, headscarves, and the bearded countenance he had left behind. He carried a tanned leather briefcase on a shoulder strap that contained a yellow legal pad, two Cross chrome ballpoint pens, a Glock 9mm pistol and three ammunition clips. In actuality, he was Harry Muneer's bodyguard. Hakim wanted him along to gain firsthand North American experience, if he was needed in any circumstance in the future.

Christian Thomason had a six-seat golf cart waiting and everybody climbed aboard.

"Just have your pilot show all your passports to the customs official, as I mentioned in our last communication," said Christian. "We don't waste your time going through the formalities. That's how they do the boats here, too. The Captain takes all the passports and fills out all the forms, Mr. Muneer."

"Well, thank you Christian," said Hakim in his adopted British English. "Is there any security for the parked airplanes?"

"Please call me Chris."

"Only if you call me Harry, Chris."

"OK, Harry. The customs office and FBO close at dark. Everything is locked up and both employees take a boat back to Coopers Town. Some jet owners have their pilots sleep aboard overnight, but there's nothing on a jet that the locals would want. There are security personnel, however, at the hotel and marina."

Hakim had acquired a talent for his British accent on his recent trip to England, and Jamaal had spoken English for so long it was hard to tell where he was from. Since the British recruits began arriving in Cameroon, Hakim, Marwan, Jabbar, Shareef, Aksleel, Naser and Abdul had formed a class each night to work on their accents with the new recruits. His compatriots were busy every day now with all aspects of the new operatives' training regimen.

The golf cart cleared the inland end of the runway and headed on a path through a thickly wooded Queen Palm section of the small island which quickly ended at the marina and hotel area. They passed a couple of private residences on the way.

"Coming up next is the large fuel dock I mentioned, at the north end of the 83-slip marina. The dock you will be leasing is the 200-foot long, two-sided 'beam-to' dock just past it," said Chris pointing — "There's plenty of room for even six 52-footers, if you add one later, plus any support boats you might need."

Hakim remembered how it looked on Google Earth, but there was no comparison to seeing it all first-hand.

They continued around the basin to the marina office, restaurant and hotel. Chris took them for a tour of the hotel and introduced Harry to the friendly manager, Carter Combs, and his assistant manager, Molly Mallory.

"Chris explained that you want to start all your cruises in Nassau, giving your clients an International Airport to fly in and out of and a night at Atlantis Resort coming and going."

"Yes, Carter," said Hakim, who was having trouble keeping his train of thought with Molly standing there. She was 5'3", with sun-bleached blond hair, and a body that rivaled Holly's, his recent consort in London. Molly was dressed in a starched white shirt, open at the neck, navy blue culottes, and hemp wedge heels. Hakim fought for composure and said, "*Th-the-**they*** will stay in the hotel each of those nights and will have the run of the casino and property. Some of them may want to extend their vacation's *b-beginning* or end and *sta-stay* at Atlantis longer."

"If our services are ever needed here, just let me know."

Molly made eye contact with Hakim and melted him with her smile.

"*Th-Thank*-you. Your n-new hotel has a *n-ni-nice* pool and TIKI BAR."

"Have you seen our 'Wrecker's Bar', Mr. Muneer? It's built out over the Atlantic," said Molly.

"Not yet," said Chris, jumping in after a long, awkward, speechless pause by Hakim. "We're headed out that way next."

Chris drove the golf cart around the hotel to the southeast end of the little island and showed Hakim two more private residences and the hotel's employees dormitory.

"How many private residences are on the island?" asked Hakim.

"Seven," answered Chris. The other three are on the west side of the airstrip overlooking the Sea of Abaco. The island is three miles long and we're driving across the widest part of it now which is only a half-mile wide."

They drove east across the same palm tree shaded trail which opened up to Barefoot Beach and a lagoon fed by the Atlantic Ocean.

"Over there are the three condo buildings you can lease," said Chris, motioning to his left. "Out on that point, straight ahead, is the 'Wrecker's Bar' — it's only open on the weekends."

They stopped at the condos and inspected each one, in detail.

"I think these condos will work out fine, Chris. But we need two sets of bunkbeds in each of the four condos in Bldg. #1. In Bldg. # 2, we'll need two bunk beds in one of the upstairs condos. The other upstairs condo will serve as an employee lounge with comfortable chairs. The whole first floor will serve as a common kitchen and dining room with tables and chairs for

16, including a carpeted meeting room across the hall with a large black board and no furniture. Condo #3 will have a queen size bed and a desk in each upstairs condo and two separate offices on the first floor with desks, chairs, and filing cabinets. Is there wi-fi service in these condo's?"

"Yes, and there's enough existing furniture here to take care of everything but the bunkbeds and office furniture," said Chris. I can also order — say, three refrigerators, two freezers, two dishwashers, and a propane five-burner stove with an oven. There's already three charcoal grills between the condos, and I can order a couple of roll-around prep tables from Nassau. You can buy all the pots, pans, skillets, and utensils you need right in Marsh Harbour."

"We'll bring some of that with us. Is there a generator on this island for emergency electric power?"

"The island's electric comes from Marsh Harbour, and the island emergency generator is only for the hotel and marina."

"We'll look into getting a portable generator. I like what I see so far. Can you show me the hangar we talked about renting?"

"Absolutely," said Chris as they all got back in the cart.

They took a more direct path back to the runway and stopped in front of two smaller hangars just south of the large main hangar.

"We'll have spare parts and supplies to store with some security."

Chris had a set of keys in his pocket and opened a side door in the hangar. He switched the overhead lights on, and the hangar was completely empty.

Hakim noticed a small office in the southeast back corner and said, "The whole hangar is clean and looks like somebody just moved out?"

"The construction company that rebuilt the hotel and restaurant, after it burnt down, used this hangar for storage and staging."

"Where is the forklift, I asked you about?"

"In the airport's main hangar — you can use the forklift any time you need it to off load your airplane or load something onto your charter boats. As long as you give them a little notice and use the airport's forklift operator."

"I'm ready to sign the lease if you will note my furnishing requirements. I realize that we'll have to buy the additional furniture and bedding. Just make a note in the lease outlining the additions and have them initial it and I'm ready to sign. Include your charges for installation of the kitchen equipment by your people. When we move in, a couple of months from now, our personnel will install the bunk beds, dining tables, chairs and office equipment. Leave one refrigerator and one freezer in the hangar. Please buy the items we need and store them in the hangar. Bill us monthly. Once we're here we will clean the condo units ourselves and only require that the hotel launder the sheets and towels. Our men will pick up and deliver the sheets and towels to the hotel. We'll need a contact for mechanical problems like air conditioning and plumbing. I also noticed that each condo building has a downstairs laundry room for our personal clothes and uniforms."

"James, you have read the original contracts, do you have anything else to add?" asked Hakim.

"We should have an extra room on the island for our jet pilots to stay overnight, and we may need extra room if a charter party ends up here because of mechanical problems or bad weather."

Hakim thought for a few seconds and said, "Chris, how about negotiating a monthly rate for a hotel room with two queens. We can use it to put up our airplane pilots if they stay over — or a Yanmar mechanic or electronics tech if we have to fly one in. I'm sure an extra room will come in handy."

"I'll make sure I have all this in writing, Harry," said Chris, adding to his notes.

"OK, we're going to fly over to our Nassau headquarters now on other business. You can email me the final contract in Nassau. I'll sign it and send it back — if any changes are needed, call me."

"Do you want to fly up to Marsh Harbour and check it out?"

"No, I checked it out on the internet and Google Earth. The supermarkets, beverage distributors, the Marsh Harbour boat yards, tradesmen and repair services are already supporting the Moorings and two other charter boat outfits, along with Abaco Beach Resort, Boat Harbour, Winding Bay, and all the other marinas, hotels and restaurants. I'm confident that the supply infrastructure is sufficient. Please buy us a Caterpillar 12,000 watt electric start diesel generator and have it wired into Bldg. #2 with a transfer switch."

Chris Thomason watched the Gulfstream lift off Spanish Cay's 4,400-foot runway. Harry Muneer and his associates would be in Nassau before he was passing behind Whale Cay on his way back to Hope Town. He'd already cleared the additions and changes with John Seamus, Spanish Cay's owner, by phone from the airport manager's office. His secretary should have the final contract ready to email to both parties when he arrived on his Albury 23, *RENEGADE,* an hour and a half later. The 40-mile trip to Hope Town would give him time to plan where he would import *Britannia's* equipment and furniture. Probably from Fort Lauderdale — where some of the items would carry as much as a 40% customs duty plus shipping. Chris always marveled at the amount of investment money that England, the United States and other foreign countries invested in the Bahamas. He'd gone to Florida

State University and studied real estate and accounting and had traveled since to Europe and beyond. But he wouldn't want to be anywhere else in the world but the Abacos, where generations of his loyalist family and relatives had survived by farming, fishing and finally wrecking. His father told him the wrecking part was where the money was made. Shipwrecks happened regularly, before the GPS was invented, in the reef-ringed Bahamas. Some speculated, when the wrecks were not plentiful enough to support the wreckers, a navigation light or two may have been moved now and then. A myth circulated that a salvaged cargo belonged 100% to the salvor. In truth, the government received 15% as import duty, laborers, brokers and warehousers got 15%, the wrecker received about 50% and the ship owner settled for 20%.

Over the years, the Thomason family had amassed a lot of what could not be made more plentiful — land. In the last 75 years they had carefully developed their Abaco legacy into an orderly vacation paradise. Now, they developed, rented, managed and brokered it.

Chris motored past Green Turtle Cay and smiled as the wind whistled through his hair and the sun made the water glisten. There were very few places in the world where a businessman could travel on an 80-mile business trip, involving a large five-figure commission, and be transported there using a 23-foot, outboard motor powered, skiff traveling at 30 miles an hour ... and where that was regarded as the normal mode of transportation.

***

Dr. Dirk Mendelsohn sewed in the last stiches around his patient's left nipple and dabbed away the last traces of blood. He stood back and admired what was probably the 3,500th pair of his famous "Mendelsohn Slopers". He'd lost track of the exact number during his 25 checkered years in the plastic surgery business. This 20-year-old pole dancer would be back at work in two weeks earning more and bigger tips, just for showing off her bouncy new "Mendelsohn's".

Since losing his license at his lucrative St. Petersburg Clinic three years ago, for reasons he considered archaic and unrealistic (re-use of silicone implants, receiving sexual favors in exchange for implant surgery and sexual harassment), Dirk's life had changed radically. He thought back to the "good old days" when he could afford to trade the "Tits for Tat" with the really good-looking dancers. He called them his "Golden Pole" girls. But they had ultimately betrayed him — the payoff was always four nights of his choice, one up front and three after. But some of the titty dancers reneged on the balance and a couple of them turned him in when he pressed the issue. There was no honor.

So, disgraced and occupation-less, Dirk reinvented himself in the nearby Bahamas. He still was a man of some means, so after a few well-placed bribes and six months attendance at The University of the West Indies Medical School, Dirk obtained a license to practice in the Bahamas.

His wife and their children remained in their Brightwaters residence. She was still the top real estate producer at her own firm, Conway Suncoast Realty, where she had forged her own lucrative career, using her maiden name Christine Conway.

Dirk advertised in women's health and fashion magazines as was his custom and had many five-star reviews on his website. But the Doctor added a new twist; he packaged five days in Nassau on Paradise Island in a hotel suite including round-trip airfare from St. Petersburg — which included a pair of silicone "Mendelsohn Slopers", for $4,900.

The benchmark for Florida quality and aesthetic breast implants has always been Dr. Daniel Diaco of Tampa. His silicone implants were simply known as "Diaco's". A pair of his creations cost $10,900. Most woman could return to a desk job the sixth day after an implant operation. Strippers and "Titty Bar" dancers averaged two weeks of downtime. How could Dr. Dirk offer medical tourism at such a bargain price?

First, he had his own plane, a single engine Piper Lance that carried six passengers and all the luggage you could fit into it. Second, he operated in a low-cost outpatient day surgery facility in a foreign country, instead of a regulated hospital in the United States. Third, he rented a budget suite on Paradise Island at a cost of $500 per week. Fourth, he used recycled silicone implants bought on the black market. U.S. medical law prohibits the re-use of silicone implants removed for any reason (i.e., women want bigger or smaller sizes in a second operation). Fifth, his patients signed a contract that absolved the surgeon from responsibility for any post-operative infections. Sixth, he was paid up-front in cash. Seventh, many women liked to hide the fact that they were having a vanity operation and could explain their absence as a vacation.

But, a few of Dirk's implant operations ended badly with fatal infections, and his medical business suffered. Dirk desperately needed more income to finance his extravagant lifestyle. He was quickly depleting his 401K and IRA retirement accounts in the United States to keep up appearances. Resilient as ever, he invested in a Nassau strip club and then started a numbers racket there with his new partner. Next, Dr. Dirk became the behind the scenes brains of an extortion, protection, and loan sharking racket that was enforced by a group of 7-foot tall Haitian illegals. Finally, he turned to even more questionable pursuits, such as financing a group of drug smuggling commercial fishermen from the nearby Arawak Springs Settlement on mystical Taino Island, near North Eleuthera.

Most people are not aware that Bahamian citizens were not allowed, by law, to gamble in their own Bahamian casinos. The numbers racket became an instant success.

Dr. Dirk melded quickly into Abaco Island and Nassau society. He became the largest donor to the annual Family Islands Regatta of native wood "work boat" racing. Each year four classes of "work boat" sloops from each major Bahamian island raced for the Championship. The Class A sloop was the largest, and most competitive, at 28 feet, with a 60-foot mast, 3-hiking pry-boards, a 32-foot boom length and a crew of 10. The races were hotly contested, and each island's pride was at stake. Dirk quickly became Abaco *RAGE'S* skipper based on his sailing skills, that were honed during his "All American" collegiate years sailing at Yale University. The regatta's rules allow four of the ten crew members to be non-Bahamian citizens in Class A. He also started a pro-bono medical clinic in Nassau that operated on Bahamian children that were born with cleft-palates. Dirk knew how to work a crowd and he became immensely popular in a truly short period of time.

***

It took longer to drive to the offices of Wilson, Egbert and Qshear, London - Nassau, than the flight from Spanish Cay Airstrip to Lynden Pindling International Airport in Nassau. Hakim and his party were cleared through customs at the Jet Aviation FBO. The law firm sent a junior partner, Dick Roberts, to pick them up in the firm's club van. New Providence Island is 21 miles long and 7 miles wide, and has a population of 248,000, which accounts for 70% of the country's total population. There are 700 islands in The Commonwealth of the Bahamas, but only 30 of them are inhabited. Nassau is the seat of the Bahamian government. It is also home to over 400 banks and trust companies. Abdul Qshear instructed Dick Roberts to set up a Ltd. Corporation for *Britannia* and establish their address and a post office box at the same building address as the law firm. International corporate banking and investment law is the firm's specialty. Dick Roberts became *Britannia's* official agent.

The van worked its way through the congested streets of Nassau. The city was crowded, and Dick alluded to big city problems of drugs and crime.

"Still, more than two-thirds of the four million-plus tourists who visit the Bahamas each year use our hotels and cruise ports."

"What about Paradise Island?" asked Hakim. "That's where our cruises will begin and end."

"Paradise Island is why tourism still works here, Mr. Muneer. It is accessible only by two bridges, the island is heavily patrolled, and the resorts all have excellent security. Tourists are encouraged not to leave Paradise Island at night."

Hakim, Jamaal and Marwan could see the large cruise ships moored in the harbor between the two islands.

"You'll be able to see the two bridges in a few seconds," said Dick, as they drove parallel to the harbor. "Mr. Willingham and Mr. Holz are waiting in one of our boardrooms for your meeting."

"We're anxious to finally meet them."

Fifteen minutes later they were in the boardroom shaking hands with "Honest Bob" Willingham and Phillip Oliver Holz.

"Well, now that everyone has met, let's get down to business. First, I want to know where we stand on the two RC-52s in the Exumas … Bob?" asked Hakim.

"Those boats surveyed out very similarly. I had the Puerto Rican yard, that is now working on the BVI boats, estimate the Exuma boats — and based on your recommendations and guidelines, these two will come in a little less than the first three."

Hakim looked over both surveys and estimates and nodded his approval.

"Looks like you lowballed them a little better than I did on the first lot. Good job! When can that yard start on the last two?"

"The two that are in Puerto Rico now are about half finished, so they could start in about 3 weeks. The Trinidad boat is almost finished. Phillip and I flew separately — he to Trinidad and I to Fajardo, Puerto Rico. The yards are making strides and are trying to earn some of the early-bird payments. If we close the deals on the Exuma boats today, we can get the paperwork finished and recorded, money transferred, and have those boats delivered to the boatyard in Puerto Rico in about two weeks."

"I should have the Spanish Cay deal done by the end of this week, so you and Phillip can hire two delivery crews to transport the first two Puerto Rico boats to Spanish Cay. We will be glad to pay you extra to make sure they arrive shipshape. I want you to inspect them and their tie-up."

"No problem, Harry," said Honest Bob.

"James and I will deliver the Trinidad boat to a training facility near Trinidad. James has an unlimited license. We haven't got the details worked out there yet, but we're close to leasing a recently closed dive camp on Little Bonaire," lied Hakim.

"Where are you getting your captains?" asked Honest Bob.

"James is using Neptune Maritime to license our captains in the United States and Bahamas. He and our captains will ferry the boats back and forth to Nassau with our own crews. James will also train our stewards, and cross-train our chefs from England. We are also using an advertising firm here in Nassau, Cruise Ad, to do our entire cruise advertising campaign. They will place ads in several U.S. and U.K. boating magazines including Yachting Monthly, Power and Motoryacht, Southern Boating, Sailing Today and Cruising World. James, Marvin and I will meet with them tomorrow morning at Atlantis before we start back to England on the Gulfstream ... Any questions? ...Then, thank you gentlemen for attending this meeting ... Mr. Roberts, will you drive us over to Atlantis? I'd like you to stay through the business part of our meeting there, so we don't get 'homered' as the Americans are so fond of saying."

"It will be my pleasure, Mr. Muneer," said Dick, smiling so hard that his eyes almost looked Asian.

***

Hakim could not believe the size and scale of Atlantis. The two high rise spires on the main pink building commanded the island's view from any location. Three other huge hotel buildings graced the manicured property, sharing its vast shoreline, a water sports lagoon and water slide rides through shark-filled tanks that defied description. Fleets of sailboats, powerboats, ski boats and wakeboard boats hugged the shoreline, waiting to be used. Hakim and his party were immediately ushered into the General Manager's office. Abram Issacs ('please call me Abram') was second in command to multi-millionaire owner Sol Kerzner, a Russian-Jew from South Africa, who started his business life as a CPA in Johannesburg. Hakim made it clear that James would be handling the business agreements for *Britannia*.

Abram took the *Britannia* group for a tour of the whole property, including the casino, and the hotel rooms. They started at the mega-yacht marina which was built on a grand scale. Abram and Jamaal negotiated at dockside for a 55-foot full-time slip that should always be available unless the weather or a mechanical problem altered *Britannia's* schedule. In that event, another slip would be made available at the monthly rate, even if an Atlantis tour boat had to be moored at the fuel dock. As they toured the restaurants, bars, public areas and terraced staircases, they noticed the large two-story aquarium that ran throughout the entire main building. While eating dinner with Abram in one of their several restaurants, Marwan and Jamaal started to recognize some of the larger pelagic fish swimming past in the enormous salt water aquarium. A huge Manta Ray went by about every ten minutes. He was recognizable by three large scars in a row on his left wing. He was bigger than two jet-skis lashed together. Some of the sharks were almost as big, with eyes the size of car headlights and mouths full of razor-sharp teeth. This ever-moving montage actually took their breath away. Motion was also constant in the lobby and on the wide staircases, walkways and waterslides. Women of all ages wearing halters, short shorts and skimpy bikinis walked by in droves. Teenagers seemed to be having fun everywhere and weren't looking at their phones. Jamaal secured a special room price for *Britannia* customers, as an excellent dinner came to an end.

"One more thing, Abram, I would like your concierge desk to give our mutual customers first-class service. Limousine pick-up and delivery to the airport. A wake up-call on their charter day, along with baggage transfer and a personal escort to our charter boat slip in the marina. Our charter steward will call your concierge desk when we re-enter the harbor so they will be met at the slip and escorted to their rooms."

Abram smiled at Jamaal and said, "That is precisely what our concierge personnel are trained to do, Mr. Raskin."

Having to make nice and negotiate with Jews was bad enough. But Hakim, Jamaal, and Marwan were totally repulsed by the exposure of female pulchritude in the public areas, and by the opulence and decadence displayed at every turn. Jamaal took it more in stride, having experienced the sights of more forward-thinking Muslims in Dubai's modern seaside resorts. Yet, all three of them never let on that they were all-in with their Islam dogma to turn back the Planet Earth's clock more than 1,400 years. They all finished the dregs of their second glass of Detoren, Black Lion Shiraz, consumed of course in subterfuge, then thanked their host and headed to their room. Early tomorrow, they would board the Gulfstream Jet and fly to Venezuela.

CHAPTER EIGHT

SETH dialed in VHF station 71 as he left Abaco Beach Resort and Boat Harbour Marina behind and headed east across the Sea of Abaco to Sea Spray Marina. Scotty Remington and Freddy Buckley, newly arrived from the airport, had joined Seth, Gene and John for a cold one at the pool bar. They all jumped aboard *TAR BABY* for the four-mile run to Elbow Key and Sea Spray. It was 3:35 in the afternoon and the Custom Boat Shootout was in its final day of competition. Most of the sixty boats competing were concentrated in *The Pocket* off Tilloo Cut. The rest were spread across the *Bridge, Brady's Bend, Wonderland* and *Jurassic Park* northeast of the Hope Town Lighthouse. The VHF radio squawked every minute or so with, "*LAYLA* hooked up, blue marlin, 3:36."... "*UNO MAS* hooked up, blue marlin 3:37."... "*WAVE PAVER*, blue marlin release, 3:39." ... "*ROSE*, hooked up 3:42 blue marlin."

The afternoon bite had started and sounded as if it would last to "lines out" at 4:30. Then all sixty boats would file back into Boat Harbour for a banquet and prizes. There seemed to be a tournament somewhere in the Abacos almost every weekend. The released blue marlin were worth 400 points, white marlin and spearfish 150 points, sailfish 100 points, points per pound for one species each of dolphin(dorado), wahoo and yellowfin or blackfin tuna over a minimum of 15 pounds. Winners won large amounts of cash in the daily and overall calcuttas, plus an array of merchandise and elaborate trophies. Seth finally turned switched off the staccato radio chatter on tournament channel 71, as Freddy and Scotty joined the conversation on the flybridge.

" I hope these tournament guys leave a few marlin for us," laughed Scotty.

"How's the fishing been, Seth?" asked Freddy.

"A little on the slow side, but this new moon seems to have clicked it up a few notches as you can hear on the radio. We've caught a couple of big marlin and some nice dorado in the 40 to 50-pound range. Billy caught a 600-pounder standing up, and Dino landed the other big marlin about 500 pounds in the fighting chair. The girls caught the big dorados."

"I haven't seen Billy and Dino in a while, how are they?" asked Freddy.

"They're both fine. Dino's getting married soon so we'll all see Dino and Zoey at the wedding. Billy is in Miami with Kitty, she got bent while we were diving the Blue Hole."

"Wow, how did they get there?" said Scotty.

"John arranged a helicopter because you can't fly higher than 500 feet with the bends. Billy called last night and said she was doing fine."

"That's good news!" said Freddy.

"We'll fish tomorrow morning, it's prime time and I bet we have a good day," said Seth with a smile. "Anything new in the 'Burg', Scotty?"

"Nothing much. Tourist season is over and the traffic's not as bad. How's Lori doing?"

"I talk to her a couple times a week. She's at her place on Torch Lake in Michigan, doing the 'Grandmother' thing. She's fine. I'll go up there the end of July when I put *TAR BABY* on the hard for hurricane season."

"How's Pam, Scotty?" asked Gene.

"Pam and I broke up a couple of weeks ago."

"Oh man, sorry to hear that, I thought you two were going to be an item."

"Things went well the first year, but then she started acting like my ex-wife. You know, trying to change me into someone she thought I should be. Pretty soon she was just a pain in the ass. She went from trying to please me into nagging me about every little thing. I started feeling down and out, and that Led Zeppelin song, *Black Dog,* started playing in my head, over and over. You know, it went from, *'Hey mama when you walk that way, I just can't keep away.'* to, *'before too long I found out, what it feels like to be down and out ... spending my money, driving my cars, telling her friends she's going be a star ... I don't know but I've been told — a big-legged woman don't have no soul!'*

"Scotty, you fucking crack me up ... but I feel your pain," said John, laughing along with Seth, Gene and Freddy.

"Hey," said Scotty. "I married the first one and it cost me big bucks ... at least this one only cost me my time and her plane ticket back to Seattle. There's millions of them out there, boys, but most of them are fucking anal ... I'm sure one day I'll find a woman that loves me as much my dog does."

Scotty's quirky sense of humor always kept the guys laughing. He was tall, sandy-haired and good looking—in other words a "chick magnet" even in his older years. He had retired early as the head of a Wall Street hedge fund, a position that had been all-consuming. He moved south to St. Petersburg and joined the sporting scene, racing sailboats, fishing and generally making up for lost time. He fit right in with the "Geezers" and their activities.

When they all stopped laughing, they were almost at the White Sound channel marker. Once the boat was backed in, moored and everyone was settled in, they took their six-seat golf cart and headed for an early dinner at Captain Jack's in Hope Town.

Back on the boat in the Hatteras's salon after dinner Seth, John, and Gene filled Scotty and Freddy in on the diving and possible treasure at Snood's Blue Hole.

"I agree with you on the camouflage net idea," said Freddy, as he inspected one of the drones that Rex had shot down.

"Seth, where are we going to get the hand-tools we'll need to excavate the limestone?" asked Scotty.

"JR tells me Jake Snood has a couple barns full of tools, tractors, front end loaders and machinery."

As John was passing out another round of Kaliks, Seth's local constabulary cell phone rang and he answered, "Hey, JR ... Winona got the information ... Really! I know her ... and she owns the house **and** the truck ... I'll fill you in when we come down ... No, tomorrow we fish, we're coming down to dive the day after tomorrow. Don't forget the tools and the camo net ... OK - and thank Winona."

"Wait until you hear this, guys, said Seth, shaking his head. "Winona heard back from Nassau, and the Winding Bay house and the pickup truck belong to Christine Conway."

"Holy-shit! I'd heard a rumor Dirk opened a practice in the Bahamas," said John.

"Who's Dirk? ... I thought you said, Christine Conway?" said Scotty.

"She's married to Dirk Mendelsohn," said Gene.

"Now it makes sense," said John. "I also heard he filed for bankruptcy in Florida two years ago and switched everything he owned into her name."

"Are we talking about Christine Conway, the realtor from Tampa Bay?" said Scotty. "She sold me my fucking house in Venetian Isles."

"Yeah," said Gene. "Her husband, Dirk Mendelsohn, was a plastic surgeon in St. Pete. He lost his medical license over re-using silicone implants and a sex scandal involving some of his titty-bar dancer patients."

"Man, I get the Dirk Mendelsohn and Christine Conway connection ... We know him from sailboat racing. They still live on Snell Isle ...but who's Winona?" asked Freddy.

"She's JR's wife," said Seth. "And, she's also the Constable in the Cherokee settlement ... she traced the house address and the truck license plate for us."

"Gotcha," said Freddy.

"We need to figure out why Dirk Mendelsohn's interested in what we're doing in Snood's Blue Hole ... I don't get it?" said Seth. "We'll start making inquiries about him here and maybe in St. Pete."

"Let's call it a night gents, fishing day tomorrow," said John, yawning.

***

The third marlin was the biggest one of the day and after a series of jumps she swam straight down. Freddy was in the chair, sitting in a bucket harness, with a Tiagra 50-wide/2-speed reel attached to a bent butt Crowder E-glass rod with a roller tip and a stripper guide before the reel. Seth told Freddy to be patient, let her run against the drag, and she'd stop down about 250 feet where it got dark and she couldn't see. Freddy took both hands off the reel and rested his arms as the bucket harness straps did the work.

As the big marlin swam down, Seth reviewed that day's earlier hook-ups in his mind: The first marlin that morning hooked up on a Black Bart purple and black "Marlin Candy" lure as *TAR BABY* trolled the *Bridge* area northeast of the Hope Town Lighthouse, in 4,500 feet of water. With the tournament over, there were only eight or nine scattered boats trolling the fishing grounds. John Harvey made short work of that 250-pound jumper standing up, releasing him in less than 15 minutes. Seth zigged-zagged back south across the *Bridge* and worked the edge of *Wonderland's* 12,000-foot depths the rest of the morning. He turned west at an area of confluent currents that had piled up some sargassum weed and the boys hooked and landed a pair of 40+-pound dorados, on blue and white islander skirted ballyhoo. The three frigate birds circling overhead were a dead giveaway.

Seth continued west/southwest working the south wall of the *Tilloo Pocket*. At the bottom of the *Pocket* in 600 feet of water, a white marlin knocked down a ten-inch Canyon Runner Ruckus lure and then tried to eat the left bridge teaser. Seth reeled in the teaser and Gene pitched one of the blue/white Islanders with a ballyhoo under and he took it. He free-spooled him for a long five-count and then slowly pushed up the drag lever, while pointing the rod tip at the fish, and he came tight. The circle hook stayed embedded in the side of the marlin's mouth as he put on a lively acrobatic show, complete with back flips. A few minutes later Scotty wired, de-hooked and released their second marlin of the day.

Seth then turned the Hatteras easterly and headed back toward the confluent currents as the tide started out. The frigates were still out there, and the weeds had broken up into several scattered clumps. They trolled amongst the weed pods, having to clear the weeds from the lures several times. But the grumbling turned to cheers when the big marlin made her move on the senior wide range, all-black, Moldcraft lure running on the right long rigger. The bite was something to see — like a tiger pouncing on a wild pig. Seth was using 400-pound wind-on leaders with #11 forged J-hooks. He felt confident his tackle would hold together.

Seth's mind snapped back, as Freddy's marlin finally stopped her free-fall into the depths. A tug-of-war ensued with Freddy pumping and reeling a few rotations, and the marlin pulling that line back out, straight down. After a few minutes of that the line started moving away from the transom.

"Get ready Freddy, she's fixin' to come back up! Get him ready, John," yelled Seth.

John slipped in beside Fred and told him, "Keep the rod in the gimbal and hold on to the rod. I'm going to unclip you from the bucket harness. When she breaks the surface, pull the rod out of the gimbal, stand up with the rod, and get out of the chair. I will put a rod belt on you. Seth is going to chase her. Move over to the starboard gunnel and start reeling. When she starts down again, move back into the chair and I'll clip you back in."

Freddy did exactly as he was told. With the rod butt secured in the rod belt's cup he reeled hard as the big fish broke the water a hundred yards out. Seth turned the boat and ran 15-mph after her. Freddy reeled hard keeping the line away from the outrigger as the big marlin jumped and surged across the horizon. Fred was short, but strong and agile. He used his low center of gravity to his advantage, just as he had as a judo champion back in his Army days. Seth and Fred got back two hundred feet of line before the marlin sounded again. Freddy climbed back in the chair and transferred the rod butt into the gimbal. John hooked up the bucket harness straps to the reels with some difficulty as Seth pulled the throttles back to idle. The see-saw battle continued for an hour. Finally, on Fred's third trip to the gunnel, Seth told him to stay put as the marlin jumped and danced in front of them. He slowed the boat and called down to Fred to keep the fish tight. Seth spun the boat, and immediately started to backdown hard on the big fish. John told Fred to move to the transom as water flew in the air and cascaded over the transom. Freddy reeled his heart out as he choked on the acrid black smoke bellowing out of the exhaust pipes. When Seth finally backed off, the fish jumped twenty feet off the transom. Freddy saw the double line leave the water and slip through the rod tip, three more winds and John had the orange leader. The old girl launched one more jump and then turned on her side as John wound in the clear mono leader with his gloved hands.

"Get a tag in her, Gene. What a magnificent fish!" said Seth.

Scotty was snapping pictures with his iPhone. John controlled the fish with both hands as Gene used the de-hooker on her. John held her head underwater as Seth sped up some to run water through the tired fish's gills. What do you think, John?" said Seth.

"She's pushing 650 pounds, look at her girth."

John released her bill and she swam slowly away. Then, with one powerful flick of her huge sickle-shaped tail, she was gone. The crew erupted in whoops and hollers and strange celebratory dance steps atypical for older men, or any men for that matter. Freddy's back was bruised by the congratulatory pounding. He sat in the chair, totally exhausted, taking it all in with a huge 'shit-eatin' grin on his face.

"Time to run in, boys," yelled down Seth. "We'll take the dorado up to Firefly tonight, and then stop and have a nightcap at Juvenal Menard's ... I want to ask him about Dirk Mendelsohn."

TAR BABY pulled up at Sea Spray's fuel dock flying three marlin flags and caused quite a stir. After fueling, Seth backed her into her slip and the boys drew a crowd. The kibitzers wanted to know how, where and how big.

"The *Bridge* and the *Pocket*," answered Seth.

Freddy and Scotty scrubbed the cockpit and hosed down the boat, while John and Gene loaded the big dorados in a dock cart and headed for the cleaning table on the other side of the marina. The Ziploc fisherman tailed them all the way over. John cleaned and filleted the fish exactly as you'd expect a doctor would ... perfect. They politely parried the Ziploc fisherman and stowed the dorado carcasses in a 55-gallon trash bag. They would dump the carcasses offshore on their way down to Cherokee Sound tomorrow morning to keep the bull sharks out of the marina. When Seth first started coming to Sea Spray everyone threw their fish carcasses in the water right at the cleaning table. Later that season a local diver, Robinson, who scrubbed boat bottoms in the marina, was bitten by a large bull shark. He almost lost his arm and it was determined that the bull shark was living off the fish carcasses discarded in the murky marina water.

Back at *TAR BABY* several captains came over to congratulate Seth. Jim Crofwell came by and offered his congratulations, and said, "We caught one blue today, Seth, about 350 pounds — had another one on, but he pulled the hook. They were definitely out there today ... any size to yours?"

"The second blue could have gone 650 pounds, she's the biggest one I ever released in Abaco."

"Too bad you weren't in the tournament."

"Those days are over for me — I don't want to kill them ... we got a tag in her though."

"I'm on the same team, Bro'," said Jim as he continued walking towards the TIKI BAR.

The Firefly was a new upscale restaurant just north of White Sound. It was built on the site of an existing estate, along with eight upscale guest cottages and a central swimming pool. A large 12-slip dock fronted the Sea of Abaco below the restaurant. After hot showers and a couple of cold ones, Seth loaded the crew aboard the golf cart and headed over the ridge past the *Garbonzo* surfing beach, then up the hill past Juvenal's and Sweeting's Grocery Store, and north past fire station #3. They turned left down Firefly's driveway. Seth took the dorado back to Chef Lorenzo as the boys ordered another cold one and watched a spectacular sunset from the semi-circular deck. As the huge red ball slipped below the horizon they were shown to their table.

"John," asked Seth. "Isn't that Chris Thomason, Todd Moran's FSU college buddy, sitting at the bar?"

"Yeah it is. He lives right down the main road from here."

"I'm going to go talk to him for a minute. Order me the lobster appetizer if I'm gone too long."

Seth walked up to Chris, who was sitting alone at the bar, and said, "Chris, I'm Seth Stone — Todd Moran's friend, I haven't seen you in almost 15 years."

"I remember you from Hideaway's and Sea Spray, but you're right—it has been awhile."

"Well, I lost my wife, Lisa, and it was hard for me to come back with all the good memories we had here."

"I understand that ... I lost my wife not too long ago."

"Well, life goes on, and I'm glad I came back — I missed your island. I see Todd at the tire business in St. Pete and he's kept me up on the island's development."

"Yeah, Todd built a big house on Hope Town Beach."

"I drove my cart by it the other day - quite a change from his first cottage, 'Finders Keepers'."

"The tire business has been good to him," laughed Chris.

"Speaking of St. Petersburg residents, do you know Dr. Dirk Mendelsohn? He and his wife bought a house down in Winding Bay."

"My real estate company handled the sale."

"Really ... how is he adjusting to 'Island Time'?"

"He spends a lot of his time doing reconstructive surgery in Nassau. But he has taken an interest in our inter-island sailboat racing competition. He's a talented sailor and has donated some serious money to update our Class A boat, *RAGE*."

"I thought only Bahamian citizens could compete."

"No, four of the ten-man crew can be foreigners. He's the best skipper we've ever seen up here in Abaco. We're hoping to win the competition this year."

"I've raced against him for years," said Seth. "He is good."

"Dr. Mendelsohn also opened a free clinic in Nassau to do cleft palate operations on needy children."

"Sounds like he's off to a good start. Are you fishing much?"

"Yes, I still have my Bertram 31, and my sons and I fish for yellowfin tuna when the moon's right."

"I remember you catching some big ones. If you ever feel like marlin fishing, come-on and jump aboard, you're welcome anytime."

"Thanks, Seth, nice to see you."

Seth sat back down at the table and John asked, "How did that go?"

"Ask me again on our way to Juvenal's."

The dinner and service was particularly good. They baked the dorado filets in a seasoned lemon butter sauce with golden-brown parmesan crusted breadcrumbs sprinkled over the top and served it with fresh green beans and scalloped potatoes. After the check was settled, the boys filed out and Chef Lorenzo shook their hands. As they reached the door the bartender shouted, **"Lorenzo — a Dungeness crab is killing all the lobsters!"**

Lorenzo moved quickly to a large salt water glass aquarium filled with local spiny lobsters and imported Dungeness crabs. Spiny lobster are valued for their large meaty tails. Dungeness Crabs have huge claws and are as big as a dinner plate. One of the crabs had broken the rubber bands holding his claws closed, and he was having a field-day with the large but defenseless lobsters.

Lorenzo yelled to the bartender, "Get the big tongs and rubber bands from the kitchen, we have to pull him out!"

Seth walked calmly up to the tank and plunged both of his forearms into the tank. He grabbed the huge crab's back fins, one in each hand, and pulled the struggling crab out of the tank. The crab tried to bite Seth's fingers with his claws, but he couldn't quite reach them. Lorenzo looked at Seth like he was crazy.

Seth said, "Watch this, Lorenzo … this is the best part."— Still holding the crab's backfins firmly with his thumbs and forefingers, Seth slipped his middle fingers under the crab's belly and gently rubbed it. Within 30 seconds the crab went totally limp.

"He's asleep now, and he won't wake up until I quit rubbing."

The bartender rushed up with the tongs and rubber bands and handed the rubber bands to Lorenzo.

Seth nodded and Lorenzo gingerly put two rubber bands on each claw, just to be safe. Everyone in the restaurant let out a sigh of relief and gave Seth a standing ovation.

Lorenzo said, "Where did you learn to do that?"

"My brother and I used to catch blue crabs in a saltwater creek in Florida when we were growing up. My Ol' Dad, Robert E., taught us to do that when a big one got loose in the rowboat."

"What's your name?"

"Seth Stone. We'll be back, Lorenzo — we like your restaurant."

"Thank you, Seth Stone, your next dinner at Firefly is on the house."

Seth handed Lorenzo his huge crab just as it woke-up and the boys departed the restaurant that was now buzzing with conversation.

"You made that look easy, Seth," said Freddy, laughing as he climbed in the cart.

"Like most things, Freddy, it's only easy if you know how."

As they passed by Hope Town Fire House #3, John asked, "So, what did Chris have to say about Mendelsohn?"

"Nothing bad. Dirk's donated some 'serious' money for updating *RAGE,* the Abaco's Class A entry in the Bahamas inter-island sailing championships and is now skippering her. He's also doing free cleft palate operations on needy island children, besides his 'reconstructive' surgery practice."

"So, he's got a 'snow job' going as our Florida winter residents like to call it."

"Apparently ... we'll see what Juvenal has to say."

They had to park out on the road when they got to Juvenal's. All the tables were busy at Juvenal's, so The *TAR BABY'S* crew gathered around the firepit, while Gene and Freddy carried some split logs over and got a fire started. Juvenal came out from behind the bar with a washtub full of Kaliks and ice for the boys.

Seth sidled up to Juvenal and said, "I need to talk to you in private when you get a moment."

"I've got one more table to serve a platter of fish, French-fries and a bowl of Cole slaw – family style. When you see me put it out, meet me in the kitchen."

Seth made small talk with the crew, then headed to the kitchen when Juvenal was finished serving.

As Seth walked in the kitchen, Juvenal said, "Pierre, I need more ice behind the bar and please restock the Kalik cooler."

"Got you covered, Boss."

When Pierre left the kitchen Juvenal said, "What's up Seth?"

"What do you know about Dr. Dirk Mendelsohn?"

"I know he's from your hometown."

"Somebody has been watching us while we've been diving at Jake Snood's Blue Hole. About two weeks ago we spotted a hovering drone watching us. We asked Jake for a guard and another truck, and he put Rex and his dog, Mozart, on site. We put Gene, our retired St. Pete detective, out on the highway. Rex has shot down two drones so far with his shotgun. After he knocked down the second one, Gene followed a suspicious truck that peeled out of hiding on the highway near the logging road that runs by the Blue Hole. He followed the truck to a house in Winding Bay. We had JR's wife, Winona, run that house's address and the truck's license plate through the Nassau Police for us, and the house and truck are owned by Christine Conway, Mendelsohn's wife."

"Have you found any treasure yet?"

"Not yet, but we have an underwater precious metal detector."

"Yeah, half the island and I heard about that when you brought it through customs," said Juvenal with a smile. "All I know is that he has ingratiated himself with the *RAGE* sailing organization, with his donations and sailing skills. Do you remember that I am part of that effort's heavy-air crew?"

"Yes, and if I were the skipper, I'd like to have your seven-foot frame out on one of those pry-boards hiking."

"He also has donated his time and surgical skills to the country's disadvantaged children. Even though I'm a second-generation immigrant and went to grade school and high school with the Alburys, Malones, Thomasons, and Roberts, my connections with the Haitian community still run deep. I hear whispers about a wealthy doctor financing illegal loan sharking, protection, gambling and prostitution rackets, all enforced by illegal Haitian immigrants who are thugs. The latest rumor has this same doctor financing a Bahamian drug ring out of Arawak Springs and Mayaguana. Crime in the Bahamas has always been fragmentized … organized crime like this is new to the Bahamas."

"Do you think Dr. Mendelsohn is behind all of this?" asked Seth.

"I couldn't prove it. But if he isn't, it would be quite a coincidence," said Juvenal. "If you find that treasure, you better triple the guards … 24/7."

CHAPTER NINE

As the Sun rose out of the east over Eleuthera, the Gulfstream G-500's wheels were up, and she was headed south to Venezuela and Orchila Island. Hakim called the Miranda Airforce Base in Caracas and gave them his heading, tail numbers and estimated time of arrival on Orchila, in the Los Roques Archipelago, 100 miles from Caracas. The 1,000-mile flight would take about 2 hours. Hakim worked in his seat on logistics and small weapons lists. Each charter yacht would be equipped with three AK-47s, three Glock 9mm pistols, grenade launcher attachments for the AK-47s and an infrared FIM-92 Stinger launcher with two warheads. The SAM's cost $38,000 each but would be a bargain if helicopters or jet fighters intervened in any situation. Both airplanes would be equipped similarly but with more AK-47s. Jamaal pored over a Waterways® chart kit of Florida and the U.S. Eastern seaboard with a pair of calipers, working on trip routes and mileages. He figured each leg of each trip at 10, 15 and 20 miles per hour, along with fuel consumption. He wanted a paper chart printed for each vessel, even though every one of the identical RC-52s would be equipped with Navionics electronic charts, dock to dock auto-routing, fuel monitoring, marina locations and service information. He knew well the hazards of relying on electric power, Wi-Fi, LTE 3g and satellites, etc. In a pinch, it was smart to have paper charts and pre-figured Intel. The RC-52 Power Cat was fast and economical at 20 miles an hour and the twin Yanmar 350 hp diesel engines used only 25 gallons per hour for both and had a range of 300 miles.

At 9 miles per hour they used only 3.22 gallons per hour and their range increased to 1,117 miles. Marwan busied himself in the airplane's galley preparing a breakfast of Koubous bread, cooked and shredded chicken and steaming cups of Teh-Tarik, a hot milk and tea drink.

Jamaal was also adding restaurants for port of call use, along with points of interest, colorful local hangouts and alternative anchorages, using cruising guides, Trip Advisor and Yelp. The time passed quickly, and the plane was soon circling over Orchila Island. Hakim could see the long military airstrip below them. The airfield's tower was unmanned, so the pilots buzzed the empty runway once, then landed. The Gulfstream pulled up in front of the largest hangar just as a small welcoming party arrived in a red jeep.

Hakim was the first man off the plane. Marwan was right behind him with his Glock pistol tucked in his waistband under his shirt. Jamaal held an AK-47 just inside the door. A large dark-haired, clean shaven Latino man jumped out of the jeep and extended his right hand.

"I am Eduardo Clemente, the head caretaker of the island."

"I am Hakim al-Rashid, Eduardo."

"Ah, welcome, Senor Rashid … we have been expecting you. Our Minister of Defense welcomes you, and he has instructed me to extend you every courtesy."

"Thank you, Eduardo."

"Senor Rashid, would you allow me and Juan, my assistant, to drive your party on a tour of our small island?"

Hakim agreed and Jamaal stowed his rifle and exited the plane. They all followed Eduardo into the red Russian UAZ3151 Hunter jeep. They toured the airfield's hangars, mechanic's shop, fueling facilities and observation tower. Next, they toured the barracks and laundry facilities which were squeaky clean.

"We have two sets of sheets, pillows and blankets for each bunk and there is a central laundry that you may use. There are 20 bunk beds in each of the barracks, each with six heads, sinks and showers," said Eduardo.

Next, they saw the large dining hall and kitchen facilities, four classrooms, six officer's cottages and an administration building that housed Eduardo's office. He lived in one of the officer's cottages and his six-man maintenance crew lived in one of the barracks. There was a manicured soccer field ringed by a running track, and a baseball diamond attesting to the Venezuelan's love of American baseball. There were assorted warehouses that garaged heavy equipment and firefighting apparatus. Leaving the military complex behind, Eduardo had Juan drive west on a one-lane paved road that ran along a ridge that bordered a white sandy beach that was protected by a reef about a half-mile offshore. He stopped about two miles from the air force base at a fenced compound and motioned towards a large sprawling two-story beachfront cottage that was surrounded by some smaller one-story out buildings.

"This is President Hugo Chavez's beach cottage. He flies in some weekends with his family, friends and his favorite bonefish guide."

On the way back, Juan ran the jeep all the way down the long runway, then out on a 25-foot wide heavy timber wooden wharf.

"This is where the 125-foot supply ship ties up every two weeks," said Eduardo.

"Will we be the only guests on the island?" asked Hakim.

"Occasionally, a squad of Russian long-range bombers comes in during an exercise and stays overnight ... we refuel them, and they leave the next morning. We extend the same courtesy to the Cuban Air Force MIG fighters."

Hakim thought this island was a perfect set-up for his training needs. He would start moving his crew here as soon as he returned to Africa. The Saudi Princes would be happy to know they were now getting free fuel flying out of Orchila. He would check out the supply situation in La Guaira and Caracas on his next trip to Orchila.

***

Dr. Dirk Mendelsohn owned 50% of the Mango Lounge, in the "Over the Hill" neighborhood in old Nassau. He was a silent partner in the now upscale strip club which sprawled into a remodeled hemp warehouse from days gone by. When he realized that his curtailed medical practice would not support his lavish lifestyle, Dirk looked at Nassau and Freeport as potential untapped goldmines. He remembered "Petite Phillippe" Moreau a local small-time gangster type who brought him several Haitian and Dominican pole dancers who needed help in the titty department. Phillippe operated the Mango Lounge as a strip club with moderate success. Dirk grew up in Tampa and understood how the Trafficante mob had taken the neighborhood *Bolita* racket away from Tampa's Cuban crime element ... they simply killed off all the principals. The Bahamas was virgin territory, they would just have to organize it there. He met with Phillippe, who was small in stature for a Haitian, but long on brains. They agreed that Dirk would finance the numbers (*Bolita*) racket and Phillippe would organize the weekly game, that would be sold in all the local bars and street corners by organized numbers runners. The bar owners would get a cut based on their sales volume. Dirk would train the bookkeeper, which would be relatively easy in this computerized world. The Bahamians, who could not gamble by law in their own casinos, would provide a steady clientele. The key was a big jackpot for a small bet. Once Phillippe agreed to the numbers racket, Dirk talked him into expanding the Mango Lounge with Dirk fronting the money. The expansion included enhanced security, a 'rub and tug' massage facility, a larger, elevated, pole dance stage and very private lap-dance booths to appeal to visiting tourist's prurient interests. This concept had been extremely popular all over Florida, especially in Tampa, for the last 40 years. He also introduced Phillippe to the loan shark business. Loan rates at 50% interest and above, and loans due measured in weeks rather than years, all enforced by Phillippe's 7-foot Haitian thugs. Dirk's money could only earn three to five percent per year in legal investments.

Dr. Dirk was averaging only three breast augmentation operations per week, and after paying for the out-patient surgery centers, nurses, patient accommodations and travel expenses his net hardly covered his cash outflow. He needed more cash flow to afford his $3500 a month Cable Beach apartment, $1200 a month Porsche payment, monthly airplane hangar rentals averaging $750 at three airports, airplane maintenance, a $15,000 per month mortgage payment for the Winding Bay Estate and a $2200 per month boat payment for a used 36-foot Yellowfin 36 Center Console with triple 300 Yamahas. His realtor wife had salary and commissions enough to maintain their St. Petersburg lifestyle, but Dirk was on his own in the Bahamas. When Dirk showed Phillippe the potential profit numbers he agreed to a fifty-fifty split.

It had been nine months since this partnership was formed and already the cash flow far exceeded their initial expectations. Payoffs were a way of life in the Bahamian Government and the underpaid police were no exception. Cab drivers touted the Mango Lounge and got a $5.00 chit per customer, handed out by the club's doormen. The high-dollar convention trade flowed in from nearby Paradise Island every night. The loan sharking profits grew exponentially, and the numbers racket got better each week as a couple of lucky players struck it rich.

Dirk wondered who controlled the lucrative drug trade in Nassau, Freeport, and beyond. His new partner Phillippe had a ready answer, Arawak Springs. Digging further produced Capt. Reltney Bender, a shadowy renegade from the Arawak Springs fishing fleet, controlled by the ubiquitous Bender family. He ran a five-boat 'fishing' operation based on remote Mayaguana Island in the far south-eastern Bahamas. He owned three DC-3 airplanes that he used to fly his 'catch' to Nassau, Freeport, and Florida.

After some research, Dirk flew his Lance to the Mayaguana airport and asked the FBO operator, Travis, to call Captain Bender on his cell phone to ask him to meet Dr. Dirk Mendelsohn at *Mel's on da Bay TIKI BAR*. He figured the FBO operator would have the Captain's number since two of Bender's DC-3's were parked at the FBO. Dirk was an average sized man, slim and wiry. He had wavy black hair and was better than average good looking. His demeanor bordered on arrogant ... like he knew something you didn't.

"Tell him I have a business proposition to run by him," said Dirk, handing Travis a $50 bill.

"I can get him, if he's around the island, *mon*. But this better be good ... Captain Bender is a busy man."

Travis dialed the number, and someone answered. Travis relayed Dirk's message and then said out loud, "A Piper Lance, NZ4735."

A couple of minutes passed on hold, then Travis hung up.

"He said he'd meet you there in 15 minutes. You can use my car ... I'll be here until 6 p.m.," said Travis, handing Dirk his keys. "It's the white jeep. Take a right at the road, it's 10 minutes on your right and there's a big sign that you can't miss."

"Thanks, but I've been there for lunch once on my way to Provo a few years back. How will I know it's Bender?" asked Dirk on his way out.

"He's big and tall, got red hair ... and his eyes are really far apart."

Dirk got settled at Mel's outdoor bar but didn't order a Kalik in case he had to fly back to Nassau. Ten minutes later a black Suburban pulled up in a cloud of dust and three men got out. The driver (Willis), was about 6'4" tall and lanky, he had long, black, slicked-back hair. He wore jeans and a T-shirt. The other two men were bigger and taller, had flaming red hair, and both their eyes were almost as wide apart as their foreheads. The biggest one, (Ferris) wore farmer's overalls with no shirt, was barefoot and weighed about 375 pounds. The other wore a T-shirt inside his overalls and a pair of Sperry topsiders with no socks. His black-billed, sweat-stained white captain's hat gave him away as Captain Bender. The lumps in their denims signaled they were all packing.

Capt. Bender strode up to Dr. Dirk and said, "I checked the registry and you own the Lance, and you came alone. Otherwise, I wouldn't be here. What's on your mind?"

"I have a business proposition for you. Petite Phillippe and I have a titty-bar, rub-joint and a numbers racket going in Nassau and we need a place to put the profits. I have an idea that could make us all more money with very little effort."

"How's that, Doctor?"

"How much could you save on the cocaine, heroin and meth you buy if you doubled your order?"

"About a third."

"I thought so. If I invested that money with you, would you return 15% of that saving to us as minority partners?"

Dirk could see Reltney crunching the numbers in his head and finally he said, "But you're charging 100% interest ... I'll have to think about it."

"What's there to think about. You pay $15,000 per kilo uncut now for 15 kilos. That equals $225,000 your cost and a $405,000 sale price at $27,000 per kilo at wholesale. So now you buy 30 kilos at $10,000 for $300,000. You sell twice as much at $27,000 wholesale equaling $810,000 instead of $405,000, but your cost is only $300,000. Profit is $510,000 instead of $180,000. You pay Phillippe and me back the $75,000, plus 15% of the new profit figure. That's cheap interest considering the risk I'm taking. What if you get caught or killed? We lose $75,000."

"But you double your money!"

"And you double your money, too. $510,000 less $151,500, which is my original $75,000 plus 15% of your new gross profit, equals $360,000. So, you make double. It's a good deal for both of us," said Dirk. "But I'll make it even better ... Phillippe and I will invite you to become a one-third partner in our new "Papaya Lounge", our sister titty-bar and rub-joint in Freeport. We're figuring a hundred grand a month profit after the first year. Our startup investment ought to be $150,000 each."

"It's hard to argue with your figures, Dirk ... I'm going to take a chance on you and Phillippe. When can I pick up the $75,000? I'm ready to make a buy in the Dominican this week."

"Come back to the airport with me. I brought the money with me in my Lance."

"Fast pay makes fast friends," said Reltney, with a crooked smile.

Captain Reltney Bender, Petite Phillippe Moreau, and Doctor Dirk Mendelsohn became partners in crime that day.

***

Two weeks later, Dirk left his Cable Beach apartment after dark and drove toward downtown Nassau in his black Porsche Cayenne. He preferred to live outside the crowded hubbub of the cruise ship-tourist district of Nassau. Cable Beach was also convenient to Nassau's airport where he kept his Piper Lance when he was in Nassau operating. This night he was on his way to a meeting with his Haitian partner and Captain Reltney Bender from Arawak Springs at the Mango Lounge in the "Over the Hill" section of Nassau. He made good time until he got to West Bay Street where the traffic congealed. Dirk turned right on Market Street and drove up the hill past the old Governor's Mansion and quickly descended into the dilapidated "Over the Hill" neighborhood where the majority of Nassau's black citizens resided. He passed by block after block of worn and weathered wooden shacks with rusting tin roofs, some the size of garden sheds and most with outdoor toilets and no running water. Here and there he passed a Hummer or a Suburban with blacked out windows. It was probably the worst slum Dirk had ever seen. He headed for Devereaux Street in the Haitian section and finally pulled around in back of the Mango Lounge and knocked on the back door. A tall Haitian named Cletus checked him out through a small portal, then opened the door saying, "Come in, Doctor, everyone else is already here."

Dr. Dirk walked into the smoky back room of the Mango Lounge with Cletus behind him. Petite Phillippe sat on a bar stool surrounded by his seven-foot tall henchmen. Captain Bender stood at the other end of the bar book-ended by Ferris, in the same pair of overalls, and Willis.

"I'm here to throw in with you boys," said Captain Bender, as he threw two burlap bags up on the bar. "Here's a bag with $150,000 in cash to join y'all as an owner of Papayas Lounge in Freeport … This other bag has $151,500 paying back your loan to me last week, including your 15% of my increased profits. I'm impressed with the Mango Lounge, and what you've done with it. There's a lot going on in here, rubbin' and tuggin', a whole show bar full of beautiful, talented dancers and a constant stream of tourists pouring in the front door. How long before we've got this going on at Papayas in Freeport?"

"Probably six months," said Phillippe. "We've got everybody greased there and the remodeling is almost done. There's plenty of single mothers lining up to dance in Freeport, wanting to make the big bucks. Your contribution should stock and carry us until we start turning a profit."

Captain Bender moved quickly across the floor and shook hands with Dr. Mendelsohn, then Petite Phillippe.

"Maybe our payments can be made at the airport or a boat dock next go around, fast and easy. No pow-wows unless we have new business to discuss," said Reltney with a smile. "Safer that way."

* * *

Hakim sent the first Gulfstream G-500 to Orchila two days after he arrived back in Cameroon. He sent ten men, with Jamaal in command. This vanguard included the camp chef, kitchen help, two bean counters and essential equipment. The jet returned the next day and after a day's layover transported ten more recruits, including more essential equipment such as small firearms and ammunition, along with Shareef, Abdul, and Naser from Hakim's original crew. The third trip to Orchila transported one of Abdullah's chefs, Umair from London, along with Yosef, his head bartender at Chennai Dosa. They would be part-timers. The fourth crossing took Aksleel, Jabbar, two more stewards and Hakim. The suitcase nukes would not leave the safety of the Cameroon catacombs until the operation was well ensconced on Spanish Cay, in the Bahamas.

Hakim had moved the *Jihad* operation in a week's time. During the move he coordinated his next move; that of paying the boatyard in Trinidad for their refit and flying Jamaal to Piarco Airport near the Chaguaramas boatyard in northwest Trinidad to pick up their training vessel. "Honest Bob" did the legwork for Hakim, arranging for a post-project survey, then personally inspecting the vessel and delivering the sizable check. The distance to Orchila was about 500 nautical miles. Jamaal and his crew would be delivered by Gulfstream jet to Trinidad and they would motor the RC-52 to Orchila, with a fuel stop about half-way in Puerto La Cruz, Venezuela, a 25-hour trip depending on the sea-state. The 50-hour or less overall trip would be a good sea trial for the RC-52 and her crew. Jamaal suggested they name the first RC-52, *TRINIDAD GIRL*.

Hakim flew into Orchila on the last flight, leaving Marwan in charge of Al-Qaeda's African operation. Once on the ground in Venezuela he turned his efforts to organizing the chefs and starting the bartending training with Abdullah's star employees, Umair and Yosef. He'd only have them for one month before he'd have to return them to London by jet. Hakim took them on a quick shopping flight to Caracas by way of Miranda Airforce Base. Antonio Mendoza, the Venezuelan Defense Minister, provided a van and a driver. Umair and Yosef bought boxes of groceries and spices, and mixed cases of top shelf whiskey, vodka, gin, tequila, rum, vermouth, fine wines, mixers and condiments.

Twice daily classes started for the six sous chefs who also were cross-trained in bartending with the waiter/stewards, during their nightly sessions. The waiters/stewards were trained in table setting and logistics by Umair, initially, then by the six sous chefs. Wine pairing was taught simply: white for fish, pork, and poultry and red for beef and red-sauced pastas. Pork and alcoholic beverages were new learning experiences for the Muslim students, but necessary to their cause. Future shopping trips would be taken on the island's supply ship which was leaving the next day but not returning until the day after. Hakim included ample quantities of tea, flour, salt, meats, pasta and sugar that would hold the camp over until the supply boat returned. One bean counter would travel on the supply boat with a shopping list and a *Britannia* credit card.

As soon as the training boat arrived, Jamaal would begin seamanship and boat handling classes, teaching helmsmanship, docking procedure, marine knots and etiquette. Everyone would be cross-trained. Jabbar, Aksleel, Abdul, Nassar, Shareef, Ameer and Rajab would be trained by Jamaal as shipwrights, navigators and licensed captains in case they had to take over a vessel in any situation. Hakim would be trained, but not certified. They would learn to troubleshoot steering and control cables, bleed diesel fuel systems, clean and change filters, repack shaft seal packing glands, change v-belts, top off engine and transmission oil, trouble-shoot auto pilots and navigation electronics, maintain 12-volt and 110-volt electric systems, service generators, maintain ship spares, change propellers underwater using auxiliary air tanks, change a starter or alternator, change leaking hoses, repair the ship's a/c system (add Freon) and maintain all pumps, to name a few tasks.

As a start, Jabbar, Aksleel, Abdul, Shareef and Naser would accompany Jamaal on the *TRINIDAD GIRL* delivery, for a firsthand learning experience. Two men would be in the wheelhouse at all times as they traveled non-stop 24/7, except for their fuel stop in Puerto La Cruz.

CHAPTER TEN

TAR BABY stuck her nose out of Tilloo Cut early the next morning and caught a snoot full of wind. Seth timed the waves and powered through a small roller just as it broke. A wall of water cascaded in the air to port and starboard, as the Hatteras muscled out of the cut and headed for deeper water.

"Good thing we got a good day fishing in yesterday, it's gnarly out here today," said Gene.

The wind was blowing 15 knots from the northeast, so the ride down south to Cherokee Sound would just be a bit bumpy.

"I don't see any rain in the forecast so it should be a good day to dive, and maybe dig for whatever is setting off the Fisher metal detector next to the Blue Hole. First, we'll have to set up JR's camouflage net in case the drone shows up," said Seth.

"Why does JR have camouflage netting?" asked Freddy.

"Two reasons," said John. "One, he uses them to construct blinds out in the open fields when he dove hunts over on Andros Island, near Congo Town, where thousands of doves are harvested each year. Two, he builds temporary blinds on Great Abaco where wild hogs are driven by precisely lit brush fires that force them towards the hunters on some of Snood's cleared land."

Gene busied himself in the cockpit, pumping up Seth's inflatable dinghy. Within an hour *TAR BABY* was idling up the shallow channel above Cherokee Settlement and across from Casuarina Point. The boys "Bahamian moored" and quickly shut the Hatteras down. Gene clamped the auxiliary outboard to the inflatable's wooden transom, then the boys loaded their diving gear aboard and headed ashore. JR was waiting at the house for them with both trucks out front.

Everyone said hello to JR, as they loaded their gear into Jake and JR's trucks.

"Rex has been patrolling around the Blue Hole with Mozart the whole time you've been up at Sea Spray. Will Gene be joining him?" asked JR.

"Yes, Gene will handle the highway surveillance and give Rex more time to check out any remote leads," said Seth.

"What about Dr. Mendelsohn?"

"I checked out Dr. Dirk with Juvenal and Chris Thomason. So far Mendelsohn has pulled off a convincing snow job, but Juvenal thinks his hands are probably dirty. There's nothing anybody can prove so far. Before I forget, did you get the wheelbarrows and tools I wanted from Jake?"

"Yes, and I told him if you find the treasure, he's got to triple the security. I've got a charter this afternoon, but I'll check in with you tonight," said JR.

The boys loaded up all their gear and started out for Snood's Blue Hole. They pulled up and found Rex parked behind the bull gate with Mozart sitting in the front seat. He opened the gate for them and said, "There's been no drones or suspicious trucks since you left."

They all drove back to the Blue Hole and started to unload their dive equipment, camouflage nets, extension ladders, wheelbarrows and hand tools. Rex and Gene helped move all the gear back to the sandy patch on the edge of the Blue Hole.

"Now listen up guys, here's the plan," said Seth. "John and I will use the metal detector to establish some boundaries for the dig we're starting today. We're going to rig the camo nets like a tent over a 20 x 20-foot area around where the metal detector senses something metal is below in the limestone. Then we'll excavate carefully like it's an archeology dig, first removing the brush, and then the 12 to 18 inches of soil covering the limestone substrate. We'll take the brush we clear away in JR's pickup and dump it way back in the woods. Then we'll come back and spread the dirt evenly in the surrounding brush and palmettos. Leave a few of the stouter pine trees up to rig the netting. There's rope, a chainsaw, shovels, picks, axes, stone chisels and hammers in Jake's truck. Unload the tools into the wheelbarrows."

Rex and Gene helped unload, and then drove out to take up their surveillance posts on the highway. Seth and John got busy with the metal detector and staked out the boundaries. Freddy and Scotty topped and trimmed branches off of taller pine trees and started cutting and clearing bushes. Seth lashed two extension ladders to the tallest remaining trees and the four of them set about rigging the camo net like an open-air circus big top.

"Time for lunch," said Seth, as he called Gene on the constable's phone that Winona supplied, and asked him to pick up lunch for everyone at Pete's Pub.

"Let's take a quick dive just to keep up appearances," said Seth. "It will cool us all off too."

After the dive and lunch everybody went back to work. Gene and Rex took two truckloads of brush to dump back in the wilderness of pines before heading back to the highway. Seth's crew skimmed the dirt and roots off the 10 foot square target limestone, and they spread that dirt out beyond the 20 x 20-foot perimeter. Seth sent Rex back to Jake's garage/warehouse for a gasoline powered pressure washer and his gas-powered Generac-CW clean water pump so they could filter and use the Blue Hole water in the pressure washer.

It took most of the afternoon to rig the gasoline powered pressure washer and water supply pump. But it worked well, and John and Scotty took turns cleaning the centuries old limestone surface. Immediately after use, Rex took both units back to Jake's warehouse and flushed both systems with fresh water.

When the clean limestone dried, Seth inspected the surface closely … there were square spaces that were bordered by weathered mortar joints. The cross joints created a large cobbled stone effect. The slight concave shape of the joints identified them as the best watertight type.

Seth pulled out his iPhone and, using LTE, Googled up limestone mortar. Wikipedia had the history of lime mortar, starting with the Egyptians, then refined by the Romans. The Romans mixed in more sand, less lime, and added ground-up lava (Pozzolan) to the limestone which allowed it to cure under water. Any Pirate Captain who understood maritime seawall construction, would know how to find and mix the ingredients. The hand-hewn limestone slabs measured a meter long by a meter wide, and the whole cache measured two meters by two meters. Seth tried to be patient, but his curiosity got the best of him. As the sun started to go down, he and Scotty start to chisel, hammer, and pry in the upper right-hand corner mortar joints.

The mortar was actually stronger than the limestone blocks and the top quarter of the limestone slab cracked, then shattered. The slabs were about 5 centimeters thick. Seth pulled the broken pieces out, while Scotty shined a flashlight into the opening. As he cleared out more of the broken limestone, he saw some small round shapes. His heart started to beat faster, and he carefully extended his hand down into the opening. He felt around and scooped up a handful of silver doubloons.

Seth opened his hand and his heart raced; as he yelled, **"Holy Shit, we've found the treasure!** He hugged Scotty and put some silver coins in his hand. The other Geezers all ran in under the tent and Scotty handed Fred and John some doubloons. Seth and John's world would never be quite the same, nor would all the Geezers who worked with him on this trip, which suddenly was far from being over. Jake Snood and JR's life's had just changed too. Seth looked down at the tarnished silver coins in his hand … just the 10 Spanish silver doubloon reales coins he was holding were worth between $50 to $80 each. At the very least they were worth $15 an ounce melted into bullion. They staged a short celebration, and then started talking about security.

Seth called Rex and Gene on their Constable phones saying, "Call Jake and tell him to triple the guard 24/7. I don't know how much silver is here, and we haven't found any gold … yet. Tell him to play it cool, but I think we've found just the tip of the iceberg. He should come over here now. I'm going to clean out the first of what I think may be 36 compartments in this cache we've found … before I call it a night. But he needs to bring serious security here right now. Both you and Gene need to scramble down here, **right now!**"

Seth couldn't wait and broke the rest of the top off the first 39-inch-square slab revealing nine equal compartments below it. The space inside each compartment was close to a half of a cubic foot and each was partially filled with the roughly minted silver doubloons. There was plenty of room for more coins to be stored in this limestone cache. Maybe the pirate had created his own safety deposit box. With his limestone and mortar skills, he could add or subtract as he wished. John, Scotty and Freddy stacked and counted doubloons as Seth scooped up handful after handful from the first compartment. When that compartment was empty, they had counted 1,250. If the other eight compartments averaged what the first did, they would have, conservatively, a half-a-million dollars' worth of silver in the first section alone. Seth emptied a small Yeti *Roadie 20* cooler and stowed all the coins in the cooler. They filled the cooler almost to the top. Seth strained as he shuffled out from under the camo netting dragging the cooler weighing about 100 pounds. With Freddy and a wheelbarrow's help he stowed it on the front seat of JR's black loaner truck. Gene, Rex and Jake all pulled up in their trucks just in time to see a drone fly over the distant treetops as dusk fell. Rex couldn't get to his shotgun fast enough to knock it down.

"Jake, go get some kind of steamer trunk or lockable strongbox and bring it out here so we can secure this treasure in your house or wherever. We've got about two to three cubic feet of silver doubloons out of the first section and there's probably another eight or nine cubic feet we haven't uncovered yet. We need as many armed men as you can muster and bring over some high-powered spotlights. Gene and John will go down to *TAR BABY* in the anchorage and come back with our weapons. We'll set up a perimeter and stay here all night with you. Check with JR and Winona and see if we can get a police presence here. There's no telling what that drone saw as it passed over here earlier. We also need to get some food, blankets, tents and whatever else you can think of to get us through the night."

"Ok!" said an almost speechless Jake Snood.

"I think we should hunker down for the night and take our time excavating and opening the other three square meter sections of the treasure trove in the morning, surrounded by proper security ... security that's ready to repel drones or whatever else might be thrown at us," cautioned Seth.

"I'm on my way," said Jake.

Rex left his hand gun with Seth. Gene gave his Glock 9mm to Scotty and left for *TAR BABY* with John. Rex headed out to the bull gate entrance on the highway to guard their first line of defense.

Seth called JR and Winona at their house, and Winona pledged one of three policemen on duty in Marsh Harbour. Then they jumped in her truck and headed for the Blue Hole with JR's jack lights, hunting rifles and shotguns, two blue tarps, and two-600 yard spools of 30-pound monofilament fishing line ... Winona joined him armed with her service pistol and two boxes of aluminum pie pans, all things Seth asked them to bring.

JR and Winona showed up first. Rex called Seth as he opened the bull gate for them. Jake Snood was right behind with two pickup trucks filled with eight armed employees, blankets and three 10-foot x 20-foot portable canopies. One of Jake's large stake trucks rolled in next, carrying two more armed men, a propane barbecue grill, four coolers full of food and drink, and two empty 24-long gun capacity electronic gun safes with interior dimensions of 14 inches x 55 inches high x 26 inch wide. Some of Jake's employees were white Bahamians and some were black. All of them had worked for the Snood Lumber Company for generations. Each one was trusted like family.

Seth was impressed when he saw the Stack-On® gun safes saying, "What a great idea, Jake. Some quick math tells me all the treasure will easily fit in both these safes if we load them horizontally. What did you do with your gun collection?"

"Well, I hid them under my bed.," said Jake with a smile. "A little quick math tells me I'm going to be able to buy all the guns I want from here on out!"

Seth got the monofilament line from JR and the pie pans from Winona. He asked Jake to have his men set up a perimeter of about 50 feet around the Blue Hole."

"Once your men establish a perimeter, let's go out another hundred feet and encircle it with the fishing line ... setting up a trip wire. Tie it to a bush every so often. If any bad guys come, they could try and overwhelm us from any direction. Tie two pie pans together, loosely, on the mono fishing line at thirty-foot intervals, so we can hear if anyone trips the mono. That way we won't be surprised. If you want to see a sample of the treasure we've found, there's a thousand coins or so in a blue Yeti cooler on the front seat of JR's black truck. My best low-ball guess is $60,000 for the cooler full."

Jake got his boys organized and 20 minutes later the trip line was tied in place. Gene and John returned with the guns and ammo from *TAR BABY*. Seth took one of his AR-15 and Freddy got the other AR-15. Both rifles had laser sights and tactical flashlights. Scotty and Gene settled for the Remington tactical 870 shot guns loaded with 00 buckshot and equipped with Fixed Star tactical flash lights with remote switches. John opted for Seth's Remington 700 hog rifle with the night scope.

"Seth, did you declare all your weapons with customs when you entered the country?" asked Winona with a smile, as she took her place on the front line. She was a stout woman and looked like she could handle herself.

"What weapons, I don't see any weapons," laughed Seth.

"Neither do I," said Winona.

Preston, the police sergeant from Marsh Harbour, finally showed up and seemed only interested in checking out the treasure. Seth suggested to Jake that he take Gene and two of his men to clean out the opened part of the cache and count and transfer those coins into one of the safes. Two of Snood's employees had already erected two of the canopies for sleeping and were installing the third one directly over the treasure site. Two other employees had the barbecue fired up back by the port-o-let on the logging road and were busy cooking hot dogs and burgers, then delivering them to the front-line troops.

Thirty minutes later, Jake Snood nestled into some waist high palmetto palms next to Seth and said, "We transferred all of the loose doubloons into one of the gun safes, then chained and padlocked it to the stake truck's flat bed. It would have taken half the night to count them in the dark. If your estimate is anywhere close, I bet we have well over $500,000 so far. Who'd have thought that the treasure would be right on the edge like that?"

"That Pirate Captain was a shrewd dude," said Seth. "Knew something about seawalls too."

They settled in for the night and kept their ears tuned-in and their eyes peeled. About two hours later Seth heard two pie pans tinkling to the west. He held his breath and heard it again. He reached over and poked Jake and put his forefinger over his lips.

Seth whispered, "Did you hear that?"

Jake Snood nodded his head in acknowledgement.

"They're coming in from *the Marls*," Seth said under his breath. "You can't hear those fucking four-stroke outboards when they're just idling. Turn your jack-light on in that direction in 10 seconds and let's see what we got coming at us."

Jake turned on his tri-pod mounted 200,000 candlepower spot light on a ten-count, and it lit up the palmetto scrub jungle around the Blue Hole and the mature pine forest in the background. The intruders were blinded and caught flat-footed.

They responded with unorganized gunfire from pistols and Uzi machine pistols. The assailants appeared to be large Haitians, six-and-a half to seven feet tall. Seth and Jake yelled, "RETURN FIRE" in unison and their western front line laid down some withering fire. The light-assisted AR-15s and tactical shotguns were the most effective. The seven-foot Haitians all stood tall in the palmetto scrub and had no cover. After their initial foray, which depended totally on surprise, they turned and ran for the cover of the pine forest. The weapons with tactical lights and laser sights had no problem dropping a few more of the thugs during their hasty retreat. As the smoke cleared, it became obvious that only two of Snood's men had been wounded, but not fatally. Also, Scotty had caught a round in his left shoulder and Winona suffered a flesh wound to her right forearm. Both were already getting first aid from Dr. John Harvey. Preston, the police sergeant, joined a scouting party that Jake Snood quickly organized to assess the dead and wounded among their assailants. Seth could hear their outboards starting up and racing off back in *The Marls* ... and he thought he heard the low growl of twin diesels idling away. He walked out towards the logging road to see how Scotty, Winona and the other wounded were doing and saw JR's black truck pulling away toward the highway. JR was with Winona and John. Winona had already called for the life squad from Marsh Harbour.

"Who are those guys leaving in your black truck, JR?" asked Seth.

"I don't know!" yelled JR, jumping up with a start. Rex was just getting out of his truck, having just come in from the highway, and Seth yelled, "Rex, follow that truck," as he hopped in on the passenger's side. He still had his AR-15 and Mozart was riding in the middle. As they pursued, the unknown driver sped up.

"I locked the bull gate when I came in, Seth," said Rex. "When the shooting started two Rastas jumped out of the bushes and shot at me, I let loose with a couple of 4-B shells from my shot gun and they ran back into the woods. That's when I headed back here."

As they neared the highway, the driver floored JR's truck, fish tailed and hit the bull gate at full speed throwing the gate out onto the highway as he headed north for Marsh Harbour. Both men in JR's truck were big and had bagged Rasta hairdos. As Rex ran up closer to them the one in the passenger seat snaked his left arm out his window and shot a pistol back at Rex's truck, missing each time. Alternately, he appeared to be talking on his cell phone. As they neared Marsh Harbour, they turned off the highway and headed for the Leonard M. Thompson Airport, just as an ambulance sped by southward with its siren blaring and lights flashing. They cut in at the FBO and started up a taxiway towards a small plane that was moving towards the main runway. Seth recognized the plane as a Piper Lance PA-32. The port side baggage door was propped open and a huge red-headed white man, with black soot smeared on his huge forehead and face, was leaning out that door waving to the men in JR's truck. Seth looked over at Rex's speedometer and he was doing 75 mph. The passenger in JR's truck had both of his huge arms holding the Yeti cooler out his window and was straining to hand it to the redhead who was leaning precariously out of the airplane wearing nothing but a pair of denim overalls and a pair of gloves. Seth aimed his AR-15 out of Rex's side window, while Mozart barked non-stop, and shot out JR's rear tires. The driver lost control of the pick up just as the plane's passenger grabbed the Yeti cooler. Seth shouted at Rex, "Get me the tail numbers on that plane," as he calmly shot the propped open door off its hinges with a hail of bullets. The large man dropped the cooler and started to fall back into the Lance. The Yeti cooler fell to the runway and broke open, spilling 1,250 silver doubloons all over the runway, as the large man disappeared inside the airplane. At that moment, the Lance took off into the night with no lights and its rear door missing.

Rex stood on the brakes as JR's pickup lurched off the runway, flipped twice, and crashed into the pine forest that bordered the runway. Seconds later, JR's pickup exploded and burst into flames. The airport lit up as a lone firetruck rushed to extinguish JR'S truck. Rex and Seth retrieved the Lance's door and stowed it in the pickup's bed, being careful not to smudge any latent fingerprints that might shed some light on this evening's activities. Gene and Freddy arrived with one of Snood's employees and spent well over an hour retrieving all 1,250 of the roughly minted silver doubloons off the runway. Both Haitians perished in the crash and the subsequent explosion of JR's stolen truck. Gene reported that four Haitians had been killed during the Blue Hole attack, and six wounded Haitian illegals had been taken into custody and were hospitalized under guard in Marsh Harbour. There were no casualties among Snood's men, just the two wounded who were taken to the new Marsh Harbour Mini-Hospital along with Scotty. Winona was not even hospitalized. The Geezers had turned the tables on the surprise attack by the unknown assailants.

"Rex, did you get that tail number for me?" asked Seth.

"Yeah, I did … NZ4735."

Seth said, "We got the NZ part on the rear door I shot off. But we'll need the rest to help clear up the criminal investigation in case that plane is never found."

"Seth, did you notice how far apart that huge red-headed guy's eyes were?" said Rex.

"I did … I've never seen anybody with eyes that far apart."

"Well, I have, and most of them live on Arawak Springs … their name is Bender."

"Sounds like that might just be a fucking start, Rex."

Preston and Winona set up a temporary morgue at Kemp's funeral home that night. The six bodies were shipped to Nassau the next day. All the constables from Treasure Cay, Hope Town and Marsh Harbour were called in to guard the wounded Haitian illegals in the hospital that night.

The criminal investigation started the next morning, bright and early. Preston and Winona, both eye witnesses, were debriefed by two homicide detectives assigned out of Nassau.

Next, the detectives questioned Seth and all the Geezers, Jake Snood, including all of his men who had participated, including Rex, in the presence of Jake's lawyer, Marcum W. Roberts. Seth, Rex and Gene passed along their suspicions about the white pickup truck and the residence where it was garaged, along with Winona's Nassau Police ownership research. Seth voiced his concern about the constant drone surveillance and who might have been behind it. Rex turned in the two drones he'd shot down as evidence. He also mentioned that the airplane's passenger hanging out of the baggage door the night before looked like he might be from Arawak Springs.

Rex relayed the Piper Lance's tail numbers. The plane had not requested permission to take-off. The consensus reason for the organized armed offensive was declared as the attempted robbery of the newly discovered pirates' treasure worth millions of dollars. The legality of the weapons used in the treasure hunter's defense was not broached.

Seth, JR, Jake, and all the Geezers were back at the Blue Hole shortly after lunch. Freddy and Gene were busy excavating the rest of the limestone sarcophagus. Their next surprise was that the lower 18 compartments of the cache were filled with gold Escudo doubloons worth no less than $300 each, not including any historical value, and would maybe fetch as much as $1,300 apiece. The gold upped the ante for everybody involved. Scores of photos were taken to help catalogue the find. Jake brought out three of his office staff to count, recount and permanently record all of the found treasure. During the rest of the afternoon, the aftermath of the previous night's activities took some predictable and unpredictable twists and turns. Jake moved the gun safes full of the doubloons to the Commonwealth Bank Vault in Marsh Harbour and added 24/7 armed guards from his own employee ranks.

Winona called JR to inform him that Dr. Dirk Mendelsohn had reported at one p.m. that afternoon, from the Marsh Harbour FBO, that his Piper Lance had apparently been stolen. He was packed and ready to fly it to Albert Whitted Airport in St. Petersburg, Florida. Detective Alex Pinder, from Nassau's Homicide Division, had been checking out Rex's tail numbers lead. He had been trying to contact Dr. Mendelsohn at his Nassau medical office and his home in Winding Bay all morning but had not received a call back. Detective Pinder's partner, Jackson Knowles, had been notified by their Nassau office of a report by Russell Bender, owner/manager of Crown Aviation from North Eleuthera Airport (MYEH), of a damaged Lance parked without authorization at their FBO that had the same tail numbers NZ 4735. Russell Bender had also tried to contact Dr. Mendelsohn. The detectives interviewed Dr. Dirk at the Marsh Harbour FBO. He told the detectives he'd been much too busy with patients and packing for his trip back to Saint Petersburg, to answer his telephone that morning. His estate's caretaker/security guard, Jacque Branlette, vouched that Dirk spent last night at home alone. The doctor stated that he would turn the airplane matter over to his insurance company. Detectives Pinder and Knowles' next stop would be North Eleuthera and nearby Arawak Springs. They would dust the Lance for finger prints and follow any leads they could find. They didn't expect much cooperation considering 75% of Arawak Springs's population of 1754 is named Bender. In the meantime, with no hard evidence to prove that he was involved in last night's debacle, and his damaged Lance in Eleuthera, Dr. Mendelsohn would be free to take a Silver Air commercial flight out of the country to Tampa.

CHAPTER ELEVEN

Jamaal gave *TRINIDAD GIRL'S* helm to Jabbar, who demonstrated that he had natural boat handling ability. He also seemed to understand the big picture better than his four contemporaries, Abdul, Naser, Shareef and Aksleel. So, Jamaal put him in command with Naser and Abdul as his crew for the night watch. They were all doing well; exhibiting no sea sickness symptoms and quickly learning to use the Navionics GPS system, which included manually marking the paper chart kit as the trip progressed. The crew constantly checked gauges and monitored the AIS system while visually scanning the horizon with binoculars for other sea traffic. Jamaal taught them that a competent captain leaves nothing to chance. He taught them the different running light patterns on various types of shipping. Freighters are lighted differently than fishing vessels or cruise ships. When this 500-mile trip was completed he would have some experienced sailors to help him train the rank and file in Orchila. Jabbar was compiling a speed, knots, rpms and gallons per hour log so they would not run out of fuel. At their present rate they would reach Puerto la Cruz, Venezuela, in another 15 hours. They had been at sea for 14 hours and were averaging 10 knots in four-foot seas. They were using 7 gallons of fuel, or 3.5 gallons in each engine per hour, so they had traveled 140 nautical miles using 98 gallons of diesel. They started with 396 gallons and had 298 gallons available for the next 150 miles. If the sea state became more favorable, they could run 20 knots per hour for 7.5 hours and still have 100 gallons left at their destination. Jamaal would sleep with one eye open, but he much preferred being out at sea to being on dry land.

***

After enduring the fucking nightmare that last night had turned into, Dr. Dirk forced himself to relax on his Silver Air flight from Marsh Harbour to Tampa. He ran the whole "Blue Hole Ambush" episode through his mind during the flight and tried to analyze what caused his carefully coordinated plan to fail.

Yesterday, he'd gotten word from Jacque, his security/caretaker at his Winding Bay Estate, that the new drone he'd purchased with enhanced telephoto capabilities was working well. Since Seth Stone and his men had returned to Snood's Blue Hole, Jacque had spotted a camo net being erected and some coins being unearthed under the camo netting. The new high-dollar drone's cutting-edge camera did not have to fly in close since the telephoto lens could focus on close-ups from 300 feet out or better. Dirk figured they better strike quickly, before Jake Snood could organize his considerable resources to guard the treasure site.

He called and ran his plan by Petite Philippe, "I'll need about 15 of your men, Phillippe, the biggest and meanest. Captain Bender is meeting me at Boat Harbour Marina tonight to drop off another drug deal payment on his way back down island. I want to cut him in on say … 15% of this treasure deal. It will be good for our business relationship in the long run. Captain Bender will give me Ferris, and two more of his crew off his fishing boat, armed and ready to rumble. I'm confident that we can surprise them if we come in by boat from *The Marls* and are armed with Uzis and Glocks. Seth's got four men with him plus Rex, one of Snood's employees, who guards the gate out on the highway. We'll sneak in and overpower them. Also, we can time our attack, so we can get Rex simultaneously. The Blue Hole is so far away from the highway or any settlement, that nobody will hear the shots. We'll kill them all and throw them in the Blue Hole, using their own dive weight belts to hold them on the bottom. Then we'll finish digging up the treasure with their own tools. Our men and the pirate's treasure will be long gone before their bodies are ever found. The earlier drone videos show they have picks, shovels, sledge hammers and masonry chisels. Late this afternoon, the video also showed Seth loading coins into a Yeti cooler. He needed help just to lift it into a black pickup truck they're using."

"Is it worth the risk? We got some good shit going on right now, Doc," said Phillippe, in his lilting Haitian accent.

"Pirate's treasure, Phillippe … think Mel Fisher. It could be worth millions!"

"What if they saw the drone?" asked Phillippe.

"It didn't get close enough … I'm sure if they'd seen it, they would have tried to shoot it down like they did before. Jacque flew it over every half-hour, but it was too far away for them to see."

"I guess your new drone is worth the big bucks, Doc. Let's do it … I'll have Cletus organize the boats and men. I'll bring the men over myself, in my new Viking 50. It's a 90-mile trip from Nassau … we'll navigate around Sandy Cay, then motor north, and meet up with you and the other flats boats inside *The Marls* at Wood Cay. The depth there is six to eight feet, east of that only two feet deep. The Viking cruises at 40 mph and only uses 96 gallons per hour. Top speed is 46 mph if we need it. Let me look at my Navionics App on my computer … the wind is 5 knots from the east, a piece of cake. Wood Cay is GPS 26⁰20'48"N, 077⁰17'07"W … write that down. That location will put us about two miles west of Snood's Blue Hole. … You'll leave from the bonefish guide's dock and ramp a half-mile below The Bae Restaurant, just off the Bootle Highway near the Airport. The guides and flats boats will meet you there. No one else will be there after dark."

"I'll go in last with Ferris Bender and his boys. But I want your best guide, in case we have to exit fast," said Dirk.

"You're going back there with the right guys. There's over a hundred small islands and countless sandbars in *The Marls*, and after dark no one else will go there. You'll go with Andre; he has a black 18-foot Hewes, with a tan deck and a 115 HP Mercury Verado. He's about six-foot-five, no Rasta, always wears a red fishing hat. Andre has organized the numbers runners for us in Marsh Harbour. Business is so good he doesn't fish Wednesdays and Fridays anymore. All the other guides work the numbers too. Take some bug spray with you, Doc."

Dr. Dirk picked up Ferris, Edmund and Volly Bender at Boat Harbour Marina two hours after dark in the black suburban he drove while in Marsh Harbour. He had Jacque drive and then wait in the Bae's Restaurant's parking lot. The windows were limo-tinted so he would be incognito. They hooked up with Andre and followed four other flats boats, empty except for their guides, into *The Marls*. It was like disappearing into a coal mine. They rendezvoused with Phillippe's Viking 50 by blinking their flashlights. Dirk stayed in cellphone contact with Jonas and Ronil who would circle in early on the south side of the logging road to take Rex out. The main attack group would move in directly at the Blue Hole on the north side of the logging road. Their phones were set on vibrate, and Dirk would alert Jonas when the main attack group was in position. They gave Jonas and Ronil a head start. Dr. Dirk burned three wine corks with a BIC lighter he'd brought in his pocket to take the shine off their white skin All the bonefish boats were powered by four-stroke engines and ran silently on two cylinders at idle. After 25 minutes they were all transported to shore. Rodney and Axon, the two head bouncers at the Mango Lounge, organized the Haitians into two assault squads and started to creep in with Dr. Dirk and the Benders bringing up the rear. They took their time and moved stealthily through the pine needle covered forest floor. Their dark clothing and dark skin made them almost invisible. As they neared the Blue Hole, they saw some light from a small campfire, but no movement from Seth's treasure divers. They moved slowly out of the pine forest and into the palmetto scrub thicket that surrounded the Blue Hole. Still hanging back in the pine forest, Dirk heard a strange metallic clinking noise. He started to yell, 'Oh Shit, GET DOWN!!'" ... but he couldn't get it out before the whole forest lit up around him. The staccato sound of automatic weapons and shotguns going off was deafening. Dirk hid behind a pine tree and watched three of his Haitian thugs fall in the palmettos around him. He and the Benders shot blindly into the powerful jacklights, then they turned and ran after the second volley was fired. Dirk felt his phone vibrating in his pocket - it was Jonas. Dirk gathered the Benders and told them to run for the boat. He answered his phone and said, "Jonas, we've been ambushed, are you okay?"

"Yes. We shot at Rex when the shooting started but we missed. He shot at us, then drove his truck towards the Blue Hole."

"You can run up the highway on foot if you want. But there's a black pickup truck, with a cooler full of treasure on the front seat, parked by the Blue Hole. See if you can steal that truck in all the confusion and meet me at the airport. It might be a better way out of there for both of you, and we'll still get some of the treasure."

"We'll try it, Boss."

Several minutes later, Dirk and the Benders were back in the Hewes™ with Andre, out of breath. Andre started the engine and said, "I'll haul ass for the ramp, *mon*. Sounded like they had an army waitin' for you."

"They cut a lot of us down," said Dirk, as four or five survivors stumbled out of the pine forest. "Wait another five minutes and if nobody else comes out, then we'll haul ass," said Dirk to the other guides.

Fifteen minutes later Dirk was in the Suburban along with the Benders, talking on the phone with Captain Reltney.

"It was like they knew we were coming; we were ambushed instead, and out-gunned ... No, we're all right, but most of Phillippe's men got shot or worse. Jacque is taking us to the airport right now ... we still may have a shot at grabbing some of the treasure. I'll know in a few minutes. At any rate, I think you should leave Boat Harbour now and head for Arawak Springs.

There's going to be a lot of people asking questions. I'm going to fly out to North Eleuthera Airport either way. You can pick up Ferris, Edmund and Volly in Arawak Springs. Ferris tells me his Uncle runs the MYEH FBO, so there won't be a problem slipping in and out of there … OK, good, he's your cousin and you'll call him too! I'll call you from the plane if I can, but from Arawak Springs for sure."

Dirk's phone vibrated, "Yeah Jonas, good you got the cooler … but now they're chasing you? … OK, we're just pulling into the airport now … I'll start the plane out towards the runway. Drive out on the runway and pass the cooler to Ferris through the rear baggage door … I know it's heavy, but Ronil is 7-feet tall and weighs 300 pounds. He can do it! When we've got the cooler, slow down and shoot the guys that are chasing you. Then I'll stop the plane … OK."

Jacque pulled the Suburban next to Dirk's Lance and asked, "Should I wait until you take off?"

"No, drop us off, then go straight back home to Winding Bay. I'll be back in the early morning … don't answer the door and put a message on the landline saying, *the doctor is busy and can't be disturbed.* I'll call your cell phone to keep you informed."

Dirk and the Benders jumped out of the Suburban and ran to the plane.

"Unchock the wheels and get in," Dirk yelled to Ferris and the other Benders.

Volly and Edmund complied, then followed Ferris inside the six-seat Lance. Dirk started her up and taxied to the runway. The black pickup truck appeared behind the plane. Ronil hung out the pickup's window holding the cooler with both hands. Ferris propped open the Lance's baggage door, as Dirk pushed the throttles forward. The plane accelerated and Ferris leaned out the open baggage door with Volly holding on to the back his overall straps. Edmund held Volly by his belt and sat on the floor.

"That other truck is catching them!" yelled Ferris.

Dirk pushed throttles all the way down.

Jonas drove the pickup inches from the fuselage and Ferris grabbed the heavy cooler from Ronil just as the plane went airborne. The pickup swerved left as a barrage of bullets were unleashed at the baggage door and the black pickup truck. Ferris was hit in the left arm and dropped the cooler. When he dropped the cooler, all the Benders fell backward inside the airplane. Dirk gave it almost full left rudder and the Lance climbed up and out.

"Ferris is hit in the arm!" yelled Edmund. Dirk handed Edmund a pair of earphones and motioned for him to put them on.

"Take Volly's belt and make a tourniquet above the wound … as soon as I get to 2,500 feet, I'll put the plane on auto-pilot and look at the wound. Get the first-aid kit out; it's next to the life raft … there's a stack of towels there too."

A few minutes later Dirk switched on the autopilot and vacated the pilot's seat.

"He has a hole in his bicep, but no broken bones or main arteries involved. Edmund, I packed and taped a compress over the wound. Let the tourniquet loose every 20 minutes for 5 minutes, until we land and get him to a doctor who can monitor him. Can you call your relatives and have transportation meet us?"

"Yes, no problem."

"Ok, everybody get in a seat and put on a seatbelt. With the cargo door shot off there will continue to be a lot of turbulence," said Dirk as he climbed back in the pilot's seat and took back the controls. "We're about 40 minutes from landing."

"How do you see this playing out?" asked Ferris. "I'm going to call my Uncle Russell now. He runs the FBO at the airport."

"I'm going to report the airplane stolen from Marsh Harbour tomorrow morning. We need to get you patched up and y'all back on board with Captain Reltney before first light tomorrow morning. He's stopping by Arawak Springs for you … I need a fast ride back to Winding Bay by water in something like a deep-vee, 36-foot center console, with three Yamaha 350 hp V8 outboards. I need to leave before dawn and do the 75 miles in less than two hours. They can drop me at Witches Point near Marsh Harbour. There's a road that runs out to Camp Abaco from the highway near the point … Jacque will pick me up and take me home like I never left my house last night."

"Since you and Reltney are partners I can make that all happen," said Ferris as he dialed up Uncle Russell.

Dr. Dirk landed on North Eleuthera unannounced but with the aid of runway lights that miraculously came on. He parked the plane near the FBO, and Dr. Dirk and Ferris were spirited away to Arawak Springs in a white unmarked van. Edmund and Volly spent the next 20 minutes wiping the airplane clean of prints. They were sequestered in a fish plant office where an emergency doctor sutured and stitched up Ferris and gave him a bottle of Vicodin to get him through the next few days. Food and drinks were served in the employee lounge. Dirk and the Benders caught some shuteye before Captain Reltney arrived and took aboard his crew. Dirk called Jacque and explained the upcoming Witch Point maneuver. Dr. Dirk apologized to

Reltney for an operation gone bad, but Reltney wrote it off to "Nothing ventured — Nothing gained." His take was an informant might have been involved, or the drone was spotted.

Dirk called Phillippe and brought him up to date saying, "I apologize, you were right in your thinking, and I was wrong. I got greedy and it cost us ten good men."

"Twelve good men, Doc. Jonas and Ronil died in a fiery crash right after you took off."

"Shit-fire, I was hoping that explosion was the truck that was chasing them … anyway, we're OK with Captain Reltney. He took the whole episode in stride and he just seems to live more dangerously then we do. But I've decided to be more conservative in the future. Like you said, we have a lot of good shit going on right now. Let's just let it work. I am leaving Arawak Springs in a go-fast boat at dawn and Jacque will pick me up in Abaco before 8:00 a.m. I'll arrive at the Marsh Harbour Airport later tomorrow ready to take the Lance to Florida. It won't be there, and I'll report it as being stolen. I have an alibi planned with Jacque and will take a commercial flight to Tampa. I don't think they have anything they can hold me for, unless there was an informant involved. It will appear that I was in my Winding Bay house all last night. You should make yourself scarce for a week or so. Some of your Haitians that were killed, or wounded might be identified."

"All of them are undocumented. They will be shipped back or buried. The ones who are alive won't give us up, they'll just get deported and will come back in a month or so and want their jobs back."

"I figured as much. I'll come back in two weeks and do a few charity operations and then resume my regular practice schedule. I'll charter a plane until my Lance is fixed in North Eleuthera. Also, the intra-island workboat sloop championships start soon. Our Abaco *RAGE* crew will start regular practices against some guest competitors that should sharpen our crew work. Chris Thomason is organizing those practices. If you need me just call on this undocumented burner cell phone."

Dirk landed at Tampa International Airport and cleared customs. He sighed a breath of relief as he caught an Uber and headed for his Brightwaters address on Snell Isle.

***

Hakim was busy on Orchila. He broke his men into three squads. The first consisted of all stewards and they outfitted the barracks with mattresses, bedding, pillows and blankets. The sous chefs cleaned the kitchen area and took stock of the kitchen equipment, pots and pans and utensils that were available. With the help of Umair and Josef, a comprehensive list of needed equipment and a weekly staples grocery list was established for the first supply boat trip. Daily table waiting, set-up and service, bartending, physical fitness (now including swimming) and cooking classes continued during the absence of Jamaal, Shareef, Aksleel, Abdul, Naser and Jabbar. When they returned in a couple more days, they would join in those classes. They all would take seamanship, boat handling, docking procedure and knot tying from Jamaal and the newly educated ship's engineers, along with their hospitality education. Also, the daily soccer game would resume. Hakim asked Eduardo if he would have the best fisherman in his crew teach his men how and what edible fish to catch in the harbor. Eduardo volunteered to have his supply boat captain buy a dozen Shakespeare rods and level-wind reels, plus sufficient tackle … chum could be generated in the kitchen so they could catch baitfish. Not only would it provide fun and recreation, but another source of food. It would also be another convincing element for blending into the marine lifestyle once in the Bahamas.

Jamaal asked Hakim to retain Phillip Oliver Holz to buy two Albury 33-foot skiffs for supply and transportation vessels once they were in Spanish Cay. The supply boats would feature two-350 Suzuki duo-prop four-stroke outboards, 350 gallons of fuel, a hardtop with dual Garmin 7612 XSV screens, 14 passenger capacity, with a 40 to 50 mph cruise capability. Phillip was able to negotiate a $235,000 each, "two-fer" price with guaranteed delivery to Spanish Cay in six weeks. Trips back and forth to Marsh Harbour could be made in any weather, and the 100-mile open sea trip to Nassau, in up to four-foot seas, was made possible by the unique Albury hull design. Christian Thomason reported that their furniture and bedding was delivered and stored in their Spanish Cay hangar. The kitchen equipment had also arrived and was being installed by one of his crews. Soon the RC-52s would start being delivered from Puerto Rico under the supervision of Phillip and "Honest Bob".

***

Christine Conway watched Dirk saunter into their bathroom in their Snell Isle waterfront home after making love to him for a solid hour. He climaxed twice and stayed erect the whole time. Christine had faked a climax during Dirk's second orgasm. He still was trim and muscular in a wiry way, but his butt had dropped a few notches from his 30's. For the last ten years, this had been his normal pattern when they had been apart for any length of time, an hour the first time, then tapering off to a half-hour every two days after that. She wondered if he was taking testosterone, Viagra, Levitra, Cialis or injections? Searching his dopp kit and luggage had not turned up any clues, so maybe he was defying the odds of a 57-year old's sexual decline. She didn't wonder why he was still attracted to her at 48, because he had created her in the image of his dream girl. When they met at Yale, she was an undergraduate and he was an intern. She was swept off her feet by his charming and persistent personality. Christine wondered what he saw in her rather "Plain Jane" looks. She did have a rather forthright and even vivacious personality, but he always said, "You have good bones." They married during Dirk's second year of residency at Duke University. Christine, a journalism major, got a job as an assistant producer at Durham, North Carolina's WSOC-TV, Channel 9. She worked hard and had a talent for writing copy and picking interesting stories. Dirk was also working hard on his plastic surgery skills. Christine was not naturally endowed physically, and Dirk finally talked her into a breast augmentation, … after all that was the type of plastic surgery he was going to do when his residency was completed. She took a week's vacation and Dirk produced his first pair of "Mendelsohn Slopers." They were immediately noticeable and attractive. Sweaters were the only garments from her wardrobe that still fit her. She bought some new, more straitlaced blouses, which helped, but they still did not diminish her new alluring look. Spurred on by his initial successful, he transformed Christine's nose and eyes into more complementing companions. A few months later Dirk put his second "Brazilian Butt" augmentation on Christine. Rhonda Starr, the first recipient, went on to become a headliner at the Cheetah Lounge in Fort Lauderdale. Six weeks to the day later … the WSOC station manager promoted Christine to the prime-time weather girl position.

As time wore on, Dirk made small corrections to Christine's lips, neck, forehead, ears and added some well-placed liposuction wherever needed. He located his practice in the Greater Tampa area after his residency and went to work in earnest. By that time Christine had moved on to a more lucrative profession in Durham, selling up-scale real estate where her local celebrity, natural sales acumen, and pleasing personality made her a success. She had no problem landing a high-end real estate job in St. Petersburg when they moved, and then launching her own company a few years later.

As time went by Christine knew that Dirk was cheating on her with his titty-bar clientele. He was almost up front about it. "Those girls are my bill boards," he'd say. Christine knew Dr. Dan Diaco of Tampa was the most famous breast augmentation doctor in the United States. He got the accolades on the radio shows. "Bubba the Love Sponge", Tampa's top shock Jock, advertised Dr. Diaco for free and his syndicated show ran a contest every Christmas giving the winning woman a free pair of "Diaco's". Christine felt that he cheated on her to compensate himself for not being #1. He told her once he would never drive on I-275 past Dale Mabry Blvd. during Christmas season because Dan Diaco rented a billboard there that asked, "ARE YOU GETTING DIACO'S FOR CHRISTMAS?" Dirk was crushed and wished he had thought of that.

In the end, Dirk had cut corners trying to have a bigger house and boat than Dan, and a bigger airplane. He lost his medical license over the recycling of silicone implants, impropriety with clients under anesthesia and surgery for sex.

Despite his peccadilloes, Dirk continued to be an attentive father to their two children. Christine would not abandon him. She felt she would have been nothing without him, and that he basically had created her. She saw nothing criminal or evil about him, and in her own mind she thought he was just misunderstood … she was in classic, total denial.

CHAPTER TWELVE

JAKE SNOOD sat in the middle of the Commonwealth Bank safety deposit box vault surrounded by overflowing banker's boxes and stacks of silver and gold doubloons. He was grinning from ear to ear.

"I always had a feeling that my Blue Hole held a pirate's treasure ... and I really thought it would be found when I let National Geographic dive it a few years ago. But they were more interested in the marine life ... and of course it never was in plain sight. What it took, Seth, was someone thinking outside of the box like you and John."

"Well, there was some luck involved, but it worked out. Do we have a final tally?"

"We have counted and recounted three times and have final tallies of 22,500 Mexican minted 1751 silver doubloons, and 13,700 Mexican minted 1715 Reales-8 Escudos, 22-karat gold doubloons. We have researched their values through the rare coin auction houses and the Krause Coin catalogues. Wholesale for the silver doubloons average $185 each. Wholesale for the Gold Doubloons is closer to $800 apiece. Of course, with professional grading and retailing like Mel Fisher has done, some will sell for 10 or 20 times that much. It depends on how you want to approach it. Professional grading is awfully expensive," said Jake.

"Well, all you owe us is 35% of the whole trove, plus our expenses which I'll start working on soon. The type of split we want is 35% of the silver and gold doubloons before any grading is done. We'll take our portion and leave the rest to you, and we'll take our expenses in cash or treasure. Some quick figuring on my iPhone calculator shows us that we're owed exactly 4795 gold doubloons, and 7875 silver doubloons ... we'll take our chances on the open market," said Seth.

"That all sounds fast and easy to me, and I'll gladly pay you cash for your expenses, whenever you get them organized."

"OK, but I am curious how you are going to handle storing your share. I never dreamed we'd be dealing with these numbers."

"My initial thought is to sell four million in gold at wholesale and put it in cash. The rest will be used as collateral for diversified investments. I'll consign some graded pieces to auction houses and store some in vaults in Switzerland, Singapore and the United States. The bulk after that will be handled by professional investment companies like Goldman Sachs, Morgan Stanley, Grand Central Investment and J.P. Morgan Private Bank."

"We're pretty much on the same page, Jake, and I thank you for your insight. I plan on shipping it to my banks and storage vault using FedEx, who is insured by Lloyds of London. We'll be storing our coins with fully insured Transcontinental Depository Services in Las Vegas, Nevada."

"You won't have to move your share of the treasure out of here for at least a month. I checked it out and this bank is fully insured. What do you hear today from the police about the people who attacked us the other night?" asked Jake.

"So far, they can't link Dr. Dirk Mendelsohn with any of the activity that happened the other night. He has a verified alibi and claims he was home in Winding Bay all night and that his airplane was stolen from the Marsh Harbour Airport. His Piper Lance was found the next morning at the North Eleuthera Airport, abandoned at their FBO. There are no leads at this point in time as to who stole and piloted it. Detectives Pinder and Knowles have not been able to establish a connection to any criminal organization among the deceased and wounded undocumented Haitians. The six wounded have been charged with armed robbery, photographed, fingerprinted and were entered in the immigration data base. They will be deported to Haiti next week and never allowed back in the Bahamas."

"Sounds like that whole investigation is going nowhere ...at least we have the treasure and none of our guys are dead," said Jake.

"Speaking of dead, is it alright for me to use your pickup truck until we go back up to Sea Spray with the Hatteras? I'll leave it with JR."

"No problem, I'm going to treat JR to a brand new truck. I ordered it from Fort Lauderdale this morning and it will come over on a coastal freighter next week. It's the least I could do for him since he's responsible for hooking me up with you, John and rest of the Geezers. If you need to move around in Marsh Harbour or want to come see me, just call and I'll send Rex to Boat Harbour to pick you up."

"Thanks, Jake. Rex is a good man."

***

Seth and John sat in the flybridge of the Hatteras, while Gene, Freddy and Scotty were bringing the last of their equipment back from the Blue Hole. Scotty was recovering from his shoulder wound but could still drive the pickup truck. He insisted on helping and was taking pictures of the Blue Hole and the treasure cache. The Fisher metal detector was below, and all the weapons were back in the secret space behind the master stateroom hanging locker. There were a few dive tanks to bring back and Freddy and Gene were giving the Blue Hole one last going over. This was the first time John and Seth could talk alone.

"I need your opinion on how we should award the shares of our final treasure count. We're going to take our 35% share ungraded ... 35% of the silver and 35% of the gold."

"That sounds like the fairest way to split with Snood," said John. "Per our original agreement, you and I split 50% of our share."

"Right, ... now we have to split the other half with our crew. Dino and Zoey, Billy and Kitty, Gene, Freddy, and Scotty. I count that at seven equal shares. What do you think, John?"

"I think that's fair since it was a team effort, and even though everybody wasn't here for the same length of time, there was always an element of danger. No arguments that way."

"You got that right! You know, we haven't been shot at since we got 'Dave the Wave' out of Cuba," said Seth grimacing.

"Yeah, I thought we were going to quit getting into these situations."

"I never thought this would escalate into a mini-war until I saw that last drone. Anyhow, Jake wants to pay our expenses for the Hatteras, your plane, Kitty's airlift, Scotty's hospital bill, dive tank air and general travel expenses with cash."

"Smart on his part and easy on us. Do you have any feel for what our share might be worth?"

"Well, if you look at rock bottom... that would be melting it down to just silver and gold bars, our 35% share of the silver would be about $140,000. Our 35% share of the gold would be worth about $1,800,000."

"So, my quarter share is worth at least $485,000."

"That's what I figure," said Seth with a smile.

"But what about Mel Fisher, Heritage Coin auctions, Sotheby's and eBay? We read all the time about gold and silver treasure coins going for thousands of dollars apiece," said John.

"You're right. Jake and I talked about that. It depends on how patient you are and who you sell to ... investors, collectors or somebody who just wants a unique piece of history ... or an unusual piece of jewelry. My take is to sell some coins that don't grade out high at the wholesale price ... if you need some cash. Then farm the rest of them out to the auction houses and try for 20 or 30 times the raw metals value ... and pay the 15% commission to the auction houses."

"That makes sense to me, too," agreed John. "What's next in the Abacos now that we've found the treasure? Do you want to go fishing down island?"

"The way I see it, we can divide and ship the treasure home in the next week. I've researched safe, fast, insured transport and storage. We'll sort it, without grading, into units for me, you and our seven partners. All of us will have separate accounts that we can draw our treasure from and do what we please. The total storage and insurance rate at JM Bullion is 5% of the raw metal worth per year. We can store it in New York or Nevada."

"That sounds reasonable. Who do we use to ship it?"

"FedEx ... and Lloyds of London insures it."

"You've done your homework as usual, Seth. What about down island?"

"As far as down island goes, I think we ought to stay in the Abacos and fish the Bertram-Hatteras Shootout that our friend, Captain Skip Smith, is sponsoring at the end of next month."

"That sounds doable," said John.

"I mean the boat is already here and it's a long trip home. There are no tournaments down island after the first week in July, unless we go all the way to the BVI. Let's take a two-week hiatus and fly home. I need to go up to Torch Lake and spend a week or so with Lori, and I'm sure Stacy would like you home for a while. I know Gene will want to come back and whatever other crew members that want to fish the Shootout Tournament can come. We'll start by inviting our treasure partners, less the ladies, and go from there. The other upside is we'll be here to take care of any loose ends from the treasure find."

"Sounds good to me, partner," said John smiling.

"Now, I'm going to run something by you that I want you to think about ... there may be a similar existing treasure scenario at the Treasure Cay Blue Hole. The problem that exists is that Blue Hole is on Bahamian National Park land. We will need to apply for an official salvor's license. In fact, we won't even go near there, with our new metal detector until we get that license. The split is quite fair … 25% to the Bahamian Government, plus all the historical items, like Arawak pottery and dinosaur bones, and 75% to the salvor. I looked it up on the internet, which cautions that it is a slow process – only 70 licenses have been granted in the last ten years."

"Now that you got me thinking about it … why not have two locations to hide your treasure?"

"Hey, and if we get a positive reading, we'll involve the police and the government before we start digging," said Seth.

"How about sneaking in during the middle of the night and taking some readings. Then we won't have to sweat the drones," said John laughing.

"Don't laugh, that's a good idea … we'll case the venue carefully partner."

"Same split as last time? And we'll probably have some minority partners."

They shook hands and Seth opened a bottle of 2009 Biale "Black Chicken" Zinfandel, from some incredibly old vines in Sonoma, California, and poured two glasses.

"To the Geezers, not many like us, and none better," said Seth, raising his glass. "Did I ever tell you the story about 'Black Chicken'?"

"I don't think so?" said John, as they clinked their glasses.

"Well, during prohibition the Biales had to open a grocery store in Sonoma to survive. Since they were out in the country, they got a lot of phone/pick up orders. The Biales still made a little wine to sell to the Catholic Church and they also exported a little. And they also did some discreet bootlegging … neighbors in the know would add two 'Black Chickens' to their grocery order and the Biales would slip two bottles of their excellent Zinfandel into their box of groceries."

"Good story Seth," said John taking a sip. "It's delicious … will you leave *TAR BABY* at Sea Spray?"

"No, the tournament venue is moving to Spanish Cay this year and I hate to think of running all the way back to the *Pocket* and *Jurassic Park* each day. I think we would be better off fishing the tournament out on *Flat-Top*. We'll reserve a slip tomorrow, moor the boat there in a couple of days, then come back early and practice out on *Flat-Top* and in the *Great Abaco Canyon*. The fishing out there should be terrific, and we just need to find out where the bait piles up. I'll start studying Roff's charts before we come back. We can rent an Albury 23 to run around in, and there's an airport right there for your Saratoga."

"I like all of that," said John.

"We'll troll back up to Sea Spray in the morning, and maybe catch our dinner on the way. One way or the other I want to talk to Juvenal before we leave for Spanish Cay and our hiatus.

Dinner for the Geezers was ashore that night, with JR and Winona, at their sprawling Cherokee Sound beach house. They had drinks and freshly caught yellowfin tuna with all the 'fixins'. Jake Snood and his wife Wyannie were there along with Rex Malone, who was Wyannie's cousin, and Mozart. Preston, the Marsh Harbour Police sergeant, also attended with his spouse, Delphine. As the sun went down the women made a fuss over Scotty, who still had his left arm in a sling. Freddy and Gene couldn't get over the vibrant, pastel, crystal clear blue waters of Cherokee Sound that changed shades every few minutes as the sun slipped slowly behind the horizon. The Bahamas beauty was dazzling. While making conversation with the ladies, Scotty questioned Winona about how she had met JR Albury.

"Well, I lived up in Hope Town, with my mother and aunt in that bright yellow house right behind the 'Cat Lady', until I got out of grade school. I knew him there, but I didn't think too much of him. My momma sent me to Nassau for high school and I saw him at a St. James Church teen dance during Christmas vacation my senior year … he had grown up and definitely caught my eye. We were married the next year by Reverend Vernon Malone, Rex's and Wyannie's uncle."

"What was your maiden name?" asked Scotty.

"Albury … I'm JR's third cousin," said Winona with a smile.

Scotty was speechless but managed a grin.

Seth took this opportunity to thank Jake for his support and explained how he was going to transport their share of the treasure out of Marsh Harbour.

"We're going to be at Sea Spray for a couple of days and then we're moving to Spanish Cay for a tournament later next month. John and I would like to meet you and JR at the Commonwealth Bank to count out our share, ungraded—as we agreed."

"Call JR when you are free," said Jake. "I'll send Rex over in a boat for you."

***

TAR BABY's anchors were pulled and stowed, and Seth idled quietly out of the Cherokee anchorage. The feeling of success wafted over them, as the salty Atlantic Ocean beckoned. But there was no feeling of closure, however, because of Dirk Mendelsohn ... Seth felt that this had only been a profitable chapter in a much bigger story.

Gene let the outriggers down while John and Freddy let out four Islanders rigged with ballyhoo and circle hooks ... two on the short riggers and two on the long. Gene flipped a large cedar plug in from the bridge and clipped it into the center/shotgun rigger. He put it 250 feet back. They spotted some birds working at the top of Winding Bay close to the *Breakers*. Thirty minutes later they had three dorados over 35 pounds in the fish box. Scotty got to watch from his seat on the flybridge as his mates made it all look easy.

As Gene pulled the outriggers up, Seth pushed the throttles up and headed for Tilloo Cut, 12 miles to the north. Forty minutes later they cleared the narrow cut and idled around Tahiti Beach with its huge palm tree grove and sugar-white sand. The shallow water was so clear over the white sand it was almost invisible. Suddenly, four jet skis raced by with bronzed men driving and bikini-clad girls hanging on for dear life. They raced and cut each other off and headed for a long dock with a boathouse that jutted out into shallow Dorros Cove. The dock was crowded with more girls and men drinking beer while they cheered the jet-skiers on.

"What's going on over there?" asked Scotty, as they headed north for White Sound.

"That's Chief Billie's house up on the hill. See that flag flying over the boat house," said Seth. "It's the Seminole Nation of Florida flag. He calls the house, *Club Fearless. 'Fearless'* was Chief Osceola's nickname back in the 1800's when the U.S. Army was trying to defeat the Seminoles. They never could defeat them ... they just melted into the Everglades."

"Well they look like they're having a great time," said Freddy. "A couple of nice sportfishes and big runabouts at the dock, too."

"Chief Billie has run the tribe from 1980 until now and is responsible for bringing legal casino gambling to their reservations. The three thousand remaining Seminoles each get paid $85,000 a year from that endeavor. Every weekend this time of year, he loads the tribe's Gulfstream G-600 up with his cronies and a bunch of Miami hookers and flies over for some fun."

Seth made the turn into White Sound and was tied up and docked in a matter of minutes. Gene plugged in the shore power and the engines and generator were silenced.

"Hey, Juvenal, *TAR BABY* here - come back," called Seth on VHF channel 68.

"Switch to 73 *TAR BABY* - standing-by," answered Juvenal.

"We want to come up for dinner tonight - we caught three dorados around 35 pounds apiece on the way up from Cherokee. You can have it all."

"How many anglers, Seth?"

"Five of us."

"Come up about 7:30. I'm roasting fresh corn and sweet potatoes tonight … and bring a bottle of that *Angels and Cowboys,* if you can spare me a glass. Best California red I've tasted this summer - over."

"You got it, Amigo - see you at 7:30 - *TAR BABY* switching back and standing by on 68."

After a dinner of grilled dorado and Juvenal's roasted sides, the crew was ready for some Kaliks and firepit time. Seth and Juvenal took two glasses of wine and sat off by themselves, while Pierre took care of Captain Chris Crash, his wife Jackie, and another couple.

"So, I heard you hit the mother lode over at Snood's Blue Hole," said Juvenal smiling.

"We're lucky to be alive, man. If we hadn't caught a glimpse of the third drone, we would have been toast."

"Preston told me you turned the tables on the bad guys."

"Well, I was hoping you could help me with that. We think Dirk Mendelsohn was involved, but because of some tricky maneuvering on his part, nobody can prove anything."

"Yeah, I know about the stolen airplane and his alibi."

"All the gunman were big Haitians. Do you know anything about them?"

"I hear from my sources that they were all undocumented and sent over here from Nassau. I've been thinking about all this and I wonder if it would be better for you to get closer to Dr. Dirk."

"What do you mean closer, Juvenal?"

"You told me you have known him in St. Petersburg for many years, and you and John Harvey sailboat raced against him often. I talked to Chris Thomason this morning after I started getting information about the treasure shootout, airplane escape and everything. I told Chris about our earlier conversation, including your suspicions concerning Dr. Dirk, and also what I've heard about him through the grapevine. Since the authorities cannot place him at the ambush and the attempted robbery, or connect him with the undocumented Haitian immigrant thugs, there's no traction. Detectives Pinder and Knowles, from Nassau, cannot find any clues that point to who stole Dirk's airplane on that same night. They told Preston the inside of Dirk's Lance was wiped clean. Their hands are tied at this point."

"Right now - I'm at a loss myself," said Seth.

Juvenal continued, "Chris acknowledges there are some known problems from Dr. Dirk's past concerning U.S. medical procedural laws and patient ethics. He wasn't convicted of a crime … but he did lose his medical license to practice in the U.S. However, almost every influential Bahamian that has come in contact with Dr. Mendelsohn is impressed with his medical skills and his generous charitable contributions of time and money. He has hit a home run starting his pro-bono cleft palate foundation and has already helped scores of Bahamian children. Important politicians have given him the benefit of the doubt."

"Yes, Chris was clear about that."

"Chris and I have come up with an idea that might bring this all to a head. We have wanted to bring in some good racing competition to try and help us win the Bahamas workboat racing regatta this year. Each of the seven highly populated islands has an entry. It's hotly contested and is a **big deal** in the Bahamas. Dirk wins against our second team very easily every race. We think if you, John, and some of your crew would race our trial horse, *TANQUERAY,* against *RAGE* in a couple of practices, it would help our team. Here's the important part … if Dirk won't agree, we think that will indicate that he may be involved in the attempted robbery and shootout. If he agrees, maybe he has nothing to hide, and you're wrong. But if he is negative, it will cast suspicion on his character."

"I see your point. None of us has ever been friends with Dirk. But he has always been treated with respect because of his sailing abilities."

"If he's guilty, he'd have to be one hell of an actor not to act weird after this latest debacle," said Juvenal.

"I would think he'd have a problem looking us in the eye," said Seth.

"Chris thinks this will work in two ways. If he agrees, he gets the benefit of the doubt … for now. If not, Chris will lobby to higher authorities in Nassau to encourage them to investigate deeper into his activities, like initiate 24/7 surveillance on him and subpoena his bank records. Financial information is hard to come by in the Bahamas because we pay no income, capital gains, inheritance, or property taxes. This country survives on customs import duties, a foreign property owner's tax and a value added sales tax. But … Dirk is an American citizen and he might be hiding funds in our offshore banking system from your IRS … you get the picture."

"I do! We are leaving the Bahamas in a couple of days for two weeks, but we're leaving the Hatteras at Spanish Cay. We are all flying back in John's Saratoga. John and I plan on bringing back at least four or five crew when we return. The Bertram-Hatteras tournament is not until the very end of next month. We can probably sail two or three days during our practice fishing time. We're going to fish a totally different area than usual, so we've allotted extra time."

"Great! Chris will be stoked."

"I know John Harvey will be up for it. We've often talked about what it might be like to sail your racing version of a workboat sloop that has only a two-foot keel, 28-foot overall hull length, and a 60-foot mast with that unbelievably long 35-foot boom. The low aspect sail plan has a **huge** sail area, considering it has a 10-foot 'J'. The human ballast, pry-board system should also be a hoot to learn and utilize. We'd want a day with you and Chris on the *TANQUERAY*, to get the crew acclimated before we go racing."

"That would be no problem," said Juvenal. "I know Dirk wants to try some new crew, too."

"Some of the Geezer's best fishermen are also great sailors. Freddy was the top America's Cup foredeck man for Charley Morgan on *HERITAGE*, back in the day. John Harvey won many National championships, and lately has won the World Masters three times sailing against the likes of Lowell North, Paul Elvstrom, Tom Allen and Ted Hood. Scotty is a good all-around sailor, and you can give us some of your backup crew. John, Freddy, and I won the U.S. Yacht Club Challenge with some younger crew in Newport Beach, California, against the likes of Rick Merriman, Larry Klein and Steve Benjamin. Scotty's arm should be healed when we get back. We won't practice fish every day, especially if it's windy, and we're going to have an Albury 23 to run around in the Sea of Abaco. I think Gene might still be spry enough to get out on the pry-boards, but maybe we should leave that for your back-up crew."

"Chris will get in touch with Dirk in St. Petersburg, and we'll see what he says. He normally stays in the States only ten days or so. We'll let you know his answer."

"OK, I'll be out of town, but it doesn't matter. Just call my cell phone. I'll start organizing a crew as soon as I hear from you."

***

Rex picked up John and Seth at Sea Spray the next morning in one of Jake's Albury 23s. They ran across to Boat Harbour in Marsh Harbour and drove with Rex to the Commonwealth Bank. The guards and bank personnel all stood at attention as they filed into the safety deposit vault. JR and Jake were already in place inside the vault. Jake opened the horizontal gun safes and exposed the piles of silver and gold doubloons.

"Gentleman, we can't do this blindfolded, so Seth, you count out 7,875 of the gold doubloons and then John will count out 4795 silver doubloons. JR and Rex will double check the numbers and load them in these canvas coin bags that the bank has provided. I'm sure you noticed the FedEx truck outside. We will load the canvas bags into these FedEx strong boxes. They will drive them to the airport and load them on their cargo plane. They've assured me that they will fly straight to Las Vegas, Nevada, where they will deliver them to your accounts at JM Bullion."

The process took about two hours. When the strongboxes were loaded and locked the FedEx driver had Seth sign the contract. FedEx was now responsible. Even though everything was insured, Jake sent two of his armed guards to the airport with the FedEx truck.

"Here's our itemized expenses. I finished them after dinner last night," said Seth. "Basically, $16,700 for fuel, marina slips, electric and water, crew food and drinks, a Bahamas cruising permit, dive tank air, supplies and ammo. $2,300 for John's Saratoga, for fuel, nominal charter fee and FBO charges. Silver Air flights and airport parking is $4,200. $2,700 for emergency helicopter service to and from Miami, plus $12,675 for Hyperbaric Chamber bends treatment. Total, $38,575."

Jake had the bank make out a cashier's check to Seth for the expenses and they all shook hands.

"God Bless you, Seth, John and the rest of the Geezers," said Jake. "You'll never be strangers in the Abacos!"

Rex Malone and Mozart ran Seth and John back to Sea Spray. They hopped off at the fuel dock.

"We'll miss you, Rex. You've become like one of us. Maybe you can steal a day and fish with us over at Spanish Cay when we come back in a couple of weeks," said Seth.

"I can only tell you one thing for sure, Seth."

"What's that?

"I want to be a Geezer when I grow up!"

"You already are, Rex. We'll call you."

Tomorrow morning Seth would drop John and Scotty off at the Boat Harbour Marina, where they would catch a taxi to the FBO for their short flight to Spanish Cay. Gene and Fred had the boat ready to go for a quick exit the next morning. The boys took a well-deserved afternoon nap and went up the hill to the Abaco Inn early that evening for some cold-ones and a leisurely dinner.

During dinner John explained how the treasure was going to be divided. Seth and John knew it was on their minds, but the Geezers were too cool to ask.

John announced at dinner, "This morning we shipped our portion of the treasure to a storage facility in Nevada. Seth and I split half of our 35 % share of the overall treasure. The remaining half will be split between seven partners equally. Those partners are Gene, Scotty, Freddy, Billy, Kitty, Zoey and Dino. Each of your shares is worth, nominally at wholesale, about $140,000."

Gene, who was taking a pull on a cold Kalik, sprayed that mouthful across the table and tried to compose himself

Freddy just shook his head and said, "Fucking A!"

Scotty, who was used to dealing in those kind of numbers, asked, "Is that just close to melt-down worth?"

Seth said, "Yes, it's all ungraded ... if you move the really good pieces through the auction houses, and you're patient, your share could easily go over a million dollars. I've also got the expense money for airline tickets and whatever else you turned in to me."

"Why did you send it to Nevada?" asked Freddy.

"It's with JM Bullion, and we all have separate accounts. You can move some or all of it. It's also double insured. I'll give you your account numbers. I already texted the info to Billy and Kitty, and Zoey and Dino."

"Wow, what did they say?" asked Scotty.

"Same thing Freddy did."

"Let's have another round and call it a night," said Seth.

Dawn broke to another perfect day in paradise, and after depositing John and Scotty in Marsh Harbour, the Geezers ran 28 miles to Spanish Cay. They started towards Matt Lowe's Cay and Man-o-War, then left Scotland Cay to starboard. Further north was Great Guana Cay, where the Nippers Bar Sunday barbecue was the Abaco's *must go to* event of the week. Nippers overlooked maybe the most breathtaking reef in the Northern Hemisphere. The dress code was clothing optional and the live island music was great. Seth called it *Adult Spring Break*. In reality, most of the time you'd wish the older women would put their tops back on. Continuing north, they ran out around dangerous Whale Cay, which was not passable in any northerly wind over 12 knots. Years ago, Seth and his first wife, Lisa, saw a Gulfstar 39 Sailmaster get rolled by large breaking waves in Whale Cay passage after it left the Bakers Bay anchorage and headed north. Seth called Treasure Cay on the VHF and reported the incident. Treasure Cay sent out a large workboat that towed the dismasted boat in. The skipper's wife did not survive. Thankfully, there were no breakers or big swells running today, and Gene turned back inside of No-Name Cay. He steered Northwest past Green Turtle Cay and quaint New Plymouth Harbor, leaving Man Jack, then Ambergris Cay, which was across from Coopers Town, on the big island, to port. They sped by Bonefish and Powell Cays who were off to starboard. Spanish Cay's rock-jettied basin and low-rise hotel soon appeared.

Gene circled in as Seth got the slip assignment over the VHF from "Sunny", the dockmaster. John and Scotty were already waiting for them at the slip. Once settled in their slip, he asked Sunny to reserve a 6-man golf cart and an Albury 23 for their return. He tipped Sunny a "Benjamin" and asked him to check on *TAR BABY* daily while they were gone. Seth pointed over to a dock near the fuel dock and asked Sunny, "What are those two RC-52 motor-cats doing here?"

"A new English charter outfit called *Britannia* is opening here in a few weeks. Those two boats were just delivered here yesterday from Puerto Rico. They expect three more to be delivered in about two to three weeks."

"Cool, where are the crews staying?" asked Seth.

"They're coming in around two weeks from now and will be staying in the old condos over near Barefoot Beach."

The boys toured the small island in their rental golf cart and had a couple of cold ones at Wrecker's Bar, that was built out over the Atlantic Ocean. Later, when they walked into the hotel's Pointe House restaurant for dinner, Sunny waved them over and introduced Seth and the crew to Carter Combs, the hotel's manager, and his assistant Molly Mallory. The three of them were having an after-work drink at the small hotel bar adjacent to the restaurant. Scotty perked up considerably, and it was obvious that he was instantly enamored with Molly.

The next morning it was wheels up at 9:00 a.m. at the Spanish Cay Airport as the Geezers bid farewell to the Bahamas for a two weeks.

CHAPTER THIRTEEN

HAKIM WATCHED THE *TRINIDAD GIRL* dock in front of the supply boat from the 25-foot elevation in front of his Orchila Island officer's cottage. Jamaal's crew moved with precision and no wasted motion … they looked professional. He'd received a call from Jamaal about an hour ago and sent the Russian jeep and driver to take them to their quarters. Jamaal was staying in the cottage next to his while Naser, Abdul, Shareef, Aksteel and Jabbar would occupy two cottages closer to the barracks.

Jamaal was dropped off and Hakim strode over to greet him.

"How was the passage?"

"A piece of cake, as the Westerners are fond of saying," laughed Jamaal. "Jabbar has the best aptitude, but they all learned quickly, and they take their responsibilities seriously."

"How did they do with navigation?"

"It's easy if the GPS is working, but I covered it up and taught them to use the compass, mark estimated distances on paper charts and use the depth readings on those charts to help dead reckon. They learn fast from me and each other."

"When will they get their certification?" asked Hakim.

"I'm sure they'll continue to learn from the classes, and the Neptune Mariners Group will be supplying our seven captain candidates on-line

OUPV/USCG six-pack captains licensing test study guides. The Bahamian government requires that they have that United States Coast Guard license to register for a Bahamas 'Type B' license. They have to pass Rules of the Road, Chart Plotting, General Navigation, Weather Systems, Life Saving Equipment and Safety exams. We will need a Venezuelan doctor to give them physicals and certify them in CPR and First Aid. All this will be sent over the internet and should be completed in the next 30 days."

"How about the "at-sea" experience requirement I read about in Neptune's brochure?"

"I can finesse the past experience and they'll be on a boat every day here and in the Bahamas. In the meantime, we will work on servicing air conditioning, marine heads, holding tanks, pumps, electronics and countless components that may need to be fixed and serviced. I will also work on assembling onboard spare parts kits and tool chests. We will be able to order those parts at Lightbourne Marine in Nassau and the tools at Ace Hardware and Pinder's Plumbing in Marsh Harbour."

"I'm learning that a large boat is a complicated product," said Hakim. "It's like a house with all the appliances, beds, tables, chairs, electric and plumbing; then add two diesel engines, a generator, propellers, fuel and water tanks, toilets and a portable septic tank."

"You are learning, my leader. How is everything going here?"

"We have cooking, bartending and house-keeping classes every day. Your seamanship classes will start in tomorrow's schedule. I added swimming in the harbor to the physical training and running. We also set up an obstacle course. There is a rifle range off to the east in a hilly section of the island and we shoot there every day. I had Eduardo buy some fishing equipment for us and we're learning to fish off the supply docks and harbor rock jetties. One of Eduardo's men, Poncho, is an excellent fisherman. We've been eating fish for dinner frequently. Eduardo has also taken me snorkeling around the reef protected lagoon near President Chavez's beach house. He taught me to use a "Hawaiian Sling" to spear grouper under the ledges in 20-feet of water."

"What is that?"

"He makes them out of strips of rubber tire inner tubes, twine, a small block of wood with a round 5/16" hole drilled in it, and a 4-foot length of ¼" stainless steel rod with a sharp barb filed on one end. I'll show you how it goes together. I have one in my cottage. Some of the white grouper we've speared were over 10 pounds."

"Sounds like fun! I'd like to try it, too."

"He has extra masks, snorkels and fins, but we should buy some in La Guairá to take to the Bahamas. The fish are good to eat, but we must all portray ourselves as watermen to help remain above any suspicion."

"That only makes good sense, Hakim. Speaking about fun, now that we're back here in numbers maybe we can start playing soccer again?" asked Jamaal.

"We'll have enough players for a real game. A couple of Eduardo's men can play if needed. Oh … I cut prayer time down to once in the morning and once before dinner. We have it in the barracks with the shades pulled down and everyone stays quiet. We will limit prayer to the same times when we get to Spanish Cay and have it in the downstairs room in the condo that has no furniture."

"It will be crowded, but its purpose will serve Allah," said Jamaal. "Anything else?"

"A squadron of Cuban MIG fighters flew in for refueling two days ago. We have made a couple of trips to La Guairá on the supply ship and have virtually everything we need. I was able to get some hand tools for your training classes and Eduardo has an extensive machine shop and tool room in the big hangar. We can borrow what we need from there. Supplies of everything in Caracas and La Guairá are either rationed or non-existent. Fresh food is becoming scarce and expensive with the constant inflation they are experiencing."

"We should only be here for a few more weeks if that. I am confident that I can whip our recruits into competent seamen in that time, especially since I have Jabbar and the rest of that crew to help me. They will learn to tie bowlines and square knots, and full bights and half hitches for the boat and dock cleats. They'll quickly learn and understand that nautical terms are precise. Bow and stern will replace front and back, and starboard and port will take the place of right and left. The time spent on *TRINIDAD GIRL'S* delivery was better than a month of classroom and simulated cruising."

"Maybe it would be wise to fly you and Jabbar to Puerto Rico to deliver the next two boats to the Bahamas in a couple of weeks along with some new crew to train? Your crew looked professional landing and docking *TRINIDAD GIRL.*"

"Thank you. Your idea makes sense from a couple of standpoints. First, we will have crew and four boats in the Bahamas. Second, we can clean and start to outfit those boats. If we fly a planeload of our personnel up to Spanish Cay, that plane can bring me back to Orchila. Then, I can deliver *TRINIDAD GIRL* to Spanish Cay with four or five crew members, while our jet flies the rest of the recruits off Orchila to the Bahamas," said Jamaal.

"Our infrastructure will be in place on Spanish Cay by that time. The beds, mattresses and other furniture are in our hangar ready to set up, and the first two RC-52s are already there. The Albury 33s should also arrive at about that time. We can always rent a boat to run to Marsh Harbour until they're delivered. I'll call Chris Thomason, our agent in Hope Town, and make sure his people have finished the kitchen installation. I talked to Dick Roberts this morning and he told me the *Britannia* advertising he set up for us has already produced nearly a hundred inquiries. He has started booking clients on various trips, starting eight weeks from now, but I can tell him to book a few in six weeks."

"I thought you and I were going to take the scouting trips first?" said Jamaal.

"We still will, but in a G-500. That way we'll check out the marinas, restaurants, and other points of interest in one-tenth the time. Water is just water; the coastline and quaint towns are the real attraction. The quicker we get the boats going, the quicker we reach our real goal."

"I'll have the navigation book on each trip done before I leave Orchila Island. I like the way you think Hakim! Let's do it."

***

Dirk Mendelsohn ended his fourth phone call that afternoon with Arenco Insurance Company. He worked his way up the chain of command until he got the response he wanted. He moved his claim from, "We'll get an adjuster there in two weeks" to, "Our adjuster will fly in there in two days". Dirk had already located a new baggage door and hinges at the Piper plant in Vero Beach, Florida. Crown Aviation at MYEH could handle the door installation and the repair of several bullet holes in the fuselage and cabin interior. A routine engine and equipment check would also be performed to check for abuse, and new tail numbers would be ordered and applied. So, no excuses by the insurance company were accepted.

At 4:00 p.m., Dirk took a 10 mg Cialis and half of a 25mg Viagra and drove north to Clearwater to pick up Desiree Cooter, one of his patient/protégées at the Oasis Club. He took her to a Sleep Inn on Ulmerton Road. They had sex for two hours under an assumed name, and he dropped her off at her night gig at BabyDolls Lounge on U.S. 19.

Dirk called these *office visits*. He got an upfront consultation (no pun intended) and half of his fee in cash before the operation, and three *office visits* afterwards. Desiree was still paying Dr. Dirk for her new 'Mendelsohn Slopers' that were making her a hot attraction every night at Clearwater's and

Tampa's strip clubs. She couldn't afford Diaco's or even the bargain Mendelsohn's. But she managed to scrape up half the cost to pay Dirk, who would let her work off the balance in trade. When their operation was completed in Nassau, these girls were in a whole different league. Only the most beautiful flat-chested girls qualified for Dirk's trade deal. The single mother, high dollar strippers lived in a fast moving, competitive, dog-eat-dog world. Florida strippers were a veritable goldmine for plastic surgeons, with Jacksonville, Orlando, Ft. Lauderdale and Miami sporting over a hundred strip clubs. But Tampa was ranked #1 in the State, and probably always would be as long as the city's convention business continued to flourish.

Dirk hopped on I- 275 and picked up his youngest son, Chauncey, at after school sailing practice at the St. Petersburg Yacht Club. Since Christine was always showing houses in the afternoon, this was his custom when he was in town. Later that evening Dirk sat out on his pool patio overlooking Snell Isle Harbor, sipping some Johnny Walker Blue Ghost, neat. His iPhone vibrated in his pocket and he took a look, *Chris Thomason*, then answered it.

"Hello, Chris," he said calmly, as his mind clicked into high gear. "What's up?"

"I heard you flew back to the states commercial, after you found your plane was stolen. Bummer, man!"

"Yes. I don't know what to think, but what a surprise. I was told there was some kind of robbery attempt targeting some newly discovered pirate's treasure at Snood's Blue Hole and some of the robbers stole and escaped in my airplane. Apparently, a pickup truck crashed and burned trying to get to my plane just as it took off. The police were a little sketchy relating the details to me and seemed more concerned about where I was that night."

"Yeah, I heard that you and Jacque were home in Winding Bay."

"Right, I was sound asleep … the Nassau police did find my Lance the next morning over in North Eleuthera, but they don't know who stole it yet. I've been working with my insurance company to get everything fixed. The police told me the rear baggage door is missing and there are several bullet holes in the fuselage. It could be fixed in a couple of weeks if I can keep the insurance people focused. Crown Aviation at MYEH seems to be a competent outfit."

"Yes, that company is owned by the Bender family from Arawak Springs. I've never heard anything but good things about their service. When are you coming back?"

"I'm planning on coming back in about a week. Chauncey has an Opti regatta in Sarasota this coming weekend and I want to see him sail. Then I have a fairly busy surgery schedule in Nassau for the next couple of months. I'll fly back on Silver Air, but I hope my plane will be repaired soon or I'll have to rent one from Marsh Harbour Airport or somewhere."

"You ought to bring your son over here to practice with the Hope Town and Nassau Opti teams this winter. Speaking about sailing practice, we have *RAGE* ready for the water after the modifications you specified were finished, and we want to schedule some practice races."

"You know I can always fit sailboat racing in, Chris."

"Well, I have an interesting proposal I want to run by you ... Last night I ran into Seth Stone over at Juvenal's. He and his crew brought his Hatteras back to Sea Spray now that the Blue Hole treasure hunt is over. He had his friends John Harvey, Fred Buckley, Scotty Remington and Gene Johnson there with him for dinner. Juvenal started talking about what great shape *RAGE* was in and John Harvey said, 'I've always wanted to sail one of those Class-A Bahamian sloops.' That gave Juvenal an idea and he said, 'It would be great practice for us to sail against you guys. Maybe you can come over and sail *TANQUERAY,* our back-up Class-A boat'. Then Seth said, 'Sounds like fun to me. We're flying home for a couple of weeks, but we'll be back to fish in the Bertram-Hatteras Shootout at Spanish Cay, and we might stay even later if the marlin are still biting.' ... What do you think, Dirk?"

Dirk's mind shifted into overdrive ... now that he realized what this phone call was really about. He had no more than five seconds to figure the pros and cons before his silence would condemn him. He knew it was a loaded question. The last thing he wanted to do was to be forced into a scrutinizing situation with Seth Stone and John Harvey, whom he considered smart guys and exceptionally good sailors. But his role-playing at this point demanded total objectivity.

"What a great idea," said Dirk enthusiastically. "That will give us some stiff competition to test our crew work and tactics. We should put better sails on *TANQUERAY* and maybe wet sand her bottom."

"Well, I couldn't agree more, Dirk," said Chris. "I hoped you would like Juvenal's idea."

"I've sailed against them in the 'States' for years. John is a great helmsman and tactician. Seth's won a lot of regattas, and Fred was crew in the America's Cup years ago."

"Juvenal will be glad to hear you're looking forward to it. Maybe this will be the year that Abaco's *RAGE* wins the championship. Call me if I can be of any help with your airplane."

"Thanks, and I'll see you soon, Chris."

Dirk ended the call, quickly threw back the rest of his Johnny Walker and poured himself another. He knew he was a rather good actor and cool under pressure, but this next scene was going to take an Academy Award performance.

***

Robert M. Thompson sat at his desk in Washington D.C. and looked at his high-resolution satellite viewing screen while scratching his chin. "Bobby" was a CIA operative, who was also the sole owner and CEO of Strategic Security, Inc., the largest Intel company in the Northern Hemisphere. One of his Intel units had just sent him a picture of the harbor on Orchila Island, an island belonging to Venezuela. Orchila Island was 100 miles north of Caracas and La Guairá in the Caribbean Sea and was part of the Los Roques archipelago. Ever since the Russians started landing their long-range bombers, refueling, and staying there overnight several months ago, Bobby had Orchila under surveillance 24/7. In the meantime, Cuban MIG jet fighters routinely refueled there during their maneuvers. It was like these communist countries were flexing their muscles or thumbing their noses at the United States.

But this new image showed a large 50 to 60-foot catamaran motor yacht docked near the end of Orchila's military airstrip and hangar complex. Bobby wondered what that type of vessel was doing there; the Venezuelan military had a 12-mile no entry zone around the island, enforced by a squadron of Russian SU-30 jet fighters at Miranda Air Force Base near Caracas. Bobby had firsthand knowledge of that area, having bill-fished there with Seth years ago out on the La Guairá bank. They'd also fished for bonefish around Los Roques, about 20 miles west of Orchila, flying out there from La Guairá in a DC-3. He messaged his satellite observers to watch the yacht carefully and to take close-up images of any personnel associated with it. He wanted to send those images to his marine specialists for identification and research.

Bobby played left defensive halfback for the University of Virginia football team when Seth Stone played right defensive halfback. They were also fraternity brothers in the Omicron Chapter of Phi Gamma Delta and the two "Fiji" brothers became life-long friends. He'd recruited Seth into the CIA a couple years out of college and they both worked against the Sandinistas in Nicaragua during Seth's first assignment. Bobby saved Seth from certain death during that espionage and Seth decided to return to the family boatyard business. They remained fast friends and he continued to fish with Seth all over the world. Bobby became an official Geezer as they got older. Seth called him often and sometimes asked for non-sensitive Intel in difficult circumstances. Bobby thought Seth should have stayed in the CIA. Little did they know that fate might bring them together again.

***

After a couple of hours of frustration, Jamaal speared his first grouper and brought it to the surface to put it in the skiff. He was grinning from ear to ear.

"I knew you'd get the hang of it, Jamaal. You're a much stronger swimmer than me," said Hakim.

"Hey, I grew up on the Nile River. You're a mountain boy, Hakim."

"Here comes Eduardo with another one. At this rate we'll have plenty after a few more dives."

An hour later they motored the skiff past Hugo Chavez's beach house and pulled it up on the beach past the day dock.

"I'll flush the engine in the rain barrel behind the garage while you two clean the fish," said Eduardo pulling the small Evinrude outboard off the skiff's transom. "Save the fish carcasses in those five-gallon buckets for crab trap bait. There's plenty of crabs to be caught in the harbor."

"It's a good thing that Chef Umair taught us how to clean this grouper before he flew back to London with his bartender Yosef," said Jamaal.

"Well, we're all bartenders now and better chefs and waiters," laughed Hakim. "I'm actually liking this saltwater lifestyle."

On the jeep ride back to the airfield, Eduardo reminded the two of them they were to have lunch with the Venezuelan Minister of Defense, Antonio Mendoza, the next day.

"He is sending a plane for you in the morning and it will leave our airfield for La Guairá at 10:00 a.m."

"We will definitely be ready to visit our gracious benefactor," said Hakim.

The plane ride aboard the old DC-3 sent by the Minister of Defense was bumpy and noisy to three passengers who were accustomed to Gulfstream jets. Hakim brought Shareef along to reward him for his excellent attitude and to act as his attaché. Shareef was large and looked menacing. The old DC-3 screamed economy, and Hakim understood that Venezuela was experiencing both serious inflation and a declining economy. Petroleum was the only product that was plentiful in the country and the government was trying to export as much as possible to help their cash flow.

Jamaal said, "I've been to Caracas a few times over the years," as they taxied to the terminal at Simon Bolivar Airport a few miles west of La Guairá. "It was built in the highlands at 3,000 feet and the east-west valley extends for 15 miles and is ringed with mountains as high as 9,000 feet. This area of Venezuela also has several extinct volcanoes. It's a beautiful colonial city that has melded in modern buildings and diverse neighborhoods around its core. The population is attractive, vibrant, and the city has an energy of its own. What I remember most are the beautiful women, suffocating traffic, moderate temperatures, and the constant party atmosphere."

"Sounds inviting. How long is the drive up to the city?" asked Hakim.

"About 45 minutes."

"What brought you to Venezuela before, Jamaal?"

"La Guairá is the country's main port and we docked there for a week or 10 days to unload, load and refuel the freighters. If I wanted to party, I would get a hotel room in the Chacao district where all the good clubs and restaurants were. If I wanted world-class shopping, I'd go to Centro Paseo, Sambil Mall or Tolon Fashion Mall. They all had multi-story world class shopping."

"I wonder how Caracas is holding up in this difficult socialist economy?" said Hakim as they got into the aging Lincoln Town Car that Senor Mendoza sent to pick them up.

"I guess we'll see for ourselves. La Guairá and the airport have had a tough time since the big mudslide back in 1999. During the rainy season, a mudslide inundated this area with 30 feet of mud. It killed 25,000 people and closed the port for almost a year and the airport for over a month. The road up to Caracas was rebuilt first. The marinas and back bay canals were filled in by the slide. So, it's hard to judge down here since the disaster, but La Guairá isn't half the town it was before the mudslide."

Forty-five minutes later they started into Caracas and the traffic was light. Their driver spoke some English and Jamaal asked him, "What happened to all the cars?'

"Plenty of gas, too little money to buy it," was his answer.

There were old cars pulled into vacant lots and alleys that appeared to be part of tent towns. The only traffic jams were caused by hordes of pedestrians and street urchins. Many businesses were boarded up and most commerce seemed to be centered on street vendors. Some shops and restaurants were open for business and apparently doing well, considering some of the crowded sidewalk cafes they passed.

Jamaal asked the driver, "Why are so many businesses boarded-up and others are so busy?"

"The only people who still have money are the government employees and the taxi drivers. Those open for business are the ones they like."

A few minutes later they exited the car in front of a large government building and were escorted by two sergeants to the lavish office of the Minister of Defense.

"Hakim and Jamaal, it is so good to meet you both. I trust that your short trip has been comfortable," said Senor Mendoza as they all shook hands. Shareef stood behind Hakim and was introduced as their attaché.

"Sit down now, I have a few questions to ask you. There is ice water next to your chairs. Hakim, do you have any problems on Orchila?"

"No sir, everything has been perfect. We are eternally grateful. We do need a doctor to furnish a general physical for seven of my men and to also teach them CPR and First Aid."

"I will send a Cuban doctor back on the plane with you today. Have Eduardo and his men been helpful?"

"He and his men have been more than helpful … above and beyond."

"That's good to hear, but now I must ask a question that President Chavez has for you. How much longer will you require the facilities on Orchila Island?"

"I think inside of six weeks would be sufficient. Our training has been progressing faster than we planned and we are anxious to move on to our next phase, your Excellency."

"I'm extremely glad to hear that, Hakim. President Chavez has some long-term plans for Orchila Island that concern one of our staunchest allies. That news will be confidential for now, but you'll no doubt hear about it soon after your departure. President Chavez also asked me if you could divulge, only to him in person, where your present mission will finally take you?"

"Again, I have to thank President Chavez for his support and generosity. But only I, Dr. Al-Zawahiri and Allah know. But you can tell him it will be an historic moment for all mankind when it is revealed."

CHAPTER FOURTEEN

STONE'S BOATWORKS was double stacked with large yachts and reverberated with the high-pitched whine of air grinders and sanders, as they belched fine dust into Florida's summertime heat and humidity. It was music to Seth's ears when all four 10 hp. air compressors were running simultaneously. His Ol' Dad, Robert E., had always said, "Sounds like money to me!" The workers were outfitted in space suits and respirators and they were cooled by the same compressed air that ran the tools. Most jobs were being done with vacuum sanders and grinders, and the initial sand blasting of the boat bottoms and running gear was confined under makeshift tarps to keep the sand under control. The business was always changing, as government regulations strove to keep the environment cleaner. His son Jeb, who now ran the yard, could foresee the day when all of this type of work, including spray painting, would be done inside huge closed sheds with 100% filtration and collection. It was all a matter of necessity and cost. After hauling with the Travelift®, the bottoms were pressure washed on a concrete wash pad that drained into a tank. Stone's Boatworks sump-pumped that waste water into the city's sanitary sewer system, while other boatyards chose to use a centrifuge and return the cleansed water to Salt Creek. Rain run off now was collected in underground tanks with weirs or small retention ponds before draining it into the creek.

Seth was stopping by the boatyard to have lunch with Jeb and to fill him in on the treasure hunt and marlin fishing in Abaco. Jeb knew some of the details from Seth's occasional phone calls, but today he'd get the whole story. First, Seth walked around the whole yard shaking hands with all the employees and inquiring about their families and health. The yard was still a big part of his life, but he was enjoying retirement and its adventures. Old habits die slowly, so he checked the checkbook and accounts receivable. The cash flow looked good. Jeb emailed him a financial statement each month and knew when to call Seth for his opinion on tough jobs. He felt that Jeb hadn't fallen far from the tree.

They left to have lunch at the Hollander Hotel, a funky boutique hotel with a tavern and swimming pool off the beaten track. The lunches and service were good and there wasn't much chance that they'd run into any friends or acquaintances which let them talk freely.

"So, you told me about the treasure hunt, but how much did you net?" asked Jeb as they sat down in a booth in the dimly lighted tavern.

"It was a longshot, but John and I figured out pirates couldn't have hidden it deep in the Blue Hole, and with a stroke of luck we found it. The Blue Hole was just a diversion, there was nothing but caves, fish and coral in the salt water. Now, to answer your question, my share is worth about a half million dollars if I just melt the doubloons into bars. If I get the coins graded and auction them, it might be worth as much as ten million or more ... it's hard to say. John Harvey's share is the same as mine, and the other seven partners, got one hundred and forty thousand minimum each,"

"Wow, I had no idea," said Jeb in amazement. "Maybe it's time for a new boat?"

"Maybe, but by the time my grandson Cullen graduates from St. Pete High, we may need that money to get him through college," said Seth ,with a smile.

"Any problems with the Bahamian Government concerning the treasure?"

"No. It was on private property and there were no 'historical' artifacts. A group of Haitians did try to steal the treasure but Jake Snood, the landowner, had plenty of guards on site so that did not work out for the bad guys. Snood runs a pine logging operation on a big piece of land. Scotty caught a stray bullet during the initial fracas, but luckily, it was just a flesh wound."

"I thought this trip was going to be safe with no danger?"

"Well, that was the plan. Nobody was more surprised than me. I'm flying up to Michigan tomorrow to see Lori at Torch Lake for a week or so, and then John and I and the rest of the crew will be flying back to Spanish Cay for the Bertram-Hatteras Shootout."

Seth and Jeb drove back to the yard in Seth's old Yukon. He let Jeb out at the front gate.

"I've got a few errands to run and I want to check on the townhouse in Treasure Island. It looks like you're plenty busy here … If you need me, call me."

"Try and keep a lid on it this time will you, Dad?" said Jeb with a smile, as he exited the truck and entered the noisy yard.

***

There hadn't been much talk, or even foreplay, after Seth drove his rental car the 70 miles from Pellston Regional Airport (PLN) to Torch Lake. He'd left Tampa (TPA) on Delta to Detroit (DTW)at 6:30 a.m. and after a layover in Detroit arrived aboard SkyWest in Pellston, Michigan at 1:30 p.m. Seth rented a Jeep Cherokee at Hertz and drove to Lori's, arriving at 3:30 p.m.

Seth swept her off her feet and never let her go. They realized immediately how much they had missed each other and vowed to make up for lost time. Lori steered Seth into the master bedroom and the couple undressed and were back in each other's arms in seconds. After their hurried initial coupling, Seth slowed down and started to gently rub Lori's back.

"You look like you have been working on your tan, girl," said Seth good naturedly.

"What makes you say that, honey?" answered Lori coyly.

"You don't have any bikini strap marks on your back or shoulders."

"Well, I'm surprised you didn't notice these," said Lori as she rolled over and exposed her lovely, totally tanned breasts.

"I guess I missed them in my haste," said Seth with a smile. "Have you been going topless on the lake?"

"Of course not, Seth. I ordered some Sunbrella™ canvas with grommets along the edges and zip tied them to the railings around the second story balcony. Nobody can see me."

"I think it's a great idea … how come your fine-looking ass is still milky white?"

"Maybe next year, *Big Boy*. You'll have to come up here more often to check me out."

"*Touché*, my love. But right now, your milky white ass is turning me on," laughed Seth as he grabbed a handful of it and rolled her back over.

The sun had gone down, and it was dark outside by the time they had exhausted each other. They showered together and then Seth took Lori to *Terrain's* for cocktails and an upscale dinner in the little town of Bellaire. They caught up on each other's grandchildren news, and Seth ... who called Lori at least twice a week while they were apart, filled in the blanks about the Blue Hole diving, Kitty's scary experience with the bends, the marlin fishing, and *most* of the details of the treasure hunt.

"When you go over for the Bertram-Hatteras Shootout, will you come home soon after it's over?"

"It depends on the weather, and whether or not we have finished sailing the Bahamian Sloops."

"Bahamian Sloops?" said Lori quizzically.

"I got a phone call last night from Abaco. It was Chris Thomason, an FSU friend of Todd Moran's ... you know my friend Todd, the St. Pete tire guy on Fourth Street. Anyhow, Chris and Juvenal Menard from Hope Town want me, John Harvey, Freddy, Gene and Scotty to practice sail against them before the Bahamas National Sloop Championships, which is a bigger deal to Bahamians than cricket or soccer. John and I have always wanted to sail one of those very unusual racing sloops. I won't go into all the details, other than to say that they only exist in the Bahamas and they are a racing version of a typical old-time Bahamian working sailboat ... with some unique solutions to ballasting and an outrageous sail plan to make them go fast."

"Sounds like more, 'Boys and their Toys' to me," laughed Lori.

"You're right on, as usual, girl," said Seth smiling.

"How about I fly over and bring the boat back with you when you're done playing?"

"Nothing would make me happier! Will you take me for a ride on the lake in your speedboat tomorrow?" asked Seth.

"How about the breakfast of champions first?"

"*Bueno,* Lori, *Bueno!*"

∗∗∗

Seth had been up and down 19-mile-long Torch Lake about 10 times in the last three days on Lori's 1996 Hacker-Craft 26 triple cockpit runabout *BOOTLEGGER.* It was powered by twin Crusader 330 hp. gas engines. Hacker-Craft is the oldest constructor of wooden hull boats in the world, still in business, and John Hacker actually invented the "V" hull. New owners have perpetuated the venerable company over the years and most of their latest hulls are fiberglass. The rest of the boats are still finished with beautiful hi-gloss varnished mahogany planks with chrome fittings and trim. It reminded Seth of his early days in the boat repair business, when Stone's Boatworks always had at least two skilled boat carpenters who could "spile" in planks and wield caulking irons to insert rolled and tarred oakum, and twisted cotton cord into the plank seams. Wooden boats were quickly becoming a thing of the past.

The Hacker was kept on a lift in Lori's double boathouse. The Torch Lake house, the Hacker, and Gudentite Tool and Die Company in Detroit were the only vestiges left of Lori's unhappy marriage to her late husband Dieter. Lori's son, Greg, who ran the family business now, kept a Malibu wake surf boat in the other boathouse slip. Seth enjoyed the past weekend with Greg, his wife Ima, and Lori's grandchildren, Rylee and Max who were all enthusiastic surfers. Lori's psychologist daughter, Gladys, also arrived Friday afternoon with her current lawyer boyfriend, Jackson Maloof, who flew up from Atlanta with her.

Lori's family left Sunday afternoon and Seth got busy on his cell phone. His first call was to John Harvey.

"Hey, Seth, how was re-entry?"

"Not too bad, John. We reacquainted quickly and had a couple of restful days, but then all the kids showed up."

"How did that go?"

"Lots of non-stop wake surfing and speedboating. Actually, it was fun, but we're worn out now and mercifully they're on their way home. I got a call from Chris Thomason; Mendelsohn wants to practice against us."

"Well, I have some mixed emotions, but racing one of those sloops is on my bucket list."

"Yeah, I'm right with you partner. Are you going to let me steer some?"

"Of course. When do you want to leave?"

"In ten days, I'll call Freddy and Gene. Will you call Scotty? ... His arm should be good to go by then. Text me so I know."

"OK, What about Billy and Dino Vino?"

"I hope they both can come. If not, maybe Doug Clorey or Norm Hogan can make it ... I'll make the calls, and someone may have to fly in later."

Seth spoke to Gene and Freddy. Gene was ready to go as usual, and Freddy was stoked about the sailing. Dino was going to be too busy through that period of time with Nitrox classes, but Billy got a 'hall pass' and called back an hour later.

"Kitty's feeling fine and she's going to an orchid show in Washington D.C. during that time. We just had a greenhouse built in the backyard and orchids have become her new hobby since she can't scuba dive anymore.

She's going to use her treasure money to fund her new hobby. I think I might buy a fishing boat a few feet longer with mine."

"I've been thinking about doing the same thing with part of my share. If you don't want to fly over with John and me from St. Pete in ten days, fly in on Silver Airlines a few days before the tournament and we'll pick you up at Boat Harbour. I'm renting an Albury 23 to run around in."

"I think I'll do that; I'll text you the flight info. Thanks, Seth."

Doug Clorey was tied up with a half million dollar condo paver job in Clearwater. But Norm Hogan, Seth's former DEA agent buddy said, "I'm packed and ready to go, man."

Monday morning Seth was jolted out of bed by a call from Bobby Thompson. Seth answered the call and walked out on the porch overlooking the lake to take it.

"Hold on, Bobby, let me get where I can talk," said Seth heading for the porch overlooking the lake … "Ok, what's up so early?"

"Early? It's 9:00 o'clock, Seth."

"That's early for us retired folks. I'm up at Torch Lake in Michigan."

"I know where you are. As long as you have your iPhone set up like a pedestrian, I can find you anytime."

"Alright, I give up, what's up?"

"You may have read about it in the newspaper, but Russia has been flying some long-range exercises with T-160 nuclear capable bombers down to Venezuela to basically flex their not-so-big-anymore muscles at the United States and show solidarity for Hugo Chavez. They've been using a well-equipped airbase they've developed on Orchila Island, which is 100 miles from Caracas in the Caribbean. The Cuban Airforce also flies their MIG fighter jets there too, for refueling. We monitor the little, unpopulated, 25 square-mile island 24/7 with our satellites."

"I remember seeing something on Fox News about the bombers and they mentioned Chavez had a beach house there," said Seth.

"Right. Five weeks ago, a Robertson and Caine 52-foot catamaran motor yacht showed up at Orchila Island's supply dock. Then about twenty new people joined the normal five-man caretaker contingent at the island airbase. The catamaran is active in the harbor and around the island every day and it appears that it is to being used to train a cadre of five-man crews."

"How does this concern me, Bobby?"

"Bear with me and we'll get there," said Bobby. "I've assigned a couple more operatives to this surveillance and they scoured previous videos and noticed two different Gulfstream G-500 jets that have made several trips to Orchila over the past 10 weeks. They also ran the jets' tail numbers through the international airport computers programs and have come up with some interesting logistics. Trips to Tashkent, London, Nassau, New York, Singapore, Monaco, Dubai, Riyadh, Amsterdam, Dhahran, Karachi, N'djamena, Spanish Cay, Las Vegas, Caracas, Hong Kong and Los Angeles. The Gulfstream owners are obscured in LLC's in Saudi Arabia and the United Arab Emirates. They probably belong to Saudi princes and our assets doubt that the princes traveled to Karachi in Pakistan, or Tashkent in Uzbekistan, or Spanish Cay in the Bahamas, or N'djamena in Chad, Africa. The rest of the cities are possible for Saudi princes abroad who are generally attracted to gambling, high-end entertainment, cocktails and Caucasian pussy."

"I'm still not getting it, Bobby."

"We concentrated on Spanish Cay in the Bahamas because our algorithms didn't show any reason for a princely visit there. And '*Bingo*' we found two more identical RC-52 catamaran motor yachts moored in its small marina. They also spotted *TAR BABY* moored on the other side of the same marina."

"Ok, you got me ... so what?"

"When are you going back to the Bahamas?"

"In about ten days, Gene, Freddy, Scotty Remington and I are flying back with John in his Piper Saratoga. Billy Chandler and Norm Hogan are flying in later. I've booked a hotel room for them. We're fishing in the Bertram-Hatteras Shootout next month."

"We did some more research and found that a new English charter boat company had been formed in Nassau called *Britannia*. They've leased space on Spanish Cay and will be opening in a couple of weeks. Two more RC-52s will be coming from Puerto Rico and we've been told that their Orchila training boat and twenty-some employees will be arriving in Spanish Cay by boat and air. Our English assets tell us all the employees are citizens of Great Britain and their own licensed captains will skipper the yachts out of Nassau. They also have a fly and stay arrangement with the Atlantis Resort on Nassau's Paradise Island, and their marina will be the embark/disembark point for all trips. They have placed ads in all the top yachting magazines. But ... it still strikes me as strange that they would train their English crew on a deserted communist controlled island and have the use of those Gulfstream jets, unless they're somehow chartering them."

"Where are they going to cruise?" asked Seth.

"They advertise five trips. All the trips are two weeks of gunkholing and exploring quaint destinations. One to Tampa-St. Pete via Key West, with stops at Everglades City, Naples, Boca Grande, Captiva, Marco Island and

Sarasota along the way, coming or going. Another trip bumps up the east coast of Florida to Charleston, including Palm Beach, St. Augustine and another similar to Savannah that includes Key West, Miami, Palm Beach and West End. There's an intra-coastal trip from Stuart to Jacksonville and the Saint John's river area. The longest trip is to Annapolis and Washington D.C., with stops at Singer Island, Jacksonville and Charleston. That trip uses the intracoastal only if the weather is bad."

"Well, the RC-52 can make 20 knots per hour if the weather isn't really bad and with a competent captain and crew, they could run all night, inside or out," said Seth.

"You know the boat?"

"Yes, The Moorings Ltd. has a charter version of that same hull in service at seven locations around the world. What do you want me to do for you, Bobby?"

"Just keep an eye on them for me and send me any head shots of their personnel you can sneak on your iPhone camera. You have a reason to be there and you won't look suspicious."

"How many situations like this are you watching?"

"More than you can count on your fingers and toes," laughed Bobby.

"Why don't you come down and fish the tournament with us, it's been a while since you fished with the Geezers. It could be like business and pleasure."

"Let me think about that, Seth. I sure would like to come. Call me when you get to Spanish Cay and I'll give you an update."

Seth spent a few more restful days at Torch Lake. Lori had cocktails and dinner for a few friends that Seth socialized with over Christmas visits, when they all raced iceboats on the lake. If it had a sail, Seth liked it, and the DN class one-man iceboats could reach speeds of 55 mph. The local iceboat club welcomed visitors like Seth. He hoped to get a ride on a Skeeter "A" class during his holiday visit this year. In the right conditions, the Skeeter could reach speeds in the 90 mph range.

Finally, it was time for Seth to head back to St. Petersburg and ultimately the Bahamas for more fishing, and possibly some low-profile treasure hunting in Treasure Cay if their salvor's license was granted.

"I'm sad to see you go again, Seth, but happy I'll see you at the end of next month when we bring the boat back together."

"I'll miss you, Lori. Why don't you go to work on that overall tan we talked about? Then you won't have to worry about bikinis when we're out in the middle of the Atlantic Ocean."

She kissed him as he started to get in his rental car.

"Don't you think about anything else, you pervert," said Lori smiling.

"Not much else, my love," said Seth laughing, as he got in the car and drove out the driveway.

***

Seth made his connection in Detroit with Delta and was in the air within 90 minutes headed for Tampa Airport, two and a half hours away. He sat up in first-class, something he decided to do now that he was at least one million dollars richer. He got comfortable after takeoff and started to plan some strategy for the upcoming Bertram-Hatteras Shootout. Skip Smith, the tournament director, had decided to work one caught dorado and one yellowfin or blackfin tuna, 15 pounds and over into the scoring each day, at a point a pound. Catch and release blue marlin were worth 400 points, white marlin and spearfish 150 points and sailfish 100 points. There was also a weigh-in kill division for blue marlin that were 101 inches and longer. Seth's boat wouldn't be doing that.

Seth knew the *Tilloo Pocket, The Bridge, Brady's Bend, the Mushroom, Wonderland, Jurassic Park, North Bar* and *Winding Bay* as well as the locals, but he had only fished *The Great Abaco Canyon* and *Flat Top* a couple of times. He remembered how he and Lisa, his late wife, had started out in the Abacos. First, Seth ordered charts from Dr. Mitch Roffer, an oceanographer in Miami. He faxed up to the minute satellite data overlaid on oceanographic charts with text analysis of current and temperature trends that show likely fishing hotspots. Seth had hooked up a fax machine/printer to his Motorola Satellite phone to receive those charts. He still had that system on *TAR BABY* and now ROFFS™ sent discounted packages to serious anglers throughout the world. Seth was only halfway through an Abacos package at the moment. But what really helped Seth and Lisa in the early days was meeting Marsh Harbour's Captain Justin Tillis. Justin was a freelance skipper who did not have a sportfish boat. He hired out at $250 a day and put visiting anglers onto fish on their own boats. Justin had fished those waters exclusively for 20 years in many different capacities: mate, commercial fisherman and captain.

Seth met him the second year that he and Lisa were at Sea Spray at the fish cleaning table. It had been a slow week for billfish, and they had only caught a couple of dorado. Their next day was no exception. So, Seth finally ran into 700 feet of water outside Tilloo Cut where he had seen locals, Captain Robert Lowe in his 32-foot Albin and Chris Thomason in his Bertram 31 chunking for tuna a few times. Seth chummed and caught some baitfish. Then he cut up some thawed mackerel from their freezer, which Lisa chunked off the transom while Seth held the boat in the same spot with the engines. Two live baits were let out from the outrigger clips. They caught four yellowfin tuna from 25 to 50 pounds before the sharks started schooling and ended fishing for the day. Lisa was hosing down the boat while Seth was cleaning the tuna when Captain Justin introduced himself to Seth.

"Sir, I'm Captain Justin Tillis. I took a party fishing on Dave Matthews Ocean 54 today and for the first time in my career, I got skunked. Dave has some friends in for the weekend and wanted to catch some fish, so he hired me, and I failed miserably. I really wanted to hook them up with at least one billfish and then, later in the day anything that swims out there. Do you think you could share one of those beautiful yellowfins you caught today? You seem to be the only boat that brought any fish to the dock. This is embarrassing for me ... Dave paid me $250, but a tuna dinner for his friends might make amends. I can make it worth your while, Captain ... ?"

"Seth ... Seth Stone ... Look, Justin, I couldn't take any money."

"No, no, I will tell you where I should have been fishing today, and that's where I'm going tomorrow with another client."

"Well, Justin, you're either the best ZipLoc fisherman I've ever run into or the most humble professional captain I've ever met. I'll go with the latter ... you can have this 35-pounder, but I'm not going to clean it for you," said Seth smiling.

"God Bless you, Seth Stone. I'm going out to *Flat Top* tomorrow. It's just below the Abaco Canyon. I'll drop the GPS numbers by your boat tonight. When you go dead north over my number, there'll be a hump, a hole, then another hump. The rest is a flat plateau about 3,000 feet deep for a square mile with 3,500 foot depths around it. When there's nothing biting and the wind is from the west, it's the place to be. The humps are where two currents converge."

Seth and Lisa caught and released two blue marlin the next day and lost a third. Captain Justin caught and released three. Later that summer, Seth paid Justin to school him out on the *Mushroom* and *Jurassic Park* fishing areas. He would call Justin, who lived in Marsh Harbour, when they flew back to Spanish Cay, to schedule him aboard for a few days, to teach Seth what he knew about the *Great Abaco Canyon* and the *Double-Dips*.

CHAPTER FIFTEEN

THE NEXT FOUR WEEKS flew by as *Britannia's* training sessions on Orchila Island transformed Hakim's Islam religious zealot recruits into hospitable nautical journeymen. Their former trades as combat soldiers, line cooks and waiters had been upgraded by a master chef, master mixologist, master at arms and a master mariner. They were in top physical condition and ready for their first assignments on the open ocean. All of them now knew how to swim, and better than half of them couldn't wait to go fishing during their free time. Hakim planned for each crewmember to participate in at least one of the deliveries of the two RC-52s in Puerto Rico to Spanish Cay or the *TRINIDAD GIRL's* trip from Orchila to Spanish Cay. The trips would serve as a baptism by fire to test their discipline and strengthen their newly acquired skills. Six of the seven captain candidates had obtained their "six pack" certification. Jabbar, Shareef, Aksleel, Naser, Abdul and Rajab were awarded Captain's epaulet shirts at a special dinner honoring their accomplishment. Ameer was still working to pass his General Navigation exam.

Hakim named the two boats that were already moored in Spanish Cay *FANDANGO* and *MERIDIAN*. The two RC's that his own men would deliver shortly were named *ECLIPSE* and *DELILAH*. All their boats were registered under the Bahamian flag with their hailing port being Nassau. Dick Roberts, their Nassau lawyer and corporate agent, handled the paperwork and considerable payments to Bahamian customs and licensing for the boats under "Honest Bob's" direction. Honest Bob ordered the vessels' names and hailing ports from a Nassau sign maker and had them shipped to the repair yards for installation during their final detailing. Thousands of vessels, including freighters and super tankers, were titled and registered under the Bahamian flag. The costs were far less expensive and the inspection rules more lax than in most other maritime countries.

Jamaal put together two crews, including Jabbar as the second captain, to deliver the Puerto Rico boats. The rest of the crews were brand new. The boats would run in tandem, which was always a good safety practice. Hakim arranged for a jet to fly them to Fajardo, Puerto Rico. Honest Bob arranged to have both boats sea-trialed and surveyed and paid the yards as agreed.

Hakim busied himself at his desk figuring the float plans from Puerto Rico to Spanish Cay. The distance was 890 miles, across the open Atlantic Ocean. If bad weather, fuel or mechanical trouble became a factor, they would be close to the Turks and Caicos and the lower Bahamian Island chain just to the west. At 8 knots (9.2 mph) the RC52's range with the 396 gallons of diesel they carried was 1,117 miles and the trip would take 99 hours or 4 full days and nights. Both the *DELILAH* and *ECLIPSE* would carry two plastic 55-gallon drums of diesel fuel lashed in their cockpits which gave them all the safety factor they needed if the weather turned really nasty or they needed to run 20 mph to a nearby port. Each drum of extra fuel would be hand-pumped into the main tank as soon as they used 55 gallons in the main tank, to keep the weight of the fuel low in the boat. All the crews had British passports, which insured there wouldn't be any customs or immigration problems.

The Gulfstream jet arrived on Orchila a couple days later and Jamaal, Jabbar and ten recruits loaded up enough provisions and drinking water for a week at sea for each boat. The RC-52 carried 265 gallons of water in her own tanks which would be utilized for showers and cleaning. The catamaran design of the RC-52 allowed for four spacious double cabins with heads and showers, crew quarters, large public areas for lounging and dining, and a full galley. A forward cockpit provided cozy seating for four. The wide and covered fan deck could easily accommodate eight to ten guests. Behind the fan deck was a large swim platform, bracketed by steps built into each transom. The swim platform was hydraulically controlled and could be lowered to the waterline. Hold downs were provided to secure a large tender, and a stainless-steel davit was installed to move it. "Honest Bob" had shipped five, 15-foot Saturn 470 inflatable tenders with aluminum roll-up floors, and five Yamaha 25 horsepower outboards to the respective refit yards. The yacht's overall spaciousness was comparable to most 75-foot mono-hull cruisers. The flybridge was equally spacious. The Yanmar 350 hp diesel engines were powerful but fuel consumption was economical, with both engines consuming only 2.86 gallons per hour at 9.2 miles per hour. The economy continued with both engines consuming 24.8 gallons at a top end of 21 miles an hour. The catamaran hull delivered a smoother and faster ride in a heavy chop than a larger mono-hull cruiser. All these features and factors were corroborated during the intense training sessions supervised by Jamaal and Jabbar while running *TRINDAD GIRL* around Orchila Island.

The two-boat flotilla left Puerto Rico the next morning in fair weather and started chugging north towards Spanish Cay at 8 knots. The on-watch crew of three, busied themselves with navigation and mechanical checks. Meals were prepared by chefs and stewards sharing responsibilities coming on and off shifts depending on the sea state.

Jamaal said to Jabbar before they split up and departed, "Our food has gotten so good in taste and quality since we started this operation, it's a wonder I haven't gained ten pounds."

"We should watch how much rich food we eat when we go to sea and don't have our everyday physical training and afternoon soccer game to burn up the calories."

"'You're right, Jabbar. Let's instruct our chefs to cut the portions 20% while we're at sea."

"*Bueno*, as our Latino friend, Eduardo, would say."

"I am going to miss the Venezuelan friends we have made. A different culture and religion ... but they are good people. I hope they find their way out of their political and economic problems. I wonder how many of them would convert to Islam after judgement day. It would be hard for me to kill Eduardo. Our Muslim religion seems to work in Democracies, Oligarchies, Dictatorships, Republics and Theocracies. But Socialism starts to break ties with all religions and Communism completely eliminates them."

"As Muslims, who believe in Islam, we are steadfast in our belief in a sublime afterlife," said Jabbar.

"That's what it's all about," agreed Jamaal. "Let's shove off."

The trip unfolded exactly to Jamaal's plan until 12:00 noon of the third day. As he checked *Passage Weather,* he was warned about Tropical Storm *Ana* heading for Havana. The present sea state was 8 knots of wind from the northeast causing a moderate chop. Jamaal checked the nearest fuel stops and settled on Rum Cay, near San Salvador. He checked his fuel usage and

ECLIPSE had used 185 gallons to this point. There were 321 gallons remaining which included the two drums of spare diesel that had been pumped in from the drums. He hailed Jabbar on *DELILAH*, who was running 100 meters west of him, on the VHF and explained the situation. At 8 knots they risked being affected by *Ana*, who was moving northwest at 15 miles an hour with 50 mph winds if they kept their current track and speed. They increased their speed to 20 mph at 25 gallons per hour and headed northwest to Rum Cay. Five hours at 20 mph would take them 100 miles further north and hopefully out of harm's way. The 125 gallons of diesel would need to be replaced, and they would leave Rum Cay with 396 gallons in their tanks, plus two full 55-gallon drums of spare fuel per boat. With that much fuel they could easily run up the leeward side of Cat and Eleuthera Islands at full speed the last 232 miles or tuck into Nassau Harbour if *Tropical Storm Ana* moved farther north. The two-boat flotilla arrived at Rum Cay's Summer Point Marina before dark and fueled up. Jamaal decided they would spend the night and leave at first light and try to run full speed, if possible, all the way to Marsh Harbour in Abaco the next day. The marina's General Manager, Benny Martin, was both friendly and helpful and was instrumental in Jamaal's decision.

Ana stayed her course to Havana and *ECLIPSE* and *DELILAH* were long gone before the rain and 25-mile outer band winds reached Rum Cay. They had smooth sailing in the lee of the big islands and were anchored behind Witches Point, near Marsh Harbour, well before dark. They had evening prayers aboard ship and a relaxing dinner before turning in.

The last 40 miles to Spanish Cay was a beautiful introduction to the Abaco Islands. They motored past Marsh Harbour and saw the red and white striped Hope Town Lighthouse towering above Elbow Cay across the Sea of Abaco. They passed Man-O-War Cay, Scotland Cay, Guana Cay and Treasure Cay on the inside. Jamaal led Jabbar around Whale Cay, which was dangerous in a north blow, then back in behind Green Turtle Cay and past a host of small uninhabited Cays, and finally to Spanish Cay across from the settlement at Coopers Town. Jamaal radioed the dockmaster, identified himself and asked to refuel before being docked. With permission granted, *ECLIPSE* landed at the large fuel dock with Jabbar following suit with *DELILAH*. Sunny and an assistant drove up in his golf cart, introduced himself and welcomed the newcomers. He and Paul helped fuel them up.

"Just sign these fuel tickets for *Britannia's* account Captain James," said Sunny. "Tie-up and plug in over at your dock with the other two RC-52s. Your two Albury 33s were delivered yesterday by Mr. Willingham and one of his associates. When you're ready, I'll show you your storage hangar and take you by your condos. Each condo has two golf carts with it … one four-seater and one six-seater. We weren't expecting you until tomorrow … Mr. Muneer called me a couple of days ago and thought that's when you'd arrive."

"We saw *Ana* coming and pulled in at Rum Cay, fueled up, then ran close to 18 knots the rest of the way here."

"Well, she stayed her course and came close to Havana, but you never know when they'll make a turn. *Ana* was very early for the season's first storm. Come up to the office when you're ready and get all of your keys."

"Add a $30 tip to that tab for you and Paul," said Jamaal knowing that dockmasters and fuel attendants depended on tips for most of their income.

"Thank you, sir," said Sunny.

Once the newly arrived RC-52s were scrubbed and cleaned inside and out, Jamaal left a two-man crew to scrub down, rinse and chamois *MERIDIAN* and *FANDANGO*, while the rest of the crew started to move in and furnish their condos. There were enough provisions aboard the boats to feed this vanguard crew for at least a couple of days. Tomorrow, Jamaal and two recruits would take a ride in one of the Albury 33s to Marsh Harbour for fresh food and galley supplies.

"Sunny, can we borrow a pickup truck to transport the furniture, bunk beds and mattresses that are stored in this hangar?" asked Jamaal.

"I've got one out back of my office," said Sunny. "I'll have Paul drive it over here to help you. We should get it all in four or five trips."

"Ok, I'll leave Alan, Sam and Basil here to load the truck. Martin, Frank and the rest of you, drive the carts back to the condos and unload these duffels. Alan, you're in charge here. Lock the hangar after the last load," said Jamaal as he headed for the condos. "Sunny, where should we leave the cardboard shipping boxes?"

"Just break them down and I'll send Paul down later," said Sunny. "We have an incinerator behind the hotel to burn them. Do you need some box cutters?"

"No, the whole crew carries these curved knives in case they have to cut a dock or anchor line quickly. They'll slice up the boxes." said Jamaal, pulling one from a leather sheath threaded thru his belt.

"Looks like that will more than do the job," said Sunny, looking at the size of the curved Damascus steel knife.

The condos were set up as specified. The first condo housed all the recruits in bunkbeds. The middle condo had the kitchen with the stove, refrigerators, and dining tables and chairs. Across the hall, a large chalk board stood against the wall at the end of the newly carpeted room. This area would be used for crew meetings and prayers. All the kitchen equipment had been installed and was in working order, including the roll-around prep tables. The upstairs of the middle condo had sleeping quarters for Hakim's lieutenants, with a crew lounge across the hall. The third condo had Hakim's and Jamaal's private quarters upstairs. A large *Britannia* reception area and desks for the operations managers, Jamaal and Jabbar, were downstairs, including a private office for Hakim across the hall.

The crews worked until dinner, which took place on the boats. Jamaal sent a coded sat phone text to Hakim in Orchila confirming their arrival and updating him on the delivery of the Albury 33s and their progress on completing the condo furnishings. He planned on borrowing the needed tools from the boats to assemble the metal bunk bed frames, which had all been moved to the condos, and then have Jabbar supervise the moving and installation of the mattresses. Jamaal would take an Albury 33 to Marsh Harbour with a chef, taking Sunny's assistant, Paul, as a guide. It would be their first visit to Maxwell's Supermarket, Jimmy's Wine and Spirits, and Direct Restaurant Supply. In addition to foodstuffs and drinking water, they needed pots, pans, skillets, utensils, plates, cups, glasses, table cloths and napkins for a start. Hakim had only minimal equipment and liquor to transfer to Spanish Cay by air. Jamaal informed Hakim he thought Spanish Cay would be ready for the entire crew in three to four days.

Hakim returned an encrypted message reading: *I will send a G-500 for you in three days, it will have some standard equipment and supplies aboard that will have to clear customs. Travel back here as soon as possible. We have five men left who have not made a long voyage, I will return with the other men to Spanish Cay the next day and you will leave with the TRINIDAD GIRL, also for Spanish Cay, weather permitting.*

***

Dirk Mendelsohn flew in from Tampa to North Eleuthera (ELH), on Silver Air to pick up his repaired Piper Lance. His insurance paid for the repairs and his airline tickets. He flew his repaired Lance the short distance (57 miles) from North Eleuthera to Nassau (NAS), parked his plane in his hangar and headed to his apartment in his Cayenne. He settled in and set up a meeting with Phillippe at Mango's later that night. The meeting wouldn't last too long, as he had a busy operating schedule at the out-patient clinic for the next three days.

After dinner, Dirk drove over in his Porsche, slipped in the backdoor and joined Phillippe in his office.

"Good to see you, Phillippe. I hope things have calmed down over the last couple of weeks."

"Our wounded and dead Haitian associates have been shipped back to Haiti and life goes on. My sources tell me the detectives are dead ended. The Haitians we lost have been replaced and our businesses have been performing well. Mango's profits are up, and the numbers racket profits increase each week. Our loan business is steady."

"How about Grand Bahama?" asked Dirk.

"Spring Break in the 'States' is driving our profits up at Papayas. We should be in the black very soon, including startup costs and remodeling. Our location near the casinos was a smart move, but we have a few good dancers over there that need your help. I'll get them on your schedule once summer rolls around. I also expanded the numbers racket to Freeport. I sent two of our top performers there to organize the runners and set-up the police payoffs. I need to give you your share of the profits this month in cash."

"I'll take care of that soon. I've got a few spots for it. What do you hear from Reltney?"

"He's going to make a big buy next week. He said he'll be contacting you soon."

"It sounds like everything is okay. I'm glad I didn't screw things up too badly. I really did learn a lesson. I'm going to continue to practice plastic surgery and further my charitable foundation and contributions. It can't do anything but enhance my cover. Also, I'm going to spend more time sailing *RAGE* and try to win the national sloop title for the Abacos this year. If I accomplish that it should make me almost bullet-proof."

"I actually hope the Nassau entry wins," said Phillippe with a straight face. Then he laughed and held his hands up saying … "No, no, Dirk … just kidding."

***

After arriving back on Orchila Island, Jamaal found his final delivery crew had the *TRINIDAD GIRL* provisioned and ready to go to sea. Her water and fuel tanks were filled, and the extra fuel drums were stowed. The five novices chosen were the only recruits that hadn't sailed on the open ocean. The trip covered 1,200 miles and required three fuel stops. It would be the longest and maybe most grueling of the five deliveries, depending on the weather. Their first stop was Cap Cana Marina, in the Dominican Republic, 485 miles due north across open ocean. At nine knots the RC-52 would burn 333 gallons of its 396-gallon fuel capacity in that distance. Two 55-gallon plastic drums of diesel fuel were lashed into the cockpit. If the weather allowed them, they could run 16 knots the last 250 miles using the extra fuel to get to Cap Cana faster. From Cap Cana, Jamaal would navigate 325 miles to Providenciales, in the Turks and Caicos Islands, and take on fuel at Blue Haven Marina, a large IGY facility with easy access on *Leeward Going Through Channel* just northeast of Grace Bay. The last leg from Providenciales to Spanish Cay, was 390 miles across the open Atlantic Ocean, staying just east and clear of the Bahamian Islands chain. If bad weather threatened, Jamaal could duck in and get leeward of Cat, Long or Eleuthera Island. Like many seasoned skippers he depended on *Passage Weather*, which was available on the internet world-wide, to predict the wind, waves and weather forecasted a week in advance. Depending on the weather and the absence of mechanical problems, the trip should take a week. *TRINIDAD GIRL* would run 24 hours a day with two watch crews alternating every four hours. The galley was stocked with sufficient provisions and the RC-52 had four spacious cabins, all with well-designed heads and showers. The Navionics and other electronic equipment were redundant, and the crew had learned to mark paper charts every half-hour and dead reckon if necessary. When this trip was completed, *Britannia* would have a whole crew that was interchangeable on any of their boats.

The night before *TRINIDAD GIRL* left for Spanish Cay, Hakim had a special dinner prepared after evening prayers and Jamaal and his crew were cheered by the remaining recruits and given Allah's blessing. The mariners cast off the next morning and the crew that was left behind made ready for their evacuation to Spanish Cay. Hakim checked with Honest Bob in Nassau and made sure the five Winslow life rafts were ready for delivery in Tampa. Bob confirmed they were paid for and ready for delivery to TPA's private jetport. Next, he sent an encrypted text message to Marwan in Cameroon on his sat phone.

"M-5 this is H-15. Purchase approximately 557 kilos of .800 millimeters thick lead sheet as follows: 15 sheets of .800 x 100 x 75 millimeters, and 5 sheets of .800 x 75 x 75 millimeters. Purchase Chinese commercial ASTM B-29 in Hong Kong. Deliver to buyer Britannia at Spanish Cay by air with no passengers. Mark crates - "Boat Ballast Material". Also, I need five cell phone-controlled bomb triggers. Contact our chief bombmaker, Fawaz Khan, in Islamabad, and have him build five two-stage triggers, one cell phone number to arm and a second number to detonate. Five different number combinations. Have Fawaz use series-8 iPhones. Set up local numbers from Tampa, Miami, Jacksonville, Charleston and Washington D.C. Instruct our Jersey City cell chief to establish and maintain these accounts. Use Verizon, they have the best coverage. Supply me with three untraceable iPhone 8's. Pick up all by G-500 and hold at your present location, to ship here in approximately two weeks. I will contact you with further instructions. Any questions?"

"No, H-15. Message received."

Hakim made further arrangements for one of the Gulfstream jets to fly them to Spanish Cay in two days. Hakim and the remaining crew had a thank you dinner for Eduardo Clemente and his crew on their last evening on Orchila.

"Our training would not have progressed as quickly, nor would our stay have been as enjoyable, if it weren't for you, Eduardo, and your crew. You helped us at every turn. We also thank you for teaching us to be fisherman. The wise Chinese philosopher, Lao Tzu said, 'Give a man a fish, and you feed him for a day. But teach a man to fish and you feed him for a lifetime'," said Hakim, standing for a toast after dinner.

Eduardo stood and said, "Good luck, *mi Amigos,* in your future endeavors, whatever they may be. We have enjoyed having you on our little island. I speak for my men as well when I say … we will sorely miss our daily soccer game when you're gone."

CHAPTER SIXTEEN

DOCTOR JOHN HARVEY BUZZED THE TOWER at Spanish Cay's Airstrip (MYAX), and saw the runway was clear. The marina was already two-thirds full, three weeks before the Bertram-Hatteras Shootout. John announced over the radio, that he was about to land and lined up his Piper Saratoga on a southwest glide path to the 4,400-foot runway. There wasn't much land on either side of the airstrip, except where the main hangar and office were located, but the runway was 70-feet wide and had turn-arounds at both ends. He noticed the aircraft parking across from the main hangar was half-filled on his fly-by. It had been an uneventful early morning flight, in perfect weather, down Florida's west coast and then across the Gulf Stream onto the Bahamas bank. The wind was light and there was frequent boat traffic below them. Spanish Cay had its own Bahamian Customs Office at the airport that processed airplane and boat entry. John and his passengers, Seth Stone, Gene Johnson and Fred Buckley would be back onboard Seth's Hatteras, *TAR BABY*, in less than a half an hour. Seth hoped that Scotty Remington would be flying in to join his "Geezer" buddies in a couple of days. His final examination of the recent gunshot wound to his left shoulder was taking place that morning.

John landed smoothly and taxied up to the main hangar where the customs office was located. Seth's iPhone dinged - it was a message from Scotty; *I passed my exam and am cleared for action, I will arrive in Marsh Harbour at 11:00 a.m. Friday, on Silver Air, ready for action.* Seth answered, *Great news, take a cab to Boat Harbour Marina. We'll be waiting at the pool bar.*

Seth said to John, "Scotty's coming in Friday."

"That's good news!" said John, smiling.

They cleared customs in a matter of minutes because their cruising permit, fishing licenses and visas were all in place. Paul and Sunny showed up with Seth's six-man golf cart and they loaded their gear and bait coolers in Sunny's cart for the ride over to the marina.

Sunny said, "I have your rental Albury 23 tied up in the second slip on the tender dock over near the hotel. She's named *BONEHEAD*. I figured you might want to run to Coopers Town or Marsh Harbour today."

"Thanks. We'll probably go to Coopers Town for essentials and really stock up in a couple of days when we go to Marsh Harbour to pick up Scotty. Thanks for checking on the Hatteras while we were gone," said Seth, as he slipped Sunny another *Benjamin*.

"Thanks, Captain. When you get settled, take a walk near the fuel dock where those four RC-52s are docked for the new charter outfit *Britannia* when you get settled. You might enjoy checking out the two new Albury 33s that were just delivered as their work boats."

"Have they started to run their charters yet?"

"No, but about half their crew is already here. Ten of them brought in two of the RC-52s from Puerto Rico last week. They've been getting their condos over by Barefoot Beach ready for the rest of the crew. The fifth charter boat is expected by the end of the week, and the rest of the crew will be flying in any day now."

"Will their charter customers be staying in your hotel?" asked Seth ... already knowing the answer.

"No, they'll pick up and deliver their passengers at the Atlantis Marina in Nassau. *Britannia*'s General Manager told me they're using their own licensed captains."

"I'm sure the International Airport and a couple of nights at Atlantis is attractive to the customers."

"Having their crew quarters and dockage here is far less expensive than anything they could find in Nassau. They've leased one holding slip at Atlantis."

"Well I hope their business is successful, and helps everyone," said Seth. "Thanks again, for keeping an eye on the Hatteras."

As Seth walked down the dock towards *TAR BABY*, he got the same smile on his face that he got every time he saw the name on her transom. He thought of his grandfather reading him Uncle Remus stories when he was just a child. He pictured the Tar Baby, fashioned out of tar and turpentine by the nefarious Br'er Fox, sitting alongside the path. Br'er Rabbit passed by the

Tar Baby saying, *"Howdy"*, and he didn't get a reply. The situation then proliferated into anger, as Br'er Rabbit said, *"If you don't answer me, I'm gonna' knock your head clean off!"* ... *and the Tar Baby, he don't say nothin'."* So, Br'er Rabbit punches him and gets stuck in the tar. The more he punches and kicks ... the worse he gets stuck. Finally, Br'er Fox comes out from behind the bushes laughing and takes Br'er Rabbit towards his cookin' pot. The cunning Br'er Rabbit says, *"You can cook me, roast me, hang me, skin me, or drown me, but please, please, ple-e-ease don't throw me in the briar patch!"*, and the rest is history.

Once everyone was settled, Seth texted Lori to let her know he was safely in Spanish Cay and sent along an emoji flurry of three red hearts and a smiley face blowing a kiss. Secondly, he sent an encrypted message to Bobby Thompson informing him, he was back in Spanish Cay and chronicled his conversation with Sunny. He also promised clandestine photos of *Britannia's* boats, the condo exteriors and their crew. Thirdly, he called Captain Justin in Marsh Harbour.

"Justin, Seth Stone. How are you?"

"I'm fine, Seth, it's good to hear from you. I heard you were back at Sea Spray."

"When can we go fishing? We moved the Hatteras over to Spanish Cay two weeks ago for the Bertram-Hatteras Shootout, and we just flew back in after a little hiatus."

"I'm sorry, Seth, I'm booked for the tournament on your friend Jim Tower's *CATTLE CALL.*"

"I already knew that; I want you to show me how you fish the *Canyon* and the *Double Dips* for a few days during the next week or so ... whenever you can."

"How about tomorrow? I'll work you in for a couple of other days before tournament week. *CATTLE CALL* isn't coming in until a week before the tournament."

"See you at 7:30 tomorrow morning, my friend. We brought plenty of frozen ballyhoo and rigged mackerel with us on John Harvey's airplane."

"I'll be there."

With that setup, Seth called Juvenal to check in about sailing. "Juvenal, Seth here. We just flew in and are settled at Spanish Cay."

"Great, when can you practice with us? Dirk got back a few days ago."

"We're fishing tomorrow, and I have to pick up Scotty at the airport the next day. I just got a message that he passed his shoulder exam. How about the day after that?"

"Saturday ... that's perfect."

"Remember, first we need a day with you and Chris and some of your crew. We need to learn the ropes before we race against your first team," said Seth.

"Chris and I figured that, so you won't race against RAGE and Dirk until the following Saturday. How many crew will you have?"

"John will skipper, and I'll trim the mainsail. Gene, Freddy and Scotty will crew."

"I will bring four crew, myself, and Chris. I'll sail with you the whole time. But Chris will sail with Dirk and the first team next Saturday."

"We'll be glad to have you, Juvenal. I read the rules, technical specifications and by-laws. It was only eight pages and they stated you can have four non-Bahamians on your crew, but the boat must be designed, built, owned and skippered by a Bahamian. How does Dirk get to be a skipper?"

"Chris has been our skipper for a number of years, but he recognizes Dirk's talent. Chris asked the regatta committee to give Dirk special dispensation for his cleft palate foundation and pro bono surgical work, and they gave it to him. We'll meet you at 9:00 a.m. Saturday over at the Government Wharf and ferry dock in Hope Town with *TANQUERAY*."

Seth had the boys work the rest of the afternoon on tackle, respooling reels with new line, pulling drags and re-rigging the big lures and teasers. The fishing they'd done earlier in the spring had taken its toll on Seth's well-used, first-rate equipment. Seth took that opportunity to ride over to Barefoot Beach and take some photos of the three condo buildings *Britannia* was leasing. He parked his golf cart just off the path near the fuel dock and took some pictures of the impressive new Albury 33s. Seth had read in one of the boating magazines that they had a top speed of 54 mph. A two-man crew was scrubbing down one of the RC-52 motor cats, and Seth took their pictures on the sly. He also managed to get photos of their transoms and names, *ECLIPSE, DELILAH, FANDANGO* and *MERIDIAN*, without being noticed. All four boats carried the hailing port of Nassau, Bahamas, and flew the Bahamian flag. The two crew members were short and trim, with neatly cut thick black hair, and had swarthy complexions. They were dressed in white T-shirts, khaki colored Columbia fishing shorts and Sperry Top-Sider boat shoes. They spoke English to each other with a clipped British accent.

Seth returned to the Hatteras and sent the pictures and his comments to Bobby's secure email. Once the tackle was ready for tomorrow's fishing, the travel-weary crew had a drink at the hotel bar and an early dinner before retiring.

***

Justin arrived aboard *TAR BABY* shortly after sunrise and was already thawing a package of frozen horse ballyhoo in a bucket of seawater. When Seth and the crew walked out to go to breakfast, he was rigging them for pitch baits.

Seth shook his hand and said, "Good to see you, Justin! We're going up to the hotel for a quick breakfast, will you join us?"

"No thanks, I already ate. I'll have the boat ready to go by the time you get back," he replied, as he shook hands with John and Gene, after being introduced to Freddy.

Thirty minutes later they motored out of the marina's rock breakwater and Seth started to turn south towards Coopers Town. The wind was light and there wasn't a cloud in the sky.

"Turn up north," said Justin. "I'll show you an inlet through the reef around the end of the island and just past Sequances Cay. We can carry 6 to 8 feet of draft through there at low tide when the wind is not blowing over 12 knots."

"I was headed down to Manjack Channel, but this will save 12 miles of running," said Seth as he rounded the end of the island.

"Just steer her north-northeast through the opening in the reef and hold that heading. It will take us to the *Double Dips* and the backend of the *Great Abaco Canyon* beyond."

White frothy waves broke over the reef on both sides of the 200-foot opening, and Seth took her right through the middle. The water shallowed to 9-feet on the depth sounder, but *TAR BABY* drew only 4-feet, 2 inches. Seth throttled her up to 22-knots, which would put them at the *Double Dips* in less than an hour. Seth's updated Roff's chart showed a two-degree sea temperature difference along the *Double Dips* and *Flat Top,* which was just a few miles east. Justin thought that would be a good place to start trolling. The *Great Abaco Canyon,* which was ten miles further out, had a one-degree temperature change that might be worth fishing later in the day.

After arriving at the *Double Dips*, the boys put out their standard spread of lures and teasers. Senior Moldcraft wide range lures with custom long skirts were on the long riggers, green and black and purple and black. Two mid-size Pakula Cockroach Jets in sizzling squid pink were deployed on the short riggers. The bridge teasers were a mirrored bowling pin, trailing a speckled silver-skirted Black Bart Marlin Candy lure off the right side and a pink squid chain on the left. A Blackflap dredge was deployed left and a TC Moldcraft squid dredge right, both controlled by Lindgren Pitman electric reels, threaded through out-rigger mounted snatch blocks. Justin rigged 50 and 80 wide Tiagra reels for pitching the circle-hooked, horse ballyhoo baits. The hook-up ratio was roughly 50-60% for lures, and close to 85% for a circle hook pitch bait in the hands of a skilled angler.

Seth zig-zagged between the two *"dips"* at trolling speed until he found the temperature break. The color difference was noticeably greener on the warm side and registered 78.4 degrees in the blended blue water adjacent to the colder 76.5 degrees Atlantic Ocean ink blue water. A few minutes later they passed under three Frigate birds as they trolled along the temperature color line when a dark shape came up behind the mirrored bowling pin.

Justin shouted down from the bridge, "Medium-size blue marlin, right teaser!"

John Harvey deftly dropped the 50-wide pitch bait over the transom and free-spooled the horse ballyhoo towards the lit-up marlin. Justin rotated the overhead teaser reel and pulled the trailing Black Bart lure away from the marlin, just as he made a move to eat it. The frustrated fish thrashed from side to side looking for his quarry. John raised the 50-wide's rod tip and made the pitch bait skip on the surface. The marlin instantly inhaled the horse ballyhoo and swam off. John flipped his reel's clicker on, and it started to sing … he aimed the rod tip right at the retreating fish, counted to six and pushed his drag lever up to strike. The circle hook embedded securely in the corner of the marlin's mouth, and the fight was on. Years ago, when all big game fisherman used "J" hooks, John would have waited longer and then set the J-hook by jerking the rod tip up. More times than not, the bait was already in the fish's stomach and the fish was "gut hooked". This practice insured a catch, but after releasing the caught fish, most of them did not survive. The new circle hooks "latch design" allowed the bait to be pulled out of the retreating marlin's stomach and would only penetrate when it latched into the corner of the fish's jaw. If the angler prematurely lifted the rod tip (jerked), the hook would come straight out of the fish's mouth. Simply put, circle hooks allowed caught fish to be released unharmed, and were now required in all billfish tournaments for live and dead baits. J-hooks were still used on lures for obvious reasons (billfish don't normally swallow lures).

Seth likes to explain it this way, "When we first started using circle hooks, everybody had trouble breaking the 'jerk habit'. Bobby Thompson especially had trouble. During a sailfish tournament on a charter boat in Costa Rica, Bobby missed fish after fish, jerking the rod each time. Totally frustrated, he asked the Costa Rican Captain, 'What should I do?' The Captain just smiled and replied, 'Senor … don't do nothing.' Everybody laughed, Bobby finally got it, and he started hooking sailfish again."

Justin guided Seth over and around the *Double Dips* several times, then trolled over to *Flat Top's* western edge and finished the day finding the one-degree temperature change in the western end of the *Great Canyon* where the depth changes from 6,600 to 12,000 feet. They caught fish in every location. Their final count: six blue marlin hooked, and four released (two jumped off) … two white marlin hooked, and one released (one pulled the hook) … and two large dorados that were on ice in the fish box.

On the back way in, Justin said, "Next time out, I'll show you how I fish the open end of the *Great Canyon* and maybe take you a little further north to fish in the cleavage of the *Big-Uns*."

"That was a good day of fishing, Justin," said Seth on the ride in. "Three days like that should win the release tournament. How about fishing with us three days from now? We've got to pick up Scotty and some supplies in Marsh Harbour tomorrow and the following day we're going sailing."

Justin consulted his pocket calendar and said, "I can do that Sunday … Who are you sailing with Saturday?"

"We're going to help *RAGE* practice. Juvenal Menard talked us into it."

"That's a hotbed of competition, *mon!*" said Justin.

"That's what we hear. We're looking forward to sailing their trial-horse *TANQUERAY.*"

The afternoon sea breeze was only blowing 8-knots, so Seth set the autopilot for the inlet that Justin showed him that morning. He'd named it *Spanish Cay-fair weather inlet* when he saved its GPS position this morning. When they were safely through the inlet, Seth asked Gene to dock the boat, then went below. He'd noticed about 15 crew members milling around on *Britannia's* docks and yachts in regular crew uniforms of white T-shirts, with a small blue *Britannia* logo, and khaki shorts. But one man was dressed in white slacks, a light blue Tommy Bahama shirt and Costa sunglasses. He stood alone on the foredeck of *ECLIPSE*. Seth stopped inside the salon and got his iPhone camera ready and snapped several photos through the port salon side window as they passed by. The whole *Britannia* crew had short cropped black hair and swarthy complexions. The man in the white slacks adjusted his Costa sunglasses and looked right at *TAR BABY* as they idled past. He reminded Seth of a young Omar Sharif. Maybe the rest of the crew, as Sunny had mentioned, had flown in from Venezuela while they were out fishing. Once docked, Freddy, John and Gene hosed the boat down, while Justin and Seth cleaned the two dorados that each weighed over 40 pounds.

"Stay for a cold one and take a couple of filets back to Marsh Harbour with you," said Seth, as Justin got ready to motor his skiff back home.

"Thanks for the dorado, but it will take me almost an hour to get home in my Paramount 21, even though I put a 200 hp. Merc. on it last year. I'll see you Sunday, my friend."

Everybody said good-bye to Justin then headed for "Wrecker's Bar", across the island past Barefoot Beach, for a couple cold Kaliks. Wrecker's was open-air and built on raised pilings out over the Atlantic Ocean. There was a nice breeze and it was a great place to watch the sun go down behind Spanish Cay. As the tournament crowd grew larger, Wreckers opened every night. The boys planned to get their showers onboard and grill the dorado for dinner when they got back to *TAR BABY*. The whole crew re-hashed their fishing day and tried to figure how they lost two of their blue marlin hookups.

John said," Really … both of them were lure bites and the average lure hookup percentage is 50%. We can make sure the hooks are sharp, and we also have the hooks all the way back at the legal limit in the lengthened skirts. Pulling lures allows us to troll faster and find more fish. But we still need a little luck to win a tournament."

As they rode back after the sunset in their golf cart, Seth noticed that all three condo buildings were lit up and three barbecue grills were smoking next to the middle condo. Seth would send his new photos and observations to Bobby when he was back on the Hatteras.

The next morning was partly cloudy and the sea of Abaco had about a foot and a half chop due to a 10-knot breeze. The "Geezers" rolled out of their bunks early and had coffee and donuts on the flybridge.

"Let's get to Marsh Harbour early," said Gene. "I've made a list of groceries and staples we'll need."

"Good thing you rented an Albury 23. She'll still go 20-knots in this chop," said Freddy.

"OK, we'll go into Marsh Harbour and dock at the public dock, then walk to Maxwell's Supermarket and load up on groceries, Kalik and whatever else we need. Then we'll motor around to Boat Harbour Marina. I told Scotty to take a cab there from the airport. He should be there in time for lunch. Let's get going," said Seth.

Scotty arrived at Boat Harbour and was filled in on their fishing the previous day and the upcoming day of sailing tomorrow.

"Sounds like we're off to a good start fishing, and the sailing sounds like fun."

The northeast sea breeze built the moderate chop off the starboard stern quarter and made the ride back to Spanish Cay comfortable. There wasn't much conversation on the way back, except when they passed Guana Cay, when they all agreed to take one Sunday off and spend that day at Nipper's Beach Bar.

The crew opted for dinner out in Scotty's honor and went to the Spanish Cay Hotel Pointe House bar for drinks before dinner. Molly Mallory was at the bar with Carter Combs and they all had a drink together.

"We heard about your treasure find over on Abaco, Mr. Stone," said Carter. "Congratulations!"

"Thank you, but please call me Seth. This trip we're just here for the Shootout, and a little sailing."

"If you need anything, Seth, don't hesitate to contact Molly or me," said Carter.

Scotty couldn't take his eyes off of Molly, and you could almost smell the chemistry. Molly and Carter left, and the crew had dinner and turned in early. They were due at the Hope Town ferry dock at 9:00 to meet Chris, Juvenal and *TANQUERAY*.

***

TANQUERAY sat waiting at the government dock as Seth and crew idled their Albury skiff towards her in anticipation. Chris Thomason, Juvenal and another large man walked down the dock to greet them.

"Gentlemen," said Juvenal in his booming voice. "Some of you already know Chris Thomason, and this is my cousin Dax."

Then Juvenal started to describe *TANQUERAY* to Seth's crew, "Her wooden hull is painted seafoam green, with a thin black boot stripe and a white bottom. The varnished, unstayed mast, is solid wood. The sloop's long boom overhangs her raked transom by ten feet. The proud bow is ten feet from her mast. The hull's overall length is 28-feet and she carries only a two-foot deep keel. Ballast is sparse in the shallow bilge, and an equal amount is attached to the outside of the small keel. Her beam is ten feet. The racing version allows unlimited pry-boards (2 x 6 inch boards x 10 feet in length) to support human ballast. They are deployed under these iron brackets bolted to the gunnels amidships and are slipped under the leeward cockpit coaming. They look like wings, don't they?" as he slid a pry-board in on each side. "Our large, athletic crewmembers slide out on these 'prys' to provide ballast, actually leverage, to fly larger sails to make the boat sail faster. And yes, tacking or gybing can become a practiced fire drill or a total cluster-fuck. *TANQUERAY* has three prys and a 'Class A' boat is normally manned by a crew of ten but may add more in heavy air. Cotton sails are legal, no Dacron allowed, and she sports only a small jib on her 10-foot "J" and a huge mainsail on that oversized boom. We bought *TANQUERAY* from Sandy Everett in Nassau a few years ago. She was a champion back in the late 70's. Sandy had her built by Walter Archer on Shirley Street in Nassau when Walter was 78 years old. Mr. Everett commissioned Charley Morgan Naval Architects in the 'States' to oversee the design. She was extremely fast in her day. Any questions?"

"Are the racing rules the same as most international classes?" asked John Harvey.

"Yes, except we start our races with all the entries anchored on the starting line. When the gun goes off, we pull anchor and sail to a mark that is always to windward. The rest of the rules are similar except we give more room at the marks … three-boat lengths. Any more questions?" asked Juvenal.

"Are all the Class A boats the same?" asked Freddy.

"They are all built to the same rule," said Juvenal, smiling. "Any other questions?"

Silence.

"OK, let's go sailing," said Juvenal, as he and Dax started to pull the main sail up the mast as two more local crew arrived and jumped aboard.

Freddy got on the foredeck and pulled up the jib and Chris steered the sloop out of the harbor, leaving the red and white striped Hope Town Lighthouse in her wake. Seth trimmed the gigantic main that was double reefed to start, while Chris worked John onto the helm. Freddy trimmed the jib. Dax and Juvenal started to school Scotty on the handling of the pry-boards. The wind was at ten knots in the Sea of Abaco with a light chop. Scotty and Dax deployed two prys. Juvenal and Gene slid out on one and Dax and Scotty slid out on the other. Seth shook one reef out of the main and trimmed it in tighter as Freddy followed suit. *TANQUERAY* came alive and the crew on the prys slid out further. Next, Chris took them through a mark rounding: first pulling in the prys, tacking, then gybing while deploying one pry to balance them downwind. Since there were no winches, extra muscle was necessary to trim sails. Late-comers, Davis and Andre, moved wherever they were needed. There were no wind or speed instruments allowed, just 'tell-tail' ribbons on the sails. Chris coached the Geezers through a few anchored start drills, and then they practiced tacking and gybing until they were exhausted. The Geezer crew had years of racing experience which shortened their learning curve, and John was in a class by himself at the helm of any sailboat. Later that afternoon, he sailed the boat into the harbor towards the government dock. Seth and Andre dropped the main on cue, and

TANQUERAY ghosted through the crowded anchorage to a luff-up stop alongside the pier as Freddy doused the jib. It had been a particularly good day of sailing.

On the way back to Spanish Cay in the Albury 23, Seth said to John, "When the sea breeze kicked in, I eased the mainsail's leech line, but the leech stayed cupped at the top."

"I noticed that. You had to ease the mainsheet to keep the boat flat."

"Her cotton sails are old and stretched out, but the rest of the boat seems solid and well-designed. Why don't we take a little tuck in the top 10-feet of the leech, so it spills the air up there when we ease the leech line."

"Right, then we won't have to ease the mainsheet and lose power in the bottom of the sail," said John.

"I have a leather palm, big needles and some white sail thread on the Hatteras ... I use them to repair my flybridge canvas. We can sew in that tuck in about five minutes at the dock," said Seth.

"It could make a difference when the afternoon sea breeze kicks in," said John.

CHAPTER SEVENTEEN

HAKIM left his condo office early in the afternoon to meet Carter Combs at the hotel to choose which hotel room he wanted to lease for the long-term. Jabbar had most of the crew busy cleaning and servicing the four RC-52s, and one crew of three men were launching, testing and cleaning each inflatable dinghy. He parked his golf cart alongside the hotel and walked through the small lobby towards Carter's office.

As he started down the corridor, Molly Mallory called out to him, "Mr. Muneer, please step into my office."

She met him at the door and said, "Carter was called away to Marsh Harbour to meet with a cruising club that wants to move down here for a week. So, he asked me to handle your room selection. Let me get my master key and we'll go upstairs."

Hakim couldn't think of anything witty to say, and even if he had, he knew he'd just start stuttering again. He just turned and walked into the elevator. Hakim followed her off the elevator on the second floor. As she walked down the hall, he started to get stiff just watching her splendid backside move from side to side. She bent over slightly at Room 203, waved the electronic key near the doorknob and a tiny green light turned on. Molly opened the door, turned on the lights and they both walked in. The door closed itself behind them.

"This room has two queen-sized beds, a full bath, a desk and a large closet. It also has a 42-inch Sony television with free satellite TV."

Hakim didn't know where to look first, but he really didn't want to look away from Molly.

"There's a view of the marina from the window, Mr. Muneer."

"Please call me, Harry," said Hakim.

"Come over to this bed, Harry, and try it," said Molly smiling.

Hakim trotted over to the bed like a puppy dog, sat down on it and bounced.

"What do you think of the room, Harry?"

"I think it will be fine."

"What do you think of me, Harry?"

"I - I don't know how to put it into words, Molly."

"Well, then we won't," said Molly pulling him towards her and kissing him. "I have wondered what it might be like making love to you from the moment we first met."

For the next half hour, Molly made love to Harry and he followed her lead. It was a different experience for a man from a Middle Eastern Muslim background. In his world, women were seldom seen and never heard. But Hakim was actually totally intimidated by her beauty and succumbed to her every whim. He hadn't figured out that Molly was a western woman who had sex on her own terms and wanted to be fulfilled during each encounter like a man expected to be. Hakim climaxed within ten minutes and normally that would have ended their first encounter. But Molly demanded alternative techniques until she too was fully satisfied. Then she quickly gathered up her garments and retired to the bathroom. Hakim concentrated on the movement of her superb derrière as she gracefully exited … and it actually brought a tear to his eye. He quickly snapped a photo of her departure with his iPhone that he'd set on the nightstand. Hakim was both elated and disturbed by the whole experience. When Molly returned her demeanor had changed.

She was all business when she said, "Will Room 203 be satisfactory, Harry?"

"Wha-well, yes - of course, whe-when can I see you again."

"I'll let you know, Harry … after all, now I know your room number," she said smiling. "Follow me down to the front desk and I'll get you the key."

As Harry rode back to the condos in his golf cart he thought, *I feel a little bit like I've just been used. But what a spectacular piece of ass!*

As he walked into the condo towards his office, Jabbar called out to him, "Jamaal just called on the satellite phone. He'll be here sometime tomorrow with *TRINIDAD GIRL*."

"That's good news," said Hakim. He put Molly out of his mind and sent an encrypted message to Marwan in Africa: *M-5, Send all the lead sheets and the five Louis Vuitton suitcases via the Gulfstream. Ship the suitcases and cell phone triggers in identical wood crates marked 'lead ballast' with cover pieces of lead on all sides. The lead linings will shield the nuclear material in those crates from radioactive material detectors at N'djamena airport in Chad and from any unlikely visual check in Spanish Cay. Have our shipping contact furnish proper paperwork and have him prepay any export and import taxes on the lead sheets to Chad and the Bahamas. Also, schedule that jet to fly to Tampa, Florida and back to Spanish Cay to pick up and deliver our Winslow life rafts. We will also need the G-500 for up to five days to check out our U.S. charter destinations. Allah be with you. H-15.*

After the new "life rafts" were installed and Hakim and Jamaal had visited all of the marinas and destination cities they'd advertised, the *Britannia* charters would begin from Nassau.

Jamaal motored *TRINIDAD GIRL* up to Spanish Cay's fuel dock the next day in the early afternoon. A small contingent of the shoreside crew arrived to meet them. Hakim had lectured the whole crew at dinner the evening before, to not act boisterous or celebratory when *TRINIDAD GIRL* arrived; "After weeks of training we have become professional mariners. We are proud of our accomplishments, but we must act professional in every situation so we will not raise any suspicion that we are involved in *Jihad*. We must behave as seasoned professionals running a 'For-Profit' charter business. Traveling hundreds of miles across an ocean is a great achievement, but for a marine professional it is just another day's work."

The welcoming crew just shook hands with the incoming crew as they filed off the boat with their duffels. They were whisked away to their quarters by waiting golf carts, while a fresh crew fueled, docked, unloaded and cleaned the boat inside and out.

After dinner that evening, Jamaal and Hakim met in Hakim's office for a voyage debriefing and an operation update.

"How was the crew?" asked Hakim.

"They all did their jobs, and none were seasick. The vessel performed flawlessly."

"We are all moved in here. The kitchen crews rotate and everyone on the crew has been cleaning and servicing the charter boats. During their leisure time, our fishermen have been supplying the kitchen with fish caught at several spots around the island."

"When are the nukes coming in?"

"Marwan is sending the suitcases on a jet tomorrow and is using the lead sheets to shield them in wooden crates marked "Boat Ballast Lead". Once unloaded, the jet will fly to Tampa and pick up the Winslow life raft order."

"We'll need the airport's forklift to unload the crates, and the life rafts," said Jamaal.

"I've already arranged for that. Jabbar was checked out on the forklift by the airport manager and I signed a waiver. Jabbar was our best heavy equipment operator on the mountain. Just like in Africa, it's amazing what a little 'dash' (bribe) can get you."

"Yes, that seems to work everywhere. I think we ought to supervise the lead lining of the first life raft cannister and its installation on the first boat."

"I had the same thought. We'll have to trim the lead sheets to fit inside the cannisters," agreed Hakim. "Then the G-500 can fly us to all the charter destinations while Jabbar supervises the 'life raft' installations on the other four RC-52s."

"Then the charter trips start for real," smiled Jamaal.

"Yes, you will supervise the boats and crews, and Jabbar will make and follow each boat's schedule, along with changing bookings when weather or mechanical difficulties called for options. That's a lot of work … we need to give Jabbar an assistant. Do you have any suggestions?"

"On this last voyage I was impressed with one of the Englishmen, Habeeb. He did very well with the detail and memory work, like plotting positions, chronicling the engine gauges and so on. He appears to have good communication and computer skills and he has a pleasant personality."

"Then Habeeb it is! There's plenty of room for another desk in the reception office."

"Each step gets us closer to detonation, Hakim," said Jamaal smiling.

***

Dirk Mendelsohn finished stitching back on his fourth patient's nipples and was finished with breast augmentation surgery for the day. It had been a busy and profitable week so far. But tomorrow, he would be back at work at the outpatient clinic performing one breast augmentation in the morning, and two pro bono cleft palate operations for his Bahamian children's charitable foundation in the afternoon. He was looking forward to giving a "sailing lesson" to Dr. John Harvey, Seth Stone and their entourage in their sparring match between *RAGE* and *TANQUERAY,* arranged by Chris Thomason and Juvenal Menard. He'd acted as though he thought the competition was a great idea. It would serve to deflect any suspicion that he'd perpetrated the attempted treasure heist at Jake Snood's Blue Hole. He looked forward to being a gracious winner this coming Saturday. John and Seth were both talented sailors, and Fred Buckley had an America's Cup crew pedigree from Charley Morgan's 12-meter *HERITAGE* campaign in the early 70's. Dirk had won and lost sailing against both Seth and John over the years. However, he felt his talent and experience sailing the unconventional Bahamian sloops, with their pry-boards, small keel, unorthodox sail plan and absence of winches gave him, and his seasoned crew, an insurmountable advantage. Just trimming the sails in brisk winds required two or three crewman working in perfect concert. He couldn't wait for this coming Saturday.

As Dirk drove home in his Porsche Cayenne, he thought of the evening ahead of him. Phillippe had transported one of their most promising pole dancers from Papayas, a Dominican named Pilar Pudenda, to Nassau for a breast augmentation. Pilar didn't have enough cash, so she would be Dirk's first Bahamian "scholarship" girl. She paid 50% cash up-front and the rest was to be paid in four cashless sex installments. Tonight, after Dirk had a catered dinner with her in his apartment, they would have their first encounter, which he now preferred to call a "consultation". She would be Dirk's only operation the next morning and would leave Nassau two days later for Freeport. He and Phillippe thought this girl would be in a class by herself once she sported a pair of "Mendelsohn Slopers". Dirk would collect Pilar's balance "in kind" on subsequent Freeport visits to check the Papaya's books. Pilar would attract more tips, lap dances and VIP room money. Papayas would attract more customer cover charges, sell more drinks and collect more VIP room rent paid by the dancer. Everybody would win.

***

The Gulfstream landed late the next day. Hakim and Jamaal watched the G-500 land, turn around and taxi to the main hangar. The customs agent arrived from her office in the hangar and glanced inside the Gulfstream at the wooden crates marked "Boat Ballast Lead". She checked the plane's manifest against her computer sheet and said to Hakim, "I wish everybody would prepay their duty. It makes my life simpler."

Hakim followed her to her office on the second floor and she stamped and returned his paperwork.

Jabbar was already unloading the wooden crates with the forklift when Hakim returned to the tarmac. Jamaal stayed in the aircraft with the pilots, and Hakim walked behind the forklift as it moved the crates into their private storage hangar. After the crates were stacked and locked up and the plane was parked and chocked, he and Jamaal took the pilots to the marina hotel for the night. In the morning, the G-500 would fly them to Tampa to pick up the Winslow shipment. While they were in Tampa, Hakim and Jamaal would check out downtown Tampa's Convention Center Marina, Marjorie Park and Westshore Marinas. Hakim had applied for the United States ESTA cards (Electronic System for Travel Authorization) online earlier using their British passports. Select countries are allowed to use this visa waiver system. He used a *Britannia* American Express card to pay the $14 fee that allowed each of them to enter the United States for 90 days at a time for business or pleasure. The electronic visa card was valid for two years and multiple trips were approved electronically almost instantly. Each of *Britannia's* crew had an ESTA card, and their British charter customers were required to have one as well.

The G-500 flew west across Grand Bahama Island at 2,000 feet the next morning. Jamaal could see the city of Freeport sprawling beneath them and minutes later West End Harbor's compact marina came into view. They started across the Atlantic Gulf Stream towards West Palm Beach to avoid some lingering thunderstorm clouds to the north. Their flight continued over expansive Lake Okeechobee to Naples, then turned northward towards Tampa. The flight's distance was 359 miles and it only took about an hour, but it gave Hakim and Jamaal their first look at Florida's West Coast.

Their jet landed and taxied to Sheltair's Jetport FBO, where Winslow had delivered *Britannia's* life rafts. The pilots supervised the cargo loading as Hakim and Jamaal ordered an XL Uber to take them into Tampa. They arranged with the driver on the way to Marjorie Park Marina for contiguous trips to the Convention Center Marina and West Shore Marina. Earlier research put the 10 best restaurants in Tampa within walking distance of the Convention Center and a 10 to 15-minute cab ride from Marjorie Park and West Shore. The quaint Ybor City Cuban/Italian section, now called "Cigar City", had added funky nightclubs to its restaurant and bar venue, which was only 15 minutes away from all three locations. Marjorie Park Marina was a peaceful protected site, 8 miles from MacDill Air Force Base which housed one of the nine United States Armed Forces Central Command headquarters. The brand new Convention Center Marina was in the middle of downtown, 10 miles from MacDill. West Shore Marina turned out to be only 3 miles from the center of MacDill, with just a few buildings in between. The damage from the nuclear blast would be minimal to the city of Tampa from that location, but it would obliterate MacDill's facilities and fighter planes, and take out the two major bridges over Tampa Bay to Saint Petersburg.

Later that day, on their way to Sarasota to look at Marina Jack's facility, Hakim said, "West Shore Marina is the best choice for our *Jihad* and has nice amenities shoreside. I'll have Jabbar make the necessary financial arrangements with their dockmaster when we get back."

Marina Jack's was a short cab ride down Route 41 from the Sarasota Airport. The marina was first-class, had a restaurant on site, and was only a block from Sarasota's sophisticated and vibrant downtown.

Jamaal said, "In a way, this little city reminds me of a miniature western version of Abu Dhabi, but the decadence is somewhat understated … Tampa was flashier."

"They're both decadent," said Hakim.

"I've heard that Key West is the worst, with 'gays' openly consorting and strip clubs full of perverts and degenerates."

"I guess we'll see for ourselves," said Hakim.

Hakim, Jamaal and their *Jihadist* followers had their feet in the 21st century, but their heads and hearts were mired in the 7th century.

Because there were no lights on the runway at Spanish Cay, they hurried back to Sarasota's airport to fly back there before nightfall. On the flight back, they watched a video tour of South Seas Plantation on Hakim's laptop. It appeared to be an upscale resort with a large transient marina, a par-3 golf course, a restaurant and bar and easy access to Captiva and Sanibel Island by bicycle or golf cart. Jamaal had the Waterway App on his iPhone and checked out Boca Grande, Marco Island and Everglades City. Boca Grande had quaint Miller's Marina, a charming old-Florida downtown and a historic hotel. Everglades City featured an upscale fishing lodge off the beaten path, where their charterers could book a guide and fish for snook and tarpon. Isolated Marco Island possessed good marinas and unspoiled beaches along with quirky bars and restaurants. Funky Goodland was right at Marco's backdoor, featuring Stan's Idle Hour Bar, the home of the "Buzzard Lope", which was a strange dance invented by intoxicated Rednecks. These locations had ample dockage and well-marked channels. They would be interchangeable depending on the weather and wind.

"Tomorrow, we'll work through the first life raft modification and install our first nuke and trigger mechanism in the lead-lined cannister," said Hakim.

"I noticed in Winslow's manual that they have a small external solar panel to maintain the life raft's EPIRB and SOLAS lights. Can we hook that up to our cell phone trigger?" asked Jamaal.

"I was counting on that. It was one of the reasons I chose Winslow."

"When do you want to install the cannisters on the RC-52s?"

"I think it will take two or three days for Jabbar's crew to assemble them. We might as well fly to Key West and then check out all the destinations on the east coast. When we get back, we'll double check the trigger wiring and make sure they'll arm with their cell phone numbers. Then I'll supervise the life raft installation on each boat. In the meantime, Jabbar's crew can pack the new rafts in the valises we bought and store them in the captain's quarters under his bunk. You can start Jabbar and Habeeb making reservations for our first round of cruises and make sure each boat has a detailed float plan and a complete set of Waterway charts on board. You can also run the Albury 33s, with some crew, to Marsh Harbour to buy provisions and essentials to stock each charter boat."

Key West turned out to be even more distasteful, reprehensible, detestable and revolting to the *Jihadists* than they could have ever imagined.

"This place is worse than Bangkok or Amsterdam," said the widely traveled Jamaal, disgustedly.

"When our religion takes its rightful place in this world and Sharia law rules, there will be no whiskey, beer and wine. The women will only expose their hands and eyes and will only speak when they are spoken to. LBGTQ's will be executed, thieves will have their hands cut off and murderers and non-believers will lose their heads. Morality and life itself will get better."

"We know that Allah is the only God," agreed Jamaal.

"Amin (Amen)," said Hakim

They'd hired a cab to take them on a private tour, and when they passed Higgs Beach near Casa Marina, it was all thong bikinis and half the women were topless. The driver drove them up and down Duval Street that morning, which was packed by people already drinking at the bars, with the strip club "Barkers" strutting out in front of the countless strip clubs touting the pulchritude performing inside on their stages. Further up Duval Street, the 'gay' men dressed in drag extolled their Drag Queen matinee shows. Loud music of all genres blasted from the bars' interiors. Traffic moved at a crawl past the Hog's Breath Bar and Ricks, which advertised a clothing optional bar on its third-floor rooftop. The Red Garter, Diamonds and Spurs, Teasers, VIP'S and Southernmost at the west end of Duval all had barker's out front lauding their naked female dancers. The 'gays' had their Bourbon Street Pub and K-West male strip clubs at the east end of Duval. Mercifully, the driver turned off at Truman Avenue, narrowly missing a large rooster and three hens strutting across the road. He took them the back way to the marinas through the quaint old Key West cottages neighborhood, driving past the above ground cemetery and down the hill to Key West Bight. They toured the marinas on foot. Hakim and Jamaal checked out the Conch Harbor Marina where the Fort Myers high-speed ferry docked, the Key West Municipal Marina, A & B Lobster House Marina and the Galleon Marina. Jamaal interviewed each facility's dockmaster and secured commercial rates. They took a quick look at Mallory Square, which was deserted during the day, but full of unusual performers every night at sunset. Their tour guide filled them in on "The Cat Man", who could actually herd cats, the high wire acrobats, mimes, living statues, musicians, clowns and freaks. Key West is where the weird turn pro! As they rode back to the airport, they passed the "Conch Train" tour for the third time on the little four-square mile island. It is hard to believe that Key West was once the largest town in Florida, growing rich on wrecking revenues in the late 1800's. Their airplane wasted no time leaving Key West behind, even though it might be their customers' favorite destination.

"Which marina did you like the best?" asked Hakim.

"I liked A&B the best, but it doesn't suit our catamaran needs," said Jamaal. "The slips are too small. The Conch Harbor Marina can handle our beam and has more large docks, better availability and their rates are $3.00 per-foot less than the Galleon. They also have a fuel dock."

"I thought the swimming pool was attractive and the pool bar had live music," added Hakim.

The flight to Miami International Airport was just a 45-minute hop. The G-500 spent most of that time in Miami's holding pattern. They finally landed and taxied to Signature's FBO where the jet was fueled. A taxi was waiting and whisked Jamaal and Hakim to the Miami Beach Marina ten miles away. It was an impressive facility that ran shuttles to South Beach which was only minutes from the marina. The marina easily met their standards, and an hour later they were on their way to Palm Beach International Airport. The plan was to rent a car and check out Ft. Lauderdale's Pier 66 (47 miles south), Singer Island's Sailfish Marina at Palm Beach inlet, then Stuart's marinas and Port Salerno's Pirates Cove Marina (40 miles north). They landed in Palm Beach in less than 45 minutes and left the jet at Atlantic's FBO. Jamaal drove Hakim and the pilots in a Hertz rent-a-car to a nearby Hampton Inn in West Palm Beach to spend the night. The next morning, Jamaal and Hakim left at dawn for Pier 66 in the rental, figuring they'd meet the pilots back at the airport no later than 3:00 p.m. to fly to Jacksonville. The pilots were free to sightsee on *Britannia's* Uber account.

Pier 66 turned out to be the place to be in Fort Lauderdale. Their catamaran slips were numerous, and their accommodations were first rate. The other Lauderdale marinas Jamaal considered were up the New River, while Pier 66 was close to the inlet from the Atlantic. Jamaal also searched for John D. MacDonald's fictious Travis McGee's boat, the *BUSTED FLUSH,* in slip F-18 while they were there. The bronze plaque marking that spot had not survived the latest reconstruction project and he found the plaque in the dockmaster's office.

Jamaal told Hakim, "I passed many lonely hours at sea reading MacDonald's novels and never thought I'd see Bahia Mar or Pier 66."

They made their deal with the dockmaster and headed for Singer Island, located on the north side of Palm Beach Inlet. The slips, showers and restaurant on the property were inviting, and their clients had access to nearby Palm Beach. They drove over the bridge, turned north and drove past Jupiter to Stuart. They checked Sunset Bay and the Harborage Marina on the

St. Lucie River, then drove to Port Salerno's Pirates' Cove, which was much closer to the inlet. Pirates Cove's rates were better and there was a hotel and restaurant adjacent to the marina. They arrived back at Palm Beach International at 2:30 and were in the air by 3:00 p.m. on their way to Savannah, Georgia. Hakim and Jamaal wanted to check out Jacksonville and St. Augustine for a full day on the way back from Washington D.C.

Savannah Bend Marina got the nod. It was conveniently located on the ICW (Intercoastal Waterway) close to downtown Savannah, a city with a rich southern history of mystery and charm. The ICW is a 3,000-mile inland waterway along the Atlantic Ocean and Gulf of Mexico coasts that runs continuously from Boston southward, around the tip of Florida, then along the Gulf Coast to Brownsville, Texas. Jamaal wanted to use the ICW during windy weather but preferred to run outside along the coast to make better time when possible.

The whole crew spent the night at the Airport Hilton, after a quick tour of downtown and dinner at the swashbuckling Pirates House Restaurant-ARGGHH!

After a good night's sleep, they took off at first light for Charleston, then to Wilmington, North Carolina, a quick stop at Morehead City and finally to Washington D.C. for the night.

Charleston International Airport was 25 minutes north of the city. The Gulfstream taxied to the Signature FBO, and Jamaal and Hakim took an Uber into town. They checked out the Harborage Ashley Marina on the Ashley River side of Charleston and the Cooper River Marina on the other side. But they chose the Safe Harbor Marina of Charleston City near the Mt. Pleasant Bridge. It had large floating docks to accommodate large boats, was close to downtown and offered a free shuttle service to its patrons. Charleston offered historic horse and carriage tours, art and maritime museums, excellent restaurants, shopping, Fort Sumter tours and nearby Boone Hall Plantation in Mt. Pleasant. The Gulfstream landed at Myrtle Beach about 2:00 p.m. They rented a car and drove to Osprey and Hague's Marina near Myrtle Beach on the Intracoastal Waterway. Jamaal chose Barefoot Marina to avoid the throngs of vacationing tourists and golfers in downtown Myrtle Beach. They flew out to Morehead City's airport, as Jamaal pored over his ICW Cruisers Guide and Waterways® charts book to prequalify that location's marinas.

They flew the Gulfstream jet into Washington D.C.'s Ronald Reagan International Airport and taxied to the Signature FBO. The crew "Ubered" to the Watergate Hotel in Georgetown. Jamaal chartered a helicopter to check out the Chesapeake Bay area the next day. Hakim and Jamaal would meet the Bell Jet 430 six-seat helicopter, supplied by Grandview Aviation, at their FBO at Ronald Reagan Airport. They wanted to fly down the Potomac River, first checking the Wharf Marina area, then flying south to Norfolk and southwest to the ICW across the Dismal Swamp to CoinJock Marina in North Carolina. While there, they'd take a look at the Nags Head-Manteo-Wanchese area marinas for an overnight stop for their charter boat before heading for Norfolk on the ICW.

The next day, the Gulfstream pilots stayed behind and got the airplane fueled while Hakim and Jamaal took off in the waiting Bell Jet Ranger. Jamaal gave the pilot his Waterways chart which marked the spots that they wanted to see. Hakim and Jamaal donned inflight headphones with microphones to communicate with the pilot. They traveled north first, flying low over the Wharf Marina, where Hakim wanted to berth the RC-52 because of its proximity to the Capitol, the White House, the Washington Monument and the Jefferson and Lincoln Memorials. The blast would take out the I-395, Route 66 and Arlington Memorial Bridges. The Pentagon and Ronald Reagan Airport would also receive significant damage in Virginia. The pilot hovered over the large, well-appointed marina and Hakim took photos of the Jefferson Memorial and Washington Monument on the near horizon.

The pilot turned south and flew down the center of the Potomac River, past Alexandria and Mount Vernon. The Bell Jet 430 cruised at 160 mph and the pilot set the helicopter down at the first marina in Norfolk in less than an hour. Waterside Marina didn't make the cut, but Ocean Yacht Marina across the river in Hampton fit the bill. Their floating slips and proximity to High Street's restaurants and the ICW won the day. The helicopter rotated out of the far corner of Ocean Yacht's generous parking lot and followed the Indian River south, past the town of Chesapeake. They followed the North Landing River east and south to Currituck Sound and into Coinjock Bay. There they found the manmade six-mile ICW canal through the little town of Coinjock leading to the North River and finally Albemarle Sound.

Jamaal told the pilot, Mickey, "Set her down behind the marina restaurant. This place is known for its good food."

"Is that the side of the canal where all the boats are tied up? There must be fifty of them."

"I'm told Coinjock Marina's restaurant is a popular place. Land in that big field behind the building and join us for lunch," said Jamaal.

Coinjock Marina's restaurant lived up to its reputation. Hakim, Jamaal and Mickey had charcoal grilled steak sandwiches with sweet potato fries, and they all agreed they'd never had a better steak.

The Bell Jet left an hour later for Roanoke Island. Mickey flew low past Kitty Hawk and its sand dunes, where the Wright Brothers launched man's first successful powered flight. The helicopter landed at Dare County Regional Airport on Roanoke after circling the island at 500 feet. The FBO agent lent Mickey a car and he chauffeured Hakim and Jamaal to Pirates Cove Marina in Wanchese on the south end and then to Shallowbag Bay Marina and Manteo Waterfront Marina on the northern half. Waterfront had the larger and newer docks and was within walking distance of downtown Manteo. Jamaal made docking arrangements there with the dockmaster.

They flew straight back to Annapolis, Maryland, and since it was a Sunday, landed on Annapolis Middle School's baseball field. Mickey called an Uber for them and stayed with the helicopter. Spa Creek Marina was in the middle of the historic downtown waterfront, near the United States Naval Academy, countless marinas, bars and restaurants. Annapolis had a vibe of its own, and they decided it should definitely be included in the trip. Jamaal made Spa Creek their outpost there. When the travel-weary duo arrived back at the helicopter, Mickey whisked them to the Ronald Reagan FBO in 20 minutes. As he landed and bid farewell, Hakim wished him luck and gave him a $200 tip.

"Mickey is the nicest non-believer I've ever met," said Hakim, as the helicopter left.

"I enjoyed being with him, too. He likes his job … he's a happy guy!"

"I'd give him **two** chances to embrace Islam," said Hakim, smiling.

Once aboard the Gulfstream, the pilots lost no time taking off for a night flight to Jacksonville. They were booked to stay at the Hyatt Regency Riverfront in the middle of downtown, 20 minutes south of the Jacksonville International Airport.

As they flew through the night, Hakim expressed his thought about what he'd seen the last couple of days.

"Both of the Florida coasts are wall to wall people, but when we're in the air the vast interior looks almost uninhabited."

"I agree … I liked the marshes and lowlands as we went up the coasts of Georgia and the Carolinas. It has a lush and peaceful feeling."

"It was interesting to see the oldest part of America, which is only 250 years old, in Virginia and Maryland. Their country is so big that you're back in the marshes and rolling hills 15 miles outside of Washington D.C. There are many pretty little villages like St. Michaels and Oxford up the countless rivers and creeks on both sides of the bay. I'm not used to all the green trees and foliage."

"You should see California with her mountains and the Texas prairies, that look more like our part of the world, but are not as hot. Most of their land is habitable because of the fertile soil, fresh water lakes and rivers, and the temperate climate," said the widely traveled Jamaal.

"There's only 300 million people here and room for many more. The United States is as big as our Middle East, although well-over half our land is not habitable, and we already have over 400 million people in the Middle East."

"I noticed the ethnic mix of people in all the cities and towns … their way of life seems to promote diversity and prosperity," said Jamaal.

"They will be better off when the world has only one religion," stated Hakim emphatically, ending that exchange.

Leaving Jacksonville at daylight, Hakim and Jamaal drove south 60 miles on State Route 17 through Florida cattle country to Acosta Creek Marina, south of Satsuma, on Route 309. Lake George would be the farthest point south that the Jacksonville/St. Johns River cruise would go. The marina was surprisingly updated with large docks and a charming southern plantation surrounding it.

Jamaal drove back towards Jacksonville along the palmetto palm and moss-draped live oak tree-lined highway and stopped just south of Jacksonville at the IGY Marina at Ortega Landing on the St. Johns River. IGY's marina facility was first class, featuring Bellingham docks for yachts to 200 feet and quick access to downtown Jacksonville. He made more arrangements there. Their final stop was east to Mayport, at the mouth of the St. Johns River where it entered the Atlantic. They checked out the highly rated Morningside Marina in Mayport, which was less than a half-a-mile from the Jacksonville Naval Station's harbor and wharfs. There were always large warships moored there. But with some luck, a visiting destroyer or a nuclear-powered aircraft carrier might be docked there on detonation day. The damage to the Naval Station and moored warships would be devastating. The little beach town of Morningside and the Naval Station were 16 miles from Jacksonville, so there would be no physical damage to the city from the initial explosion. But if the suitcase nuke were detonated in the early afternoon the easterly sea breeze would spread the deadly radioactive fallout over the whole city. Jamaal made the preliminary arrangements with the marina's efficient dockmaster.

As Hakim and Jamaal napped in their seats, the G-500 crossed over the choppy, deep blue, Atlantic Gulf Stream, with two hours of daylight left. In the coming days, there would be no time for naps for these two as the *Britannia* charters started their path towards detonation day.

CHAPTER EIGHTEEN

SCOTTY REMINGTON looked forward to his first day of marlin fishing since he was wounded at the Snood's Blue Hole skirmish almost a month ago. Seth had his local captain friend, Justin, aboard as *TAR BABY* headed northeast out of the unmarked Sequences Cay Inlet just north of Spanish Cay. His shoulder felt strong again and Scotty hoped to test it today. They were starting a 30-mile run that would take them a little over an hour at the 46-foot Hatteras's 26 knot cruising speed. Justin wanted to troll the south drop-off of the canyon where the 15,000-foot bottom graduated up to 4200 feet in less than 3 miles. The easterly flowing current and prevailing northeast wind would hold the bait in that constant upwelling. Seth's daily Roff's chart showed a 75.3º to 77º temperature change in that area along with a color change from blue to deep Bahamas blue, validating Justin's local knowledge.

When Seth reached their destination, he slowed to 8-knots and Gene swung out the outriggers. The cockpit crew deployed two mirrored teasers off the transom, then let out four marlin lures through the four outrigger clips. Seth used 50 pound rated, extra- wide Tiagra reels clamped to 7-foot Crowder bent butt rods fitted with roller tips and reel strippers. The crew added a mud-flap dredge on the right side and an extra pink Moldcraft pink squid chain in lieu of a dredge on the left. Both bridge teasers were also squid chains.

"Why so many squid chains, Justin?" asked Seth.

"We've been seeing a lot of sperm whale pods out here in this deep water the last two weeks. Sperm whales will eat 2,000 pounds of squid a day, so you can imagine how much giant squid is around. Marlin like it too, and we've been finding squid in the big dorado's stomachs when we clean them."

After an hour of zig-zag trolling, Seth spotted some birds on his radar about three miles away.

"Pull the lines and teasers in, I've got some birds working ahead of us about three miles," shouted Seth to the crew below.

"Do you want me to pull the outriggers up?" asked Gene, when the crew had the spread reeled in.

"No, I can run with them out at 18-knots in this sea-state," said Seth.

Ten minutes later the crew could see the shearwaters, boobies and terns diving and wheeling around above the bait school. Higher up, a few frigates circled looking for significant scraps.

Seth slowed down to trolling speed and the crew put the spread back out. As he trolled along the edge of the bait school, two dorados attacked both Pakulas on the short riggers. Scotty and Fred set the hooks and reeled them in. John gaffed each one in turn and put them on ice in the fish box. Seth trolled further out from the bait-school and on his second pass a marlin bit the Moldcraft purple and black on the right long rigger. Scotty set the hook and climbed into *TAR BABY'S* Pompanette fighting chair. "Looks about 250-300lbs, Seth," said Justin.

Scotty flipped off the screaming clicker and let the greyhounding marlin run against 12 pounds of drag. John and Freddy cleared the remaining rods and cockpit teasers. When the marlin's initial run was over, Seth circled the boat 180-degrees and ran after the fish. When Scotty had reeled about 350 feet of the line back on the 50-wide Tiagra reel, Seth turned *TAR BABY* back down sea and waited until the fish came tight. Then he began to back on the fish aggressively. Scotty reeled with all his strength to keep the marlin on the surface for a quick release. John put on his leather gloves and grabbed the leader as Scotty wound the double line onto the reel. Seth idled the boat forward slowly on one engine, as John grabbed the 400 lb. mono-leader. Gene loaded a tagging stick and stuck a tag in the lit-up marlin's shoulder. Then he helped John dehook the marlin and sent him on his way.

"Your crew is awesome, Seth," said Justin. "And, excellent boat handling on your part."

"Thanks. It's nice when everything works," said Seth, over the congratulatory hoots and hollers coming from the cockpit. "How's the shoulder, Scotty?" yelled Seth down to the cockpit as Scotty danced around the fighting chair like he was on "Soul Train".

"Never been better, Captain, never been better," giving Seth a thumbs up.

Justin's kind words must have snake bit the boat because the following two hook-ups were disastrous. The next hook up started with a larger marlin coming up behind the pink squid chain bridge teaser. John grabbed the 50-pound pitch rod and freelined the circle-hook armed horse ballyhoo back to the lit-up marlin, as Justin quickly reeled the teaser up and away. The marlin inhaled the horse ballyhoo and sped away. John freelined the reel's spool for a full five seconds and slowly pushed the drag lever to strike. Nobody was home! He lifted the rod tip high, making the bait skip on the surface, just in case the fish had just missed it … but nothing happened.

"The fish is gone!" shouted Justin from his vantage point on the flybridge.

John reeled the ballyhoo to the transom and pulled it out of the water. All that was left was the ballyhoo's head. It was the dreaded **sancocho**. He hung his head in embarrassment.

"Hey, John, shake it off. Sometimes you do everything right and they still don't hook-up. You'll get the next one," said Seth. "Let's get the spread back out, boys."

They trolled another hour and finally got a hookup on the left long green and black Moldcraft wide-range. Freddy got into the chair, while John and Scotty cleared the cockpit. After the marlin's initial run, the fish swam down deep. He tried to reel him up and it turned into a stalemate. When Freddy reeled in a few feet of line, the big fish would take it right back. He kept at it and seemed to be gaining when the line suddenly went slack.

"Pulled the hook?" asked Gene.

"I don't know," said Freddy as he reeled the slack line in. When the line was finally all reeled in, all that was left was the 400-pound monofilament leader.

"Looks like the crimp fitting failed," said Gene.

"That's enough for one day, boys. We know there's fish here. We'll have Justin fish with us a couple more times before the tournament. When we get back to the dock, we're going to check every crimp and swivel on our lures and all the double-line Bimini knots. Tomorrow we sail as a trial horse against *RAGE* and Dirk Mendelsohn. We'll run up to Hope Town in the Albury 23 right at first light. So, let's have an early dinner on board the boat tonight. We need to be well rested."

The ride in was subdued, but they all knew it couldn't be perfect every time out no matter how hard they tried. They'd check everything and make it right.

***

Gene steered the Albury 23, *BONEHEAD*, through the early morning mist. They ran south past Green Turtle Cay, and watched the sun come up in the east behind the string of cays. The early morning sunlight shone pink on the east side of Great Abaco Island parallel with their starboard beam. As the sun slowly rose, the Sea of Abaco changed from dark blue to a variety of pastel blue shades depending on the depth. Seth had two thermoses of hot Costa Rican Tarrazu coffee, and Scotty brought a bag of Bahamian Johnny Cakes and a jar of Guava jam he'd procured from the hotel kitchen's baker the night before. The boys were enjoying the ride in the Albury 23, planing in the swash channel close behind Whale Key, while leaving *Don't Rock* to starboard. They soon left Guana Cay in their wake and had the Hope Town Lighthouse in sight. There was little or no wind or chop, but a fleece pullover made the early morning trip more comfortable.

They idled into Hope Town Harbour and headed through the throng of moored boats to the Government dock, as the Albury ferry boat left the dock for Marsh Harbour. Juvenal was already there with *RAGE'S* back-up crew hanking on *TANQUERAY'S* sails. Gene docked the Albury and Freddy cleated her off. Then the Geezers climbed aboard the venerable old sloop in anticipation of a great day of racing.

"You already know my cousins Dax, Andre, and Davis. This big fellow in the red shirt is another cousin of mine, his name is Wilguens ... we just call him 'Willie'."

"What's the weather forecast, Juvenal?" asked Seth.

"No rain, sunny, light to moderate air this morning with the usual afternoon sea breeze around 15 knots. A weak low is approaching, so the wind may pipe up a little more. We'll have one race this morning, then lunch aboard. I made some hoagie sandwiches at my restaurant earlier and we have a couple coolers full of Kalik stored under the gunnels. This afternoon, we'll run two more races after the sea breeze kicks in."

"Where's *RAGE?*" asked John Harvey.

"She's sailing over from Marsh Harbour Boatyard. We dry sail her from there," said Juvenal, smiling.

"You guys don't miss a trick!" said Seth laughing. "John and I want to make a minor modification to the mainsail. If it doesn't work out, we can take it out later."

"No problem, go ahead. These sails have already seen better days."

The crew continued to get the boat ready to sail, while John and Seth stitched the little tuck into the top 10-feet of the huge mainsail's leech. Fifteen minutes later Seth, Scotty and Andre hoisted the main and Freddy unfurled the jib. John steered as the sloop ghosted away from the dock and made its way past The Edge and Captain Jack's, both popular restaurants, and the Hope Town Lighthouse. He carefully tacked his way out the circuitous and shallow entrance channel.

They would meet *RAGE* in less than an hour in front of Scotland Cay. The race course would be in the confines of the Sea of Abaco between Man-O-War and Great Guana Cay. Once out in the Sea of Abaco, past Point Set Rock, there were 15 miles east to west and 4 miles north to south of consistent 12 foot depth.

John tacked and jibed his way down to Scotland Cay, affording Scotty and Gene plenty of practice on the pry-boards with Juvenal, Dax, Willie and Davis coaching them at every turn. Andre helped Seth with the mainsail considering that there were no winches. Soon, John saw the anchored committee boat's flags flying, as *RAGE* sailed towards them downwind. As the boats passed, Dirk Mendelsohn on the helm and Chris Thomason in the cockpit waved and saluted. John and Seth returned the salute. Chris shouted for John to anchor near the committee boat and indicated they would follow suit. The wind was blowing about 8 knots from the southeast. John continued to windward and luffed-up about half a mile from the east end of Scotland Cay, just downwind of the committee boat. Scotty tossed the anchor in as Juvenal, Dax and Willie backed the mainsail. Scotty felt the anchor grab in 12 feet of water and cleated the rode. Dirk turned *RAGE* upwind and tacked to windward and finally anchored a few boat lengths to *TANQUERAY'S* port side. Each boat had a VHF radio and was given the distance and compass heading to the first mark, 3 miles away to windward. The first race would be a windward-leeward-windward, 9 miles total. Considering the current wind speed, the race should last about two hours and would be influenced by a strong incoming tide.

The committee boat blew an airhorn, signaling a 10-minute warning. Another airhorn warning was sounded at five minutes, and five minutes later a 10-gauge shotshell starting cannon was fired. Dax and Juvenal pulled the anchor and as the sloop moved forward, Willie coiled the line in the forward cockpit. As the anchor broke free the sails were trimmed. John started on starboard tack and Dirk chose to start on port tack. Port tack proved to be favored and only one pryboard was used on each boat. Dirk finally tacked over to starboard, as started to get headed by the breeze, and ended up three-boat lengths ahead of John. *TANQUERAY* was eating *RAGE's* 'bad air' so they tacked away. When Dirk tacked back, he still maintained his three-boat length lead to the mark. He tacked around the windward mark, then gybed and called for *RAGE'S* mainsail to be fully eased. Dirk used one pry-board to reduce wetted surface and sailed down to the leeward mark "wing and wing", almost by the lee.

John gained a couple of boat lengths by gybying twice but was still behind at the leeward mark. Dirk covered John at every move upwind and gained four-boat lengths on that final leg by gassing *TANQUERAY* the whole way with dirty air. The boats anchored up for lunch after the finish and the committee waited for the inevitable sea breeze to kick in from the east northeast.

As Dirk ate his lunch, he rehashed the race in his mind; He knew John was a talented skipper, but he was surprised at how close the race had been. If he hadn't picked up the port lift just as they were pulling anchor he might have lost. He felt he would win by a larger margin when the sea breeze kicked in for the next race and RAGE'S lighter dry-sailed weight and excellent crew work became more of a factor.

The northeast sea breeze arrived on schedule and both boats sailed down to the old windward mark, that would now be the new leeward mark, and anchored. John was determined to watch for wind shifts and not be distracted by the anchor pulling. The wind had increased to a brisk 15 knots. The first airhorn went off and then the second. John had his watch set on countdown so the cannon shot wouldn't startle him. This time both boats started on starboard tack, and once up to speed both utilized two prys with four men out on them. Dirk tacked underneath him, and *RAGE* had to steer down to miss *TANQUERAY'S* transom. John knew that Dirk had tacked to test John's crew, hoping for a foul-up. But he didn't take the bait. There hadn't been a port wind shift, so John stayed his course. Finally, Dirk tacked back and was clearly four or five-boat lengths back.

"You're a cool customer, John Harvey," chortled Juvenal from his vantage point up on the aftermost pry-board. "You didn't fall for no bullshit there, *mon.*"

"We're getting headed now," said John loudly. "Get ready to tack on a three count. One-Two-Three!"

Juvenal, his cousins and Scotty slid off the boards as John threw the helm over. They shifted the boards to the windward side like they were mere toothpicks, ducking under the swinging boom and quickly repositioning the pryboards. As the sloop picked up speed, they slid themselves outboard over the choppy water to keep the boat flat. *TANQUERAY* easily sailed across *RAGE'S* bow gaining another boat length on the lift.

John rounded the windward mark with a six-boat length lead, and he could hear Dirk scolding his crew as they passed *RAGE* coming upwind to the mark. *TANQUERAY* maintained her lead after *RAGE* rounded the windward mark and sailed downwind. Seth pointed out a wind shift and John decided to gybe, worried about *RAGE'S* lighter weight downwind. During the gybe, Freddy lost the jib sheets and Scotty fell off the newly set downwind pry-board but caught himself with his hands. Andre went forward and helped Freddy retrieve the sheets, but Andre's weight forward slowed the boat, which was compounded by Scotty's feet and legs dragging in the water as he held on for dear life. If a crew member falls overboard, the rules demand that the boat must retrieve him. Juvenal and Dax somehow retrieved Scotty, but the damage was done. Dirk gybed around the leeward mark and started the final leg to windward, three-boat lengths ahead of *TANQUERAY*.

John settled into a rhythm on the last leg. He concentrated on keeping the boat in its groove. As the wind increased a couple of knots, the chop increased another foot on the Sea of Abaco. There were five men out on the pryboards trying to keep the boat flat. Flat was fast, heeled was slow. Seth reached up and eased the leech line on the gigantic main. The mainsail spilled air out the top of the main like a chimney in a fireplace. He and Andre trimmed the main in a few inches, and the boat came alive. *TANQUERAY* started to punch through the chop and gain speed. Slowly, John gained on *RAGE*, who was heeling more than *TANQUERAY*. Dirk tried to steer up and gas John with dirty air, but he was too late. John "rolled" *RAGE* and Dirk was gassed. *TANQUERAY* powered over the finish line almost a boat length ahead. The crew on *TANQUERAY* didn't celebrate, they quietly gave each other a thumbs up. They had accomplished the unthinkable … or was it just a fluke?

Dirk thought it was a fluke. He thought they were toast after their cluster-fuck downwind. He chastised himself for relaxing on the last windward leg. He should have put a third pry-board out there with more crew to keep RAGE flatter. Dirk wished he'd never mentioned wet-sanding TANQUERAY'S bottom.

Neither crew nor skipper had much time to think about the last race because the committee boat called for anchoring over the VHF. After an equal start, the race was almost dead even after the first windward leg. The sea breeze had shifted towards the north a few degrees and had freshened to 17 knots. Each boat took a reef in its mainsail. Dirk rounded the windward mark first with a three-boat length lead. The boats tacked more often on that windward leg, and the crew work was efficient on both boats. John pulled closer on the downwind leg when the wind shifted to the north another 10-degrees. As they sailed up the last windward leg, the wind steadily increased to 20 knots and the chop slowed their progress again. Seth eased the mainsail leech line for a second time and John called for another prybar with two men out. Gene and Davis slid out on it. *TANQUERAY* picked up speed and power and John quickly tacked on a header … Dirk was in the middle of putting out another prybar and had seven of his crew out on them. John tacked back as the lift petered out, and *TANQUERAY* and *RAGE* were neck and neck with the finish boat in sight. Seth felt a puff on his cheek, but instead of easing the main, he eased the leech line a few more inches and the boat powered through it.

Chris Thomason felt the same puff and started to ease *RAGE'S* main. Dirk screamed at Chris to trim it tighter.

There's no fucking way I'm to going to lose this race to these guys, thought Dirk. *It would destroy my credibility in the Bahamas.*

He set his feet on the cockpit sole and pulled on the tiller with all his strength trying to hold the boat on course. The boat heeled precariously in the strong puff … Suddenly, the forward pry-board broke in two, dropping three large crewmembers into the water. The sudden loss of leverage started a broach. Chris dumped the mainsail, but it was too late. *RAGE'S* bow spun into the wind, the jib backed, and her free-swinging boom swept across the transom. The boom hit Dirk squarely in the head, knocking him overboard.

Freddy saw it happen and shouted, **"They just crashed and burned, we've got to go back and help them!!"**

Seth quickly eased the main. Juvenal and the rest of the pry-board crew slid back into the cockpit. They took a second reef in the main and John gybed the boat around and *TANQUERAY* picked up the three crew members that were bobbing in the water. Seth called the committee boat, who searched the area for Dirk in vain. Chris came aboard *TANQUERAY* and sailed back to Hope Town. The committee boat finally gave up the search and towed *RAGE* and her crew back to Marsh Harbour. On the way back to Hope Town, Chris told Seth and Juvenal that when the 32-foot solid wood boom hit Dirk's head, it sounded like a baseball bat hitting a cantaloupe.

The Royal Bahamian Defence Force and a U.S. Coast Guard Search and Rescue helicopter started their search for Dr. Dirk Mendelsohn's body within the hour. They searched for three days, but he was never found.

It was a long, quiet and reflective ride back to Spanish Cay in the Albury 23. No matter how fierce the competition was, and whatever animosity that was felt towards Dirk for his suspected responsibility for the Blue Hole shootout, none of the Geezers wished for that kind of tragic outcome. Just winning that last race was all they hoped for. They showered and grilled the remaining dorados from yesterday's fishing for dinner. There was no conversation, just quiet reflection.

Finally, Seth said, "Tomorrow, we'll just take a day off, recheck our tackle again and rest."

That moved John to say, "We hate to see a great competitive day on the water end in tragedy. Whatever else we might of thought about Dirk, he was a great sailor and competitor. I'll give him a toast for that."

John raised his Kalik bottle and clinked it with the all the Geezers assembled in *TAR BABY'S* cockpit.

Gene was tired and turned in early, and Scotty and Freddy headed for the hotel bar. John and Seth grabbed two wine glasses, a bottle of Turley Juvenile Zinfandel from the salon wine cooler and headed for the flybridge for a post-mortem.

"This is a nice wine, Seth," said John after taking a long sip.

"I thought we deserved something special, even though everything didn't turn out all right."

"I have a lot of mixed emotions, but the leech tuck was the deciding factor."

"Juvenal's Haitian crew was impressive."

"So was *RAGE'S* first team."

"Dirk would have creamed us in light air," said John.

"You're right, her sails were better and dry sailing any race boat gains you a substantial weight advantage."

"Do you miss sailboat racing, Seth? We haven't done it for a while."

"Not really. Near the end, when we still raced all the time, the whole scene was changing so quickly."

"I didn't like the subjective judging on the water in the big regattas," said John.

"They started that because of the litigious professional skippers who armed themselves with notebooks full of rules decisions. I remember when we won the U.S. Yacht Club Challenge in Newport Beach back in the 90's. As our skipper, you spent more time in the protest room then you did on the water. But we brought one home for the St. Petersburg Yacht Club."

"Those guys had to win, so they could sell sails. There are a lot of professional sailors these days getting paid by boat owners and sailmakers to win. But, it's still one of the only major sports where amateurs get a chance to compete against the professionals."

"Well, I guess we have Bahamian sloops off our bucket lists now. I'm going to call our lawyer in Nassau, Monday, to check on our salvage permit. I'm itching to search the perimeter of the Blue Hole on Treasure Cay to see if our pirate friend hedged his bet," said Seth.

"If history is a teacher, I'd say that patience is a virtue," said John with a smile. "Maybe we won't get shot at this time?"

CHAPTER NINETEEN

Jamaal was on his way to Marsh Harbour on a supply run with two crewmen aboard. Shareef and one of the chefs followed in the other Albury 33. The first *Britannia* charters would leave from Nassau at the end of next week. Hakim and Jabbar were busy installing the first new 12-man Winslow "life rafts" on *ECLIPSE*. The first installation had not gone smoothly due to the added weight of the lead shielding and the suitcase nuke. A standard 12-man life raft and fiberglass cannister weighs 165 pounds. The lead/suitcase nuke in the same cannister weighed 365 pounds. The "life raft" was transported from their storage hangar to the fuel dock, secured with polyester sling straps, beneath the raised ends of the forklift's 6-foot long forks. All the new stainless-steel life raft cradles had already been bolted in position thru the foredeck of each catamaran, and the old Ocean Master 10-man life rafts were stored in the hangar. As Jabbar positioned the "life raft" over the cradle from the dock, one of the polyester slings failed and the falling cannister damaged the deck. Hakim and Jamaal were supervising and they both kept their cool. The broken polyester straps were quickly replaced with new ones and they lifted the "life raft" clear. Jamaal calmly moved *ECLIPSE* back to her berth and replaced her with *MERIDIAN*.

The second installation attempt went smoothly, and Hakim already had Sunny, the dockmaster, on his phone contacting a fiberglass repair tech in Treasure Cay to fix *ECLIPE'S* foredeck. Hakim stayed to oversee the remaining installations and Jamaal headed to Marsh Harbour with his shopping crew.

The Albury 33, powered by her twin Suzuki 350 hp dual-prop outboards, ran through the Sea of Abaco's early afternoon chop with little effort. Jamaal put her through her paces and ran the seaworthy center-console up to 50 mph. Both boats also easily handled the return trip's load of countless bags of groceries, coolers of frozen foods, dozens of cases of Kalik, water, whiskey, mixers, fine wine and soft drinks. They'd also bought bags of charcoal, staple supplies, kitchen utensils, paper goods and an array of hand tools for each charter boat. Each boat was packed to the gunnels, but the overloaded Alburys cruised back at 35 mph.

The supplies were stored in the hangar, along with other necessities already stocked there by Honest Bob and Chris Thomason. Extra refrigeration and storage shelving awaited. Spare parts kits and oil for the Yanmar diesels had been shipped in previously from Mastry Engine Center in St. Petersburg. Custom embroidered *Britannia* sheets, pillow cases, shams, blankets and bedspreads were shipped from Yacht Bedding in San Diego, California under Honest Bob's supervision. He also procured custom *Britannia* monogrammed, nonslip, unbreakable dinnerware, utensils, drinkware, placemats, cookware and complimentary sun visors. All the professional luxury charter touches were supplied by Welcome Aboard Co. Honest Bob also ordered five Weber-Q1400 electric grills for the RC-52s that could be deployed on the fantail and stored in a lazarette locker. When they returned all the boats, with the exception of *ECLIPSE*, were now equipped with new "life rafts".

The crew stored the perishables in the condo refrigerators, freezers and coolers. The balance would be stored in the hangar. In the morning, the RC-52, *MERIDIAN* was stocked, then motored the 120 miles to Nassau's Atlantis Marina for *Britannia's* inaugural charter. Two days later, Captain Samuel (Shareef) and two of *Britannia's* cross-trained crew took three British couples on the Florida West Coast/Tampa cruise. Three days after that, Captain Adam (Abdul) and his crew would leave Atlantis on the *FANDANGO* for the East Coast/Charleston cruise. Then the first Washington D.C. three-week cruise was scheduled to leave on *DELILAH* a week later, followed by a Jacksonville-St. John's River cruise and so on.

Jabbar and Habeeb were making their reservation schedules under Jamaal's supervision, while constantly monitoring weather situations on NOAA that might call for marina cancellations and port-of-call changes. Jamaal had equipped each RC-52 with a Garmin GPS locator beacon that would be monitored on the computer screens in *Britannia's* Spanish Cay office and also in Jamaal and Hakim's offices. Each charter yacht was also equipped with a portable satellite phone. In any personnel emergency, Jamaal or Jabbar could replace a captain, a steward or chef in under 48 hours using their Gulfstreams or a domestic airline. Perishable items would be replenished by the chefs as needed, in locations vetted by Jabbar and Habeeb. Systems were in place to turn the charter vessels around between charters, servicing engines, repairing equipment, cleaning and restocking each yacht. An onboard washer and dryer facilitated changing bed linens and towels every three days during the charter.

In the coming days and weeks, the constantly revolving crew left on Spanish Cay would fall into a regimen of early rising, silent group prayers in the condo, breakfast, assigned cleaning and maintenance chores on the boats and condos, fitness training, personal grooming, fishing, silent nightly group prayers, dinner and then early to bed. Some days there would be twenty men in the condos, other days only six to ten, depending on how many charters they were running.

"Tonight, before the first charter boat leaves, we will perform our final cell-phone trigger test," said Hakim.

"Our initial tests, when the triggers arrived, proved they worked. Each one armed from your cell phone and then they all passed the detonation test when you dialed those numbers," said Jamaal.

"We will test each RA-230 trigger wiring circuit by arming it. Then I will know beyond any doubt that they're operational."

"But once it is armed on the bomb ... it cannot be disarmed," said Jamaal.

"Precisely," said Hakim, smiling.

All the triggers armed immediately, including *ECLIPSE'S* which was in the storage hangar. Hakim returned his detonation iPhone to the safe in his office where he kept his other two spare iPhones.

"Are all the arming and detonation phone numbers in those iPhones' contacts list?" asked Jamaal.

"Yes, they are listed in contacts under the target cities names, Washington D.C., Tampa, Charleston, Jacksonville and Miami. There is no other information other than those numbers in the iPhones. You should know this if something happened to me and you had to carry on by yourself."

"When will the deck repair on *ECLIPSE* be finished?" asked Jamaal.

"It should be done in a couple of days. The fiberglass repairman is being paid double-time to complete it by then."

"That should fit in nicely with our charter schedule, which is filling in fast."

The next day *MERIDIAN* left for Nassau, sailing east then south in the protected Sea of Abaco. She exited through *North Bar* channel, just north of Little Harbour, into the Atlantic Ocean some 50 miles from Spanish Cay. Shareef sailed a southerly course to Providence Island and soon encountered a line of morning thunder showers. He throttled back to 12-knots in the four-foot sea. An hour later the weather cleared, and he pushed the throttles back up to 18-knots until he entered Nassau's busy harbor later that afternoon. Jamaal and Hakim nervously checked the GPS monitors every 15 minutes for the duration of the seven-hour trip. A day later, Hakim called Shareef on his sat phone as he approached Florida's coast and Miami.

"How did things go at Atlantis?" asked Hakim.

"It all went very smoothly. Our passengers and their luggage were delivered to the boat at 6:15 a.m. by two bellman in golf carts. We introduced ourselves and they chose their cabins. Their luggage was stowed while I gave them a safety briefing and we cast off before 7:00. The steward served them beverages and breakfast as we left the harbor."

"How was the weather and sea state?"

"Except for the choppy Gulf Stream, the conditions were ideal. It took us eight hours. We'll be docked at Miami Beach Marina in 30 minutes and the charterers can sample South Beach tonight. We'll start down to Key West tomorrow and travel inside or out, depending on the wind."

"You've looked at the alternate routes?"

"Yes, Jamaal showed me the inside course down Biscayne Bay, through Jewfish Creek to Florida Bay, then west using the northside channel to Key West. We'll leave Miami after lunch and stop at Faro Blanco in Marathon for the night and make for Key West the next day," said Shareef.

"Recommend the Barracuda Bistro for dinner in Marathon."

"Right, I've got that here in Jamaal's travel notes."

***

The days flew by quickly after *FANDANGO* left for Nassau with Captain Abdul for the cruise to Charleston. Two days later *DELILAH* left for the first cruise for Washington D.C., with Axel (Aksleel) in command. A few days later *MERIDIAN* turned back south after two days in Tampa and headed for Sarasota. ECLIPSE'S deck repair was completed and her Winslow "life raft" was finally installed on her foredeck.

As his Spanish Cay crew shrank in size, Hakim joined Jamaal and Jabbar to help on their all day shopping trips to Marsh Harbour. He enjoyed the 'back and forth' boat ride in the Albury 33 and the long lunches at some of Marsh Harbour's finer restaurants.

Captain Nathan (Naser) headed *ECLIPSE* over to Nassau to pick up his Jacksonville trip clients. *Britannia* was busy on all fronts.

Shareef reported that the *MERIDIAN* charterers were raving about their night in Goodland at Stan's Idle Hour, where they learned the "Buzzard Lope" dance from the resident "Rednecks".

Shareef shared that piece of information during a routine sat phone check-in that morning with Jabbar, saying, "Goodland has strange music, and even stranger people, out in the middle of nowhere. But our British clients reveled in it."

***

After fueling the Albury 33s, Jamaal and Hakim left Spanish Cay Marina early, along with a number of sportfish boats who were headed out to the fishing grounds. Both Alburys were headed on yet another supply run to Marsh Harbour to replenish their supplies for the next round of charters. During the 50-mph ride to Marsh Harbour, Hakim stood next to Jamaal at the T-top helm and said, "Your planning for these charters has been impeccable so far. Not just the courses, fuel planning and supply logistics, but the local color aspect and alternative travel plans. I think we could run this business at a profit."

"Thank you, Hakim. I think we have to provide a professional product to avoid any suspicion. We don't look like these people."

"I think they are used to seeing Filipinos working hospitality positions on all the cruise ships. And our British accent English is helpful."

"But still, the product must be excellent."

"I agree. I like having the GPS tracking you suggested. It helps us keep on top of the details. But when we get close to detonation day, we'll turn those beacons off."

"That was my thought, too. We may need to move our boats around to achieve our objectives."

"Captain Rajab (Ray) and *TRINIDAD GIRL* are halfway to Nassau to start our second west coast trip tomorrow and *MERIDIAN* has just passed her coming back this way after dropping off her passengers at Atlantis," said Hakim looking at the GPS tracking app on his iPhone.

"We were running a half day late, and the conditions were calm, so I had Shareef run all night from Key West," said Jamaal.

"*MERIDIAN* will be back here well before dark. I like the daylights saving time they use in the United States and Bahamas. So, we get three crewmembers back for a few days. Where does she go next?"

"Charleston," said Jamaal as they sped past Scotland Cay and started to angle towards Marsh Harbour.

Later that afternoon, as they unloaded the supplies into three taxis at the Union Jack Public Dock, Hakim's iPhone dinged. He dug it out of his pocket, and it was a message from Molly Mallory. *It's been too long since I've seen my Omar Sharif look-a-like. Meet me at 6:30 tonight in 203 for fun and games, MM.* He crammed the phone back into his pocket.

"Anything important?" asked Jamaal.

"No, just spam," said Hakim. He had decided soon after their last unsettling encounter not to succumb to her charms ever again. He was steadfast while they loaded the supplies in the boats and left the harbor.

By the time they got to Guana Cay, he started to weaken. And when Jamaal slowed to navigate through the swash channel behind Whale Cay, he snuck a couple of peeks at the iPhone photo he had taken of her walking naked into Room 203's bathroom. As they cleared Green Turtle Cay, he glanced at his watch to see how close it was to 6:30 p.m.

Twenty minutes later, they were back in Spanish Cay. While they were transporting the new supplies into their freezers, refrigerators and storage racks, *MERIDIAN* arrived at the fuel dock. The remaining crew on the island refrained from a celebratory welcome as ordered and acted professionally. But they were anxious to hear about the whole trip from Captain Shareef, steward Punjab and chef Khalid. Being late in the day, *MERIDIAN* would be cleaned inside and out in the morning. The main engines would be checked and serviced, including the dinghy's outboard. The engine and rudder shaft seals would be checked, along with the marine heads and showers. All the boat's equipment, lights, galley stove, oven and electronics would be double checked, and any repairs or replacement needed would be performed. The storage hangar was stocked full of spare parts and equipment.

After the boat was fueled, Shareef docked *MERIDIAN* at *Britannia's* dock and the whole crew headed for the condos. Once behind the closed doors of the crew's lounge, Shareef and his crew related a blow by blow report of the cruise to their compatriots.

Khalid described his time ashore in Key West in graphic detail, "You won't believe this, but the prostitutes and strippers are everywhere on the main street called Duval. As Punjab and I walked several more blocks to the east, the homosexuals were everywhere, and most of them were in the streets dressed as women. We came back to the boat as fast as we could on a ride, they call the 'Conch Train'. The smell of pork 'Hot Dogs' was in the air everywhere we went … it made me sick."

"Captiva, Boca Grande and Sarasota were more civilized, and the people seemed normal and very wealthy. Tampa was a busy big city with a lot of traffic jams. Everybody has a car. We took a tour in an Uber and some parts of that city reminded us of Beirut. But others were upscale. Downtown had 'skyscrapers', but older and smaller than those in Dubai," said Shareef.

"What about the navigation aids?" asked Jamaal.

"Everything is marked and lighted. Traveling at night is easy. The markers in the intercoastal waterway and the sea buoys all have flashing codes."

"What about Miami?" asked Jabbar.

"It reminded me of Caracas, except it was flat with islands and taller buildings. Everybody looked Latino and rich," said Shareef.

"Time for silent prayers now, with dinner in a half an hour," said Hakim.

As the crew filed out of the lounge, Hakim looked at his watch and said to Jamaal in the foyer, "Supervise the prayer meeting, Jamaal. I have to take care some business that can't wait."

Jamaal watched him go down the steps, in the fading light, and take a golf cart towards the marina.

CHAPTER TWENTY

THE CELEBRATION OF LIFE for Dr. Dirk Mendelsohn was more like (*Death Benefits*), but Seth, John, Gene, Scotty and Freddy attended the afternoon service out of respect for his family. The gathering was held in world-famous Randolph Johnson's art gallery and bronze foundry in picturesque Little Harbour. Pete's Pub (Randolph's son) catered the event. Reportedly, Little Harbour was Dirk's favorite place in the Bahamas. Seth passed the time playing an **oxymoron** mind game, while he sized up the participants. Painfully, the minutes went by like hours. Dirk's wife ,Christine Conway, (*Alone Together*) and their two sons, Dirk Jr. and Chauncey (*Clearly Confused*) were there. Chris Thomason pointed out a smattering of Nassau politicians (*Honest Thieves*), who had flown in and congregated together. In another corner there was a gathering of tall, well-dressed Haitians (*True Rumors*) that nobody knew, who'd arrived in a brand-new Viking 50 sportfish. Across the room, three unmistakably huge, red-haired, Benders (*Jumbo Shrimp*) from Arawak Springs were ogling a couple of attractive, buxom young ladies (*Real Illusions*) who were wearing sky-scraper high heels and their little sisters' skirts. *RAGE's* crew (*Controlled Chaos*) was in full attendance, including Seth's friend, Juvenal, and his cousins.

A local minister, the Reverend Vernon Mallory (*Religious Tolerance*) gave a short non-denominational eulogy concentrating on Dirk's medical and philanthropic contributions to the Bahamian people. Mercifully, liquid refreshments were served at that point. After seeing the eclectic collection of mourners, Seth was more than convinced that Dirk was behind the Blue Hole Skirmish and more. But it really didn't matter anymore, since "Just Desserts" had been served. The St. Petersburg contingent (*Ageless Seniors*) paid their respects to Dirk's family and left for the long ride back to Spanish Cay in Seth's Hatteras. There were no plans for a service in St. Petersburg. The whole situation reminded Seth of the last stanza of a poem about death that he remembered from his English Lit class in college, "From the cold tomb

... Only the actions of the just – Smell sweet and blossom in their dust."
James Shirley: Death the Leveller.

After returning to Spanish Cay, Scotty, Fred and John headed for the hotel's Pointe House Restaurant bar. Gene checked the tackle and frozen bait in anticipation of another practice day with Captain Justin tomorrow, while Seth took his sat phone up on the flybridge and called Bobby Thompson in Washington D.C.

"Bobby, I haven't been ignoring the charter outfit here. They have started their charters and most of the boats are gone right now. We've either been fishing or sailboat racing every day since we've gotten back."

"How's the racing going? You guys must be a little rusty. I thought you gave that all up ... too much work, right?'"

"You got that right. But we were given the chance to sail one of the Bahamian work sloops that they race. You've seen them, huge mainsail, shallow draft, with hiking boards. John and I have always wanted to sail one. We've been helping some local friends tune up for this year's championship by sailing against them. It's a big deal here."

"How did it go?"

"We sailed well, with a lot of help from their spare crew. But you know John Harvey, there's none better. It was fun and we got better each race, but there was an unfortunate accident on the last leg of the last race. A hiking board broke in some heavy air and spilled three of our competitor's crew into the water. The boat spun out of control, and the boom came across and hit their skipper squarely in the head. He was knocked overboard and hasn't been found."

"A tragedy!"

"Yeah, we just got back from his funeral. We knew him from St. Pete. He recently became an ex-pat doctor in the Bahamas, when his license was revoked in the U.S. We've sailed against him for years. I don't count him among my friends, but he was a worthy competitor."

"What was his name, Seth?"

"Dr. Dirk Mendelsohn."

"Well, it's like you always say, 'It's all fun and games until someone gets their eye poked out or worse'. Keep your eye on *Britannia* for me. We've decoded their boat's GPS beacons and so far, the boats are traveling to the destinations that they advertised."

"OK, Bobby, will do!"

Seth rounded up Gene who was just finishing pulling the drags on the Tiagra 50-wide reels and headed for the Pointe Bar in the hotel. John and

Freddy were sitting at a table with Carter Combs and Sunny, while Scotty was engrossed in a conversation, over martinis, with Molly Mallory at the bar.

"We're going to leave the dock a 7:30 tomorrow morning and head out for our last practice day with Captain Justin," said Seth, pulling another chair up to the table.

"You guys are way ahead of the curve," said Sunny. "Shootout boats and crews will be crowding in here the rest of the week."

"We have Norm and Billy flying in two days from now, and we'll practice again with our full crew starting two days before the tournament."

"I don't know about you guys but that 60-mile trip each way to Dirk's wake on *TAR BABY* wore my ass out," said Gene. "I'm up for an early to bed night."

"I'm with you, Gene. I'm glad we didn't take the little Albury 23, but it's still been a long day," said Freddy. "How about an early dinner."

Seth and John agreed, and John clued in Scotty at the bar.

Sunny left for Cooper's Town and Carter headed for his house on the southeast end of the island.

"I'd like Molly to join us for dinner." said Scotty.

"The more the merrier," said John, smiling.

The dinner conversation centered around fishing, and the Geezers mixed emotions about attending Dirk's wake.

Finally, John said, "I think we would have been conspicuous by our absence, since we were still in the Abacos and were present at his demise."

"Well put," said Seth as he signed the dinner check to his marina account. "Let's head for the boat."

"I'll be down in a little while ... I want to buy Molly an after-dinner drink," said Scotty to Seth while the rest of the crew filed out.

Seth smiled knowingly, and said, "*TAR BABY* and the tide waits for no man."

"I won't be late," said Scotty with a grin.

***

Seth and Captain Justin waited up on *TAR BABY'S* flybridge with the engines idling. They checked their watches ... both read 7:30 a.m. Seth called down to John, Gene and Freddy to throw off the mooring lines, and Justin eased the Hatteras out of her slip. As he idled around the other docks towards the marina breakwater exit with some other "early-bird" boats, they spotted Scotty running out to the end of the fuel dock, waving his arms and jumping in the air. He was too out of breath to yell. Seth just laughed and Justin steered towards the fuel dock. *TAR BABY* slowly glided by, and Scotty, still in his funeral clothes, jumped into the cockpit red-faced and gasping for air. John and Gene caught and steadied him.

When Scotty finally composed himself, he yelled up to Seth, "I told you I'd make it!"

Seth laughed again and said, "Ah-Scotty, the things we do for love."

Captain Justin headed for the fair-weather inlet off of Sequances Cay. Their destination was 12 miles due east to the *Double Dips*.

As they'd passed the fuel dock Seth noticed *Britannia's* two Albury 33s at the gasoline pumps on the south side. Four of their crewmen were wiping the morning dew off the gunnels and decks while the boats were being fueled. "Omar Sharif" was standing on the dock talking to a tall, dark, burly man wearing sunglasses and a captain's hat. With that snapshot in his mind, Seth headed for the cockpit to hear about Scotty's exploits. As soon as he was safely down the ladder, Justin pushed the throttles up to the boat's 26-knot cruising speed.

Right away, the curious crew started to question Scotty.

"Where did you take her, Scotty? There isn't much on this little island but mosquitoes," said John smiling.

"I didn't take her anywhere. She took me."

"Really, does she have an apartment or what?" asked Gene.

"She has a master key for the hotel rooms and took me up the backstairs to Room 203, a plush room with two Queen-size beds. We indulged in a little foreplay and then she asked me if she could tie me up and spank me."

"You're shitting me, right," said Seth.

"No, I'm telling you … it fucking blew me away."

"So, what did you do?" asked Freddy expectantly.

"I told her that wasn't my thing, but how would she liked to get her bottom spanked?" Molly said, 'that would have been my second choice'."

"So, what happened then?" asked John

"Well, I slowly took off all her clothes and had her lay face down on one of the beds spread eagle. I tied her wrists to the bedpost with two bath robe sashes and tied her feet apart with a hair dryer cord and my belt."

"What did you spank her with?" asked Freddy.

"With one of my Sperry Topsiders®, of course. I whacked her until her exquisite behind was bright red, and she still begged for more. When I finally untied her, she was all over me like a blind starving dog."

"What did you do for the rest of the night?" asked Seth.

"I've never been with a woman with appetites like hers. Did you read 50 Shades of Grey?"

"I started it," said Seth. "But I put it down after two chapters."

"I had the same reaction," said John.

"Then I guess all 125 million copies that were sold around the world must have been read by women. Men ... there might be something there for you to learn. Anyhow, I was down and out about 3:00 a.m. When I woke up at 7:20 this morning she was gone."

"Well, that's one for the record books, Scotty," said Seth shaking his head. "Why don't you get in your fishing togs, while the rest us get the tackle ready? We'll be at the *Double Dips* in twenty minutes."

Seth climbed back up the ladder to the flybridge and took over the helm from Justin. Fifteen minutes later Justin spotted what looked like a flock of working birds on *TAR BABY'S* radar.

"Steer east-northeast 086 degrees, Seth, and we should see some birds working on the *Dips,"* said Justin as he took Seth's Canon 10x42, stabilized binoculars from their case.

A few minutes later Justin said, "There they are ... and there are five or six Frigates circling above the working birds."

Captain Justin let the outriggers down as Seth throttled the Hatteras down to seven knots. Freddy and Gene let out the Moldcraft lures on the long riggers, while John and Scotty put the dredges in and then the transom teasers. Justin positioned the right and left bridge teasers, while Freddy and Gene deployed the short outrigger Pakula lures. John Harvey double-checked the pitch baits and rods.

Seth zig-zagged along the edge of the school of skipjacks, and a few minutes later Scotty was in the fighting chair battling a yellow-fin tuna that bit the left Pakula. It appeared to be a big one, because Scotty was sweating like a fat man at a buffet. The crew cleared the other tackle efficiently, and twenty minutes later a 150-pound tuna was gaffed and pulled through the open tuna door.

A soaking wet Scotty was congratulated by the whole crew, who loved to eat sashimi and grilled tuna.

Scotty got out of the chair grinning, looked up at Seth, and said, "Can I take a nap now?"

Everybody cracked up, and Seth said, "Get out of here, you asshole. We'll see you in a couple of hours!"

"You can call me Mr. Asshole," laughed Scotty as he headed for the salon.

The crew knew they were in the right place and put the spread back out quickly. Twenty minutes later, John fed a pitch bait to a nice marlin who'd come up behind the left bridge teaser. With the help of some good boat handling, John caught and released that 275-pound blue marlin in 15 minutes. An hour later, Seth trolled by a floating piece of wood, and Freddy hooked a 40-pound dorado on the right Pakula. He brought the feisty fish to gaff 20 minutes later. The middle of the day didn't produce any fish, but the crew enjoyed a light lunch in the cockpit and cracked a couple of "cold ones". Scotty appeared for lunch and was his old composed and humorous self again. About 3:00 p.m., Scotty fought and bested another large dorado on the left Pakula and retired for another nap. Forty minutes later, Gene hooked a big marlin on a green and black Moldcraft wide-range on the right long outrigger.

"Get in the chair, Gene," yelled Captain Justin. "I saw the bite and she's a big one!"

Gene slipped into the fighting chair while the reel's clicker screamed.

"Push the drag lever up to strike," yelled Seth, as he gave the boat a little throttle to help set the hook.

Gene pushed it up and the marlin started to greyhound behind the boat.

The crew whooped and hollered as they cleared the other rods and teasers. The marlin was pulling line at an alarming rate. This was a 50-wide reel, not an 80 or 130-pounder. There was plenty of line, but they couldn't put more pressure on the fish until she started to tire. John clipped Gene's reel into the bucket harness's straps and that gave Gene's arms a little relief. Finally, all the gear was back in and the big fish jumped a couple of times and slowed down.

"Get ready to reel, Gene," yelled Seth. "I'm going to go after the fish."

Gene was a proficient captain himself and understood the drill. Seth turned the boat 180 degrees and throttled up to 10 knots. Gene started reeling and within a matter of minutes they had most of the line back. Seth spun the boat around and started to aggressively back down on the big marlin while Gene continued to reel. He did not want to let this fish start down in 5,000 feet of water. Sea water constantly splashed over the transom as Seth backed relentlessly. The boat's exhaust pipes belched acrid smelling black smoke. The scuppers couldn't handle the volume and the cockpit started to fill with sea water. Seth knew the big fish was tiring because she was swimming against the waves and current the whole time.

All of the quick turns and engine revving woke up Scotty. He stepped out of the salon door, still half asleep, to check it out. The boat hit a swell and Scotty lost his balance in the ankle-deep water and hit the deck. Being Scotty, he started to feign swimming across the cockpit.

Fifty feet from the transom, the marlin tried to sound. But it was too late, Gene finished the fish off with persistent short uplifting jabs with the rod while reeling on the downstroke. John put on his leather gloves as the leader came through the rod tip and he took control of the fish. The big marlin jumped, and John had to dump the leader to avoid being pulled overboard. Gene immediately reeled up the slack and John grabbed the 400-pound leader once again. This time John got some wraps and took control. She half-heartedly jumped close to the cockpit, then John led the tired fish up the starboard side of the boat. Scotty put a tag in her shoulder, while Freddy continued videoing the entire catch and release. John removed the hook from her jaw, and Seth kept the boat moving water through her gills. John finally released her, and she slowly swam away to fight another day. Gene had caught this magnificent fish in just over 20 minutes. Seth and Justin agreed this marlin weighed at least 550 pounds. The crew started high-fiving and broke into an unrecognizable end zone dance. Gene's back got slapped until it hurt.

The crew settled down and put the spread back out as Seth worked that area for another 30 minutes. A small marlin came up behind the right bridge teaser and Scotty tried his luck at bait and switch. The teaser disappeared and Scotty placed his circled-hooked horse ballyhoo right in front of the lit-up fish. But after an aggressive bite and four seconds of free spool with the reel clicker on, he only came up with the dreaded *sancocho.*

Scotty took it in stride, *that's why they call it fishing instead of catching,* and Seth decided to call it a day. During the ride back to Spanish Cay, the crew watched the video that Freddy had taken over and over.

"What a fish, Gene! I hope we catch a few of those in the tournament," said Freddy.

"I can't see enough of that!" exclaimed Gene, laughing and pointing at the video. "Scotty swimming in the cockpit."

"Hey," said John. "The last jump that fish took ... I thought she might end up in the cockpit with us. Good thing she was tired."

Up on the bridge, Seth thanked Justin for his help, "I'm confident now that you've given me a good feel for the *Canyon* area. Good luck in the tournament to you, Jim Tower and *CATTLE CALL.*"

When they motored past the breakwater, there was *MERIDIAN* tied up at the fuel dock. When they passed the fuel dock Seth saw the two Albury 33s at *Britannia's* dock and a crew was unloading bags of groceries and supplies, large coolers, and cases of bottled water, soft drinks, and Kalik. He was sure Bobby was watching all the action from above at that very moment. But he made a mental note for his next report.

The marina started buzzing when *TAR BABY* backed into her slip in Spanish Cay flying two blue marlin release flags and one tuna catch flag. The crew already had a couple of Kaliks on the way in, and once tied up, they said their goodbyes to Captain Justin and started to rinse the tackle and scrub the boat. When everything was back in its place, they drew for showers on the boat. The line at the marina showers wound all the way around the TIKI BAR. John drew the first shower and Gene drew the last. Gene and the boys watched the marlin video in the cockpit until the iPhone's battery died.

Gene put his arm on Seth's shoulder when Seth walked through the salon door towards the shower, "I never thought I'd catch a marlin that big on 'fifty-pound' at my age," said Gene. "What a thrill … I can't wait to show my wife the video."

"Helen will be proud. We make a good team, Gene, whether we're on the helm or in the fighting chair," said Seth with a smile. "I feel good about this tournament."

A little later, as Gene undressed to finally take his shower, Seth called down the stairs, "Gene, we're going to walk down to Wrecker's for some drinks. No hurry, we'll leave the golf cart for you to bring down. Take your time in the shower."

***

Wrecker's Bar was packed with fisherman. It was just getting dark when they walked in, and it had taken so long to order a drink that Seth went ahead and ordered a cold one for Gene. There were so many conversations going on it was hard to hear. Seth and John said hello to a number of fisherman that they knew who were in for the tournament from Florida and South Carolina.

Freddy said, "What's taking Gene so long? We've been here for forty-five minutes. His beer's getting warm."

"Maybe he called Helen?" said John.

"Maybe we ought to check on him?" said Scotty.

"Let's give him ten more minutes," said Seth, as Big Jim Tower walked up to say hello.

Seth shook his hand and asked, "Just get in, Big Jim?"

"Yeah, we just made it before dark. We're only a couple of slips down from you. Saw your flags … you had a good day!"

"We fished with your Captain Justin today. He's been helping us with some local knowledge. You're in good hands," said Seth.

"If you remember, you're the one who told me about him."

"Well, I guess I did."

"Did you see Gene on *TAR BABY*?" asked Seth.

"No, I didn't, but there was a big crowd at the TIKI BAR. That's why we came down here."

"I better go check on him," said Seth. "Good luck practice fishing tomorrow, Jim."

"I'll go with you, Seth," said Freddy.

Seth and Freddy walked back up the cart path, past the condos, through the tall palm trees and out on the dock to the Hatteras. There was still a line for the showers next to the crowded TIKI BAR. The 6-man golf cart was gone, and Gene wasn't on *TAR BABY*. Gene's iPhone was charged, but still on Seth's charger. There were no recent calls. They both checked the TIKI BAR, but he wasn't there, and the very busy bartenders hadn't seen him.

"Let's head for the hotel bar and restaurant," said Seth.

They found Sunny and Carter at the small hotel bar. Molly walked in right behind Freddy and sat at the bar.

'We've lost track of one of our friends. Do you remember Gene?" said Seth to all three. "He was supposed to meet us at Wrecker's with the cart, but he's not on the boat and our cart is gone."

"Maybe he ran into friends?" said Carter. "He was the former police detective, right?"

"Gene would have brought them to Wrecker's ... and he's not a ladies man," said Seth, glancing at Molly.

"Can you lend us a cart ... and maybe get your security working on it?"

"Of course, ... Sunny, go get them a cart. I'll call Kendall and start him working on it immediately. We have a couple extra men here for the tournament. Molly ... check with all the employees in the dormitory, on the chance someone saw something."

Seth met Kendall and provided a description of Gene and messaged a photo of Gene to his phone. Freddy mentioned their cart number was 37 and was navy blue.

Kendall said, "All the rental carts are navy blue."

Sunny delivered a loaner cart from security, which was green.

"Fred and I will pick up our crew at Wrecker's, then we'll start looking for Gene and our cart. Put 727-439-6661 in your phones. Call me on my cell if you find him."

Carter handed Seth his card with Kendall's cell phone written on it saying, "Call either of us if you find him. We'll be scouring the island for him."

Seth and Freddy rode down to Wrecker's and passed a couple carts full of fisherman returning to the marina. They found Scotty and John where they left them.

"Did you find him" asked John.

Seth said, "No." And explained everything they'd done so far. They left the bar, and all rode back to the boat for flashlights and a spotlight. As they the passed the condos, Seth noticed two men starting charcoal fires in their metal barbecues. Other fishermen walking on the paths were overtaken, and a couple of carts with single drivers rode east. They got the lights and rode on all the paths on the south end of the island where Carter lived. All four of them walked Barefoot Beach shining their flashlights and then checked the four residences' driveways and grounds just south of the airstrip. The golf cart crisscrossed the runway back and forth, as Scotty shined the spotlight from the front seat into the scrub jungle and checked around the hangars. At the narrow northern top of the island they walked four abreast through the scrub and on a narrow path. Sandspurs and brambles took their toll, but they kept looking until they ran out of island. Scotty panned his spotlight out over the water at the end of the island.

"Shine your light back to the left, Scotty," exclaimed John. "There's a little sunk boat or something out there."

Scotty zeroed in and said, "It looks like the sun roof on a golf cart."

"I can see the windshield and part of the steering wheel now," said John.

Seth emptied his pockets and put his iPhone on the path and waded out. He shined his flashlight on the blue cart and said, "It's number 37 ... but I don't see Gene."

"Don't touch anything," yelled John.

"That's what Gene would have said," said Seth as he waded back to shore.

Seth called Carter Combs ... ten minutes later, Kendall, Sunny and Carter arrived.

"I've called the Constable in Cooper's Town and he's asked us to tie two lines to the cart and secure them to some bushes or trees on the shore . He called Nassau and they will send two detectives and a forensic team over here tomorrow morning. Can you provide a better picture of Gene Johnson from your phone photos?"

"We'll come up with one," said Seth. "We'll get some line, then sweep the island one more time, before we leave it for the police in the morning."

Another sweep didn't turn up anything new, so Seth and the crew returned to the Hatteras.

"Should we call Helen?" asked John.

"Let's wait until the morning, this may be the last good night's sleep she gets for a while," said Seth. "Let's find a better picture of Gene and we'll send it to the boat's printer."

"Aren't Norm and Billy flying into Marsh Harbour tomorrow? Maybe they should cancel," said John.

"Thanks, I almost forgot," said Seth. "No, I think it would be better if they came, for a number of reasons. We may find Gene, and still fish the tournament ... If we don't find him, we'll probably leave. I'll need two crew to help me take the boat back to St. Pete, and whoever's left can fly home with you. Also, Norm is retired DEA and he will be a big help. Why don't you pick them up at Boat Harbour in the Albury at 2:00 p.m.?"

Freddy found a good picture of Gene with a fish and photo-shopped it into a head shot. Seth printed several copies and delivered them to the front desk for Kendell and Carter, and the crew called it a night.

CHAPTER TWENTY-ONE

Hakim parked his golf cart, then hurried through the busy hotel lobby, and walked up the back stairs to the second floor. He approached Room 203 and knocked on the door. The room key was in Jabbar's desk, but he needed to be discreet for many reasons. He almost turned to leave before knocking a second time, and Molly opened the door.

"I wondered if you were ever coming," said Molly smiling.

He brushed past her quickly and said, "Please close the door ... I had trouble getting away. We have a lot going on."

"But you have time for me, Harry ...don't you?" said Molly seductively.

"I made time," said Hakim, as he started to feel a little light-headed.

Molly stepped towards him and kissed him on the lips, while groping him with her right hand. He pulled her close and kissed her hard. Molly stepped back, pushing him away.

"Take off your clothes and pull down the bed while I freshen up, Harry," said Molly as she sashayed towards the bathroom.

Molly returned a few minutes later wearing only a black bra and said, "Roll over Harry, we're going to have some fun and games first."

Harry wasn't sure what she meant, but he already had a throbbing erection, so he complied. She had a hand towel in one hand and her white leather belt from her Bermuda shorts in the other. She climbed up on the bed and put her left hand on the back of Hakim's neck. She doubled her belt in her other hand and smacked Hakim's butt with a medium blow. It didn't really hurt much, but he jumped a little in surprise.

"Why did you do that?" asked Hakim sternly.

"You liked it, Harry, didn't you!"

"Not really."

"If I told you it turns me on would you like it?"

"I don't know."

"If I told you it would make me have crazy sex with you, would you like it?"

"I'm willing to try it, Molly," said Hakim as his loins felt like they might explode.

Molly folded the hand towel into a small square and said, "Put this between your teeth and bite hard and don't yell." Then she proceeded to whack his buttocks hard until they were bright red.

Just when he felt like he was going to pass out from the pain, Molly stopped and said, "Roll over!"

Hakim rolled over and Molly mounted him. He didn't last long and when he started to moan loudly, Molly stuck the towel in his mouth again. She knew the next time; he'd beg her to beat him harder.

It was the most intense orgasm he'd ever experienced. Molly let him rest for a few minutes, then she laced her belt around his neck and led him, like the puppy dog he'd become, through a litany of intimacy that pleased her. Hakim thought he noticed a pronounced pattern of fresh zig-zag bruises on Molly's exquisite buttocks during one encounter, but she yanked his head to a more intimate location before he could confirm that. When Molly was finally satisfied, she rolled off the bed and headed to the bathroom.

As Hakim dressed to leave Room 203, his cellphone vibrated in his pocket ... it was a text message from Jamaal; *Leave your meeting ASAP! We have a serious situation to deal with immediately. Meet me at the storage hangar. JR.*

He kissed Molly on the cheek as she repaired her lipstick and said, "Thank you for an enlightening evening. I have to leave right now!"

"I will call you soon, Harry."

Hakim hurried down the back stairs, navigated the lobby, then sped in his golf cart towards their storage hangar on the runway. It was pitch dark as he followed the path through the palm trees, and all he could see were the lights in a couple of the vacation homes south of the runway where the trees gave way to palmetto thickets. He was at once exhilarated by his latest encounter with Molly and disgusted at his lack of will power. Mohammed had taught him that Allah would forgive his sins if he atoned, and Hakim was now banking on his upcoming *Jihad* service to Allah and Islam to get him into heaven.

Jamaal was waiting for him at the side door of the hangar and said, "Come inside quickly, we can't take the chance of being overheard."

Once inside the hangar Jamaal continued, saying, "During prayers Ameer and Waheed started to argue over a prayer space. Ameer has been depressed because he hasn't passed his Captain's test and Waheed called him a worthless dog. They started fighting and crashed into the door to the outside and it flew open. None of us had time to react. At the same time, a fisherman went by on the path outside in a golf cart on his way to Wrecker's Bar and stopped to watch the commotion. He saw the rest of us kneeling and praying. To their credit, Ameer and Waheed immediately ran after the infidel, who turned and headed for the airstrip. They almost ran him down on foot, but he had a 6-man cart which was fast. Both of them chased him to the north end of the runway where he abandoned his cart and is hiding in the scrub jungle."

"Waldils Gabbaas!(Sons of Dogs)", shouted Hakim in Arabic, losing all control. **"I will kill those fucking idiots myself!** (reverting to English)."

Hakim quickly regained his composure and asked Jamaal, "Is anybody else looking for him besides Ameer and Waheed?"

"I sent Jabbar and Shareef with orders to help find and kill the infidel. We need to make him disappear. They will text me when they've got him."

" A good move, Jamaal. But we should find his golf cart and run it into the water," said Hakim, thinking clearly.

"That's a good idea! They'll text me when they find him. Let's take some gloves and flashlights."

Jamaal and Hakim drove up the runway with no headlights and found the path at the north end where the runway ended. Only a couple of green mercury vapor lights were on at the main hangar. They found the cart at the end of the runway with the keys still in it. Hakim got in and drove through some mowed grass and finally ended up on a short path that led to the end of the island. At that point, Hakim drove the cart into the water at full speed. He left it in about three feet of water and waded ashore. They cut some brush and obliterated their foot prints in the sand on their way back. Jamaal turned their cart around and started down the runway. As they passed the main hangar Jamaal's cellphone vibrated. He read the message to Hakim; *come a hundred meters past the south end of the runway, flash your phone light three times, Shareef.*

Jamaal passed the south end of the runway and estimated 100 meters, then stopped and flashed his cellphone flashlight three times. They heard a rustling sound in the palmetto scrub just ahead. Shareef's large form suddenly appeared out of the darkness carrying something in his left hand.

Shareef said in a low voice, "The infidel killed Ameer and Waheed, and I killed the infidel," as he held the severed head up by its hair.

"Where is Jabbar?" asked Hakim.

"Jabbar is hiding the bodies in the brush. What do you want me to do next?"

"We need to have all three bodies disappear," said Hakim looking at his watch. This dark of the moon tide is high right now."

"It's about a three-and-a-half-foot tide," interjected Jamaal, while trying not to lose his lunch.

Hakim and Shareef were used to beheadings, but it was Jamaal's first encounter with the real thing.

"Jamaal, drive over to our hangar and get more vinyl gloves, some bleach, a few plastic garbage bags, a hatchet and two hacksaws," said Hakim. "How far is it to the dead men, Shareef?"

"About 75 meters to the east."

"When you get back, Jamaal, drive the cart into the palmetto scrub and join us on the beach. We're going to let the outgoing tide and the sharks do our work. All the blood will concentrate them quickly."

When Jamaal arrived at the beach 15 minutes later, the bodies had been carried back to the ocean's edge. Shareef and Hakim started to dismember the bodies, while Jabbar waded out with the parts and flung them further out into the Atlantic. Jabbar put all the dead men's clothing in a garbage bag. They'd burn them in a charcoal barbecue grill later tonight.

"Jamaal, go cut some brush and check the area where Jabbar hid the bodies for blood stains. Then sweep the area for footprints with the brush you cut," said Hakim.

"You won't find much blood," said Shareef. "The infidel bled out in the water, and Ameer was drowned with his neck broken. Waheed was clubbed with a stick from behind and his skull was fractured."

"Sounds like the old infidel was a tough guy," said Hakim

"He obviously had training and courage ... I grabbed his hair from behind while he was concentrating on drowning Ameer and sliced his head off with my serrated scimitar. But he was definitely a warrior."

"Speaking of heads, double-bag his head in those garbage bags. I want to put it in the freezer in our hangar."

"Why?" asked Jamaal.

"After we unleash the Holocaust and we are all hiding safely in Africa, the real experts will scour this little island. They will probably find it. I want them to know who they're dealing with. Until then we will only have a missing senior citizen who probably had a heart attack and drove his cart into the ocean. Like I said, the strong easterly ebb tide and the sharks will do our work for us."

Jamaal said, "The charts I have studied show that 100 meters off this beach the ocean depth quickly drops to 20 fathoms past the barrier reef."

"Now, let's bleach the tools and our hands and sweep the sand once more before we go back and reassure our crew. We should burn all our clothes too, just to be safe." said Hakim.

"We'll get the grills going next the condo. two to grill the chicken and fish, and the third to burn the clothes," said Jamaal. "I'm getting hungry."

Hakim had a meeting with the remaining crew, while Jabbar and Shareef grilled dinner and incinerated all the clothing.

"Ameer and Waheed are dead," said Hakim to the crew assembled in the meeting room. "Both of them were killed by the infidel. Shareef killed the infidel. The dead are all in the ocean now and will not be found. Our two dead brothers unnecessarily endangered our holy *Jihad*. If they had not been killed by the infidel, I would have killed them. As soon as tomorrow, there may be police asking questions of everybody on this island. If they ask where Ameer or Waheed are, we tell them that they are on a cruise. If they ask more questions, you saw or heard nothing. Beyond that, tell them to ask James (Jamaal) or Harry(me). Any questions …?"

"OK then, this situation shines a light on this island and everyone on it. Prayer time is suspended until we are all safely back in Cameroon. We are going to have to speed up our *Jihad*. It makes no difference when we do it as long as we succeed. Some targets may not be where we want them, but there is no bad time to launch this Holocaust. We could all be safely back in Africa in close to two weeks … if Allah wills it."

After a quick dinner of fish and chicken, Hakim checked the ashes in the clothes burning grill and instructed Shareef to scoop all the ashes into a five-gallon bucket and dump them in the ocean. Then Shareef burned some new charcoal, so it matched the other grills.

Next, he and Jamaal worked far into the night to plan a schedule to quickly complete their *Jihad* during the next two weeks. If the coming investigation found two of their men missing, and a passport check and the location of their entire work force was requested, they might only have a matter of days before any suspicions might be confirmed. Hakim doubted the Bahamians could move that quickly, but he also didn't know what kind of connections the missing fisherman's family might have in the United States.

Jamaal's counsel was, *prepare for the worst and hope for the best!*

The office condo was set up as an all-night war room. Hakim, Jamaal, Jabbar and Habeeb pored over the four RC-52s GPS locations and plotted their eventual timelines to their scheduled destinations. The other two condos were dark, and their crews were sleeping, but the third condo had blankets tacked up over the inside of the windows and sliding glass doors on the office level to hide the interior lights. After a couple of false starts, Jamaal finally thought he had a plan that would work.

"First, we have to realize that we are only going to do this once," said Jamaal. "We may have to fake engine trouble or a sick crew member, to make it work. When the holocaust becomes a reality, *Britannia* goes down with it. The four of us and all of our crew don't exist. We all have fictitious passport identities."

"That's true, Jamaal, even the lawyers who set us up and brokers who bought our boats do not know our real identities," said Hakim. "We will live to fight another day."

"I can see *ECLIPSE* leaving Washington D.C. and ending up in Jacksonville at the Mayport Marina on Holocaust-day," said Jamaal. "*TRINIDAD GIRL* will take her time arriving in Tampa after stops in Key West, Marco Island, South Seas Plantation in Captiva, Sarasota and St. Petersburg before docking at West Shore Marina in Tampa. We will cite possible bad weather during their return trip for the extra stops on the way to Tampa. *DELILAH* will motor down the east coast from Jacksonville, staying in St Augustine, Port Salerno, Palm Beach, Fort Lauderdale and be in Miami for *Jihad* day. *MERIDIAN* will just be pulling into Charleston after stops in West End, Singer Island, Jacksonville, and Savannah. I will expedite *FANDANGO* when she returns from her Charleston charter tomorrow morning. After she's been serviced, we'll equip her with two 55-gallon plastic fuel drums. We can run day and night with one fuel stop in Wilmington, North Carolina, then sail straight through to Washington D.C. I'll need a crew of three."

"How long will it take you to get to Washington?" asked Jabbar.

"Fifty-two hours to Wilmington, North Carolina in good conditions, on the first leg. We'll run at 9 mph for 12 hours at night and 13 mph during the day for the first full two days and transfer our drum fuel as soon as possible when we have calm seas. During the last 75 miles we'll have enough fuel to run at 21 mph if the seas permit. It's 550 miles from here to Wilmington. There's a good fuel stop there, and I plan to run the next 450 miles outside to the Chesapeake Bay and Washington D. C. That avoids navigating the intercoastal channels at night and any drawbridge malfunctions. The fastest we could make that distance, running at 9 mph at night, would be close to 36 hours. Four days to Washington at best."

"What if there's bad weather?" asked Hakim.

"Five days, depending on the weather's severity," answered Jamaal. "We have enough fuel, with the drums to run the entire 900 miles to Washington

D.C. without a fuel stop. But we couldn't run faster than 9mph, and it would take more than six days with bad weather all the way."

"That area's weather forecast for the next two weeks shows nothing tropical, just local thunder storms," said Habeeb.

"We'll get *MERIDIAN* and Shareef's crew on their way to Nassau at dawn tomorrow to pick up their Charleston charter, and hopefully we can turn around *FANDANGO* in a day and be on our way to Washington," said Jamaal.

"I'll contact *ECLIPSE, DELILAH* and *TRINIDAD GIRL* by sat phone in the morning and explain our new plan of attack. I'll also schedule both Gulfstreams for our getaway plans. Our extra personnel can burn all of our records and correspondence in the barbeque grills and we'll take only our personal effects and weapons on the Gulfstream Jets. We'll stop at Spanish Cay on our way back to Africa and pick up the four crewmen and our computers we left here," said Hakim. "Will Jabbar go with you, Jamaal?"

"I think it would be better for Jabbar to stay here with Habeeb. They will have to change and make reservations and monitor each yacht's progress to its target. Also, if we have a personnel problem, Jabbar can be flown there since we'll have the jets standing by. I'll use Jabbar wherever I need him. We will use Abdul and his present crew on *FANDANGO* ... they know the boat. Let's turn the lights out and take the blankets down. We should get some sleep now ... we're going to need it."

***

The next morning came quickly and Hakim's first order of business was putting the *Camel Hair sport coat 50 long $500, 941-555-1212*, ad in the New York Times Sunday newspaper classified section, for Al-Zawahiri. He handled that through an encrypted email account, using a Bank of America debit card account assigned to a deceased American citizen named Jason Dodd. Al-Qaeda's cell in Jersey City arranged for that.

Next, he systematically called his captains on their sat phones. Hakim called Naser on *ECLIPSE*, Aksleel on *DELILAH* and Rajab on *TRINIDAD GIRL* and brought them up to speed on the whys and wherefores of the new attack plan.

"Counsel your crew, Rajab, and use subterfuge if needed, to reach and keep your vessel at the attack location. Jabbar and Habeeb will help you with reservations and planning. I will personally call you at least twice; once when I want the GPS beacons turned off and again when I set the detonation time and tell you when to Uber yourself and your crew to the FBO at Tampa International Airport. After you turn off your GPS beacon, use your sat phone to keep Jabbar apprised of your location hourly. Your Gulfstream will pick up *ECLIPSE'S* crew first in Jacksonville, then your crew in Tampa, and then *DELILAH'S* in Miami. Your jet will leave Miami and fly directly to Orchila Island in Venezuela for fuel and then non-stop back to N'djamena in Africa."

"When are you going back, my leader?"

"I will be on the other G-500 that will pick up Shareef's crew from *MERIDIAN* in Charleston, and *FANDANGO'S* crew and Jamaal from the Dulles Airport's FBO outside Washington D.C. I want to see the nuclear mushroom cloud over the infidels' capital when we fly out of the airport, 26 miles away from ground zero. I will set off all five bombs when we are cleared to take off from that airport. We'll stop in Spanish Cay and pick up our remaining crew members and follow you to Venezuela."

The plan was in place and each minute brought them closer to Holocaust Day and the fulfillment of Hakim's dream to become the greatest Islamic terrorist the world had ever known. He would dwarf Isis's Al-Baghdadi, the blind Iman-Rahman, Boko Haram's-Shekau, Bin-Laden, and Al-Zawahiri.

***

That afternoon two detectives came by the office asking questions about a fisherman missing from the marina. They questioned Jabbar and he had no information to share. Then they asked to speak with Hakim.

"Mr. Muneer, I'm Jackson Knowles and this is Alex Pinder, my partner," said Jackson while showing Hakim their identification. "We were sent over here from Nassau to investigate a missing person's report filed on an American fisherman, Mr. Gene Johnson, a retired police detective from St. Petersburg, Florida."

"Have you ever seen Mr. Johnson?" asked Detective Pinder holding up his picture.

"I can't say that I have," said Hakim.

"We've received the full cooperation of the hotel, marina, and airport staffs, and interviewed their employees and searched their facilities. Constable Archer, from Coopers Town, and our forensic team are now searching the private homes and boats in the marina. They should be here shortly to inspect these condos. The only other building we haven't searched is your rental hangar. Would you mind opening it for our inspection?"

"Not at all, we just keep parts and supplies in there," said Hakim.

"James," called Hakim out to the front office, "Would you get the key and open the hangar for the detectives."

Jamaal retrieved the key from his desk and stood by the front door.

"And," said Detective Knowles. "We'd like a list of your employees and their passport numbers. We also need to know their whereabouts last night. I understand everyone at *Britannia* charters is a British citizen."

"Yes, and actually most of them are out on four extended charters right now. I'll get Herbert to make a list for you while you search our hangar."

"Thank you, just routine you know."

"I understand, Detective. Any leads?"

"We found Mr. Johnson's golf cart out in the water off the north end of the runway, but there's no unusual finger prints or any other clues. He might have had a heart attack and just fallen out of the cart. There was a strong tide last night."

"I hope you find him. I'll have your list waiting when you return."

After the detectives left with Jamaal, Hakim told Jabbar, "Fit your Glock 9mm with its silencer. I have mine in my desk drawer already set up. If the detectives get lucky and find the infidel's head in the freezer, we'll have to kill them. I emptied a 3-gallon ice cream container last night and put his head in it. I don't think they'll go as far as opening up the ice cream."

"What flavor?" said Jabbar.

"Vanilla."

"Good, I like the "Moose Tracks."

"You're getting decadent, Jabbar," laughed Hakim.

The detectives returned satisfied and picked up their employees list that placed Waheed aboard *TRINIDAD GIRL* and Ameer aboard *DELILAH*. Eight employees are in port and seventeen out to sea. If a role call were requested, *Britannia* would pass.

CHAPTER TWENTY-TWO

SETH wiped a tear off his stiff upper lip, as he watched the forklift pull the 6-man electric cart out of the water. Gene had taught him that immersion in water does not wash away fingerprints. He watched with interest as the Nassau forensic team tried to find some prints. It turned out there were none except his, Freddy's, Scotty's, Gene's, Sunny's and Bristol's, one of the marina's assistant dockmasters. The detectives from Nassau were the same team that handled Dirk's plane disappearance, but they seemed more competent and confident investigating this type of case. At the end of the day their best guess was a heart attack caused the cart to run into the ocean and an unconscious man fell into the water. The strong new moon tides supported their conclusion.

Seth drove the loaner cart back to the marina. John was just pulling in with Billy Chandler and Norm Hogan in the Albury 23 from Marsh Harbour. After briefing Norm and Billy, Seth went inside the Hatteras to call Gene's wife, Helen. It was one of the hardest things he ever had to do. He made sure John called his wife, Stacy, and that she was already on her way to Helen's before he called. There were no words he could think of that were adequate.

"Helen, this is Seth. I have bad news … Gene is missing. We found the golf cart he was driving in three feet of water. We have not been able to find him. The authorities are theorizing he may have had a heart attack or seizure and fallen out in the water. This is a small island with very deep water around it."

Helen was crying and could not speak.

Seth continued, "We are going to stay here for a while and see if an expanded water search of the area by the Marsh Harbour police turns up anything. Nassau sent a whole team of detectives and forensic people over here to deal with the situation. I don't have to tell you how sorry I am, and how devastated I am after losing my best friend. I will come back to St. Pete whenever you choose to have a service. And if you need anything at all, you know that I'm here for you, Helen"

Helen blew her nose, composed herself and said, "He loved you, Seth. You should know that. If he had to die, I'm glad he was having fun with you and his friends. His whole working life, I worried every time he went to work that some drugged-out criminal was going to kill him. I'll be all right … Gene left me secure, especially after receiving his treasure share, and I have my daughter and my grandchildren … My door bell's ringing."

"I know … it's John's wife Stacy. She's there for you. We need to stay in touch. John can fly us home in a day."

"Thank you, Seth."

Seth took Norm out to see where the cart had run off the end of the island. On the way, he took him past Wrecker's Bar and Barefoot Beach.

"I brought you out here so we could talk in private. This information is classified, so you can't talk freely about it. But I value your experience and opinion. My friend Bobby Thompson, who was my teammate at Virginia and later recruited me into the CIA for a short time, discovered I was fishing here and asked me to keep an eye on *Britannia Charters* who just opened for business. Bobby owns a major security firm that gathers information for our CIA. *Britannia* is one of eight or ten operations he is currently monitoring for possible terrorist threats. I've sent him pictures of their charter yachts and he has been monitoring their movements. They are housed in the three condos that we just passed."

"What makes them suspicious?"

"Their personnel, who are all citizens of England but former Middle East immigrants, were trained on an island owned by Venezuela that is being used as a fueling stop for Russian and Cuban military aircraft. Also, they travel in Gulfstream private jets registered to Middle East aircraft charter companies," said Seth. "They have five identical charter yachts. But, right now only one is at their dock. I'll take you by it before I show you where our cart ended up."

They rode past *FANDANGO,* who had just arrived and was being scrubbed and serviced by four crew members.

"An impressive catamaran motor yacht," said Norm as they passed by the RC-52, "And, the crew is all clean cut and shaven."

"Does that surprise you?"

"Yes, long hair and beards are part of their religion. As is, the five calls to mandatory prayers each day."

"I haven't seen or heard anything like that while we've been here."

"Maybe they're all Christians or atheists, but it makes me suspicious," added Norm.

Seth rode along the runway to the north end of the island and showed Norm where the cart entered the water.

"I guess I could buy into the senior citizen heart attack scenario, Norm, but Gene didn't have any health issues. He was as healthy as a horse."

"What did the surveillance cameras on the island show?" asked Norm.

"The only security cameras are in the new hotel's lobby and corridors. This is a small unsophisticated island."

"If I were you, Seth, I'd call Bobby and tell him about our conversation."

***

Seth called Bobby on his sat phone from the privacy of his cabin. He explained what had happened to Gene, and his subsequent conversation with Norm Hogan.

"That's it in a nutshell, Bobby. Like I said, Norm is retired DEA and ran their New Orleans office before he retired. We both smell a rat here."

"It's very possible that Gene saw something and was caught checking it out. It's hard for people in police work to turn those instincts off. I'm going to fly two of my operatives in there tomorrow morning with a plan to flush these guys out if they're bad guys. Can you put them up and provide a cover for them?"

"Yes, I've got Billy and Norm in a room in the hotel, I'll move them on *TAR BABY* and give your guys the hotel room."

"I'll have them dressed like fishermen. Their names are Rick Walsh and Erwin Clark. I'll call you early tomorrow morning with Rick and Erwin's arrival time. In the meantime, we're tracking four of *Britannia's* charters ... the fifth one is in your marina."

"You're right, Bobby, but it looks like they're getting it ready to leave again. I'll talk to you tomorrow morning."

Seth got the whole crew together in the Hatteras's salon and explained that Bobby was sending two CIA agents to Spanish Cay disguised as fisherman. Seth, Norm and Bobby all agreed that *Britannia* could possibly be a front for terrorism.

The two agents would blend in with *TAR BABY'S* crew but would dig deeper for the truth, with the Geezers help.

"Are we going to go fishing?" asked Billy, smiling.

"Good question! The tournament is out. But if something develops with *Britannia,* we'll go fishing so we don't look suspicious to them. Otherwise, we'll fly home for Gene's funeral when the date's set … some of us in John's Saratoga and some commercial. Then John will fly me and a delivery crew back to bring *TAR BABY* home. If anybody wants to leave now, that's OK too."

They all wanted to stay and see how the agents worked out.

***

Seth's sat phone rang at 7:00 a.m., it was Bobby.

"Rick and Erwin are two of my best operatives. They'll land in a King Air at 11:00 this morning … both of them are pilots," said Bobby. "Follow their lead. Also, there will be backup standing-by in Freeport."

"OK, Bobby."

Rick and Erwin arrived on time. Seth reserved them a golf cart and they met outside airport customs. Bobby must have shown them a picture because they came right over and high-fived and hugged Seth like an ol' buddy. They wore mirrored Costa sunglasses, were dressed in well-worn Columbia fishing clothes, and their Sperry topsiders weren't new. Erwin had on a red baseball cap with a small American flag on the front over white block lettering reading, "MAKE MY DICK GREAT AGAIN". They acted like ugly Americans do … wherever we go. They threw their duffels in the cart and Seth drove them to the hotel to check into their room. Rick and Erwin would fit right in.

"Check us in, Seth, and then we want to meet your crew on your boat. You can fill us in on any local knowledge when we get there," said Rick.

"Bobby told us you worked for "The Company" with him back in the day," said Erwin.

"Yeah, and I found out I wasn't cut out to do your work," said Seth smiling.

"According to Bobby, you were damn good," said Rick.

"Well, I'm just a raggedy-assed old boatyard owner, boys. That's why you're here."

When they arrived at the Hatteras, Rick and Erwin continued their glad-handing act with the crew in the cockpit as they all moved inside.

"Now that we're all introduced, we've only seen this little island on Google Earth and our own satellites … We'd like to go sight-seeing after lunch. We're most interested in *Britannia's* storage hangar and condo/office setup. We also want to retrieve some gear and weapons that we left hidden in the King Air that we parked."

"Let's have some lunch at the TIKI BAR and then we'll ride around, which won't take long," said Seth.

They sat down at a large table and ordered lunch. After that there was a long silence. Rick piped up and said, "Have the marlin been biting?" … and everyone started talking at once.

After lunch, Seth and Norm took Rick and Erwin for a ride around the island. Seth showed them the condo complex, coming and going from Wrecker's Bar. They passed by Britannia's storage hangar on a trip up and down the runway when he drove them where Gene had allegedly driven into the ocean. Seth stopped on the way back at the King Air.

"Just to double-check, Bobby told us there was no camera surveillance on this island except in the hotel lobby and hallways," asked Rick.

"That's what the two detectives from Nassau told us," said Seth.

Erwin retrieved two more small duffels from the King Air.

"We need to see the inside of the *Britannia's* office condo. We can scope out the rest of their layout after dark, watching their movements and inside lights pattern." said Rick.

"We just can't walk in their office, can we?" asked Norm.

"I've got an idea," said Rick. "But take us past their charter yacht first, I'd like to size up their crew."

Seth rolled past *FANDANGO* while she was being loaded with groceries and bottled water.

"I see what you mean, Norm. I've never seen middle-easterners so clean cut, unless they were interviewing for a job. Once they're hired and past probation, the facial hair returns … drive us up to the hotel, will you Seth?" said Rick.

Seth stopped in front of the hotel and Rick went inside. Ten minutes later he returned with a *Britannia* brochure in his hand.

"Where did you get that?" asked Seth.

"From the tour desk … you can go fishing, sailing, get ferry tickets, go scuba diving, shelling, parasailing, catch a tour boat to Green Turtle for the day and so on."

"Why didn't I think of that?" said Seth.

"Let me take the cart alone and I'll meet you all back at the Hatteras," said Rick.

Rick parked the cart and walked into the *Britannia* condo that was marked OFFICE. A door to the left was open. A pleasant looking man sitting behind a desk turned from two computer screens on a credenza and said, "Hello, I'm Herbert, how can I help you."

"I saw your charter boat *FANDANGO* in the marina, and I asked the hotel concierge desk where it sails to. He handed me this brochure and sent me down here."

"As the brochure states, we offer crewed charters to Tampa, Jacksonville, Charleston, Savannah and Washington D.C. They are two weeks long, except the Washington charter takes three weeks. They are all gunk-holing adventures with overnight stops in many interesting locations, coming and going, like Miami, Key West, Boca Grande, Sarasota, Manteo and Myrtle Beach to name a few. There is a captain, chef and steward aboard and the onboard food, drinks and wine are gourmet quality. All the charters begin and end in Nassau at Atlantis. Each charter yacht has three equal double guest cabins and heads, and a RIB inflatable launch for exploring. Six guests per charter is the maximum."

"Sounds terrific. I'm down here to fish in the upcoming tournament, but a cruise like this would be perfect for a family vacation. How far ahead should we book?" asked Rick as he looked past Herbert into a rear office. "We're booking next spring right now," said Habeeb, as Rick paced back and forth.

"Are your crews Filipino, like on the big cruise ships?"

"No, sir, we're all British."

"I should've known from your accent, Herbert. Do you have any more printed information you could give me?"

"Just this seasonal rate chart," said Habeeb handing it to Rick. "There are many more pages of information and photographs on the internet at britanniacharters.com."

"Thanks for the info, Herbert, I'll run it by my family."

As Rick left, he noticed a rear door in the hall and a closed door directly across the hall marked PRIVATE.

Back in *TAR BABY'S* salon Rick and Erwin clued in the crew.

"Tonight, we want to gain entry to *Britannia's* storage hangar to check it visually with a Geiger counter and a Flir-440 handheld radiation detector. We can do that around midnight, but we need two lookouts after we pick the lock and are inside the building. We will put our cellphones on vibrate and you will text us if necessary," said Erwin. "We also want to watch the condo's interior lights from the front and back to track the room occupancy patterns … especially in the office building upstairs bedrooms. Rick is our locksmith and safe cracker. He spotted a safe in a back office, and he figures the private office may have one too. We need lookouts there to alert him to possible discovery with a vibrating text."

"You guys don't waste any time," said Billy.

"Well, history has taught us that when these terrorist attacks are ready to go, they go down fast," said Rick.

Rick and Erwin went back to the hotel to get some rest. They would all have a late dinner aboard the Hatteras. Seth's crew rested and nobody had a cold one.

After dinner, Seth played the video of Gene's last marlin fight a couple of times in his honor on the big LED television. Rick and Erwin watched intently at the close-knit, efficient teamwork that was necessary to catch a 550-pound marlin in that short period of time and release her unharmed. Quite a few tears were shed that evening as stories were told about Gene's police prowess in Key West, the Turks and Caicos and Cuba. They would all miss him, but those fond memories of his strength and character helped them with their grief.

Seth, Norm and Scotty went along with Rick and Erwin at midnight to the hangar.

Freddy, Billy and John walked east armed with Glock 9mms, and took up positions around the condos. They would watch the *Britannia* crew and warn Seth if someone started their way. No one was moving about at that hour, but as Seth hid his cart in the palmetto scrub south of the hangar, he noticed that *FANDANGO* had left the dock. All of them were dressed in dark clothing. Seth armed Norm and Scotty with Smith and Wesson .38 police specials. They all had Rick's and Erwin's cell phone on autodial as they tri-angulated their look-out positions. It took Rick less than 10 seconds to pick the hangar's side door entrance lock. A long 15 minutes went by before the two slipped back out the door, relocked it, and melted into the palmetto scrub.

Back at *TAR BABY*, Erwin said, "We found five old Louis Vuitton suitcases and cut off scraps of lead in a wooden crate marked, BOAT BALLAST. It was covered by some tarps. The Geiger counter and Flir picked up traces of nuclear material and radiation. This is serious shit!"

"What else is in there?" asked Seth.

"There were five identical, older, life rafts stacked in a corner, cartons of spare boat and engine parts, 20 or more 5-gallon pails of engine oil, cases of oil filters and galley supplies. Also, a freezer full of food, shelves of kitchen and cleaning supplies, boxes of linens, bags of charcoal, stacks of bottled water and soft drinks. A refrigerator was full of foodstuffs, and cases of beer and wine. We took pictures of it all," said Erwin.

"Erwin and I will join the surveillance crew that's watching the condos … we'll text them that we're coming. An hour or so from now we'll all meet back here and plan my creepy crawl. Seth, if anything happens to us in the meantime, call Bobby about the nuclear traces and radiated suitcases. We'll wait in case there's more useful information in their offices. I only want to wake him up once tonight," said Rick.

An hour later, they had pieced the condo information together and decided there was only one man in the office condo upstairs bedrooms. All the bedroom room lights were out now. All the lights were out in the other two condos except for the front porch lights, and they figured there were only four or five men in those two condos. Freddy, Billy and John went back to the condos with Erwin and took up their hidden positions. Rick slipped down the north shoreline behind the condos and approached the office condo from the rear avoiding the front porch light. He picked the lock on the rear door and crawled down the dark hallway. Herbert's office door was open. Rick bypassed Herbert's desk and crawled into the back office where he'd seen a safe. The safe had a tumbler lock and Rick pulled a stethoscope out of his fanny pack. *Right*, 3 turns … he could hear it click, *Left*, 2 turns slowly- another click, *Right*, 1 turn back and it opened. His pencil light showed nothing but pistols, ammo and a stack of passports from different countries. He took a photo of each one and put it all back in the safe and locked it. Rick then crawled across the hall and picked the lock on the office door marked PRIVATE. He quickly located an electronic safe in a closet. He took a small circular neodymium magnet (available at any Home Depot) out of a small shielded pouch in his fanny pack and placed it on the upper left corner of the electronic safe's door. It stuck to the steel door tightly. Rick moved it around until he heard the lock's electronic solenoid click. He pushed down the door's handle and opened the safe. He carefully returned the powerful magnet to its pouch. Rick found more pistols, three identical iPhone-8's and more passports, all of them British. He turned on each phone. Each phone had five phone numbers from five different area codes in their contacts. That was the only information on the iPhone and each phone had exactly the same information. He recognized 301 as Washington D.C. and Miami's 305. He took pictures of the iPhone contact lists and the passports, then returned them all to the safe and locked it. The office desk tops were littered with scribbled notes with their yachts' positions and fuel usage charts. Rick knew Bobby was tracking them by their GPS beacons. He silently exited by the rear door, locking the door behind him. Rick eased up the north shore and was soon making his way through the palm trees towards the marina. He stopped behind a palmetto bush and texted the lookouts in unison, *A-OK see you at the boat*.

Now it was time to call Bobby!

CHAPTER TWENTY-THREE

FANDANGO WAS 135 MILES CLOSER TO WASHINGTON D.C., twelve hours after leaving Spanish Cay. The north flowing Gulf Stream current was giving the RC-52's 9 mph speed a 3.5 mph boost as she motored northeast. Jamaal had drained one 55-gallon diesel drum into the RC-52s fuel tank and would try to run the rest of the way to Wilmington, N.C. at 20 mph(23.5 mph with the Gulf Stream), while keeping the other 55 gallon in reserve if the weather got sloppy. At this rate he would make his Wilmington fuel stop in 32 hours and Washington D.C. 24 hours after that, even with some night running at 9mph. With no charter stops to slow them down, *FANDANGO* might even get to D.C. a day before Shareef motored *MERIDIAN* into Charleston harbor. Jabbar emailed and booked *FANDANGO'S* reservations with the Wharf Marina dockmaster, relaying that they were picking up charter guests there.

***

Hakim was pleased with Jamaal's progress. Shareef was also taking advantage of the Gulf Stream current, as he headed *MERIDIAN* up Florida's east coast. Shareef's next stop was Singer Island, then two other charter stops before docking in Charleston. Hakim thought they would both arrive at their final destination within hours of each other.

He walked across the hall and said to Jabbar, "The jets should arrive here late tomorrow. When our jets land, I will give the order for our yachts to turn off their GPS beacons. I want Habeeb to take our captain's sat phone calls each hour and manually update their position on each float plan on his computer. If I need to see it, he can send me a screen-shot."

"Who will supervise on the other jet, Hakim?"

"You will, Jabbar. Habeeb can hold down this office if we need anything. My jet will stop to pick up Habeeb and the remaining crew on our way to Orchila. My plane will have fewer people aboard. We will disappear into thin air, as the infidels are fond of saying. I can't wait to see the mushroom cloud over Washington D.C."

"Allah be with you, my leader," said Jabbar.

******

BIG JIM TOWER came by *TAR BABY* early, on his way to breakfast with Bill Scotch and "Cheech" Montana.

Seth met him in the cockpit and Jim said, "We came by to pay our respects to Gene. He was a great guy and we'll all miss him!"

"Thanks, Jim, Gene liked all of you, too. It doesn't look like we're going to stick around for the tournament."

"I can only imagine how you all feel," said Jim. "We're waiting for Captain Justin to come over... he's running a little late. How about letting me take Billy and Norm fishing with us today. We're short-handed until the end of the week. I've got Spanky Browne and Toby Warner coming in later this week."

"They're good fishermen. I know Billy and Norm will jump at the chance to fish with you today. I'll roust them up and we'll join you for breakfast."

Justin showed up during breakfast and Billy and Norm were stoked to be fishing. As Seth, John and Freddy walked back to the Hatteras ... Erwin and Rick drove up in their cart.

"Let's go inside the boat," said Rick. "Bobby has moved this operation's surveillance to Level-One. The nuclear traces and radiated suitcases may mean these "Englishmen" could really be terrorists. They might have five small nuclear bombs from two to ten kilotons. Bobby says there was some chatter on the black-market internet about Russian suitcase nukes about six months ago. But it's been quiet since then. His team also noted that the five iPhone numbers I found, are from these area codes: Charleston(843), Jacksonville(904), Tampa(813), Miami(305) and Washington D.C.(301). Our analysts think these numbers may be part of a cell phone trigger system that the Middle East terrorists favor. All the numbers are activated through Verizon accounts. Bobby never liked the Gulfstream jet situation, it smelled of Saudi money ... and the Venezuela connection speaks for itself."

"What about the foreign passports you found and photographed," asked John.

"All of the passports from Africa, Afghanistan, Syria, Arab Emirates, etc. are forgeries, and the photos were taken with their beards and mustaches. But that's more like suspicions confirmed. Bobby also noted that the last boat, that left late yesterday, is steaming straight for the upper east coast towards Cape Hatteras."

"The cell phone triggers bother me," said John. "If they have that capability, how can we stop them?"

"Bobby's tracking all five boats closely. If they dock a boat in each of those iPhone area code cities in the same time frame, he will invoke a SOP-303 order with Verizon," interjected Erwin.

"What's a SOP-303?" asked Seth.

"After 9/11, Congress and George W. Bush passed a law that the Department of Homeland Security could force telephone providers to turn off cell phone towers in specific areas if a perceived threat exists, without a court order. It's been used twice to my knowledge, once in New York City's four major tunnels, and the other in San Francisco's subway stations," said Rick.

"That makes me breathe a little easier," said Seth.

"I'm going to sit on Barefoot Beach and drink a couple of Kaliks. But really, I'll be keeping my eye on the condos," said Erwin. "Later on, I'll ride over to check on our King Air and scope out the airport."

"I'll hang out here, if it's all right with you, Seth, in case Bobby calls on the sat phone," said Rick.

"Sounds like a plan," said Seth. "We all could use some R & R, and there's always something to fix aboard this boat."

Late that afternoon, CATTLE CALL returned to her slip with four flags flying from her starboard outrigger halyard. Big Jim, Billy, Norm, Cheech and Bill Scotch arrived with a cooler of cold ones, while their boat was being cleaned by Justin and Jim's mate, Tommy.

"Come on aboard. It looks like you had a good day!" said Seth.

"It started out slow," said Jim. "But Justin spotted some birds as we trolled six miles east of Flat Top. There's a lone mountain peak out there that comes off the 3500-foot bottom up to 1500 feet. The birds were working, and the fish were biting. Cheech reeled in a 250-pound blue marlin that bit a Black Bart "Marlin Candy". We released him in 15 minutes. Billy hooked a white marlin, about 100 pounds, on a circle hooked ballyhoo after the fish knocked down both short riggers. He came up again behind the bridge teaser and Billy pitched the bait. We all got to see that bite. Later, Norm caught and released another blue marlin about 125 pounds. He hooked it on one of those Pakulas you like so much. Then we got into some 50-pound yellowfin tuna. Everyone caught at least one of those, and we kept them. Justin and Tommy cleaned them on the way in and put them on ice. You're all invited to dinner tonight at 7:00 o'clock."

"We accept ... Jim ... this is Rick, another friend of mine," said Seth. "Can we bring Rick and my other friend Erwin along? He's checking out his King Air at the airstrip right now."

"Nice to meet you, Rick ... Sure, we've got lots of tuna to grill."

The dinner aboard *CATTLE CALL* was great and everybody relaxed. The Geezers slept better that night, and Rick and Erwin seemed to be comfortable in any situation.

***

The next morning brought a flurry of activity to Spanish Cay. Most of the tournament sport fishing boats left the marina before 8:00 to practice fish. A small fuel tanker arrived, docked at the fuel dock, and began pumping fuel into Spanish Cay's above-ground storage tanks. Rick and Erwin arrived at the Hatteras at 9:00 and reported that two Gulfstream G-500s were parked beside their King Air across from the main hangar. Before Rick could get up in *TAR BABY'S* flybridge to make a sat phone call to Bobby, his own sat phone rang.

"Yeah, Bobby, hold on a minute," said Rick. "Let me get to where I can talk."

He scaled the ladder and disappeared forward. When he came back down, he gestured for Seth to go inside the cabin.

"I told Bobby the two *Britannia* Gulfstreams were here. He said one of his satellite scanners had already reported that to him. Bobby also told me the jets arrival coincided with all five RC-52s GPS beacons being turned off."

"What do we do now?" asked Seth.

"Bobby has assigned five satellite scanners to track each boat, 24/7. But they're hard to follow at night, especially in the Intercoastal Waterway and in populated areas."

"Why don't they get the Coast Guard to send a gunship and helicopters after each charter boat and collar these guys?" said Seth.

"I asked the same question and Bobby said, 'They have a built-in hostage situation with the charter clients, and their *martyrs go to heaven and get 52 virgins* religious beliefs encourage them to detonate if law enforcement gets too close'. He also pointed out that all their bombs always have a tamper and manual detonation switch," said Rick.

"So, what's the solution?"

"Bobby thinks the fact that two jets came in indicates they will try to collect their five crews before they detonate. The cell phone triggers make that possible. When all five boats are in their five area code localities, he will pinpoint their positions and have Homeland Security invoke SOP-303. Verizon will turn off the cell phone towers near each of them. If the jets land at nearby airports to collect the terrorist crews, that will further support his time-line theory. When the terrorists dial the detonation numbers, they will get a 'no service' reading on their cell phone. That will give local authorities time to evacuate at least a five-mile area around the nuclear armed RC-52s. Then the bomb squads can try to defuse or remove the nukes. Bobby will have the FBI corral the terrorist's Gulfstreams, with all the bad guys aboard, at their last airport FBO stop," said Rick

"I should have thought of all of that, but that's why Bobby makes the big bucks," said Seth. "What does he want us to do?"

"If this whole thing unfolds like Bobby thinks it will, he wants us to detain any terrorists that remain here and turn them over to the authorities in Marsh Harbour. He says you have plenty of large plastic tie-wraps, pistols, rifles, AR-15s and even a couple grenade launcher. Pretty impressive for a sport fisherman," said Rick laughing. "He definitely wants to know when the Gulfstream jets leave."

"Hey, I'm just an old, raggedy-assed, boat yard owner," said Seth smiling.

******

Jabbar took the G-500 pilots to the hotel by golf

cart, then put their two co-pilots in Shareef's and Abdul's room. When they were settled, he went back to his office.

Shortly after his return, Hakim walked in and said, "Things are starting to fall into place. Right now, I want to look at the charter boat location chart that Habeeb has been updating from the hourly sat phone calls."

They walked around Habeeb's desk and checked the progress of each RC-52.

Habeeb updated them out loud, starting with *TRINIDAD GIRL*, "She is just leaving Marina Jacks in downtown Sarasota, on her way to St. Petersburg. *ECLIPSE* already left Savannah for Sea Island, Georgia and should easily make Mayport Marina, next to the Naval Station near Jacksonville, by tomorrow afternoon. *DELILAH* is nearing Palm Beach, and she will make Miami tomorrow, either inside or outside, in this good weather."

"Allah seems to be with us," said Hakim smiling.

"Look at *MERIDIAN*," said Habeeb moving her pin with his computer's mouse. "Shareef called in just before you came in and he is passing by Hilton Head Island right now. He is going to anchor in a cove off the intercoastal near Kiawah Island tonight. With only 30 miles left to go tomorrow, he should be in Charleston by midday."

"Jamaal has made amazing time with the help of the Gulf Stream's northerly current and the ideal weather. He already made his fuel stop in Wilmington and has been running at top speed today. He'll run at 9 mph all night, and still be able to run at top speed up the Potomac River to Washington and have fuel left over. I predict *FANDANGO* will be there in the early afternoon tomorrow," said Jabbar.

"Allah be praised," said Hakim. "I can't wait for the simultaneous detonation in five major cities. The day after tomorrow will teach the infidels that they will never be safe from Allah's wrath."

"So, that's when we leave this island, Hakim?"

"Yes, we will know when all five boats are tied up at their destinations. The hourly phone calls will stop once they're docked and call us. I will call each of them back later and give them a time to be at the airport FBO's to meet us and the Gulfstreams. The four boats with charter guests will develop a minor engine complication like a failed alternator or fuel pump, and the captain will suggest that the charterers go sight-seeing or go into town for lunch while he gets the part. The chef and steward will accompany him to restock the galley. But they will take an Uber straight to their airport FBO."

"When will we load our weapons on the Gulfstreams?" asked Jabbar.

"Tomorrow night. Each of us will travel with a minimum amount of personal effects and our British passports. Today and tomorrow we will gather up any essential files and the Middle East passports. We'll leave those documents and the computers on the island with Habeeb. I will collect them when we pick up the last of our Spanish Cay operatives."

"I am feeling both apprehension and excitement leading up to our *Jihad's* consummation," said Jabbar.

"That's natural, Jabbar. Every real warrior feels that on the eve before a major battle," said Hakim.

***

Both of the Gulfstream jets left Spanish Cay Airstrip mid-morning in clear skies and bright sunshine. Jabbar's plane headed for Jacksonville International Airport and its Signature fixed base operators facility. After landing and picking up Naser and his crew, they would head for Tampa International Airport's Sheltair FBO to retrieve Rajab and his crew. After a short flight to Miami International's Tursair FBO, they would collect Aksleel and his crew, then top off their fuel tanks and take off for Venezuela's Orchila Island.

"I wish I could see the explosion in Jacksonville from the air," said Naser, who was sitting next to Jabbar as they taxied to the runway to take off for Tampa. "The British aircraft carrier HMS Queen Elizabeth and the USN Destroyer Roosevelt are docked in Mayport right now."

"Hakim wanted us to be on our way before he detonated," said Jabbar. "I'm sure we'll see plenty of pictures of all the destruction on the plane's satellite television on Al Jazeera's network before too long."

Five minutes later, the Gulfstream was airborne and headed south to Tampa.

***

After picking up Shareef and his crew at the Charleston International airport's Atlantic Aviation FBO earlier, Hakim landed at Dulles International Airport. The G-500 taxied to the Jet Aviation FBO at the north end of the airport. Once the plane was parked and being fueled, Jamaal and his three man crew climbed aboard.

Hakim greeted him warmly saying, "What a masterful job of navigation and fuel management, Jamaal. Allah will be proud!"

"Thank you, Hakim. I was lucky the weather held, and I had the Atlantic Ocean's Gulf Stream to help me. Also, the Yanmar engines and my crew were up to the task."

The fueling was completed and the pilots started the engines. Hakim's sat phone rang and he answered, "Ok, Jabbar ... no problems ... incredibly good. We'll see you in Cameroon."

As the plane taxied towards the runway to take off, Hakim walked forward and asked the pilots to tell him when they were cleared for takeoff. He sat down in his seat and pulled down his tray table from the seat back. Hakim pulled his three iPhones from his duffle and set them in a row on his tray table and turned them on. He brought the numbers up in contacts under H. There was HC for Charleston, HJ for Jacksonville, HM for Miami, HT for Tampa, and HWDC for Washington D.C. The co-pilot said they were cleared for takeoff.

Hakim speed dialed the HC number, by just touching it with his finger.

The phone changed screens and read **NO SERVICE**. He quickly brought up HJ and got the same response.

He yelled towards Jamaal, "Stop the pilot from taking off! Have him return to the FBO, claiming engine problems!!"

Jamaal rushed forward and stopped the takeoff, while Hakim tried HM, HT, and HWDC. They all ended with the same result, **NO SERVICE**. He tried the numbers on the second phone ... **NO SERVICE**. His mind was working overtime ... He hadn't come this far to fail, but obviously there was a problem with the triggers ... or maybe the Americans had somehow figured out his plan. But he could not fail ... the bombs were protected with a tamper device and maybe that would make them detonate. Hakim felt his dream of immortal fame and entrance into Islam's heaven as their greatest martyr slipping away. The tamper switch was not a sure thing. But the manual switch on the bombs was another possibility. He would leave the Gulfstream with Jamaal and find a way to detonate the Washington D.C. nuke. That single prize would still elevate him into heaven and eternal infamy as the world's top terrorist.

As the Gulfstream taxied back to the Jet Aviation's FBO, Hakim heard sirens. He looked out the windows and could see several police cars and SWAT vehicles racing up the runway towards them with their lights flashing and sirens blaring. The sound of helicopters filled the air.

"STOP THE PLANE, ordered Hakim. "Shareef, break out the AK-47s. Get down on the tarmac and lay down some fire. Shoot those helicopters down with the SAM's that we have. Jamaal, get a couple of those grenade launchers out there and stop the SWAT trucks and police cruisers. We'll go to the marina and detonate ... and fight to the death for Islam!"

Shareef launched a FLM-92 (SAM) at the nearest helicopter and turned it into a falling ball of fire. That one shot slowed the infidel's offensive down to a crawl. Jamaal set two men up with grenade launchers, at each end of the plane and their lobbed grenades started two of the SWAT trucks on fire, while they intermittently fired regular ammo from those same rifles. The other four terrorists laid down a withering cross fire with their AK-47s, wounding some of the police officers and disabling their vehicles. Hakim had an AK-47, a Glock 9mm pistol and a couple of hand grenades. He motioned to Jamaal to follow him. Getting away depended on slipping past the police, who would soon encircle them, leaving surrender or death as their only options. Hakim knew Shareef would not surrender.

As he and Jamaal ran behind Jet Aviation's facility, he yelled to Jamaal, "We have to get back to *FANDANGO* and detonate."

They ran across Airport Drive and into the Budget Car Rental lot. A new customer was driving out and Hakim stepped in front of the SUV with his AK-47 leveled at the windshield. The driver stopped short and Jamaal pulled him out of the car and knocked him out cold. They jumped in the SUV and drove down the Dulles Access Road to Interstate 495. They traveled south for 15 minutes and then turned east on RTE 66.

"We need to ditch this car soon. The police will be looking for it by now," said Hakim. "Let's get off on RTE 29 ... it looks like more of a backroad on this car's GPS."

They drove through Falls Church, and then Cherrydale before they ran into a roadblock. All the traffic was coming out of Washington D.C., no traffic was going in.

"Park the car up this side street while I check this out. Look in the back for any luggage while I'm gone."

Hakim walked two blocks and saw carloads of people pouring out of the city over the Francis Scott Key Bridge. There were ambulances and firetrucks parked along the road in the far east lane. They were poised to go into Washington, but the other three lanes were open for outbound traffic.

Hakim walked up to the barricades and asked a policeman, "What's going on here, officer? I need to get to Georgetown."

"Not until we get the all clear. We're evacuating everyone out of downtown. Only emergency vehicles can get through."

"Why?" asked Hakim.

"Some kind of terrorist bomb threat ... don't you listen to the radio?"

"No, I just got back in town, but thanks, I'll turn it on now."

Hakim walked back to the SUV and said to Jamaal, "Somehow they found out what we were up too. They're evacuating downtown."

"That might give us some time. They won't let a bomb squad try and diffuse it until everybody's gone," said Jamaal.

"Wait a minute, the policeman I just talked to has given me an idea," said Hakim. He said, 'Only emergency vehicles can be let through'. There's a whole line of EMT ambulances up there pointed at the bridge. Let's take one and make a run for the marina."

"There won't be too many guards around the marina, not with them thinking that a bomb might detonate. But I'd feel better if we took our AK-47s with us!"

"The only luggage in the SUV is a carry-on roll-around suitcase. We can't fit them in there."

"Yes, we can. I'll take the barrels off and put both of them in the suitcase with the stocks and ammo clips we have left. I'll reassemble them while we're driving to the marina," said Hakim.

Once they were ready, they walked towards the bridge dodging the cars and masses of humanity that were flowing over the bridge. They slowly walked down the long line of EMT vehicles and spotted one with the back door open and two attendants sitting in the opening, smoking. Jamaal nudged Hakim and he nodded. They walked up to them, trailing the rolling suitcase.

"Are you guys in the market for some bargain cigarettes?" said Jamaal, pointing towards the suitcase.

"We might be," said the shorter of the two.

"What brand do you smoke?" asked Jamaal.

"Marlboros," said the taller one.

"We've got those for $3.00 a pack, 10% off for a carton," said Jamaal, rolling the suitcase closer while he turned his head from side to side. "Let me show you in the truck … there's too many cops around here."

"Hop in, but hurry up," said the shorter one.

They all hopped in and closed the doors. Jamaal started to open the suitcase as the attendants watched expectantly. Hakim hit the short one in the back of his head with the butt of his 9mm. Jamaal grabbed the taller one by the neck and slammed his head into the side of the truck twice.

They stripped off the attendants dark blue jumpsuits and put them on. Then trussed and gagged the attendants with their own adhesive tape and threw two blankets over them next to the gurney. Jamaal started the truck and pulled out into the east lane with the siren blaring and lights blazing. He threaded the ambulance towards the bridge, and yelled to the police at the barrier, "**Heart attack in Georgetown!**"

The police pulled the barrier back and let them pass. The ambulance drove in a stop and start mode as the oncoming traffic tried to pull over. Ten minutes later, Jamaal turned right on the other side of the Potomac River on Maine Street SW, as Hakim finished   reassembling the AK-47s. Jamaal remembered how the Uber had driven them out and turned at Blair's Alley SW. A few minutes later, he took a left at Wharf Street SW. There were four armed National Guard soldiers clustered around a Jeep at the entrance to the marina docks.

Jamaal pulled up, with all the lights blazing and the sirens blaring, and screeched to a halt. Both of them jumped out of the ambulance, ran around and opened the back doors. They pulled out the two AK-47s and killed all four of the astonished guardsmen. Hakim and Jamaal ran down the dock and boarded *FANDANGO,* as distant sirens screamed in their belated pursuit of the terrorists.

"I didn't think it would end this way. I wanted to be alive to see the aftermath. But I will see you in heaven, Hakim."

"I'll welcome your company in the after-life, my friend. There's nothing left to say but, **ALLAHU AKBAR!"**

With that said, he opened the life raft cannister, reached behind the raft, and flipped the manual detonation switch. Milliseconds later a bright blinding flash was seen for miles and supersonic winds and fire vaporized everything within a half-mile radius. An ominous mushroom cloud could be seen from over 30 miles away.

WILLIAM VALENTINE

AFTERMATH

At the one to two mile radius of the nuclear blast most residential buildings collapsed, and the concrete commercial buildings were damaged by fire after all their windows were blown out. Depending on the wind velocity, the radiation fallout reached out five to six miles. The radiation level in the one-to-two-mile radius would render those areas uninhabitable for as many as three years or more. Casualties were counted at 1,600 souls. Among the dead were military, law enforcement and emergency personnel. Also, the homeless population, drug addicts and others who just did not heed the call to evacuate, perished.

The mastermind, Hakim Al-Rashid, a young Afghanistan Al-Qaeda operative, died as he and his Egyptian compatriot manually detonated the Washington D.C. nuclear device. Four identical devices were prevented from detonating by timely work by the U.S. Government Intelligence and Homeland Security services, negating cell phone detonators in Miami, Tampa, Jacksonville and Charleston. The U.S. Air Force had a squadron of F-16 jet fighters(1,500 mph) intercept a Gulfstream G-500, owned by Saudi Prince Faisal bin Abdul, that carried ten escaping Al-Qaeda operatives bound for Venezuela near the Dominican Republic. The squadron forced the Gulfstream G-500 to land at near-by Muniz Air National Guard Base outside of San Juan, Puerto Rico.

Four Al-Qaeda operatives were taken into custody by Bahamian Police, at the *Britannia Charters Ltd.* facility on Spanish Cay, in the Abaco Islands. They are awaiting extradition to the United States on terrorist charges. *Britannia Charters Ltd.* is suspected as being a multi-million-dollar front created by Al-Qaeda. Another Saudi owned Gulfstream jet was blown up at Dulles International Airport in a fierce fire fight to the finish near the Jet Aviation Service FBO. All six terrorists perished along with two charter pilots. The heavily armed terrorists shot down a police helicopter, and disabled several SWAT and police vehicles, causing seven fatalities and ten wounded. The physical and radiation damage to the United States' capitol city of Washington D.C. is still being assessed.

The 932-foot visiting aircraft carrier *HMS QUEEN ELIZABETH II*, and the 506-foot (DDG-80) destroyer *USS FRANLIN D. ROOSEVELT* both put out to sea, immediately. All citizens and shoreside military personnel were evacuated from a five-mile radius of Mayport Naval Station near Jacksonville, Florida. A U.S. Naval Explosive Ordinance Disposal Squad was jetted there from nearby Panama City's Eglin Air Force Base, and successfully disarmed the first nuclear device. Squads were then deployed to Charleston, Tampa, and Miami to disarm those devices as well.

.

EPILOGUE

AS THE DAMAGE reports filtered out of Washington D. C., and the large scope of the original terrorist plot became known, a nation's fear quickly turned into righteous indignation. On the second day the major television news outlets showed video clips, taken from a helicopter, of the Washington Monument with its top half broken off like a tree after a tornado. There were shots of the White House's roof with sections blown off, some columns were askew, all the windows blown out, and the West Wing burned to the ground. The Thomas Jefferson Memorial was gone, and the Lincoln Memorial was severely damaged. The east side of the Pentagon on the Virginia side of the Potomac was destroyed. The nation's capital building's dome had been blown off and was fire damaged. The Supreme Court building was damaged beyond repair. By the third day it was reported that 3,000 cherry trees, gifts from Japan which surrounded the tidal basin, had been vaporized. There would be no Spring Cherry Blossom Festival in the foreseeable future. The Smithsonian Museum was in ruins, along with the National Museum of Art, the National Museum of Natural History and many other national treasures. A ground swell of public opinion demanded retaliation. The United States Congress, as a whole, agreed and reiterated, "Enough is enough!"

By this time, Bobby was in the CIA's New Orleans office with Rick and Erwin and had been all over the computers that Seth and the Geezers corralled when they took down the terrorist skeleton crew left on Spanish Cay. The four terrorists the Geezers helped capture were still being held in Marsh Harbour, but the terrorist's computers were taken by Rick and Erwin to New Orleans the next morning in their King Air. Those computers proved to be a treasure trove of information.

A 20-kiloton, low yield, nuclear warhead was launched from an atomic powered submarine submerged in the Indian Ocean during the dead of night. It exploded on top of Al-Zawahiri's compound in the mountainous outskirts of Karachi, Pakistan, the fourth most populated city in the world. A fair warning to the double-dealing Pakistanis.

Several missiles, including two "bunker buster" nuclear bombs, delivered by stealth bombers, hit Iran at the same time and the Ayatollah's modest home in Teheran ceased to exist, along with their nuclear weapons program.

A 40-kiloton nuclear warhead was dropped on Orchila Island, 100 miles north of Venezuela, as a warning to Cuba, Russia and the failing communist government of Venezuela. The island no longer exists.

United States' stealth bombers dropped two nuclear "bunker busters" bombs on Al-Qaeda's mountain fortress outside of Koussei, Cameroon. The mountain is now just a hill.

The Russians, Chinese and the whole world felt and understood the American people's resolve. Hopefully, the constant thirst for world domination would turn inward, and the despotic leaders of aggressive countries and sects would redirect their efforts towards improving the lives of their neglected citizens.

***

The ten terrorists being held in Puerto Rico were charged, arraigned, and sent from San Juan, Puerto Rico to Guantanamo, Cuba to be questioned and await trial.

Warrants were issued by the Department of Justice for Saudi Arabian Princes Faisal bin Abdul and Khalid bin Rahman, who were the owners of the Gulfstream G-500 jets used by the terrorists. The FBI followed the money trail to round up the operation's financial backers. All sales of U.S. weapons and spare parts to Saudi Arabia were suspended. All financial aid and treaties with Saudi Arabia were put on hold until this investigation was completed, and all perpetrators were handed over for trial. *Oil independence in action.*

***

Pilar Pudenda was discovered at Papayas Lounge in Freeport, on Grand Bahama Island, by Telemundo producer Joaquin Rodriquez. She will appear six days a week as Inez Martinez in *Mariposa De Barrio,* video-taped in Miami.

***

Bobby told Seth that he and the Geezers had helped save close to 400,000 lives. The computers they retrieved could lead to eliminating Al-

Qaeda world-wide. Roundups were already occurring in London, Jersey City and Dearborn, Michigan.

Seth, John, Scotty , Norm, Billy and Freddy flew to St, Petersburg for Gene Johnson's funeral. It was a solemn event, finished off by a real celebration of life ... full of fond memories and stories about Gene's adventurous life.

Later that week, as John made plans to fly Seth, Freddy, Penelope and Lori back to Spanish Cay to bring *TAR BABY* back home, their Bahamian lawyer called Seth to tell him he had their treasure salvors permit in hand.

"I guess we ought to wait and fly back over in a few weeks when tournament fishing is over," said Seth. "The boat's as close to Treasure Cay as we would want it. We'll rent that Albury 23 again and do a little sleuthing with our new Fisher metal detector one night and see what happens."

"Sounds like a plan," said John, smiling.

***

Detective Pinder had a crew of six men from the Marsh Harbour Police Station move all the furniture and equipment out of the Spanish Cay condos and into the storage hangar with the rest of *Britannia's* equipment. Carter Combs was anxious to move the original furniture and appliances back into the condos and start renting them again. Detective Knowles job was to catalog all of *Britannia's* desks, chairs, furniture, beds, appliances and kitchen equipment. The two Albury 33s were already back in Nassau and were being outfitted as police boats. When all the other confiscated items were marked and cataloged, they would be shipped to Nassau on an island coaster. The Nassau Police Department would keep any items they could use and put the rest up for sale in their monthly public auction.

"Jackson, have a couple of those guys unplug and defrost the freezers and refrigerators in here and clean them out. We don't need any of the frozen food, or the stuff in the refrigerators. None of it is evidence. Put it all in those black 55-gallon plastic bags and burn it in the hotel's incinerator. I wouldn't trust it anyhow, with all the power outages they have here," said Detective Pinder.

"OK, Alex, once that's done maybe we can catch a plane out of Marsh Harbour and get back to Nassau this afternoon, " said Detective Knowles.

***

Because of the damage to so many buildings, and the dangerous radiation zone that would not be usable or rebuildable for at least three years, the seat of the United States Government was temporarily moved to the University of Missouri campus in Columbia. Their current students were transferred to Mizzou's St. Louis and Kansas City campuses. It was a good deal for both Mizzou and the U.S. Government because of dwindling admissions at the Columbia campus due to a continuing student diversity issue. The Government leased the entire campus, including two 13,000-15,000 seat fieldhouse/arenas, to house the Senate and House of Representatives. There were more than enough rooms for the House of Representatives and their staffs in 28 large dormitory buildings and 30 multi-story married student apartments. These buildings also had the capacity to house the essential employees of all the other government agencies who lost their facilities in Washington D.C. The Senate, and their staffs, found plenty of living space in the 40 fraternity and sorority houses. The Supreme Court moved into the Mizzou Law School building. The University's housing could serve 30,000 people. The POTUS resided in the former University President's home. The FBI and the DOJ moved into two of the 50 large classroom buildings that are on the campus. All the major federal agencies established offices there.

The University's Student Union personnel provides meals for them all, and there are free gyms and workout rooms available. There is an 18-hole golf course on campus. A large university hospital occupies the center of the campus. There are over 100 bars and restaurants to keep the legislators and agency workers fed and inebriated. There are only 28 small (70-100 rooms) hotels and they are insufficient to house the 12,000 lobbyists that are based in Washington D.C. Illicit trysts require ingenuity, since hotel rooms are at a premium. Flying in and out of Columbia, Missouri commercially is difficult.

With distractions at a minimum, it was no accident that Congress passed more legislation to benefit the United States citizens during their first year in Columbia than in the ten previous years combined in Washington D.C. They also found numerous ways to decrease the National Debt by more than a trillion dollars.

BAHAMAS SURPRISE

WILLIAM VALENTINE